TF102548

GW00656393

CROWN WARS

CROWN WARS

Peter Ling

SEVERN SH HOUSE

This first world edition published in Great Britain 1996 by
SEVERN HOUSE PUBLISHERS LTD of
9–15 High Street, Sutton, Surrey SM1 1DF.
First published in the USA 1996 by
SEVERN HOUSE PUBLISHERS INC., of
595 Madison Avenue, New York, NY 10022.

British Library Cataloguing in Publication Data

Ling, Peter
  Crown Wars
  1. English fiction – 20th century
  I. Title
  823.9'14 [F]

  ISBN 0-7278-4926-3

Typeset by Palimpsest Book Production Limited,
Polmont, Stirlingshire, Scotland.
Printed and bound in Great Britain by
Hartnolls Ltd, Bodmin, Cornwall.

For Sheilah – as always

With many thanks to Sheila Black and Andrew Ellis for their research, help and encouragement, and to Norman Longmate, whose chronicle of life on the Home Front – 'How We Lived Then' – was invaluable.

The Minster Family Tree - as at July, 1939.

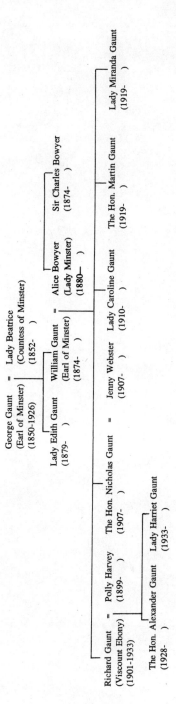

George Gaunt = Lady Beatrice
(Earl of Minster) (Countess of Minster)
(1850-1926) (1852-)

William Gaunt = Alice Bowyer
(Earl of Minster) (Lady Minster)
(1874-) (1880—)

Lady Edith Gaunt
(1879-)

Sir Charles Bowyer
(1874-)

The Hon. Nicholas Gaunt = Jenny Webster
(1907-) (1907-)

Lady Caroline Gaunt
(1910-)

The Hon. Martin Gaunt
(1919-)

Lady Miranda Gaunt
(1919-)

Richard Gaunt = Polly Harvey
(Viscount Ebony) (1899-)
(1901-1933)

The Hon. Alexander Gaunt
(1928-)

Lady Harriet Gaunt
(1933-)

Chapter One

Thursday, 22 June to Sunday, 23 July 1939

Jenny couldn't get back to sleep.

She had been lying awake since dawn, listening to the chorus of birds. Now she could hear girls' voices from the floors below, and the clatter of mops and dustpans as the maids began their rounds before breakfast. She jumped up and ran to the open window, to see the sunlight striking across the lawns. Throwing off her nightdress, she shivered with delight. Today Nick would be back in England.

When she had bathed and dressed, she hurried downstairs and took the last flight at a run, wondering what time Nick's ship would berth at Southampton. How soon could she expect to see him?

As she opened the door of the breakfast-room, her father-in-law walked in through the french windows and greeted her: "Jenny, my dear! You're up bright and early."

The Earl of Minster held out his arms, and she kissed him, saying: "So are you."

"I never sleep as well when Alice is away. Besides, I wanted to take a look at those carnations I planted out last night – they all seem to be flourishing."

Now in his mid-sixties, he was a fine figure of a man. Although the heart attack he had suffered some years ago had slowed him up a little, William, Lord Minster, was still the master of Crown House. He strolled across to the table, already laid for breakfast; a pile of mail awaited him, and he glanced through it, sorting the letters.

"Two for Polly – one for Mama – one, two, three for me – ah, and here's one for you . . . by airmail."

Jenny guessed that Nick must have written before he left Canada. She tore open the envelope and began to read:

"Halifax,
  "Thursday, June 15th.
  "Dearest Jenny —
  "A brief line to tell you that I love you – and that we are on our way home. The trip has been gruelling but very worthwhile; their Majesties have stood up to the strain extremely well – thirty days touring all over Canada, with a side trip to the USA thrown in.
  "Dinner tonight at Government House, and tomorrow the 'Empress of Britain' sails for Southampton. We're due to arrive on the 22nd, and then I shall be with you again. . . ."

Today their Majesties had not been lucky in the weather; after blue skies and sunshine on the return journey, when the cruise-liner dropped anchor in the Channel, an English sea-fret cast a chill over everything.

On the main deck, Nicholas narrowed his eyes, trying to see through the mist. He could just make out a blurred shape across the water – the destroyer which had come to meet them. A little nearer, a pinnace covered the last hundred yards between the two ships. A full-scale welcome awaited King George and Queen Elizabeth when they went ashore; but before that, there was to be a personal and private meeting – a family reunion.

Lieutenant Christopher Gaunt, RN, one of His Majesty's equerries, felt a stab of envy. He and Jenny had set their hearts on having a family of their own, but five years ago Jenny miscarried, and had never become pregnant again. The doctors had done their best to be reassuring; there was no reason why she should not bear a child satisfactorily – they must simply be patient – and wait.

2

An open bulkhead door led to the royal suite, and now Nicholas sprang to attention as their Majesties stepped out on deck.

"Not much longer now," said the King.

Queen Elizabeth took her husband's arm, murmuring: "We've only been away a month, and it feels like a lifetime. Whatever happens, I mustn't cry – the girls would never forgive me."

They heard the engine of the pinnace ticking over as it drew alongside; moments later, the Princesses scampered up the companionway. Margaret was the first to appear, running along the deck and shouting: "Hello!" Lillibet tried to be grown-up and walk slowly, but then she too broke into a run, calling out: "Mama – Papa – hello!" They threw themselves into their parents' arms, everyone talking at once; the family was together again.

Some Ladies-in-waiting followed at a discreet distance, but Nick was watching the Princesses. They seemed to have grown, even in a month; the affectionate nursery-name of "Lillibet" was too childish for this graceful thirteen-year-old – though she was still dressed in the same demure schoolgirl style as her nine-year-old sister.

She hugged her father and mother, while Margaret was doing most of the talking, as usual: "Were you seasick? Are your cabins through there? Will you take us all round the ship?"

The King swung Margaret up into his arms, laughing: "You little monkey – you always want everything to happen at once! Very well – c-c-come on —"

But the Queen reminded him softly: "Don't forget the presents."

"Presents?" Margaret's sharp ears caught the word: "For us?"

"Yes – for both of you – from the Captain and the crew."

Nicholas beckoned the youngest crew-members, who saluted the Princesses, handed over two large parcels, then took two paces back and saluted again.

Tearing off the coloured wrapping paper, the girls found

3

two identical nightdress-cases in the shape of giant pandas; the pandas at Regent's Park Zoo were universal favourites.

"You'd better not take them round the ship with you – they might get lost," the Queen warned them. "Nicholas – would you mind —?"

"Perhaps I could look after the pandas?" suggested a familiar voice.

"*Ma—!*" exclaimed Nick, in amazement – and the Princesses giggled.

Alice, Lady Minster – one of Queen Mary's Ladies-in-waiting – curtsied to their Majesties, who welcomed her as an old and dear friend.

"This is a surprise for us too," said the Queen. "*Two* family reunions!"

"I came down by train with the royal party this morning, ma'am," Alice explained. "Her Majesty is waiting to meet you when you go ashore at Southampton, but she was kind enough to suggest that I might like to help Miss Crawford bring their Royal Highnesses out to join you."

At her shoulder, the nursery-governess bobbed a curtsey, and the Queen drew her into the group.

"Crawfie – how are you? I want to hear all the news; I believe we're all to have lunch in our suite . . ." Putting her arms round the two girls, she added: "Everyone's gone to a lot of trouble on your behalf – they've been blowing up balloons all the morning!"

". . . After lunch, the King and Queen invented a kind of tennis with balloons, and when that began to pall the girls decided to give the balloons their freedom, and let them out of the portholes – much to the delight of all the other shipping in the Solent." Then, seeing William's quizzical expression, Alice broke off and sighed: "I know, I'm talking too much – and it has been a long day. . . . What time is it?"

"Late," said her husband. "High time for bed."

"I can hardly wait; why are strange beds never so comfortable? Even our bed in London isn't as cosy as this one."

When Alice was in attendance upon Queen Mary at Marlborough House, she stayed at the family's town-house in Eaton Square. William missed her whenever she went away, but he rarely grumbled; he knew how much she enjoyed her occasional duties at Court.

Somewhere outside in the night, a bird began to sing.

"Listen . . ." Alice went to the window and pulled the curtains open; their bedroom was on the first floor of Crown House – a seventeenth-century manor set in rolling parkland and gardens that were William's pride and joy. In the darkness, the nightingale poured out its liquid song.

Taking a deep breath, she said: "I can smell the roses . . . It's so lovely."

"And so are you." William came over and stood beside her. "As lovely as ever."

She leaned against his shoulder: "I'm an old hag – I shall be sixty on my next birthday."

"You're still the most beautiful woman I ever saw," he told her. "And I'm a very lucky man."

"Sssh. . . ." A shadow crossed her face: "Don't tempt providence."

"Is it tempting providence to give thanks for happiness?"

"It feels selfish to be happy, when there are so many terrible things happening. You never talk about the crisis – Germany – Czechoslovakia. . . . If the worst came to the worst – if we had to go to war against Germany – what would happen to us?"

"Nothing. We shall come through it – don't worry."

She turned, looking up into his face: "How can you be sure?"

"Whatever happens, we shall come through. I've started to make plans, in case of an emergency – but it's too late to start discussing all that now. Let's go to bed."

She closed the curtains, saying sadly: "Our nightingale's stopped singing. Nothing lasts, does it?"

Later, as they lay in bed, William asked: "What are you thinking about?"

"I can't help remembering Richard. . . . One day he was here, strong and well and so much alive, and then suddenly –

5

he'd gone. And now we hardly ever mention him. You never talk about him – Polly has thrown herself into her work – she's so busy running her business and looking after her children, it's as if she'd forgotten she ever had a husband."

"I don't believe Polly's forgotten him. . . . Not for one moment."

Richard Gaunt, Viscount Ebony, had been the Minsters' eldest son. He had worked hard, running the home farm, and he played hard, giving and taking love where he found it, sharing his easy pleasures with so many pretty girls. One of those girls had been Jenny Webster, the housekeeper's daughter; at nineteen, Jenny had fallen under Richard's spell – and in time he left her, just as he left all the others.

All except Polly.

Polly Harvey was a chorus girl, whom he met in London. When he learned that she was pregnant, Richard realized that he loved her, and they were married very quickly. A few months later their son, Alexander, was born, and five years after that, she conceived another child.

By then the novelty of being a faithful husband had begun to wear thin, and Richard started taking his fun on the side; he became involved with the bored, lonely wife of a local JP. When the gossip began, Richard came to his senses and told her the affair was over; after a violent quarrel, Viscount Ebony was found dead, with a bullet in his brain. The resulting scandal made newspaper headlines and rocked Crown House to its foundations.

Polly went into a long decline; when her daughter Harriet was born, she rejected both children, wanting to be left alone in her grief.

So it was Jenny who looked after Alex and Harriet. She had long since shaken off her infatuation for Richard and given her heart to Nicholas; they were married only a year before Richard's death.

Remembering those dreadful times, Alice whispered: "When Richie died – it was like the end of the world."

William held her tightly: "That's what I'm trying to say. We got through it somehow – life went on."

In time, Polly found a new interest; she started a marriage bureau in the nearby market town of Medford; the business prospered, and she began to hold up her head again. Eventually Jenny was able to pass Alex and Harriet back into the care of their mother, and life returned to something like normality.

"I'm certain we shall be all right, in the end," William concluded. "We must prepare for the worst, and hope for the best."

"I suppose so." Alice cuddled a little closer to him. "All the same . . . I wish that nightingale hadn't stopped singing."

One floor above, in another darkened room, Jenny and Nicholas lay together – alert and awake, with every sense tingling and responsive – mind, body and spirit at their highest pitch – exultant, triumphant. . . .

At last, all passion spent, they clung together. For a while they did not speak, but held one another in darkness and silence. Then Nick whispered: "The best part of travelling is coming home."

"The very best." She smiled, lazily teasing him. "All right – *now* you can tell me about Canada."

He shrugged: "Oh – it was a real triumph for their Majesties. They showed the Canadians they could be 'just plain folks' – going to barbecues, eating hot dogs, and all that. Of course they fell for the Queen, hook, line and sinker. In Washington, one of the Senators congratulated His Majesty on being 'a darn good Queen-picker' – that went down very well."

"How long were you in the USA?"

"Only a few days. When we visited the White House we were offered cups of tea, because the President said: 'My mother doesn't approve of cocktails" – and the King said: 'Neither does mine . . .'."

Jenny smiled: "Queen Mary might come round to them in time, like your Grandmama."

"Old Bea – drinking cocktails?" exclaimed Nick. "I don't believe it!"

"It's true – Polly persuaded her to sample a dry martini, and now there's no holding her."

At eighty-seven Lord Minster's mother, Lady Beatrice, was a formidable old lady. She occupied her own small suite in Crown House, and her sitting-room commanded the best view of the gardens. Crippled by arthritis, she did not often venture out, but complained vigorously to her family: "I won't be left out of things – d'you hear? I won't be overlooked!"

It had always been difficult to overlook the Dowager Countess of Minster.

"She listens to her wireless every day, so she always knows the news before anyone else." Jenny's smile faded as she added: "What *is* the latest news, Nick? Is there any hope of a settlement with Germany?"

Nicholas chose his words carefully: "I don't believe any kind of agreement is possible now – between us and the Nazis."

"You mean – there will be a war?"

"I'm afraid so."

"Does that mean you'll be going away?"

"I don't know. I'm based in London until the middle of July at least."

"Then I shall come up to Eaton Square. . . . What's happening in July?"

"The King is going to visit the Naval College at Dartmouth, and I'm to go with him. It will be like old times." During the General Strike of 1926, Nicholas had thrown up his degree course at Oxford and gone to Dartmouth to train as a Midshipman. "After that, their Majesties are off to Scotland, and I'll be due for some leave – so we'll have lots of time together. Do you want to go away somewhere? Paris, perhaps?"

Jenny put her arms round him. "Let's not go anywhere. Let's stay here – with the family."

Nicholas knew what she was thinking; if war broke out, it might be a long time before they could all be together again.

"Will the twins be here? And Caro?" he asked.

His sister Caroline was three years younger than Nick; she had been a successful journalist on the *Daily Argus* until

8

she disagreed violently with her employer at the time of the Spanish Civil War – Caro's sympathies were always with the underdog. Now she was married to Scott Hanson, the foreign correspondent for a New York daily paper, and a regular columnist for a left-wing weekly.

"I don't know what Scott and Caro are up to – I don't even know if they're in England. The last I heard, they were dashing about between Berlin, Paris and Rome."

"How about the twins?"

Martin and Miranda were born on the same day, twenty years ago; there was a strong bond between them, and although they had quarrelled, on and off, ever since their nursery days, they shared a special understanding which somehow excluded everyone else.

For the moment, they had been separated; Martin was finishing his second year at Oxford – following in Nick's footsteps, he was reading English and history at Wadham – while Miranda had been sent to an expensive and exclusive finishing-school near the French alps. Though they were far apart, they rarely wrote to one another, or telephoned; perhaps they did not need to.

"Martin's due to come home in a day or two. Miranda's staying out there for the summer; she wrote and said she wanted to visit Aunt Edith."

"I wonder why – she's never shown much interest in Aunt Edie before."

"Well, it will make a nice change for Edith and Grace. They don't see many people, tucked away in their corner of the Pyrenees."

At ten o'clock on a July morning, the Mediterranean glittered in brilliant sunlight.

"It's going to be another scorcher," said Grace Duncan.

She had been out of England for five years, and away from her native Scotland a great deal longer than that, but the Highland burr in her voice was as strong as ever.

"Yes – another lovely day," agreed Lady Edith.

Shielding her eyes, she looked along the station platform. Shimmering in the heat, the railway-tracks converged in the distance, as they disappeared into a tunnel.

Grace glanced at her watch: "The train's late."

"Better late than never," said Edith brightly. "I'm really looking forward to seeing Miranda. I wonder if we'll recognize her; she was only a schoolgirl when we left Crown House."

"She's a schoolgirl still, by all accounts. Where's this boarding-school she's at? Somewhere near Annecy?"

"That's right – but she's a young lady now – she was twenty on her last birthday."

"Mmm. You sent her one of your water-colours and she never wrote back to thank you – I hadn't forgotten that."

Edith bit her lip: "I expect they have exams in the summer

Lord Minster's sister, Lady Edith had been a lonely, unhappy child, ignored by her father and bullied by her mother, Lady Beatrice. She had withdrawn into a sad, isolated existence, until at the age of forty-eight she met Grace Duncan, who was headmistress of the little school at Ebony – the village at the gates of Crown House. Worlds apart in background and upbringing, they had become devoted to one another, and chose to spend the rest of their lives together.

When Grace retired from teaching they left England, settling in the foothills of the Pyrenees. They soon got to know the people of Collioure, the nearby fishing-port, but they saw very few English visitors; Miranda's arrival was an important event.

"It's very nice of her to take the trouble to visit us," said Edith. "Such a long way – right across France —"

Grace lifted her head: "Listen now – would that be the train?"

The rails began to sing with a high metallic note; a whistle blew, and the locomotive emerged from the tunnel.

"Here it comes!" exclaimed Edith happily.

They watched the train come in, slowing to a stop with a squeal of brakes and a hiss of escaping steam. They watched a few passengers alight, and then they watched it draw away, gathering speed as it disappeared with a last mournful whistle into another tunnel.

Stricken, Edith turned to her friend: "What happened? Where is she?"

"Seemingly she changed her mind," said Grace.

"Oh, surely not! She may have left a message for us at the Post Office."

But there was no letter or telegram for them in the pigeon-holes behind the counter. They tried to telephone the boarding-school to ask whether Mademoiselle Gaunt had left Annecy as arranged; and waited until the operator informed them that there was no reply from that number.

"I suppose the school must be closed for the holidays," Grace concluded. "Let's go home."

Leaving the village, they climbed the stony path to *Mas-Lou* – the semi-derelict farmhouse they had converted into a comfortable villa – and Edith fought back her tears.

"I mustn't be silly . . . But I had been looking forward to seeing her – I haven't seen any of the family for so long."

Grace squeezed her hand, and they held hands all the way up the path, like children.

The next day was sunny again and the sky was as blue as the sea.

"Would you fancy roast duck for supper tonight?" Grace enquired, after breakfast. "I intended it for last night, in honour of our visitor – it will only be wasted unless I cook it today."

Edith looked crestfallen: "I suppose we'd better have it – though I don't feel very hungry."

"There's plenty of work to be done in the garden," Grace told her. "I dare say we'll both have an appetite by supper-time."

The two ladies had done their best to create an English garden, though it was flanked by palm trees and mimosa, with bougainvillea throwing a riot of purple across one white-washed wall. All the morning they worked companionably, side by side, until Grace realized that the sun was directly overhead.

"It's high time we had a breather. There's a jug of orange juice in the cooler; let's sit on the terrace, under the vine."

11

At that moment they heard the squeak of the garden gate, and someone called: "Aunt Edie – are you at home?"

Miranda came down the path, carrying a suitcase. Laughing and crying at the same time, Edith rushed to meet her, while Grace followed more slowly.

"My dear – how wonderful – how well you look – and so tall, I'd never have known you . . . And here's Grace —"

As they shook hands, Grace asked if she would care for some orange juice.

"Gorgeous – I'm simply parched after the journey – it's quite a trudge from the station, isn't it? I lost my way twice, and had to ask – I rather pride myself on my French by now, but the people here have such thick accents, I could hardly understand them."

"That's because French isn't their first language; they speak Catalan among themselves." Grace offered the visitor a wicker chair, and Miranda threw herself into it.

"What a heavenly garden – and what a pretty cottage. Did you do it all yourselves? Goodness, you are marvellous."

Edith gazed at her niece – long-limbed, brown-skinned, her short blonde hair bleached almost white by the sun – and said: "We're so glad you managed to get here; we were expecting you yesterday – did we make a mistake about the day?"

"Oh, no – something cropped up at the last minute, so I stayed at school for one more night. . . . Sorry about that."

Grace returned with a jug and three glasses, saying: "That's odd – we tried to telephone, but there was no reply. I thought the school must have closed for the summer."

"Oh – really?" Miranda looked disconcerted, then turned back to her Aunt: "Perhaps it was a wrong number. . . . Have you heard from the family lately? How are they all? How's Martin?"

"I had a letter from your father last week; Martin's visiting some of his Oxford friends. . . . It's so good of you to give up your holiday to come and stay with us."

Miranda shrugged: "Well, you know – since you're both in France too. . . . Though I won't be staying here very long, actually."

"Oh? I thought you said – till September?"

"Well, no – I'm going back to school early – I've got so much reading to catch up on . . . and I promised I'd help Monsieur Lafitte at the stables during the vacation, mucking out and so on. . . . He gives us riding-lessons." A silence fell, and after a moment, she went on in a different tone: "If there's a war – what will you do? Stay here – or go back to England?"

"A war?" Edith stared at her. "Oh, I know people are talking about a crisis – but we don't take it seriously, do we, Grace?"

Miranda looked astonished: "The French newspapers are full of it. And Alain – Monsieur Lafitte – is making preparations already; that's another reason I want to get back there – I feel I ought to do something to help."

That night, when they went up to bed, Edith sat at the dressing-table, unpinning her long hair which she wore braided into a bun by day.

"You don't think it's true, do you?" she asked. "About the war?"

"Certainly not." Grace was unbuttoning her blouse. "Remember all that fuss last year, when Mr Chamberlain had to fly off to see Herr Hitler? It will all blow over."

Slightly reassured, Edith began to brush her hair: "All the same, Miranda seems very anxious to get back to her school."

Grace pursed her lips: "I fancy there could be another reason for that – rather more pressing than rumours about the war."

"What do you mean?"

"Did you not notice how often she mentioned the name of the riding-master? It strikes me that Monsieur Alain Lafitte must be a very charming gentleman."

On another day, in another country, Nicholas stood on the deck of the royal yacht, *Victoria and Albert*. Their Majesties were having better weather on this voyage.

Their visit to the West Country was to cover the weekend, and they reached Dartmouth on Saturday morning. The Officer in Charge of the Royal Naval College, Captain Dalrymple-Hamilton, came out to meet the royal visitors and escort them ashore. He was presented to them by the King's cousin, Lord Louis Mountbatten – known within the family as "Dickie" – who had been a Dartmouth cadet himself, and was enjoying this nostalgic return to the scenes of his youth.

"But I'm afraid there's a slight problem," he explained, when he had performed the introductions. "I'm sorry to tell you there's an epidemic going round the College – two epidemics, actually – mumps *and* chicken-pox. A lot of the lads are in the sick-bay, and the rest are in quarantine."

The Queen's face fell. "You mean we can't take the girls round the College? They're going to be awfully disappointed."

"The M.O. thinks it would be better not to run any risks."

"They c-c-can't stay on board the whole weekend!" protested the King. "They'd be bored stiff."

"No need for that," said Dickie Mountbatten. "The Captain has made arrangements for the Princesses at his house; he's got a young family himself, so there's a play-room – toy trains, a tennis-court – plenty to keep them amused, and no danger of infection."

So the King and Queen inspected the College, while the Princesses were entertained at the Headmaster's house.

King George enjoyed his tour round the College and insisted that the old "punishment book" should be brought out. Turning the pages, he regaled the company with a recital of his youthful misdeeds.

Later, when he and the Queen were alone, he confessed: "It's strange – I used to hate this place, but when I look back it all seems to have been tremendous fun. I suppose unhappy memories fade eventually; that's why we talk about the g-g-good old days."

On Sunday morning, their Majesties attended Divine Service at the College Chapel, then returned to the Captain's House for a family lunch. In the afternoon they played croquet with the Princesses, while Nicholas took a stroll round the front of the house, grateful for a few moments of peace.

Hearing the crunch of footsteps on the gravel, he looked

up and saw a tall fair youth approaching, and asked: "Can I help you?"

"I've been invited to tea," said the Senior Cadet. "My uncle says I've got to entertain the girls."

"Your Uncle —?"

"Uncle Dickie – Lord Mountbatten."

"Ah – they're all in the garden – let me lead the way."

They walked round and joined the others; when the eighteen-year-old boy had been presented to the Royal Family, he joined in the croquet game. Tea and sandwiches were brought out, though the younger members of the party elected to have lemonade and biscuits instead; Lord Mountbatten's nephew amused himself by jumping over the tennis net several times, and by teasing Princess Margaret, much to her indignation.

At thirteen, Princess Elizabeth was too old for teasing, but she could not take her eyes off the young blond Viking; throughout the afternoon he was aware of her steady, concentrated gaze.

When it was time for the family to return to the yacht, the quarantined naval cadets, who had scarcely caught a glimpse of the Princesses, made up for lost time by sailing down the River Dart in every vessel they could lay hands on – old rowing-boats, dinghies, canoes, even a leaky, flat-bottomed barge – determined to give the visitors a royal send-off.

They kept pace with the *Victoria and Albert* as far as they could, along the winding river, but gradually fell away one by one, until only a single rowing-boat remained.

In the stern of the *V and A*, the King turned to Nicholas and asked: "May I borrow your glasses? Who's that boy, trying to keep up with us?"

Nick passed his binoculars to the King, who exclaimed: "I thought as much – it's Dickie's nephew, showing off again. . . . What's he trying to do – drown himself?" He attempted to wave him away, but the boy waved back enthusiastically. "Look at him – grinning all over his face . . . Tell the damned young fool to go back. . . . What's his name?"

"Philip," said Princess Elizabeth.

Chapter Two

Wednesday, 9 August to Sunday, 3 September 1939

Alice put down her pen and read through what she had written.

> *"Crown House. Wednesday, August 9th.*
>
> *"Dear Miranda —*
>
> *"Still no word from you! We can't help being a little anxious. Aunt Edith wrote and told us that you had gone back to Annecy, but we never get any answer when we telephone the school, and we haven't heard from you since you left Collioure. No doubt you're working hard on your French grammar, but even a postcard would be nice.*
>
> *"We are all making plans for the future. As you can imagine, there's a great deal to be done. Your father has called a family conference, and we have to gather in Grandmama's room at eleven o'clock – so I daren't be late. . . ."*

"I won't have black curtains on my windows!" Old Bea's bony hand tightened on the handle of her cane, and she banged the floor crossly. "I won't live in a funeral parlour!"

William sighed: "I don't think you quite understand, Mama. We have to obey the official orders." He read aloud from the latest batch of government pamphlets: *"At the first sign of*

16

hostile aircraft approaching, a warning will be given by a fluctuating or warbling signal from the sirens. . . . Obscure all lighting; during hours of darkness, no light whatever must escape from any windows. . . ."

"We don't have to black out all the windows, surely?" asked Polly. She had left her secretary in charge of the marriage bureau, and now she could hear her children squabbling outside on the lawn. "Just the rooms we use at night, I suppose?"

"And all the passages and staircases?" William raised an eyebrow. "We can't blunder about the house in pitch darkness. Besides, next winter it will be impossible to keep the place warm; there's bound to be a fuel shortage."

"Do you think the war will go on that long?" asked Jenny.

Lord Minster smiled wryly: "In 1914, people said it would all be over by Christmas – but it was four years before they signed the Armistice."

"So what's the answer, Pa?" said Nicholas. "Are you planning to close part of the house?"

"It seems to be the only solution," said his father. "Your mother and I have been discussing ways and means with the staff."

"I had a long talk with Lilian and Hawkins," Alice explained. Lilian Brooks had been the housekeeper for seven years, but Mr Hawkins, the butler, had worked at Crown House since he was a junior footman, forty years ago. "The younger ones will be leaving us anyway," she continued. "The men are being called up for military service, and the girls want to work for the war effort as well. There are plenty of jobs going at the munition factories."

"Better money and shorter hours," sniffed Old Bea. "But what are you going to do about my windows?"

Lord and Lady Minster exchanged glances, and William said: "You won't be in these rooms, Mama. There will only be a skeleton staff to run the house, and that will leave some empty rooms in the West Wing, above the kitchens. Alice and I are going to move into the housekeeper's flat; it has a pleasant little sitting-room and two good bedrooms – we shall take one, and you shall have the other."

17

Lady Beatrice put her hand to her heart, then said in a shocked whisper: "Are you suggesting I should live in the *servants' quarters* . . .? No, no – somewhere else – the Lodge Cottage perhaps —?"

"We can't turn Ken out," said Polly. "The Lodge is his home."

Ken Stubbs was the farm manager; originally employed on the royal estates at Sandringham, he had moved down from Norfolk to run the home farm at Crown House, and had proved to be the right man for the job.

"Things have come to a pretty pass when a farmhand merits more consideration than the oldest member of the family. . . ." Old Bea tossed her head. "Stubbs is a bachelor – what does he want with two bedrooms?"

"That's been taken care of," said William. "Dennett is going into Ken's spare room; which leaves the chauffeur's flat vacant in the garage block for Polly and the children. . . . If Polly has no objection?"

"Fine," said Polly. "The kids will love it . . . but what about Nick and Jenny?"

"As long as I'm wanted at the Palace, we shall be at Eaton Square anyway," said Nick.

Old Bea glared at her son: "So – you've got everything arranged, haven't you?"

William said, with more confidence than he felt: "I'm sure it will work out very well. We must start moving as soon as possible; there will be no time at all, when war is declared."

A silence fell, broken by Alice: "A few weeks ago, we were saying: '*If* there's a war . . .' Now it isn't 'if' any longer – it's 'when' . . .".

Nicholas and Jenny moved up to Eaton Square in the middle of August. They did their best to prepare the house against possible attack, converting the cellars into an air raid shelter, fitting blackout material to the windows, and stocking up provisions as if they expected a siege.

"It took me ages to get round Sainsbury's this morning,"

said Jenny. "And when I got home at last, I found I'd left this beastly object behind, so I had to go all the way back for it."

The "object" was a brown cardboard box with a long loop of string that could be slipped over the shoulder. Inside was a black rubber mask, with canvas straps to secure it in position and a metal filter, honeycombed with holes, to breathe through. Jenny had tried to practise wearing it, and found it hot, smelly and claustrophobic.

"You needn't carry it about with you all the time," Nick told her.

"But they say we'll have to, when . . . I mean if – you know. . . . Only I keep losing the wretched thing."

Nick kissed her gently: "You hate all this, don't you?"

"Well . . . I don't really care what happens – as long as we stay together."

Next morning Nick was summoned to the palace; His Majesty had decided to cut short his holiday and return to London. The Queen and the Princesses were staying in Scotland for the time being. This meant that Nicholas had to report for duty every morning, sometimes working until very late. Jenny only saw him at breakfast – or at supper, when he was often too tired to eat, and picked at his food.

What good was she doing, she wondered, alone in London? She rang Crown House every evening, and learned that Lady Minster was helping to organize lodgings for the evacuees, and Lord Minster had become an ARP Warden.

"I told him he's raving mad," said Alice. "The doctor said he mustn't do too much, after that heart-attack, and now he's out every night, going to meetings, fitting gas masks, distributing leaflets. . . . What are you and Nick up to?"

"Nick's busier than ever – I know I should be doing things too, but somehow. . . ." Then, as the front door bell rang: "I must go – there's someone at the door, and we don't have parlourmaids any more. . . . We'll talk tomorrow."

Hurrying downstairs, she opened the street door. Nick's sister Caroline stood under the portico, her hair tied up

19

in a scarf, a raincoat over one arm and two suitcases at her feet.

"Is this a bad moment?" she asked. "You're not just going out?"

"No – of course not – come in."

As the front door shut, Caro went on apologetically: "I hope you don't mind, but I thought – if it's all right with you and Nick – I might dump myself on you for a while. . . . A sort of aging evacuee."

Jenny laughed: "I can't think of anything nicer. Nick's out all day, and I never see a soul. How did you know I was here?"

"Martin dropped in last night; he was between trains, on his way back to Oxford."

"He's still going up, next term? I thought he might be conscripted."

"He should have been, but they decided to let third-year students take their finals – it's a 'deferred call-up'." Over cups of tea, she explained that Scott had disappeared on another foreign trip. "He said travelling's getting rather problematic, so I'm supposed to sit in our little flat in Chelsea while he whizzes about, having a whale of a time."

"Couldn't you get a job of your own? They might take you back on the *Argus*, if —"

"If I grovelled a bit and swore I'd never sing the 'Red Flag' again? Yes, they probably would; and then I'd find myself writing 'A Hundred Ways With Rice' or 'How to Knit Your Own Air-Raid Shelter'. . . . No, I want to do a *real* job."

"I keep seeing advertisements for volunteers," said Jenny. "Ambulance drivers – the Fire Service – switchboard operators . . . Only I can't decide which one to choose."

"When I was in Spain, I worked in a hospital for a while – only as a dogsbody, but I'm quite used to mopping up blood and messes. I'd like to start again and do it properly – have some training, get some qualifications. . . . Why don't we both volunteer?"

"I don't know if I could face nursing; if anyone died on me. . . ."

"Well, there must be other jobs. Anything's better than sitting about, doing nothing."

Caro's enthusiasm was infectious, and Jenny exclaimed: "You're right – I must get out of this house and *do* something. I've been feeling very peculiar lately; like when someone lights a firework and you're waiting for it to go off. . . . Do you remember the firework parties at Crown House? I remember you dancing round the bonfire – but then you grew up and moved to London."

"And I landed a job on the *Argus* – and got sent to Spain. . . . That was where I met Scott again."

"I remember that summer. One afternoon I took Alex to the Picture Palace in Medford. When the newsreel started, there were pictures of the Civil War, and he said: 'Is this where Auntie Caro is? Will we see her?' I couldn't wait for the Silly Symphony to come on; it was so awful – buildings being blown up – people running away – the bombs falling. . . ."

She did not tell Caro that, even now, she sometimes lived through those scenes of devastation in her nightmares. Reaching for the teapot, she said: "Let's have some more tea."

While she refilled the cups, Caro gazed out of the window, at the sunlight on the plane trees in the Square, saying: "It's funny to think I lived here, when I first came to London." In her mind's eye, she saw a different window, and a different view. "But I soon moved to another address."

"Somewhere in Primrose Hill, wasn't it? I know your parents were terribly shocked – you were Living In Sin With An Older Man. . . ." Jenny smiled; it all seemed so long ago now. "He was an old friend of the family, wasn't he? – I can't remember his name."

"Paul – Paul Weyman. Oh, he was very kind – very sweet – but it didn't last."

"Do you still keep in touch?"

"Goodness, no. I walked out on him; I don't suppose he ever forgave me. . . . I wonder what he's doing now? He used to work at the television studios, in Alexandra Palace – perhaps he still does." Suddenly restless, Caro turned and studied herself in the mirror over the mantelpiece. "God – I'm twenty-nine –

21

practically ancient. . . . If we're going to put our names down for hospital jobs, we'd better do it soon."

Outside Broadcasting House, Portland Place was a hive of activity; workmen were constructing a barrier of sandbags to protect the main entrance – inside, anxious people milled about, bumping into one another, and waiting for directions.

"They said I should report here at eight-thirty – I've been here ever since, and there's no sign of any transport. . . ."

"The DG told me himself that the train was due to leave Paddington at ten – it's nearly one o'clock now, and there hasn't been a word from the Fourth Floor. . . ."

"My secretary's gone off with the filing cabinets, so she's got all the addresses – but they won't do her a scrap of good, because I've still got the keys. . . ."

Stepping out of the lift, Paul Weyman surveyed them unsympathetically. At least these radio people knew what they were supposed to be doing; Drama and Variety and Children's Hour were all moving to the West Country, to carry on broadcasting from makeshift studios in secret locations. Working in television, he had no such luck; the studios and transmitter at Alexandra Palace could not be set up anywhere else.

Pushing through the swing doors, he emerged into the sunlight in time to see a cab disgorging a passenger. As the driver flicked up the "For Hire" flag, Paul lunged forward, yelling: "Hey! – taxi —!"

At exactly the same moment, an elderly gentleman gesticulated and shouted: "Cabbie —!"

They collided on the pavement, and the other man said: "My cab, I believe . . . Good lord – Weyman!"

"My God – Charlie Bowyer," said Paul. "It's a small world."

"It is indeed." Sir Charles Bowyer reddened, looking about for another taxi. "Very tiresome."

"You're not going to the club, by any chance?"

"As a matter of fact I am, but —"

"Then we'll go together." Paul held the door open, and told the driver: "The Pall Mall Club."

22

As they bowled along Oxford Street, Paul said: "Under the circumstances, I think we might bury the hatchet, don't you?" Charles shifted uncomfortably: "I suppose you're right."

Before her marriage, Lady Minster had been Alice Bowyer; Sir Charles was her brother – he and Paul Weyman were both members of the Pall Mall Club, but they had not spoken since the unpleasantness over Paul's liaison with Caroline.

Paul continued: "Just to show there's no hard feelings – why don't you have lunch with me?"

"That's extremely civil of you," Charlie admitted. "Actually – I've just been having a very unprofitable meeting with my broker; the Stock Exchange seems to be quite hysterical at the moment."

"So does the BBC. I've had an equally unprofitable meeting at B.H. – Broadcasting House. They're evacuating the radio staff to the country, but no such luck for us television chaps. They just say we must 'sit tight and await further instructions . . .' We never know from one day to the next how long we'll be on the air." Seeing Charlie's blank expression, he changed the subject: "And how are the family at Crown House? What are they all doing?"

"Alice has joined the WVS – she's very busy now, as a billeting officer; and William is with the ARP"

"What about the girls? How is – Caroline?"

Paul found it hard to say her name; it was still painful to think of Caro.

"She's volunteered to train as a nurse – and Jenny's at the same hospital, helping in the canteen. But as for Miranda —"

Charlie broke off as the cab drew up outside the Club, and Paul prompted him: "You were saying – Miranda . . . ?"

"Well, in actual fact – nobody seems to know where Miranda is."

Alice sat at a table, surrounded by lists of names and addresses, trying to work out a foolproof system for billeting the evacuees.

The sitting-room in the housekeeper's flat was hardly spacious, and by now it was so cluttered – address books,

23

maps, typed lists and pamphlets filled every flat surface – it was practically impossible to find anything. To make matters worse, Lady Beatrice was installed in the adjoining room. She played her wireless set at full blast all day, and insisted on keeping the door open. If there were any important announcements, she always called Alice to her bedside, and between bulletins she often summoned her with urgent requests for cups of tea or biscuits.

And all the time, Alice worried about Miranda.

Why had she ignored their letters and telegrams? And why was there never any reply from the boarding-school? William tried to persuade her to look on the bright side, pointing out that, at twenty, Miranda was quite capable of fending for herself, and no doubt she would turn up when she felt like it.

For Lord Minster had problems of his own. He had been promoted from the post of Air Raid Warden, and was now District Organizing Officer for the Weald of Kent (South Medford Division.) Since he spent so much time taking or passing on orders, he had to have access to a telephone, so he worked in the library, where his desk and chair were the only pieces of furniture not shrouded in dust-sheets.

Crown House was being systematically closed up; the furniture had been removed from all the principal rooms and stored away, together with the pictures and *objets-d'art*. The carpets were rolled up and put into the attics, and the bare boards in the corridors set up unfamiliar echoes.

Alice was trying to decide how many children she could reasonably expect the Vicarage to take in, when she recognized the sound of William's footsteps. Surely it couldn't be lunchtime already?

He was smiling when he came in.

"Good news," he said. "I've just been talking to Miranda."

"Miranda—?" Alice jumped up, sending billeting forms flying in all directions. "Is she holding on? Let me speak to her —"

William stopped her: "Holding on – all the way from France? It would cost a fortune."

"She's still at school? Then we can call her back —"

24

"No – she was calling from a telephone kiosk; the new term doesn't start till next week."

Sick with disappointment, Alice sank back into her chair: "But – where has she been since she left Collioure? Edith said she had to go back to look after the horses —"

"She's staying with a married couple who work at the school. She sounded very happy, and she's determined to finish her course. She said if Martin can do his Finals year, she's entitled to do the same."

"But it's not the same thing at all; once we're at war, it will be so difficult to travel."

"She assured me she's perfectly safe where she is. Nothing can get through the Maginot line."

"You should have been firm with her – oh, I do wish you'd called me – if only I'd been there when she phoned. . . . You must *do* something!"

"I certainly shall; I'll get on to the Post Office engineers right away – they must install a telephone in this flat."

"That's not what I meant – you must do something about Miranda —"

Lady Beatrice's voice broke in: "Speak up, Alice – I can't hear when you mumble. What's that about Miranda? I want to know what's going on."

"Nothing's going on, Mama!" snapped Alice. "She's in France, that's all." Lowering her voice, she added: "I shall write and tell her to come home immediately – before it's too late." But it was too late already.

On Friday, the first of September, Hitler's army marched into Poland.

In south-east England, the evacuation scheme went into operation; the railways ran special trains, and the London termini were crowded with bewildered children. Name-tags pinned to their coats, they clutched suitcases, teddy bears and gas masks; and distraught mothers choked back tears, trying to pretend they were going off for a lovely holiday.

25

Alice was busy all day, meeting parties of children off the trains at Medford and escorting them to their new homes.

The King went to Downing Street to see the Prime Minister, and the Queen returned from Balmoral to join her husband.

At the Alexandra Palace studios, Paul Weyman interrupted the rehearsal of a television play to address the cast: "I'm afraid this production has just been cancelled. A state of emergency has been declared."

On the little black-and-white screen, a Mickey Mouse cartoon was being transmitted. When it ended, the screen went blank. Television services had been suspended indefinitely.

On Saturday, September the second, radio broadcasts too were curtailed; national and regional programmes merged into one. Most of the staff had already left Portland Place for a secret rendezvous in Bristol or Bangor. The work of sandbagging public buildings continued; barrage balloons sailed in the sky like celestial silver pigs. The streets were filled with soldiers carrying kitbags, reporting back to their units.

Sunday, September the third, was another beautiful summer's day.

Lord and Lady Minster went to Matins at St Peter's, Ebony, as usual; but the service was interrupted soon after it had begun. One of the churchwardens carried a portable wireless up the aisle, and it was switched on. At eleven-fifteen, the voice of Neville Chamberlain was heard:

"I am speaking to you from the Cabinet Room at Number Ten, Downing Street. . . ."

In Eaton Square, Jenny listened to the wireless; Sunday was her day off from the canteen – Caro had an early shift at the hospital, and Nick was on duty at the Palace, so she was on her own.

"I have to tell you now that no such undertaking has been received, and that consequently this country is at war with Germany. . . ."

Eight minutes after the Prime Minister had finished speaking, the air raid sirens sounded throughout London.

Jenny opened the french windows and stepped onto the narrow balcony, looking down into the square. The noise of the siren went on and on, making the air tremble with its high-pitched wail. A solitary policeman rode past on a bicycle, with a cardboard notice attached to his back which read: *"Take cover."*

Jenny looked up at the sky, and waited for the first enemy plane to come into view; would it drop bombs – or poison gas? Should she hunt for her gas mask – or go down and shelter in the cellars?

She could not think what to do. She could not move. She could only stand there, looking up at the sky, waiting for the nightmare to begin.

Now she knew what that strange feeling was – the feeling which had been haunting her. She recognized it at last; it wasn't excitement, or anger, or impatience.

It was terror.

Chapter Three

Monday, 11 September to Saturday, 30 September 1939

"Two baked beans on toast, one bacon and egg, bread and butter, and three cups of tea, please, miss."

Jenny scribbled on her pad, and gave the order number to the ambulance driver on the other side of the counter.

"There you are – number one-seven-two – I'll call you when it's ready."

Then she pushed through the swinging service door into the kitchen, where she passed the order on to one of the cooks.

One-seven-two. . . . She had served one hundred and seventy-one meals since she came on duty, and it was nearly half-past eight; only another half-hour, and she could go home.

This was the busiest time of day in the basement canteen. The day staff at the hospital were snatching a meal before going off-duty, and the evening shift were fortifying themselves against the long night ahead.

It wouldn't be so bad, Jenny told herself, if it wasn't so noisy. In the kitchen, the cooks had to shout to make themselves heard above the clash of pots and pans, the splash of washing-up water in the sinks, and the continuous roar of gas jets burning in the ovens or under the grills.

The canteen wasn't much better; apart from the chatter of the nurses and ambulancemen, a wireless loudspeaker seemed to play the same dance tunes over and over again. "Roll Out the Barrel" and the chirpy optimism of "We're Going to Hang

Out the Washing on the Siegfried Line" were firm favourites – but the one Jenny hated most was "Little Sir Echo".

Back at the counter, while she waited for order one-seven-two to be dished up, she made herself useful by cutting bread and butter, pouring milk into thick white cups, and refilling the huge metal teapot.

The words of "Little Sir Echo" ran through her head with maddening persistence: *"Won't you come over and play?"* . . . Too many songs seemed to be about loneliness.

"Number one-seven-two!" she called out, loading plates of food on to a tin tray.

"Ta very much." The ambulance driver moved along the counter, to pay the cashier. Immediately, another customer took his place.

"Next, please," Jenny began. "Number one-seven-three – oh, hello, Caro!"

She hadn't recognized her at first; the probationer nurses all looked alike in their uniforms.

Caro smothered a yawn: "Sorry – I'm not awake yet; my alarm didn't go off, and I thought I was going to be late, so I rushed out of the house in a panic – and now of course I'm early. . . . Still, that means I've got time to eat."

"What would you like? The Irish stew is quite good."

"For *breakfast*—?" Caro winced: "Just tea and toast, please . . . I'll be glad when I finish this turn of night duty."

"So shall I." Jenny poured another cup of tea and began buttering toast; it had been made some time, and was warm but leathery.

"But you do twelve to nine!" Caro stared at her: "That's practically civilized."

"No – I mean I'll be glad when you're back on days. I hate going home to an empty house."

"I suppose it must get a bit dreary, when Nick's away." Caro helped herself to a dollop of marmalade from an open jar. "I can't think why they keep a full staff on at nights; the wards are half-empty anyway. They send the patients home the minute they're fit to stagger – Sister Collinson says they have to keep the beds empty, for war casualties."

Jenny frowned: "Are there any?"

"No – unless you count people falling down steps in the blackout, or tripping over sandbags. But once the raids start, we'll really be busy. . . . You know, I'm quite looking forward to it. The war hasn't started yet; ever since that false alarm the first day, it's been really boring."

Jenny wondered how she could treat it so lightly. At the end of August, they had both volunteered for hospital work; Caro had been taken on as a probationary nurse, and Jenny was assigned to "Staff Catering" – which turned out to mean working in the canteen. Her hours were long, and the work was monotonous, but according to Caro, ward duties were equally uninteresting: "I'm supposed to be training for my nursing certificate, but it's just like Spain all over again – I'm really a dogsbody."

Jenny forced herself to concentrate on the task in hand: "Next, please – number one-seven-four. . . ."

Half an hour later she was free to go. She went to her locker and took off her overall, which always seemed to smell of frying fat, then climbed the stone steps and said goodnight to the porter, on duty in his glass-fronted cubbyhole.

"Good night, miss – mind how you go."

She let herself out of the building, through inner and outer doors that blocked any chink of light, and emerged into cool night air. Waiting until her eyes became accustomed to the darkness, she opened her handbag and took out a torch, the lens covered in two thicknesses of tissue paper held by a rubber band. Its dim glow showed her the edge of the kerb, and she began to pick her way along the pavement to the main road.

Occasional cars and buses crawled through the darkness; their offside headlamps were heavily screened, giving out a feeble glimmer. At the crossroads, the traffic lights could just be seen; the red, amber and green circles had been covered in protective shields, with small coloured crosses in the middle.

Jenny wondered whether she should catch a bus – but there was already a queue of travellers waiting at the stop; at this time of night the service was infrequent, so she decided to walk.

Caro had seemed so certain air raids were bound to happen

30

eventually; everyone at the canteen complained that nothing was happening – how could they be so casual about it?

Once across the river, she skirted Parliament Square, heading for Birdcage Walk. As she passed the surface shelters, she imagined herself taking refuge there during a night attack – penned in with a crowd of frightened strangers, listening to the planes overhead, and the bombs whistling down. . . .

But she would not let herself think about that. Taking deep breaths, she walked on, and smelled grass and leaves and blossom in St James's Park – it reminded her of Crown House, and her spirits rose.

Even the searchlights sweeping the sky above Buckingham Palace did not depress her; they were helping to keep enemy planes away. If only Nick had been on duty at the Palace – or better still, waiting for her at home. But she did not even know when she would see him again.

The words of "Little Sir Echo" came back to her: *"You're always so far away. . . ."*

When she reached Eaton Square, she fumbled in her bag for her key. Once inside the house, she relaxed, and switched on the hall light. Passing her reflection in the long mirror above the console table, she averted her eyes; she always looked tired and worn nowadays.

As she was about to go up to the first floor, she paused, listening. Had she imagined it – or was that a sound from the basement?

Yes, there it was again – the creak of a floorboard – and the chink of metal. . . . But tonight the house should have been empty.

Most of the staff at Eaton Square, like those at Crown House, had left to do National Service. The housekeeper, Miss Kendall, had taken on the cooking and cleaning, with the help of a "daily" who came in every morning to do the heavy work. But this was Miss Kendall's night out; she would not be back until tomorrow.

Another sound from below stairs forced Jenny to take action.

"This isn't like being afraid of air raids – it's only a burglar," she told herself. "I can deal with this."

31

The umbrella stand in the hall contained a heavy walking-stick, left behind by Lord Minster years ago; Jenny took a firm grip on it, and descended the basement stairs.

The kitchen was empty, but the door to the big, old-fashioned larder stood ajar, and she heard someone moving about inside. As the door swung open, she raised the walking-stick to protect herself, and —

"Good gracious!" exclaimed Lady Minster, dropping a tin of sardines. "You frightened the life out of me!"

When Jenny explained, Alice began to laugh: "I'm sorry, I should have warned you – but it all happened at the last moment. I thought you'd be at the canteen, and Caro would be asleep, so I didn't telephone. When I got here I decided I'd make myself some supper." She picked up the tin: "Sardines on toast – would you like some?"

Jenny shook her head: "I couldn't eat a thing – but I'll make us some coffee."

Sitting at the kitchen table, eating her scratch meal, Alice went on: "You see, I had a call from Marlborough House; Queen Mary wants me to help her get ready for the move."

"The move —?"

"They say it would be be too dangerous for Her Majesty to stay in London, because of air raids —"

"Of course," said Jenny. "That's understandable."

"She didn't want to go, but they persuaded her she should be packed off to the country, like our other national treasures!" Alice sipped her coffee. "For one terrible moment, I thought she'd decided to honour us at Crown House – but thank heaven, she's going to the Beauforts, at Badminton, for the duration of the war . . . So I've got to get Her Majesty packed up and delivered to Gloucestershire."

Jenny smiled: "You should be used to dealing with evacuees by now."

"Yes, we've had a few problems at Ebony," Alice agreed. "Did I tell you about poor Mr Wilkinson?"

Mr and Mrs Wilkinson, who ran the general store beside the village green, had offered to take in some evacuees from London, so Alice installed two small boys, the sons

32

of a Limehouse docker, into their spare bedroom above the shop.

"The trouble started when some chocolates disappeared; then Mrs Wilkinson discovered a box of peppermints, several tubes of winegums, and a bottle of ginger beer hidden under the boys' bed. They promised not to help themselves again – and the next day they took a whole jar of sherbet lemons – so Mr Wilkinson walloped them with the back of a hairbrush."

"Did it do any good?"

"None whatever; so he wrote and told the boys parents he was having a few problems, and their father came down to sort things out. He was twice the size of poor Mr Wilkinson, and he threatened to break his neck if he ever laid a finger on the little darlings again. And after he'd gone back to London, Mr Wilkinson found the cash register had been cleaned out. . . . Apparently it runs in the family."

Changing the subject, she asked suddenly: "What time does Nicholas get home? Is he always this late?"

"He's gone away – on a special assignment. He couldn't tell me any details; it's terribly secret. All I know is that he was going across to France."

Alice's face changed: "Our family seem to be drawn to France. William wrote to Edith, inviting her to come home and stay with us, but she said she and Grace were very happy where they were, and anyway the war couldn't possibly touch them. . . . And as for Miranda —"

When she hesitated, Jenny asked: "Is there any news?"

"The school's reopened now, and they answer their telephone, thank goodness. Mandy's determined to stay on for her final year, and the headmistress assured me all the girls are perfectly safe – but I can't help worrying."

It was nearly midday when HMS *Kelly* reached Cherbourg.

On deck, Nicholas watched as she manoeuvred skilfully through the fishing-boats, past the harbour arm. Up on the bridge, Lord Louis Mountbatten – the youngest Captain in the Royal Navy – was in charge of operations;

Nicholas admired his control of the ship, and felt like a passenger.

He was not a member of the destroyer's crew; he was here on behalf of the King, acting as personal escort to an important visitor.

When the ship docked, he went ashore, together with Lord Mountbatten and Randolph Churchill – an incongruous figure in the uniform of a Hussar officer. A car took them to the Port Commander's house; a large pile of luggage stood on the front steps, ready to be taken on board. Through the open doors, two figures appeared; the Duke and Duchess of Windsor.

It was not an easy meeting. The men wore strained smiles, and tried to appear at ease. The Duchess, immaculate in a grey Chanel suit, her raven-black hair knotted at the nape of her neck, did not attempt to conceal her irritation.

"Put my bags into the car first." She rapped out her orders to the chauffeur: "And for Pete's sake take care – that pigskin marks if you so much as *breathe* on it."

Awkwardly, the Duke shook hands with his cousin, Lord Mountbatten.

"Good to see you, Dickie," he mumbled.

"You know Randolph, of course," said the Captain, as Churchill stepped forward.

"Of course." The Duke's practised eye ran over his cavalry uniform, and he snorted with laughter: "Good God, man – you've got your spurs on upside down! Anyone would think you'd never ridden a horse in your life!"

Randolph Churchill flushed angrily; but at least his sartorial slip had broken the ice. Some years earlier, David, the Prince of Wales, and his cousin Dickie had been very close; but their friendship had cooled since then.

Lord Mountbatten continued: "I'm not sure if you know Lieutenant Gaunt?"

"Gaunt – yes – we must have met somewhere." The Duke held out his hand, and Nick wondered whether to remind him of a weekend at Royal Lodge, Windsor, when he and Jenny had been guests of the Yorks, and the King and Mrs Simpson dropped in for tea, uninvited. That meeting too had been

34

fraught with difficulty, so he said nothing – but the Duke went on triumphantly: "Now I remember – you're Alice Minster's boy! How is she? Tell her I hope to see her when we get to London."

The visitors from England exchanged glances; the Duke was about to return to his native land for the first time since he renounced the throne.

When war broke out, he and the Duchess remained in their villa at Cap d'Antibes, and the Duke sent a series of messages to his brother in London, saying that he would be glad to serve in any post His Majesty might consider suitable.

Having taken advice from his ministers, the King replied that he would be pleased to see his brother and discuss the possibilities. Winston Churchill, one of the Duke's supporters at the time of the abdication, was now First Lord of the Admiralty, and he dispatched Captain Mountbatten to Cherbourg, to ferry the Windsors to England, with his son Randolph as his representative, and Nicholas representing His Majesty.

The *Kelly's* return journey took six hours, and Nicholas joined the guests of honour at dinner in the principal saloon. The Duke seemed to be rather withdrawn, lost in his own thoughts, while the Duchess kept up a stream of inconsequential chatter.

Nick guessed that at some point the Captain had taken the Duke aside, making it clear that he must not expect hospitality at Buckingham Palace during his visit to England, and that the Duchess would not be received by the Royal Family.

When they reached Portsmouth, the town was in darkness; after the destroyer berthed alongside the harbour wall and the gangplank had been run out, the authorities waived the blackout regulations and switched on the jetty lights long enough for the visitors to go ashore, across a red carpet. The band of the Royal Marines struck up the national anthem, and the Duke inspected the guard of honour.

Then Nicholas accompanied the Duke to the limousine, where the Duchess had waited throughout this ceremony.

In silence, the two men took their places; the Duke sat next to his wife, and Nick pulled down the folding seat opposite them.

"Where are we going?" the Duchess wanted to know.

"Mr Churchill has arranged for you to stay here tonight, at Admiralty House," Nick replied.

"My God – that sounds like Navy blankets and lumpy mattresses!" she grimaced. "I thought the Metcalfes had invited us to stop over at their place?"

Major "Fruity" Metcalfe was one of the Duke's closest friends; he and his wife, Lady Alexandra, had offered them the use of their house in Ashdown Forest, or the townhouse in Wilton Place, during their stay in England.

"That's right, ma'am," Nick agreed. "But it's too late to drive to South Hartfield tonight; the Metcalfes look forward to seeing you both tomorrow."

"Hmmm." Wallis nudged her husband: "You're very quiet, honey – what are you thinking?"

The Duke stirred himself, saying wistfully: "The shorter version, by God. . . ."

"The *what* —?"

"The shorter version of the anthem. The Monarch gets it all the way through – minor royalty only get the first six bars. . . . You know, I'd rather got used to having the full treatment."

On Wednesday, Nick accompanied the Windsors to South Hartfield House, then went up to town and reported to Buckingham Palace.

On Thursday, the Duke travelled to London for a meeting with his brother; their first meeting for three years.

In the King's private sitting-room, Nicholas noticed signs of strain in His Majesty's face; a muscle twitched in his cheek, and he drummed his fingertips on the tabletop.

"How was David when you left him?" he asked.

"He seemed very cheerful, sir. He's done nothing since he left England; he looks forward to having a job to do – it's a chance for him to start again."

"To start again? He c-c-can hardly hope to do that." The

King lifted his head, hearing voices along the corridor. "There he is – will you please g-g-go and bring him in?"

His Majesty's stammer, which had been so much better recently, was more noticeable today.

In the corridor, the Duke was accompanied by Sir Walter Monckton, his counsellor and mediator for more than twenty-five years.

"His Majesty is waiting for you, sir," said Nicholas.

"Ah. . . . . What sort of mood is he in?" asked the Duke.

"He is very well, sir."

"That's not quite what I asked – however. . . . Don't go away, Walter."

The Duke walked on alone; the door opened, and they heard him say: "Bertie – dear old chap—!" before it shut again. Nicholas and Sir Walter prepared for a long wait.

"The Duke is delighted to be back," said Sir Walter. "I understand he's been offered a choice of possible jobs; the one that most appeals to him is in Wales – Deputy Regional Commissioner in charge of Civil Defence."

Nicholas said cautiously: "I was under the impression that His Majesty was considering a post abroad —?"

"Oh, you mean Paris? – Yes, liaison officer between the War Office and the French General Headquarters. He mentioned that too, but I think he'd prefer to remain in this country."

Some time later, the door opened again, and the King's voice echoed down the passage: "There's no urgency, David. Think it over, and discuss it with the War Minister – Hore-Belisha's expecting you at his office tomorrow at four."

"Thank you, Bertie."

The Duke marched briskly along the corridor; when he rejoined Sir Walter, he grinned broadly, saying: "I think it went all right."

Nick excused himself and returned to the sitting-room. His Majesty watched his brother leave, then asked: "Did you happen to catch what he said to Monckton?"

When Nicholas told him, he muttered: "'Went all right'—? Only because I kept off contentious topics – that's why it 'went all right'!"

He crossed to the windows, looking out on to the Palace gardens; a breeze had sprung up, bringing down some yellowing leaves, but he did not see them.

"He wanted that job in Wales – but it wouldn't do. He even suggested a short tour round the British Isles, to meet the people again – and he proposed taking his wife with him. . . . Can you imagine what sort of reception she'd get? Especially in Scotland; the people of Aberdeen have long memories – they won't forget the time he cancelled an engagement there, in order to be with his lady . . . I shall tell Hore-Belisha to make it clear to David – he must accept Paris – nothing else will do." He turned to Nick, with a faint smile: "Nobody seems to realize the position I'm in . . . My ancestors succeeded to the throne on the death of their predecessors; but *my* predecessor is alive and kicking – very much so!"

Throughout the week, Alice was extremely busy at Marlborough House. Persuading Queen Mary to leave London had been no easy matter, but the most difficult problem was deciding which of her treasures should go into store; each object had to be examined, discussed and admired.

All too often, Her Majesty would conclude: "Oh, no – this is *too* enchanting – I can't be parted from it. . . . It won't take up much room – have it put with the rest of the luggage."

Every day, the luggage became more cumbersome; and every day Alice added another vehicle to the procession which was to leave London. Limoges vases, Meissen figures, crystal and silverware were all wrapped in tissue paper, boxed and labelled; nothing but the heaviest pieces of furniture would be left behind.

On Friday evening, when every single item had been carefully packed, she put away her notebook with relief and said: "If Your Majesty will excuse me – I don't believe there is anything more to do tonight."

"If you're quite sure we haven't overlooked anything . . . ?" The Queen sounded doubtful.

"If anything is left behind, I can bring it down to you later, Ma'am."

"Thank you, my dear; you have been a great help. Tomorrow we must make an early start; we have a long journey ahead of us."

They said goodnight, and Alice was about to leave when an equerry knocked and entered, announcing: "His Royal Highness the Duke of Windsor is here, Your Majesty, and hopes very much that you will receive him."

Alice saw expressions of shock – joy – and a flash of anger chase each other across the old lady's face. Her lips quivered, and Alice took a step towards her, but the Queen waved her away: "No, no – I am perfectly all right. . . . But I had not expected – there has been no talk of David visiting me." An awful thought struck her, and she asked abruptly: "Is my son alone?"

"Yes, Ma'am."

"Very well; please show the Duke up." She turned back to Alice: "You may go, my dear – I must see him alone. Do not worry; I am quite calm."

Alice left her sitting there, her back ramrod-straight, awaiting the arrival of her eldest son.

As she descended the staircase, she met the Duke on his way up. Recognizing her, he recalled the nickname he'd given her, many years earlier: "The Duchess of Dillwater, as I live and breathe!" He took her hand for a moment. "You've been with my mother? How is she?"

"Her Majesty is wonderful, sir; the same as ever."

"Of course – she never changes. . . . Forgive me, I daren't keep her waiting. Wish me luck!"

When he smiled, Alice saw the boyish Prince of Wales once more, but when his smile faded, he became a troubled, middle-aged man.

The next day was blustery, and as they drove down to Badminton in the royal Daimler, the high, old-fashioned vehicle was buffeted by strong gusts.

"The countryside looks very—" Alice began, then saw too late that Her Majesty's eyes were shut.

The Queen roused herself immediately: "Did you say something, Alice?"

"Nothing of any importance, Ma'am. You must be tired; it's been an exhausting week."

"Oh, no – I enjoy going through my collection. . . . But I did find yesterday evening a little trying."

Alice ventured to ask: "Did His Royal Highness stay very long?"

"Not long. We did not have a great deal to say to one another. I understand Bertie has found work for him in Paris – David said he would have preferred to remain in England, but I told him that was out of the question."

Alice said gently: "Isn't it natural, Ma'am, that he should want to meet his family again? To pick up old friendships – old ties?"

"He no longer has any ties with us. He took that decision himself, three years ago; he has no place here now." The old lady continued implacably: "It would be very wrong – and most unfair to Bertie. David has always had the knack of whipping up popular support; it would be disastrous if the nation were to feel a divided loyalty . . . and that woman will never be welcome here."

For some minutes there was no sound but the purr of the engine and the breeze rattling the windows. When the Queen spoke again, her tone was gentler: "I cannot tell you how grateful I am for your help – for all you have done, over the years . . . and I'm very sad, now we must say goodbye."

"Goodbye — ?"

"Oh, we shall meet again, of course. But as long as this war continues, I shall have no official duties. I must remain quietly at Badminton, out of the public eye – so I shall not require your attendance. . . . And no doubt you will have a great deal to do at home, now you have joined the Women's Voluntary Service."

"Yes, Ma'am – I expect I shall. But after the war, I hope I may be able to attend you again, when things get back to normal."

Her Majesty pressed Alice's hand, and her eyes were glistening.

"Let us hope so indeed," she said.

Certainly there was plenty to be done at Crown House. When Nick and Jenny came down for a weekend, they were startled by the changes that had taken place.

They found Alice making up a double bed in one of the rooms in the west wing. She wore a shapeless overall, and her hair was tied back under a duster.

"I hope you'll be comfortable," she said. "I was going to run the carpet-sweeper over these rugs, but I haven't had a spare minute – as soon as I've finished the bed, I —"

"Don't worry – we'll see to the bed," said Jenny. "Come on, Nick, give me a hand with the sheets and blankets."

Rather surprised, he obeyed, asking: "Doesn't Lilian make beds any more?"

"No, we all do our own – anyway, Lilian's gone into the village for the weekend shopping – when she gets back we're going to start the lunch; she's a better cook than I am. And of course we both have to look after Grandmama. I swear she waits until we're in the middle of mashing potatoes or making omelettes, and then she rings her bell. As a rule, she's dropped something on the floor and wants it picked up. . . ."

"It sounds like sheer bloody murder," said Nick. "You must be worn out."

"Well, let's say I don't need rocking to sleep at night!" Alice admitted. "But it's the same for everyone nowadays – and to be perfectly honest, I rather enjoy housework."

"That's because it's still a novelty," Nick teased her.

"That's not fair! – Your mother's always worked hard!" Jenny straightened the counterpane and stepped back, adding: "There – that's one job finished. What else can we do?"

"Oh, you're not here to work, Jenny; why don't you go out and enjoy the sunshine? William's in the garden – I know he wants to talk to you. And Nick – you can come and pay your

41

respects to your grandmother. She'll be highly indignant if she thinks she's being ignored!"

Lord Minster was walking slowly along the herbaceous border, conferring with Ken Stubbs, the estate manager. As Jenny approached, William's face broke into a smile: "My dear – it's so good to see you."

Mr Stubbs echoed these sentiments, adding: "I'll leave the rest till later, sir – we'll talk after lunch."

He tucked a notebook and pencil into his breast-pocket, and walked off towards the farm.

"It's good to be back," said Jenny. "But I shouldn't interrupt when you're busy."

"Oh, we're all busy nowadays."

"Yes – Lady Minster was telling me about the work she's taken on – cooking, cleaning, making the beds —"

"That's only part of it. She puts in three or four days a week at the WVS – did she tell you she's joined their Volunteer Car Pool – running errands, chauffeuring people about and so on?"

Jenny stared at him: "But she hasn't driven a car for years!"

"She said it seemed ridiculous not to, when she could make herself useful. So she had a few extra lessons, to brush up her skills – she says the worst part is driving at night, with those dim little lights—" Then he frowned: "Perhaps I shouldn't have mentioned it. Forgive me – that was tactless of me."

Taking her arm, he led Jenny to the stone seat at the end of the long walk, and they sat side by side in the sunshine. They were both remembering a winter night, long ago, when Alice had driven Jenny's mother up to London; the car overturned on a patch of black ice, and Mrs Webster was killed instantly. It was nobody's fault – but Alice had given up driving after that.

"I'm glad you told me," Jenny said quietly. "I can imagine what it meant to her. . . . She must be very brave."

Gazing down the long perspective of the border, she welcomed the calm beauty of the garden, letting it flow over her.

"The dahlias are better than ever," she said. "I never saw such a blaze of colour. I suppose you'll lift the tubers when they finish flowering, and store them for next year?"

When William spoke, he chose his words carefully: "I don't know when we shall plant dahlias again," he said. "Ken Stubbs and I have been co-opted on to the County Agricultural Committee. One of our jobs will be to go round the district, looking for extra land to be turned over to cultivation. Our lawns must be ploughed up; we'll be planting vegetables instead of flowers. We were just discussing it when you joined us."

"Your beautiful garden . . ." Jenny didn't know what to say.

After a moment William continued in a different tone: "I'm glad you're here, Jenny; I've been trying to remember a line of poetry – I don't know who wrote it – something about '*all things lovely* . . .'" Where does it come from?"

"It's by Walter de la Mare; I learned it at school." She quoted the words: "'*Look thy last on all things lovely, every hour . . .*'."

"That's it. I was sure you'd know it."

He put his arm round her shoulders, and they sat in silence, looking at the sunlit garden.

Chapter Four

Thursday, 21 December to Monday, 25 December 1939

"No *guests*?" Lady Beatrice sat up in bed, swathed in shawls and propped against pillows, rigid with disapproval. "We always have guests in the house at Christmas – I never heard of such a thing!"

"But the house has been shut up, Mama," Alice said patiently. "We've no room for guests. Except family – Martin and Miranda will be coming home as usual. Caroline too, I hope; it depends on the roster at the hospital."

"And Nicholas and Jenny?"

"No, Nicholas is on duty at Sandringham with the Royal Family – and they've invited Jenny as well – isn't that nice?"

The old lady was unimpressed: "They should be here; it's the season for family reunions."

"Not this year, I'm afraid. Families must expect to be split up at a time like this. . . . Besides, we only have two spare bedrooms now; Miranda and Caro will have to share – they won't like it, but that can't be helped – and it will be so wonderful to see Mandy again."

"You should invite some of the neighbours to luncheon on Christmas Day. I should like to see some new faces for a change – I'm stuck in this poky little room —"

Alice, who knew this recurring grumble by heart, said: "I think that might put too much strain on the kitchen, Mama.

44

I'm already having problems, trying to work out menus for the weekend."

"I can see this is going to be an exceedingly dreary holiday." Old Bea sulked, sticking out her lower lip: "I suppose I shall be forced to rely on my wireless set for company."

"Well, I'm very sorry about that, but I really can't stay and talk all the morning – I've a million things to do. Why don't you read the newspaper?"

"I've lost my glasses," retorted the old lady. "And I can't manage that nasty small print without them, so —"

She was interrupted by Lilian Brooks, who tapped at the half-open door, saying: "Excuse me, my lady, but were you wanting to go through the shopping-list with me?"

"Yes, I was – I must," said Alice gratefully. "It's going to be enormous."

"You can do that quite well without her, Alice," snapped Old Bea. "Come here, Brooks – I can't find my spectacles, and I want you to read the newspaper to me. . . . Clearly, mind! – I can't abide mumbling."

Lilian looked helplessly at Alice, who sighed and surrendered.

"Very well, Lilian . . . I'll make a start on the list myself."

When William came indoors, she was still wrestling with the Christmas Day lunch, and turned to him for advice: "Do you suppose everyone will expect turkey, or would a goose make a nice change?"

"It's up to you, my dear – I don't mind either way," he replied, imagining that he was being helpful. "Could you leave that for a moment, and come out to the yard? I've been practising my lecture on 'How to Deal with Incendiary Bombs', and I'm not sure whether the demonstration with the stirrup-pump is entirely clear. If I run through it with you —"

"William, I'd simply love to see your demonstration another time, but I must get this shopping-list finished. Couldn't Ken Stubbs help you?"

"He had to go into Medford; I don't know what time he'll be back, it depends on the buses. Surely Lilian can see to that? – dammit, she is our housekeeper."

Alice pointed at the closed bedroom door and whispered: "She's reading to your mother. Looking after Mama is becoming a full-time job; I think she hides her glasses on purpose."

Then the telephone rang, and Alice picked it up. Having an extension phone installed in the flat was certainly an advantage, but the already overcrowded room had become more cluttered than ever, as piles of papers and pamphlets and assorted items of ARP equipment accumulated around it.

"Hello – Crown House – Lady Minster speaking."

"Mummy – it's me – Miranda!"

It was a crackly line, but her daughter's voice was instantly recognizable, and Alice's heart soared.

"Darling – how lovely to hear you – William, it's Miranda! . . . Are you in England already? Do you want me to meet you at the station?"

"No, you don't understand – I'm still in France – at Annecy."

Alice's heart plummeted again: "But darling – I thought you'd be on your way by now – what's happened?" Miranda hesitated, and Alice was afraid they'd been cut off: "Hello – are you still there?"

"Yes. . . . The thing is – the trains out here are pretty chaotic now, and I'd hate to get stuck halfway. You can't rely on the timetable; they keep cancelling trains because of moving troops up to the Maginot Line. But heaps of the girls are staying here for the holidays – the first snow began falling this week, and we're hoping to get in some skiing. . . . So I decided not to come home this Christmas – you don't mind too much, do you?"

"Well, of course I *mind* – we're all longing to see you. . . ." Alice felt disappointment like a lead weight inside her; she took a deep breath and tried to be sensible: "But if you really think that will be best. . . . We'll just have to look forward to Easter instead. And it won't be long before you're home for good, will it?"

Beside her, William asked: "What is it? What's wrong?"

"Daddy's here – he'd like to have a word – I'll pass you over."

When he finally rang off, William put his arms round Alice and held her tightly, murmuring: "Never mind . . . as you say – she'll soon be home for good."

Hundreds of miles away, under a slate-grey sky heavy with snow, Miranda replaced the antiquated telephone in its upright cradle. The parents were both being so *nice* about it, which made her feel even worse. She wished she hadn't lied to them – skiing was the last thing she wanted to do. . . . Anyway, Alain would never let her.

For a long time she continued to sit at his desk, struggling with the burden of guilt and deception – but how could she tell her parents the truth? They would never understand. . . . Mummy had talked about her going home for good – how could she explain that she might never go home again?

On the last Thursday before Christmas, Medford was busier than usual. Although there was no Christmas tree in the market square this year, and no coloured lights strung between the buildings, the pavements were crowded and Ken Stubbs had to keep side-stepping as he made his way up the High Street.

The shopkeepers had done their best; the plaster reindeer and Santa Claus figures had been dusted off, and there were cotton wool snowballs and crêpe paper garlands filling the window-displays – behind criss-crossed sticky tape intended to prevent flying glass, in case of an "incident" – and someone had stuck a "Merry Xmas" sign over the entrance to the air raid shelter.

Ken had done his Christmas shopping early; not that there had been much to do – since his wife left him for another man, some years ago, they had not been in close touch. Once a year they sent one another polite messages of goodwill on cards decorated with robins and holly, but that was as far as it went. The only presents he had bought were for the Minster family; bath salts for the ladies, boxed handkerchiefs for the gentlemen, and clockwork toys for young Alex and Harriet. In a jeweller's window, a single rosebud carved in ivory caught against it. He had no wish to embarrass her.

Thinking of Polly, as he threaded his way among the passers-by, he suddenly stopped short – for there she was, only a few yards away – as if his thoughts had conjured her up.

Then he scolded himself for such nonsense; of course, her office was in the High Street. His first instinct was to turn back, but he saw she was carrying some heavy cardboard cartons, and courtesy outweighed caution.

He stepped forward and raised his tweed hat: "Good morning," he said. "Can I lend a hand?"

"Oh – Ken! – hello. . . ." Flustered, and a little breathless, Polly smiled and said gratefully: "That would be a godsend – can you spare the time?"

"Of course I can. Where do you want these boxes?"

He took them from her, and she pointed to her little saloon car, parked across the street.

"Could you dump them in the boot? Thanks ever so much." Her smile dazzled him. "I ought to warn you – there's plenty more where those came from."

It took about twenty minutes, and a great many trips up and down the stairs to the first-floor office, before the car was fully laden; the boot and the back seat overflowed with parcels, box files and card indexes.

By the time they had finished, the two rooms above the dress shop looked very bare. Only a few pieces of furniture remained; the removal men would be coming to collect those later.

"I couldn't very well let them shift the paperwork," Polly explained. "It wouldn't do if they got nosy and started reading about my poor old clients!"

She swung a bentwood chair towards Ken and continued: "Sit down, and I'll make us both a cuppa – I reckon we've earned it." There was a gas ring by the hearth; Polly went and found a kettle, filled it at the tap in the back room, then put it on to boil. "This is the first time you've been to my office, isn't it?" she asked.

"It's the first time I've been to a marriage bureau," he said.

"Ah, but this isn't a marriage bureau any more – I've sold the rest of the lease. . . . How do you like your tea?"

"Just as it comes, thanks."

Ken watched her spoon the tea into the pot. At the age of forty, Polly was as full of life as she had been twelve years earlier, when Richard, Viscount Ebony, picked her out of a chorus line and made her his wife. She had kept her figure; her short, curly hair was a warm chestnut brown, untouched by grey – her sparkling eyes and tip-tilted nose were vivid with humour and mischief.

Feeling he had let the silence go on too long, he asked: "Are you moving the office to new premises then?"

She looked at him in surprise: "No, I'm packing it in – didn't you know? That's why I'm taking all this stuff home; the files can go into one of the attics till the war's over . . . I thought I'd told you."

"No. But we haven't had much chance to talk lately."

"No, we haven't." She frowned at the fireplace, saying: "Come on – boil up, kettle."

When Ken had arrived from Sandringham to work on the home farm, Polly had been one of the first to welcome him, helping him to settle in to the Lodge Cottage; they made friends quickly, and enjoyed each other's company. Polly knew Ken was lonely, and noticed Lilian Brooks had taken a shine to him; she did what she could to encourage the match, and they became engaged – but after a while the engagement was called off. Ken told Polly it had been a mistake; he confessed he'd never really loved Lilian – how could he, when he had been in love with Polly from the moment he set eyes on her?

Polly had been touched and embarrassed, and told him as gently as possible that she could not return his feelings. Since then, they had remained on good terms, but had not sought each other's company.

"So – why are you giving up the Bureau?" he asked.

"My secretary left last month; she's gone to work in a munitions factory. And business had fallen off lately. People aren't looking for life-partners any more – they don't want to take on any more commitments – or p'raps they're too busy to feel lonely."

Ken looked at her: "Do you really think so?"

Ignoring this question, she went on: "But it wasn't only that. Everyone else seems to be answering the call of King and Country – so I thought – why not?"

"You'll be taking on another line of work, then?"

"I'd like to. My trouble is, I don't really know what I'm cut out for. I've been on the stage – I can run an office and drive a car, and that's all."

"I can't believe that. You could do anything you wanted, if you put your mind to it."

"Like what? I tell you, I'm useless; I've never done anything worthwhile – unless you count bringing up two kids . . . And I needed help doing that, as everybody knows." She busied herself with the teapot, then produced a tin of biscuits, saying: "Help yourself . . . So if you hear of anyone looking for a middle-aged mother of two, to do part-time war work – let me know."

As they drank their tea, Ken said: "Matter of fact, I've just been answering the call of King and Country myself, in a manner of speaking."

"Oh? How's that?"

"That's why I came into Medford today – to register for National Service. All men between the ages of 18 and 41 – I just scrape in, at the top end."

She looked really shocked: "You mean they're going to take you for the army?"

"I hope not – I don't relish the idea of sharing a barrack-room with a load of strangers. But according to this chap in the office, I'm not likely to be called. For one thing, by my next birthday I'll be too old – and anyway I'm doing my bit already, working on the land and serving on the Agricultural Committee – so they'll probably leave me where I am."

"Well, that's a relief; I don't know what we'd do without you . . . Are you ready for another cup? There's plenty more in the pot."

"Thanks all the same, I'd better be getting back; His Lordship will be wondering what's become of me." Ken rose to his feet and pulled on his overcoat. "Thanks for the tea – it was very welcome."

"And thank you for all your help. It was nice seeing you – and talking . . . We must do it again, one of these days."

When he left, Ken ran down the stairs two at a time; suddenly he felt very happy.

At the turn of the year, the daylight hours were depressingly short – by teatime on Christmas Eve, it was almost dark.

Alice shivered, and turned up her fur collar; she was on her way to the chauffeur's old flat, above the garage. When Dennett moved out, into the Lodge Cottage, Polly had moved in, and Alice was hoping to find her on her own.

She knocked at the yard door, and Polly called down: "Who is it?"

"Only me. May I come up?"

"Yes – it's not locked – give it a good shove!"

Alice climbed the narrow staircase, finding Polly in the sitting-room. She was kneeling in front of the fire, with an assortment of toys and sweets and two pairs of long woollen socks spread out on the hearthrug.

"You've caught me doing Santa's work for him," she explained. "The children are having tea with Great-Grand-mama, so it seemed a good opportunity."

"I had the same idea." Alice began to unpack her shopping basket. "I picked up a few odds and ends the other day, when I was in town – I thought they might fill a few empty corners."

"Bless you," said Polly. "I've made a start with a tangerine and an apple in the toe, and a sugar-mouse and a little gold net of chocolate money . . . Then there's a water-pistol for Alex, and a tiny kaleidoscope for Harriet."

Alice was puzzled: "But – *four* socks – for two children?"

"Oh, the two empty ones will be tied to the ends of their beds. Then, when they're safely asleep, all I've got to do is sneak in and swap them for the other pair – already packed with goodies."

"Why did I never think of that?" Alice wondered. "I always did it the hard way."

Polly went on: "Of course Alex is really too old for Father Christmas – but he insists on hanging his stocking up. I'm not sure about Harry; she talks about Santa Claus coming down the chimney, but I have a suspicion she only says it to keep me happy . . . I just hope I've got enough things to fill them all the way up – nothing's worse than a Christmas stocking with a sag in the middle."

"And they're such long socks – where ever did you find them?"

"They belonged to Richard," said Polly easily. "He used to wear them with plus-fours – they were all the rage."

"I thought you gave all his clothes away, after. . . ." Alice left the sentence unfinished.

"I got rid of most of them – but I kept these socks – and a few shirts and ties – I don't know why . . . I still miss him, even after all this time."

"Christmas has never been the same without him." Alice looked into the heart of the fire, seeing her son's face. "But this won't be a proper Christmas anyway, with so many of the family missing. Caro can't get away – Nick and Jenny are at Sandringham until after Boxing Day – Miranda's still in France – and now it looks as if we'll be without Martin as well."

Polly glanced up: "I thought you said he was definitely coming home?"

"He said he'd be here this morning, but there's no sign of him."

"It's a rotten shame," said Polly fiercely. "People can't get about the way they used to. I hate this beastly war."

"So do I. Thank goodness you're still here, Polly. We'd be absolutely wretched without you and the children."

They continued to fill the stockings; Polly was just adding some striped peppermint sticks, when they heard the yard door slam.

"They can't be back already!" she gasped, scooping up stockings and presents.

"It doesn't sound like the children," said Alice, as footsteps climbed the stairs.

The door swung open, and Martin walked in.

"Hello, Ma – Polly – Grandmama said I'd find you here. . . . Any chance of a cup of tea? I'm frozen."

Alice hugged her youngest son: "Darling – I'd almost given you up! You said you'd be here before lunch."

"I should have been, but the trains are running late; the one I was on ground to a halt somewhere outside Sevenoaks. I've been sitting in an ice-cold carriage for hours, and if I've got frostbite, I shall sue the Southern Railway."

Polly scrambled to her feet, saying: "I'll make some tea."

"Marvellous . . . Oh – hang on – I met a weary postman coming up the drive, finishing off his rounds." Martin held out a handful of mail: "One for you – one for me – and heaps for Ma and Pa. . . . Yours looks rather exciting; an airmail letter from California. I had a squint at the address on the back – who's Dorita Rose, and what's she doing in Los Angeles?"

"Dorita—? Gawd – I haven't seen her since my wedding day; she was one of the gang who came down to the reception. Dorita Rose was her stage name – she's really Dot Patterson. We were in the same dressing-room at the Pavilion. . . . Good old Dot – fancy her remembering."

She went off to the kitchen, tearing open the flimsy envelope as she went.

"Well, Ma – and how are you?" Martin studied his mother critically: "You're not getting enough sleep – too much gallivanting round town, I bet."

"I don't do much gallivanting now," Alice smiled. "I went up to town last week to do some shopping – but I don't go to Marlborough House, since Her Majesty moved to the country."

Martin threw himself into an armchair: "It seems very peculiar, finding you and Pa and Old Bea pigging it in the servants' wing – and Polly and her brood living in the garage block."

"It's rather fun, actually. And it's the only practical solution – we can't go on living in the past."

"Yes, this war's a damn nuisance." Martin stretched his legs towards the fire. "I'd been thinking of buying myself a sports car – then I wouldn't have to rely on those lousy trains."

"Could you afford a car, out of your allowance?"

"I was going to ask Pa to pay for it, for my twenty-first. I thought it would be sensible to have it now, rather than wait for my birthday. . . . But now they've started rationing petrol, I wonder if it's worth all the bother."

Alice looked at her son; long-limbed and handsome, yet with his untidy blonde hair he still had the look of a schoolboy.

"Where's Mandy?" he asked suddenly.

"I don't really know – I told you, we haven't heard from her since she telephoned."

"You said she'd decided to stay in France for the holidays – you didn't say why."

"I suppose the travelling would have been difficult . . . and she said something about skiing . . . I do hope she's all right."

"Of course she's all right. In fact she's very happy."

"Why do you say that—?" Alice stared; sometimes the strange rapport between the twins made her uneasy. "How can you possibly know she's happy?"

Mockingly, he brandished a picture-postcard: "This was in the batch I got from the postman. She says she's having a wonderful time."

Polly returned from the kitchen, still frowning over her airmail letter, and saying: "The tea won't be long."

"How is your friend?" asked Alice. "Not bad news, I hope?"

"Oh, no—" Polly flashed a smile: "Dot's doing nicely; she's in Hollywood now. She's given up dancing and landed herself a job in the movies. She says if we saw a picture called "Wuthering Heights", she was the servant who brought in the candles."

"These theatre people are all the same," said Martin. "All they ever talk about is what they've been doing, or what they're going to do next. Doesn't she say anything else?"

Polly hesitated before replying, then said lightly: "Oh, no – just Christmas greetings – that's all."

*　　*　　*

54

In Norfolk, another tea party was in full swing.

The entire staff at Sandringham – indoor and outdoor – had assembled in the servants' hall, as they did every Christmas Eve. Cups of tea and slices of cake were handed round, while the servants were called up to the top table, and the King and Queen handed out their presents.

At His Majesty's side, Nicholas read out the names from a typed list, while Jenny stood in the background, watching.

"Mr and Mrs Herbert Robinson – a Norfolk turkey."

Red-faced and shy, a middle-aged couple advanced and shook hands with the King and Queen, who wished them both a very happy Christmas. Nicholas passed them their turkey, and the Robinsons backed away awkwardly, bumping into each other.

"Mr Joseph Parfitt – a side of ham."

"Home-cured, from our own piggeries," the King told Joe, one of the gamekeepers.

When the party was over, the Queen waved goodbye to the staff and their Majesties slipped away, followed by Nicholas and Jenny.

"It's an old-established c-c-custom – I hope this won't be the last time," said the King, as they made their way through the house. "Though God knows where we shall be next year."

There were to be no more holidays at Sandringham until the war was over; after Christmas, the Royal Family would move to Windsor.

"After all, Royal Lodge is our real home," said the Queen gently. "We've always been happy there."

"Yes – but I shall miss this old place," said the King. "Still, it has to be done." He turned to Jenny: "Did Nicholas tell you about the exhibition we went to, at the Ministry of Agriculture? We saw that Lord Minster has begun work already on the grounds at Crown House . . . I can imagine how he must be feeling."

When they reached the main hall, they stopped to admire the tall fir-tree, cut that morning from the plantations; the Princesses were helping to add the finishing touches, hanging silver balls and flying angels from the branches.

"Doesn't it look splendid, Mummy?" asked Margaret proudly.

"Wonderful, darling," agreed the Queen. "And have you put out all your presents on the table, ready for tomorrow?"

This was another Sandringham tradition; each year, a large oak table in the main hall was divided into squares by red velvet ribbons. Within each square, the family and their guests built up a little cache of presents, to be ceremonially unwrapped on Christmas Day.

"Those are your places." Princess Elizabeth pointed out two squares to Nick and Jenny. "We've put your presents in already – if you've brought any from home, they must go in your squares as well."

"Good gracious, Bertie – some extra parcels have appeared in our squares!" exclaimed the Queen. "I think I recognise Lillibet's handwriting on the labels."

"Presents for parents?" The King smiled: "That's very generous."

"But where did they come from?" The Queen explained to Jenny: "I took the girls shopping on Thursday. . . . But how did you manage to buy presents for us when I wasn't looking?"

"We didn't," said Elizabeth. "We bought them with our pocket money when we were in Scotland."

"Crawfie took us to Woolworths in Aberdeen," Margaret chimed in. "We wanted to surprise you."

"And you certainly did." The Queen put her arms round her daughters, adding: "But now I'm going to whisk you both upstairs – it will soon be time for bath and bed, and I can see someone waiting to talk to your father."

She led the girls up the broad staircase, and the King turned to greet the newcomer who had just entered the hall.

"Ah – Mr Weyman – good evening. I hope you had a good journey from London?"

"Not too bad, sir. I drove up with our engineers; they're already in your study, setting up the microphone."

"Ah, yes." The King drew Nicholas and Jenny forward. "This is Mr Paul Weyman from the BBC – Lieutenant Gaunt – and Mrs Gaunt."

"Mr Weyman is an old friend of our family, sir," said Nicholas politely. "He served in my father's regiment during the last war."

"I remember coming home on leave, and being introduced to you when you were still in the schoolroom, Nicholas," said Paul. He glanced at Jenny a little uncertainly, and she helped him out: "We met briefly at Crown House – I wouldn't expect you to remember."

"Well, if your chaps are ready, we mustn't keep them waiting," said the King.

"Thank you, sir. I'd like to run through your speech this evening, to check the sound levels, and get a rough timing."

"Very well. There's one small alteration I want to make – something I'd like to add at the very end . . . Nicholas – would you mind? You'll find a book on my bedside table. . . ." They went up the stairs, and Jenny heard His Majesty say as they disappeared: "This is always an ordeal for me; I can't begin to enjoy C-C-Christmas until it's over."

At the foot of the stairs, Jenny broke the silence by saying to Paul: "I think someone said you worked in television?"

"I did – until Alexandra Palace closed down. Now I've been shunted back to radio; and as I used to work on the royal broadcasts, I've got my old job back this year." Keeping up the conversation, he asked: "How are Lord and Lady Minster?"

"They're both very well."

"Good, good. . . ." He paused: "And – how is Caroline?"

"Caro's fine; she's training as a nursing auxiliary. I see her almost every day – we work at the same hospital."

"Really?" After another silence, Paul said: "Would you give her my love?"

That night, as they were getting ready for bed, Jenny asked Nick: "Should I tell Caro – or not? You don't think it might upset her?"

Nick shrugged: "I imagine she's got better things to do than waste time brooding over Mr Weyman. . . . She's happily married – she's even got a worthwhile job to do."

Something in his tone made Jenny look up: "What makes you say that?"

Pulling on his pyjamas, he said: "Two years ago, I chucked my job on the farm because I was bored – I couldn't wait to get back in uniform. Now there's dear old Pa, ploughing up the estate, digging for victory – and here am I, fetching and carrying sides of ham and bedside books . . . I'd say my father is doing more for the war effort than I am – wouldn't you?"

Christmas Day at Crown House dawned bright and clear. After lunch, Alice, William and Martin joined Lady Beatrice, to listen to the King's broadcast.

The children were impatient to get out into the sunshine; Alex had been given a new bicycle with stylish dropped handlebars, and Harry was the proud owner of her first fairy-cycle. Polly excused herself from the family group, saying she would bring the children back at teatime.

They went out on to the drive, and Alex showed off his prowess, circling round on the gravel, executing figures of eight. Harriet was more cautious, and Polly had to stay close beside her, holding the back of the saddle.

Gradually Harry got her courage up, and demanded: "I want to try on my own – don't hold me!"

By the time they met Ken Stubbs, outside his cottage, she was feeling more confident, and he congratulated her.

"You're doing fine!" he said. "Keep it up, and you'll be racing your brother in no time."

"Stay and watch me," Harry commanded. "I'm going all the way to the gates and back without falling off."

Ken and Polly stood under the trees while she pedalled doggedly away.

"You must be proud of her," said Ken.

"I'm proud of them both – that's what makes it so hard to decide . . . Can I ask your advice?"

"Why – what's the problem?"

"I've been worried sick, since the post came yesterday. And I don't like to bother the others."

Keeping an eye on Harriet, she told Ken about the letter from California: "It wasn't just Christmas greetings, Dot's married

58

to some American film producer – I can't remember his name – but they've got a big house in Beverly Hills. She says she'd like us to go and stay with them till the war's over – me and the kids. We wouldn't have to worry about anything – and the children would be safe."

"Mummy, mummy – did you see? I did it!"

Harriet's voice rang out in triumph; she had reached the gates. At the same moment they heard another voice, through the cottage window:

". . . a new year is at hand. We cannot tell what it will bring. If it brings peace, how thankful we shall all be. If it brings us continued struggle, we shall remain undaunted. . . ."

Ken's lodger had turned on the radio; the King's voice carried clearly across the crisp, wintry air:

". . . we may all find a message of encouragement in the lines which, in my closing words, I would like to say to you . . . *I said to the man who stood at the gate of the year, 'Give me a light that I may tread safely into the unknown,' and he replied, 'Go out into the darkness, and put your hand into the Hand of God. That shall be to you better than light, and safer than a known way . . .'* May that Almighty Hand guide and uphold us all."

In the west wing, Lady Beatrice switched off her wireless-set. Alice gripped William's hand; they were remembering other wars, other challenges.

Martin's thoughts were very different. For some time now, Miranda had been on his mind; he was aware of her all the time. He had no idea what she was doing, but he knew what she was feeling. Mandy was happy enough – no doubt of that; he knew she was carried along on a tide of joyful emotion that he could not share. But beneath that emotion there was fear as well. He sensed that she was trapped in a situation beyond her control – she seemed to be a prisoner. . . .

He could not understand it. He only knew that something was terribly wrong.

Chapter Five

Monday, 1 January to Wednesday, 29 May 1940

"Don't go so fast, Alex," called Polly. "Wait for us!"

The garden was unfamiliar under an eiderdown of snow. It was the afternoon of New Year's Day, and Alex dragged a brand-new, streamlined sledge with steel runners – Harriet's sturdy toboggan had been in the family for years. Polly could remember Alex sitting on it when he was three years old, sailing down the gentle slopes below the summerhouse.

"Brrr – it's perishing out here," she said. "Let's pop into the farm office for a minute and get warm by the stove."

"Oh, no – we'll soon warm up once we start whizzing about," said Alex impatiently.

"You go on without me then," Polly told him. "I want to have a word with Mr Stubbs first." They raced off happily, churning up the snow, while she shouted after them: "And whatever you do – don't break your necks!"

Then she turned aside, making for the farm office.

Ken Stubbs had an Ordnance Survey map of the district spread out on his desk; he looked up with a smile as Polly walked in.

"Hello – I saw you all setting off with the sledges. I'd have come out to join you, only I'm waiting for his Lordship; we're driving over to Ashford, for a meeting at the County Office."

"On New Year's Day? Don't they ever give you any time off?"

"You should know by now – farmers don't have holidays!

We've got to put in our recommendations for the new ploughland areas. I dare say we shan't be too popular, but that's all part of the job."

She warmed her hands at the stove, saying: "I mustn't stop long either; I've got to keep an eye on the kids. Still, Alex is pretty good with Harry."

"He's a sensible lad." Ken began to fold up the map. "Have you told the family yet – about America?"

"No, not yet. I know it's silly, but – I still feel bad about it. . . . Like we were running away or something."

"Now then – we've been through all that. You're doing the sensible thing; you're acting in the best interests of the children – that's what matters."

"I know – but I keep thinking how upset William and Alice are going to be."

"They'll want what's best for their grandchildren; you know that."

"I suppose so . . . I'll try and tell them tonight, but —"

She broke off as the door opened again, and William came in, stamping the snow off his boots.

"Hello, Polly – I thought you'd gone winter-sporting."

"I let them go on ahead – they don't seem to mind the snow and ice, but that freezing wind goes right through me."

"You'd better get used to it – according to the barometer, this spell of weather is here to stay. . . . Well, Ken – are you ready to face the committee?"

"Yes, sir – as ready as I'll ever be." Ken reached for his overcoat, as Polly moved to the door.

"Sorry to run away so rudely, my dear," said William. "But I'll see you this evening, I expect."

As a rule, the children had their supper at about half-past six. Tonight, Polly gave them sausages and mash, and put Harry to bed at seven-thirty; then she left Alex to read, or listen to the radio, while she went to join her in-laws for a more grown-up meal at eight o'clock. Alex grumbled about being treated like a child, but Polly pointed out that grown-up conversation was very boring, and he wasn't missing much.

For once, Old Bea had decided to join the family at the dinner-table, so the sitting-room was quite crowded.

"This is the soup I made from the turkey carcass," Alice said, ladling it into bowls. "I'm afraid inspiration ran out after that – but there's plenty of cold ham and pickles."

"Not for much longer," William remarked gloomily. "Once rationing begins, we shall have to tighten our belts."

"Don't remind me," said Alice. "From next Monday we'll be using those horrible little books. . . . Four ounces of bacon or ham a week – I can't bear to think of it."

"I never heard such rubbish," growled Old Bea. "We've still got the livestock – we can slaughter our own pigs if we want to, I presume?"

"There are rules and regulations, Mama," William reminded her. "And as you know, I'm on the Agricultural Committee, so —"

"All the better; you can change the rules to suit yourself," said the old lady. "I hope you don't propose to let your family starve, just for the sake of some absurd regulation?"

"I'm sure we shall manage very well," said William firmly, bringing the discussion to an end. "Whatever happens, the important thing is that the children won't go short."

Irritably, Old Bea wiped a dribble of soup from her chin: "Oh, yes, of course," she sniffed. "I realize I'm an old woman, so naturally I don't count. . . . The younger generation always get preferential treatment – Alex and Harriet must come first!"

Carefully, Polly put down her spoon. Looking at no one in particular, she said: "Actually – I was going to tell you about the children . . . I've had an invitation from that friend of mine in America. She wants me to take them over to Hollywood and stay there for the rest of the war – and I've sort of decided we ought to go . . . I think it's the right thing to do."

For a few moments nobody spoke, and then Lord Minster said: "I'm afraid I must disagree with you. In my opinion, it would be very wrong to take Alexander away. You may do whatever you think best for Harriet, but you mustn't overlook the fact that my grandson is Viscount

62

Ebony, and in due course he will take my place as head of the family."

Old Bea chimed in: "Quite right! – the idea's outrageous. I'm surprised at you, Polly – you'd be setting the boy a bad example."

Polly's cheeks were very pink, but she lifted her chin, determined to stand up to her in-laws.

"They're my kids, and it's up to me to decide what's best for them. . . . I'm sorry, but quite honestly – it's none of your damn business."

They all began to talk at once, until Alice's voice cut through the argument: "I think it would be a good idea to take some time and think this over quietly. If we try to decide anything now, we shall only get upset and say things we might regret afterwards. Why don't we sleep on it, and see how we feel about things tomorrow?"

William and Old Bea were inclined to go on arguing, but she cut them short: "William . . . Let's talk about this later – not now – please!"

Polly closed the discussion by standing up and saying: "Anyway, there's nothing to talk about. I've already made up my mind."

Then she pushed back her chair and walked out of the room.

Alice followed her quickly, catching up with her on the half-landing and saying: "Polly dear – you haven't even finished supper – do come back and sit down."

"I don't want any supper – it'd choke me." She was trying hard to keep her temper, but it wasn't easy. "How dare they tell me what to do? I don't care about Alex being head of the family some day, and all that stuff – if a bomb lands on Crown House, there mightn't be any family left – and there might not be any Alex . . . I want my kids alive and well – that's all I care about."

Alice nodded: "I know. Let me try and talk to William. And – if this is any consolation – I'm sure I'd feel exactly the same, if I were in your place."

Polly flashed a grateful smile: "Thanks – it's not much fun, having them going on at me. I'm glad you understand."

"Of course I do. Incidentally – to be severely practical – have you done anything about booking passages to America? Foreign travel is very difficult now, and you'll have to apply for visas and things from the Embassy as well."

"I haven't done anything yet, but —"

"Then I think you should, as soon as possible. In fact – why don't you come up to town with me? I had a message from the Palace this afternoon, saying that Her Majesty wishes to see me, and I'm going to London on Thursday morning. We can keep each other company."

Polly said that would be wonderful, and went off to the garage flat, looking a great deal happier while Alice returned to the supper table.

As she entered the room, Old Bea snorted: "I never heard of such a thing – it's our patriotic duty to stay at our posts in time of war. I was very shocked – it's not like Polly, turning tail and running away – I call that cowardice in the face of the enemy!"

"Mama, don't talk such balderdash," said Alice calmly, leaving Lady Beatrice momentarily speechless. Turning to her husband, she continued: "My dear, I know you feel very strongly about this, but I'm afraid I'm on Polly's side. Alex and Harry are the most important things in her life; they matter to her a thousand times more than the family title or the family honour – and if she thinks she can save their lives by taking them to America, she has every right to do so."

"War or no war, the boy is eleven years old; it's time he began to learn about his responsibilities," said William doggedly. "I shall speak to Polly, and try to persuade her to change her mind. Apart from anything else – the boy has no father; it's up to me to act *in loco parentis* and help to guide him along the right path."

"No, William. You heard what she said; her mind is made up, and you've no right whatever to try and keep Alex here. Besides, I agree with Polly; I'd rather our grandchildren grew up in America or in Timbuctoo, than risk them facing death in England – and I told her so . . . and if you two go on bullying her, I'll never forgive you."

Old Bea and William were both taken aback by Alice's quiet determination.

After a moment, William said in a different tone: "Perhaps I was being hasty. . . . But – why *Hollywood*, for heaven's sake? If her only concern is the children's safety, couldn't she find somewhere a little nearer home?"

Old Bea followed her son's lead, asking: "Surely there are places in England where they wouldn't come to any harm? How about the West Country – Devon or Cornwall, perhaps? Or Gloucestershire? That must be reasonably safe, or they wouldn't have sent Queen Mary there – poor woman, she needs somewhere quiet and peaceful at her age. . . ."

Alice did not remind her mother-in-law that she was in fact Queen Mary's senior by some fifteen years, but concluded firmly: "I've already told Polly that I think she's doing the right thing. And I've promised to take her to London with me on Thursday, so she can start making their travel arrangements – and that's that."

Nicholas had been checking through the desk diary with His Majesty, bringing next month's public engagements up to date; on the way back to his office, he took a short cut through one of the public ante-rooms.

A woman in a charcoal-grey suit sat alone on a little gilt chair, and Nick glanced at her in passing – then blinked, and looked again.

"Polly!" he exclaimed, in amazement. "What on earth are you doing here?"

She looked up, grateful to see a familiar face.

"I'm waiting for your mother," she told him. "We drove up this morning – she's got an appointment with the Queen – we're both going on to the American Embassy later, and she said I could come in here and wait." Polly lowered her voice: "The only Palace I've ever been in was the Palace Theatre, Manchester. . . . Between you and me, I'm scared stiff."

"I suppose it is rather impressive until you get used to it. . . . But the novelty soon wears off, I can tell you."

"Really? But it must be so exciting to work here, right at the middle of things. I mean, this is where everything happens, isn't it?"

"Don't you believe it. Out on the minesweepers and the troopships – that's where things happen. All we do is sit and read the newspapers, and wait for the news to come through. . . ." Nick changed the subject: "Are you staying at Eaton Square tonight? Will you have dinner with us?"

"No, I've got to get back, because of the kids – thanks all the same."

"That's a pity; I know Jenny would love to see you . . . I wonder why Ma has been summoned to town – did she say?"

"I don't think she knows herself. It was just a phone message, saying the Queen wanted to see her." Polly looked at her watch. "I wonder how much longer she'll be."

In the Queen's private sitting-room, Alice put down the typewritten list she had been studying, and said: "It's going to be a big job, Ma'am."

"I'm afraid it is – that's why I thought of you." The Queen smiled: "You were so marvellous, organizing everything at Marlborough House. This is going to be a similar problem – only more so."

It had been decided that for reasons of security, large parts of the Palace would be closed for the duration, and the contents of the State Apartments were to be removed to places of safety.

"Some of the bigger pieces have been sent away already, but there's still an awful lot to go – the pictures and porcelain and so on. Everything has to be crated up and stored in the cellars at Windsor Castle; and it needs someone in charge who knows what's what. . . . But of course if you're too busy, I shall quite understand."

"Well, I have got my WVS duties – but I'm sure I can make time somehow."

"Bless you, Alice – I know you'll do it splendidly. In fact – since Queen Mary doesn't require your services any longer, I was rather hoping I might add you to my list of 'occasionals'. So many of the Ladies-in-waiting have other calls on their time now – may I include you in the team, as First Reserve?"

"I'd be delighted, Ma'am."

"Then we shall both be delighted." The Dresden clock on the overmantel began to strike eleven, and the Queen asked: "Would you like some coffee?"

When Alice said that her daughter-in-law was waiting for her, the Queen exclaimed: "But you must ask her to join us – Jenny and I are old friends."

Alice explained that it was not Jenny who had accompanied her to town; and a few minutes later Polly – in a state of shock – found herself dipping a nervous curtsey, while the Queen said: "Of course I remember you; we met years ago, when the King and I came to stay at Crown House. Such an eventful weekend; we've never forgotten it. Lillibet was still very young – and Margaret had only just learned to walk."

Feeling that she couldn't remain tongue-tied for ever, Polly forced herself to ask: "I hope the Princesses are well, Your Majesty?"

"Oh, yes – Margaret had a little cold, but she's over the worst of it now. We left them at Sandringham, though they will be moving down to Windsor in a few days." Pouring coffee, the Queen went on: "We've been rather concerned about them lately; it's so difficult to know what one should do at a time like this. We had several kind invitations from friends in Canada, suggesting that we might like to send the girls over there, out of harm's way . . . But in the end, we had to refuse."

Polly put down her coffee-cup, as Her Majesty continued: "I wrote and said that we were immensely grateful, but it wasn't really possible. You see, the children wouldn't want to leave without me – and I can't leave without the King – and the King will never leave."

On the way out of the Palace, Alice and Polly found Nicholas waiting for them at the side entrance.

"I've ordered a cab to take you to your next appointment," he said. "I thought you might be cutting it a bit fine."

"Thanks ever so much," said Polly. "Only we won't be needing it, actually."

"But Polly – the man's expecting you, about the visas —" began Alice.

"I'll ring up and apologize; I'll tell him there's been a change of plan. I don't want the kids to go to America after all; I want us to stay in England – all of us – together."

They drove back to Ebony that afternoon, and before supper, Polly went down to the Lodge Cottage.

Ken opened the door, and said: "I thought you'd gone to London?"

"I came back . . . I'd like to talk to you – can I come in?"

"Of course you can. I'm on my own; Mr Dennett's gone over to the pub." He led the way into the little parlour and threw another log on the fire. "How did you get on at the Embassy?"

"I didn't go. Lady Minster took me with her to the Palace this morning, and I met the Queen. She gave us coffee, and – this might sound a bit daft, but – she made me feel as if staying in England was the most important thing. . . . Important for me, and for the kids as well. After all, it's their war too; when they grow up, they might never forgive me if I'd taken them out of it." She added quietly: "That's what I came to tell you."

Ken walked to the fireplace and stood with his elbows on the mantelpiece. He prodded the log with his boot, settling it into the fire.

Eventually Polly said: "I s'pose you think I'm crackers."

He turned to face her, and his eyes were as bright as the leaping flames in the grate.

"I think you're doing the best thing," he said. "I'm glad you're not going away."

In their sitting-room, Alice had been telling William about Polly's change of plan.

". . . So you got your own way in the end," she finished wryly.

"Hmph!" He grunted noncommittally, frowning at his hands; his nails were chipped and rimmed with dirt. "I suppose you still think I was wrong to argue with Polly. . . . But I was looking ahead – thinking of the boy's future —"

"Nobody can look ahead, the way things are now. I simply wanted her to be free to choose; we couldn't make up her mind for her. But if she's happy to stay – then I'm happy about that too." Alice came closer, adding: "Your hands are filthy – what on earth have you been doing?"

"Trying to clear a blocked drain in the yard – it had frozen solid. I'm just going to wash." He stood up, hesitated a moment longer, then asked: "Did you mean it – when you said you'd never forgive me?"

She looked into his eyes and smiled: "I don't know. . . . Probably not."

While Polly decided not to leave England, Miranda had taken a different decision.

She sat on her bed, in a dormitory partitioned into four small cubicles. None of the other beds was occupied, but Miranda didn't mind that; she enjoyed the unaccustomed luxury of space and silence. Last term, when she was sharing with three other girls, she had been continually irritated by their silly gossip and giggling. They only talked about idiotic things; clothes, and make-up, and parties, and boyfriends. But now they had all departed – to Paris, to Texas, and to the Gulf – all they ever wanted was excitement and glamour, but Miranda had been trying to find something else. She needed a purpose in life – and she believed she had found it.

Outside, big flakes of snow whirled past the windows as the winter evening closed in. Their shifting patterns made her feel sick and dizzy; she looked away, concentrating on the fire that crackled in the grate. At this time of the year, she couldn't stop thinking about Marianne. . . . It was almost exactly a year since the accident.

On her bedside table there was a snapshot of a nineteen-year-old girl, laughing and carefree. Miranda had taken the photograph the day they all went skiing. She would never forget the look on Alain Lafitte's face when they came home that night; when they told him that his daughter had had a very bad fall. . . . They tried to get a doctor – but Miranda had known at once, from the hideous way her head lolled sideways, that it was hopeless.

A studio portrait of Marianne, taken by a photographer

in Annecy, had a special place in the Lafittes' house. A candle burned before it, and there were always fresh flowers in a vase.

If only she could make Martin understand . . . Not for the first time, Miranda had begun a letter to him, and now she read through what she had written:

"Les Gentianes,
Pas-de-Loup,
Annecy, France.

"Friday, Jan. 5th. 1940.

"Dear Martin —
"I am supposed to be doing my preparation for an essay, but French Literature can wait; it's more important to write to you.

"I know you are worrying about me. I should have written to you long ago, but it's so hard to say what I have to say. I should write to Mummy and Daddy as well, but that's even more difficult. I can never hide anything from you; that is why you are the first person I must tell.

"Before Christmas, when I phoned home and spoke to Mummy, I told her I'd decided to stay here for the holidays – I said lots of the other girls were staying on as well, but the truth is, most of the others had gone. The parents came down to take their daughters home, and now there are only a handful of us left, and the Head says she will have to close the school. It's high time she retired anyway. The whole place is so old-fashioned, and most of the girls are ghastly snobs.

"There was only one girl I really liked, and she wasn't a boarder – Marianne Lafitte, the daughter of M. Lafitte, who runs the stables and gives riding lessons. He's very nice, and so is his wife; Marianne was my best friend – until she died last winter, in a skiing accident. I was terribly upset – and you can imagine how the Lafittes felt. Their whole world fell apart.

"I went to see them every day, and tried to do what

70

I could to help – which wasn't much. At least we were able to talk about Marianne, and remember her, and for a while we all felt a little bit comforted. That's why, when the holidays came along, I made excuses not to go home. I stayed with the Lafittes during the summer; they let me sleep in Marianne's old room. I've become very close to them now – like one of the family.

"So I'm going to stay here. Even if the school closes, I shall go on living with the Lafittes. Perhaps I'm helping them to get over their loss. It's nice to feel I'm doing something useful; there's nobody in England who needs me.

"There's you, of course – but that's different. We're together anyhow, even when we're in different places. But I don't belong at Crown House any more. Mummy's always been so busy, rushing off to London every five minutes – and Daddy's never been close to either of us, has he? I suppose it's because there was a long gap after Caro, before we were born; I always feel he somehow lost touch with us when we were little. I'm sure he hasn't missed me at all since I've been away.

"I feel closer to the Lafittes now than to the Minsters – all except you, Marty. Very soon we shall both be twenty-one, and then we can live our own lives. Soon I must find a way of telling the parents that their youngest daughter is leaving home. . . . In fact I've left already, though they don't realize it yet. I'm never going back —"

The letter broke off at that point, and Miranda's heart sank as she realized that she could never send it. It would put Martin in an impossible position; how could he keep this news to himself? Perhaps she had been secretly hoping he would tell the family; perhaps she wanted him to break the news for her . . . but that would be a mistake. Once her parents heard what she planned to do, they would rush out here to plead with her – argue with her – try to drag her back . . .

She couldn't risk that. Better to wait till her birthday; after that, she could declare her independence.

She glanced at her watch. Soon it would be time for supper; she must run down the lane to the stables. She pictured the Lafittes waiting for her, facing one another across the red-and-white checked cloth – turning gladly to her as she entered the room – smiling, loving, welcoming – as she slipped into the empty place at the table. . . .

She tore the sheets of notepaper across, again and again, and threw them into the fire.

In England, it seemed as if winter would drag on for ever; when spring came at last, the prospects were no brighter. At the beginning of April, the German forces invaded Norway and Denmark; at the beginning of May they moved again, sweeping across Holland and Belgium.

On Friday, the tenth of May, as enemy troops were being parachuted into the Low Countries, Mr Chamberlain resigned and the King sent for Winston Churchill, inviting him to form a coalition government. On Saturday, Mr Churchill announced the names of his new cabinet; himself as Prime Minister and Minister of Defence, Chamberlain as Lord President of the Council, and Lord Halifax as Foreign Secretary.

When Nicholas arrived for work, he met Lord Halifax entering the Palace gardens through a private gate in the south-west wall.

They knew one another slightly; they lived in neighbouring houses in Eaton Square, and Lord Halifax – a personal friend of His Majesty – was permitted to take a short cut through the grounds each morning, on his way to the Foreign Office.

As the two men walked under the trees, they came face to face with the King, taking a stroll after breakfast. Guessing that His Majesty might wish to speak privately to his Foreign Secretary, Nicholas excused himself and walked on, but by the time he reached the entrance to the Palace, the King had caught up with him.

"I was hoping I might see Halifax – I wanted to tell him

how sorry I was not to have him as Prime Minister," he said. "We have known one another a long time – and he understands how I feel about Winston."

"Don't you think Mr Churchill is the right man for the job, sir?" asked Nicholas.

"I don't say that; I'm sure he will do very well. My reservations are entirely personal; there have been occasions when he and I were not in agreement."

At the time of the Abdication, Winston Churchill had supported the King's marriage to Mrs Simpson; during the Munich crisis, he had been outspoken in his condemnation of Mr Chamberlain's attempts at appeasement. It was hardly surprising that His Majesty should have misgivings about his new Prime Minister.

"Well," he said, as they walked up the steps into the building: "We shall see how things work out."

Throughout the weekend, the news grew steadily worse; after nearly nine months of deadlock, events in Europe were moving at last. The Dutch and the Belgians were not strong enough to resist the German invasion, and Hitler's troops pushed on.

When Nicholas reported for duty on Monday morning, he found the King already at his desk; there were dark circles under his eyes.

"I didn't sleep very well," His Majesty explained. "And when I finally dropped off, I was woken at five o'clock by a long-distance telephone call. Queen Wilhelmina of the Netherlands insisted on speaking to me; she begged me to send our aircraft to help defend her country. . . . I passed the message on immediately – but I'm afraid it may be too late."

Within a few hours, the King's daily schedule had to be abandoned. Before lunch, Prince Bernhard and Princess Juliana arrived from Holland with their daughters – Princess Beatrix, aged two, and Princess Irene, only nine months old. The Prince apologized for imposing upon the King's hospitality without warning, but said that events were now moving so fast he had had no option. As soon as his wife and daughters were in safe hands, he returned to Holland to continue his country's fight for survival.

He had scarcely left the Palace when the telephone rang again; once more Queen Wilhelmina wished to speak to His Majesty.

Half an hour later, the King summoned Nicholas and gave him his instructions: "Her Majesty was speaking from Harwich; tell them to bring the car round – we have to meet her at Liverpool Street."

Puzzled, Nicholas asked: "Why didn't Prince Bernhard tell us the Queen was on her way to England?"

"He didn't know. When the rest of the family left, the Queen insisted on staying – but she soon discovered that was a mistake. The Germans would have had no hesitation in holding her as a hostage, to force the capitulation of the Dutch army. When she realized that, she decided to leave The Hague, and managed to get on board a British destroyer at Rotterdam. She asked the Captain to take her to Flushing, where there is a strong contingent of Dutch troops, but the German Navy was bombarding the coastline, so the Captain took her to Harwich instead. When she telephoned, she was still determined to go back to her own country; I managed to talk her out of that, though it wasn't easy – she's a determined old lady. I told her that her daughter and her granddaughters were here already, and invited her to join them – and at last she agreed."

By teatime, three generations of the Dutch Royal Family were reunited; Wilhelmina wept a little at the sight of her grandchildren, saying: "It is very foolish of me, but I cannot help remembering – in a few weeks time, little Irene was to have been christened in Amsterdam Cathedral, but now. . . ." She wiped her eyes: "God only knows what will happen."

Queen Elizabeth took her hand, saying: "Might I make a suggestion? Our daughters were christened here, in the Palace. We should be honoured – and delighted – for Irene's christening to take place in our Chapel."

For the first time since their arrival, Princess Juliana managed to smile, as she said: "Thank you . . . Bernhard

74

and I would appreciate that – very much. And now – I am sure Her Majesty would like to wash and change —"

Queen Wilhelmina exclaimed: "Oh, I should have told you – I did not bring any luggage with me. I have nothing to wear but the clothes upon my back – and a tin helmet, which the ship's Captain gave me."

"Please don't worry," said Queen Elizabeth. "My Ladies-in-waiting will provide everything you need. Nicholas – your mother is working in the Long Gallery – could you ask her to come and help us?"

It was nearly midnight by the time Nicholas and Alice reached Eaton Square; Jenny was waiting up to give them supper, but they were too tired to eat. Nick managed half a cup of cocoa, then pushed it aside.

"Sorry – I must go up to bed, before I fall asleep on the kitchen table. . . . One way and another, this has been rather a busy day."

One evening at the end of May, Jenny sat in the basement kitchen, talking to Caroline and struggling with a shapeless mass of khaki wool.

"What's it supposed to be?" yawned Caro, who was on nights again, and had only just got up.

"A balaclava helmet," said Jenny. "If I ever finish it, which doesn't seem very likely."

"I never knew you were a knitter?"

"I'm not – that's the trouble. But everybody at the Canteen seems to be knitting comforts for the troops, and I began to get a guilty conscience. My mother taught me to knit when I was quite small – but she had a natural talent for it, and I was always hopeless."

"If you hate it that much, I should give it up."

"It seems so feeble; I keep gritting my teeth and remembering what Mr Churchill said last week – '*I have nothing to offer but blood, toil, tears and sweat . . .*'."

Caro grinned: "There you are – he never said a word about woolly balaclavas. . . ." She dived into the larder, adding: "I'm going to make myself some breakfast before I go out – if I won't be in anyone's way?"

Jenny raised her voice: "Help yourself – this is Miss Kendall's night out. She's gone to see *Gone With The Wind* for the second time; she says she likes a good cry."

"I may have a good cry myself – what's happened to our marmalade? I was going to make some toast."

"We finished the last pot yesterday – it's in short supply, because of the oranges. Have a bacon sandwich instead."

"Can't – I polished off all my rashers yesterday."

"Pinch a slice out of Nick's ration – he won't be needing it this weekend."

"Honestly? Well, if you're sure. . . ." Caro reappeared with a slice of bacon, which she put under the grill. "How is he, anyway? I haven't seen him lately."

"Neither have I," said Jenny. "He's gone away for a little holiday."

Caro stared at her: "You're joking. . . ."

"I'm not. He said he'd been working terribly hard, and he'd got a few days leave due to him, so he rang up an old Naval chum with a motor yacht, and they've gone for a sailing holiday on the Thames."

"Whereabouts on the Thames?"

"I haven't the remotest idea. He was rather mysterious about it."

Caro was suitably indignant: "What a sneaky thing to do. . . . All right, he has been working hard – but he's not the only one. If he needed a holiday, why couldn't he take you with him?"

"I'm on work of national importance – the Canteen couldn't possibly spare me," Jenny said grimly.

They were interrupted by Lady Minster, who had just come home after another long day at the Palace.

"Mmm – that smells good," she said wistfully. "I don't suppose there are any spare rashers, by any chance?"

"Let's finish up all the bacon," said Jenny recklessly. "And we'll make some more toast – as long as the butter lasts out."

They sat round the kitchen table and enjoyed an impromptu

meal that was partly breakfast and partly supper, while Alice passed on the latest news. "I'm desperately worried about Miranda," she said. "Since Belgium collapsed, the German army is getting closer to France all the time . . . I heard today that the Military Mission in Paris have been given orders to destroy all their records and leave immediately – most of the staff are making for the Channel ports. . . . Except the Duke of Windsor; he and the Duchess have closed up their house in Paris and dashed off to their villa – I suppose he thinks they'll be safe on the Riviera."

Jenny tried to reassure her: "Oh, I can't believe France is really in danger —"

Lady Minster's face was drawn tight with anxiety: "I hope to God you're right – but the British Army have fallen back all along the Belgian coast. They're trying to raise a fleet of little ships to ferry the men back to England. Of course it's practically impossible – the whole of the British Expeditionary Force is stranded out there – but every boat that's fit to go to sea has been called into service . . . sailing-boats, tugs, motor yachts – even the pleasure-boats that run up and down the Thames —"

She broke off: "Why – what's the matter?"

Jenny and Caro looked at one another. They knew now where Nicholas was spending his holiday.

Chapter Six

Thursday, 30 May to Thursday, 11 July 1940

It must have been Thursday morning, and well after midnight because there was the luminous blur of a false dawn in the sky; but Nicholas had lost count of time long ago.

All that mattered was the job in hand.

He stood in the bows of the motor yacht *Gloria*, helping the men clamber aboard. Most of them were half-dead with fatigue and lack of nourishment – some still wore full uniform and equipment, sodden with sea water and heavy as lead weights – some, trembling with cold and shock, were half-naked and barefoot – but they were all determined to get away from the hell-hole of Dunkirk.

Nick called back to Pat Kernan, at the stern: "How many more can we take?"

"We've got twenty-five – no, thirty – I reckon there's room for another fifteen." Pat's voice was hoarse and toneless; under stress, his Old-Etonian drawl had disappeared. "Twenty at the outside."

"Right! Next chap – give me your hand. . . . Try and pull yourself up by the rope – easy does it."

The night sky was broken by glaring columns of fire and the men's faces shone with salt water and black oil, glistening in the reflected light of the flames.

"Get below, man —!" Nick heard Pat barking orders, guiding the next survivor through the open hatch to join his comrades. "Find yourself room to stretch out; lie down and stay down – understood?"

78

The work had been going on for over twenty-four hours. At first it had seemed simple enough; a flotilla of small boats plying to and fro, picking up men who stood waist-deep in the surf, and ferrying them out to the destroyers waiting in the deep channels. As soon as one load of soldiers was safely delivered, the boats returned to start another journey.

Nick didn't have time to think what he was doing – no time to stop, though his mouth was dry and he was desperate for a drink. He only knew that the work had to be done.

Two weeks earlier, the BBC had announced on the nine o'clock news: " . . *An order requesting all owners of self-propelled pleasure-craft between thirty and one hundred feet in length to send full particulars to the Admiralty within fourteen days. . . .*"

Pat Kernan was a keen amateur yachtsman, having been trained by his father, a retired Naval Captain, living on the Suffolk coast. When the old man died, Pat inherited the family estate near Southwold, together with his father's pride and joy – the MY *Gloria*.

"Christened after his other passion," Pat told him. "He was potty about Gloria Swanson too."

Pat and Nick had met at school, and again as cadets at Dartmouth, when they were commissioned as midshipmen. Postings to different sections of the fleet had kept them apart, though they managed to keep in touch; now Pat was deskbound at the Admiralty, but early on Monday morning he had called Nick, saying: "The old girl's ready to put to sea, and I need someone to crew for me – how about it?"

Nick applied for the leave that was due to him; on Tuesday morning they collected the *Gloria* from her mooring at Orford Ness and made their way south to the Thames Estuary, then followed the coast down, past the North Foreland and Ramsgate, until they reached Dover.

Pat went ashore for instructions, while Nick took on provisions and attended to refuelling; a couple of hours later Pat returned with a set of charts.

The obvious way was the short crossing to Calais, then along the French shoreline, but this route was known to be heavily mined. Until it could be swept, their best bet was to double back to the North Goodwin lightship, and make the long crossing from there – fifty-five miles instead of thirty-nine, but with a better chance of getting through.

They reached Dunkirk on Wednesday morning, and joined the rescue operation immediately.

All that day the work continued, and the little boats sailed to and fro in the sunlight; as they toiled on through the night, they were no longer sweating but shivering.

Several times, enemy aircraft flew overhead, swooping down and firing machine-gun bursts that made the surface of the water boil, and sent men diving for cover under the shadow of the keel. Some of the planes dropped bombs to disperse the rescue ships; a few scored direct hits, and at first light on Thursday, the sea was littered with flotsam, and half-submerged vessels stuck out of the water like broken toys.

There were floating bodies too; men too weak from exhaustion or wounds to survive – dark shapes that drifted through the water, occasionally breaking the surface.

Nick saw the face of a corpse that rolled over on the crest of a wave and seemed to stare at him with wide-open eyes, the gaping mouth calling silently, as if to say: *"Remember me. . . ."*

Another day passed, and another night, bringing a sea-mist. Nazi planes dropped flares to light their targets; an unearthly glow spread over the beaches – and still the men lined up, waiting for rescue.

Once, Nick heard the sound of a shot; on the wooden jetty a man with a corporal's stripes on his sleeve and a service revolver in his hand stood over a dead dog.

When the corporal reached the head of the queue half an hour later, Nick helped him scramble aboard, then asked: "Why did you shoot the dog?" – a plain question, not an accusation.

"I picked her up in Belgium; she came all through the retreat with me. I knew I'd never be able to bring her on the ship, and I couldn't leave her behind. There's no food there – the dogs are all half-mad, attacking each other – if she hadn't been ripped to pieces, she'd have starved to death. So I put her to sleep; it was the only —" Then he jerked his head up: "*Christ almighty —!*"

Overhead, a German plane hurtled towards them with a high, howling scream; it seemed as if it must crash on top of them, and they ducked instinctively. At the last second it pulled out of the dive and disappeared into the night sky; a second later the bomb it dropped had exploded, demolishing the end of the jetty and scattering the men who were lined up, waiting. Their bodies were flung in all directions, and in the light of the flares, the sea turned red.

"Bastards! Bloody bastards!" screamed the corporal. Uselessly, he shook his fist at the sky, while bomb fragments rattled on to the deck like hailstones.

Nick's legs were shaking and the palms of his hands were wet – but the job still had to be done.

When another boatload of passengers were aboard, he turned to check the numbers with Pat – but Pat wasn't there.

A medical orderly said: "Your mate got hit by shrapnel . . . I patched him up as best I could."

In the stern, Pat lay unconscious; his face covered in blood and a field-dressing plastered across his forehead.

"He's lucky it missed his eyes," said the orderly. "But he'll be spark out for a while. Can you manage on your own?"

Nick had no choice. He knew he could not keep the rescue work going single-handed. He could just about manoeuvre the *Gloria*, and with luck he might even be able to follow the sea charts well enough to steer a homeward course.

"Right, then," he said. "Next stop – Dover."

From the moment Alice had inadvertently solved the riddle of Nick's disappearance, Jenny lived through forty-eight hours of nightmare.

It was a waking nightmare, because she hardly slept at all.

81

She went to bed each evening, hoping to blot out the fear that paralyzed her, but sleep was impossible. Sometimes she fell into a restless doze, but then she was troubled by images of Nick – Nick wounded, Nick drowning, Nick dead. . . .

On Friday morning, the news of Dunkirk appeared in the press; and though the rescue was hailed as a great success, *The Times* added a cautionary note:

> *"Operations of this nature cannot be carried out without loss. His Majesty's destroyers, Grafton, Grenade and Wakeful, and certain small auxiliary craft have been lost. Next-of-kin of casualties are being informed as details become available."*

Jenny tried to convince herself that no news meant good news, but on Saturday she could not leave the house; she rang the Canteen to say she was unwell – it wasn't a complete lie, for lack of sleep was taking its toll. All the morning, she stayed close to the telephone; willing it to ring, yet dreading the message she might hear.

It was almost noon when the bell shattered the silence; she picked up the receiver, her heart thumping.

"Jenny —?" It was Nick's voice. "I just thought you'd like to know – I'll be home for supper."

She grabbed a shopping-basket and hurried out, managing to wheedle a tin of pink salmon out of a sympathetic grocer, explaining that her husband was on his way home. With a bottle of wine, a bowl of salad and a couple of hard-boiled eggs from Crown House, it would make a feast.

When Nick arrived, she was shocked by his appearance; he was grey with fatigue, his face scarred by small cuts.

"You're hurt —" she began, but he grinned wearily.

"I didn't get round to shaving for three or four days; when I did, my hands were rather shaky – and it was a lousy blade."

Later, he explained that Pat had been injured: "But he's going to be fine – they patched him up pretty well, and when he came to he remembered an emergency bottle of brandy in

82

one of the lockers – that helped a lot! Only one problem – I was in sole charge all the way back."

"The engine had taken a hell of a beating, and halfway across it packed up altogether. Luckily we had a couple of Royal Engineers unit on board, and they took the engine to bits, while we drifted on the tide and I hoped to God we wouldn't collide with anything. After an hour or so they got her firing on a couple of cylinders, and we managed to crawl home somehow. I damn nearly ran us aground on the Goodwins – but we finally limped into Ramsgate some time this morning."

After supper they went to bed early, for they both had a lot of sleep to make up; naked, they lay in one another's arms, and Nick whispered: "I think we're both too tired tonight . . . better get some sleep, and perhaps – tomorrow morning – when we wake up. . . ."

"Yes, of course – let's just hold each other – and sleep."

But gradually, in spite of their exhaustion, their bodies took control, and they soon found they were helpless – swept away on a tide of overpowering excitement.

"I need you – I want you. . . ." Nick breathed the words in Jenny's ear, as they slipped into the rites of love.

"Yes —" she agreed: "Yes – oh, yes. . . ."

And then there were no more words.

Next morning Jenny stayed in bed, lazily content, watching as Nick began to get dressed. Seeing that he was pulling on his dress uniform, she asked: "Do you have to report for duty at the Palace?"

"Sort of." He sat on the bed to tie his shoelaces. "Actually – I came to a decision while I was away. I'm afraid you may not like this, but. . . ."

She knew what was coming: "You're going back to active service. That's it, isn't it?"

"I shall ask His Majesty if he will release me from my duties as equerry . . . I can't stay in London, with everything going on out there." He turned to her: "I hope you won't be unhappy about it. It's what I have to do."

She took his hands in hers and tried to smile. She longed to argue, to protest that he mustn't put himself in danger again, to beg him to stay with her . . . And she heard herself saying: "Yes, of course . . . I understand."

His Majesty was graciously pleased to assent to Nicholas's request, and the Admiralty were duly informed. Within a matter of days, Nick was posted to HMS *Kenilworth* – one of the oldest destroyers in the Navy – and granted seven days embarkation leave before joining the ship.

On the second weekend in June, Nick and Jenny went down to Crown House, to spend a few days with the family.

The weather was glorious; Polly put bathing-slips on Alex and Harriet, and they splashed in the shallows at the edge of the lake, squealing with delight and sending up rainbow showers of spray.

Sprawled on the grass beside Polly and Jenny, Nick said: "I wish I'd had the sense to bring my bathers down with me – for two pins, I'd strip off and dive in myself."

"And scandalise the entire family?" said Jenny. "Don't you dare!"

Polly said wickedly: "Go on, be a devil – I'll tell the kids to look the other way!"

Nick laughed: "It's a tempting thought, but I haven't got a towel either. It won't give a very good impression if I go aboard *Kenilworth* with a streaming cold."

"Well, never mind – perhaps you'll be shipped off to a tropical island," Polly consoled him. "Drop us a postcard if you finish up on a golden beach in the South Seas. . . . Do you know where you're going?"

"No – and if I did I wouldn't tell you," retorted Nick. "Haven't you seen the posters? – '*Careless Talk Costs Lives!*'"

"I dare say you're right – I never could keep my trap shut." Polly sighed: "Oh, dear – you two make me feel completely useless. All I do is sit here, looking after the kids and enjoying the sunshine. I must start looking for a part-time job."

"I think you're doing a wonderful job already," Jenny assured her. "Alex and Harry are looking so well and happy."

As they watched, Alex plunged headfirst, to emerge dripping a few seconds later, shaking himself like a dog.

"Did you see me, Mummy?" he demanded. "Look! – I can swim under water! Nick – Jenny – watch me!"

Jenny laughed and applauded enthusiastically; beside her, Nick was watching too, but he was no longer smiling. As Alex broke the surface again, shining and triumphant, Nick saw another face rising from the water – a wide-eyed face, with a gaping mouth that seemed to say: "*Remember me. . . .*"

The following weekend, news of Dunkirk was superseded by other headlines. On 16 June, the French Premier, M. Reynaud, resigned, and the elderly Marshal Petain formed a new government.

On 17 June, he sent a message to Herr Hitler, with the Spanish Government acting as intermediary, requesting a peaceful settlement, and the cessation of hostilities.

On 18 June, General de Gaulle, who had set up his headquarters in London, broadcast a message to his countrymen:

"*France is not lost – one day she will rise again, and conquer. . . .*"

But in the eyes of the world, France had fallen; and as the German army moved across their territory, Frenchmen everywhere wept, watching their country being torn apart. Hitler's troops pushed down from the north, and the people fled in their thousands – abandoning their homes, taking whatever they could carry, in old hand-carts or perambulators.

In London, Alice reported to the Queen that everything of value within Buckingham Palace had been removed to places of safety; it had been a rush job – even the Crown Jewels, now under lock and key in the vaults beneath Windsor Castle, had been hastily wrapped in newspaper.

"It's been a race against time," said Her Majesty. "And we are immensely grateful. Do sit down, Alice – you look quite worn out."

They were in the royal air raid shelter, for there was a daytime "alert" in progress – a cream-painted room, previously occupied by the housekeeper. Now there were steel shutters on the windows, and the ceiling had been reinforced with steel girders, though it would still be inadequate against high explosives.

Alice sank on to the sofa and tried to smile: "I am a little tired, ma'am . . . and a little worried."

"Of course you are – we're all worried," said the Queen. "You know we're moving into Windsor Castle ourselves? We'd prefer to stay at Royal Lodge, but they say that's impossible to protect – the Castle has its drawbacks, but at least it's a fortress! As soon as France fell, the King decided we must move. . . ."

Then she saw the look in Alice's eyes, and exclaimed: "My dear – I'm being very thoughtless – you have some of your family in France. . . . Do forgive me."

Alice struggled to control herself: "William's sister Edith and her friend are in the Pyrenees – probably out of harm's way . . . But my youngest daughter is still at a finishing-school near Annecy, and we've had no news of her at all. I've sent cables – I've tried telephoning – but there's never any reply."

The Queen said quietly: "Please tell me if there's anything I can do – anything at all."

Alice bit her lip, then began again: "I was thinking – would it be possible for me to speak to the Duke of Windsor, at his villa? He might advise me what to do – if you could give me the telephone number —?"

It was a difficult request to make, since David's name was seldom mentioned within the Royal Family.

After a moment, the Queen said: "Of course I'll give you the number – though I don't know that he will be there. But anything is worth trying."

When the "All Clear" sounded, Alice returned to the Queen's office. At this stage, France and England were still – technically speaking – maintaining diplomatic relations, but it was far from easy to put a call through. After several false starts, she finally succeeded, but then she had to wrestle with various members of the Windsors' staff before they would pass her on to the Duke.

At last she said in desperation: "Tell him it's the Duchess of Dillwater!"

The long-standing private joke did the trick, and the Duke's husky tones came over the line: "Good God, Alice – is that really you?"

As briefly as possible, she explained about Miranda.

David sounded harassed: "I only wish I could help – but there's nothing I can do. You've picked a bad moment; we're just about to move out ourselves. We should never have come down here – we're heading for Spain – the cars are at the door, and Wallis is just rounding up the dogs."

In the background, Alice could hear some hysterical yapping, and the strident voice of the Duchess exclaiming: "David, the luggage is all in – come on, let's go!"

"I tell you what – I'll leave messages with our chums here – and I'll call the American Consul at Nice – I'm sure he'll think of something. . . ."

"For Pete's sake, David —!" Wallis was getting fretful: "Will you get off that phone?"

"I must go . . . I hope everything sorts itself out – good luck – goodbye!"

And he hung up.

On 20 June, Lyon surrendered to the German motorized columns, and bombs fell on Bordeaux. Two days later, the terms of the armistice had been hammered out, and were accepted. France was to be divided into two zones: "Occupied" in the north and west – "Unoccupied" to the south-east, with a demarcation line running roughly from Bayonne on the Atlantic coast, across the country to the Swiss frontier.

On 24 June, Edith walked out of Mas-Lou, trying not to cry. The garden, which they had worked on for so long, was looking at its best.

"It seems dreadful to leave it on such a lovely day," she said. "Just as the white roses are coming out. Once we've gone, the garden will turn back into a wilderness."

"Don't give way, dear." Grace was briskly practical: "You

know this is the only thing to do. It's far too dangerous for us to stay in France."

"But the villagers are our friends – they'd never let anything bad happen to us – it's not as if the Germans were going to march in —"

"We could still be interned as enemy aliens. But as you say, we have good friends here – I've arranged to leave the keys with Monsieur le Curé; our house will be in safe hands. . . . We shall come back some day, when this terrible business is all over." Holding her head erect, Grace locked the front door behind her and said: "That's done. Let's be on our way."

Lugging their suitcases and an old carpet-bag, they made their way along the goat-track to the main road, where an ancient taxi waited for them. Pepé, the driver, spat out the butt of a Gauloise, mopped his bald head, and put the luggage into the boot, while the old ladies settled themselves in the back seat. Then he climbed in, started the engine, and said: "Le Perthus?"

"If you please." Le Perthus was the frontier-post on the mountain road which linked France and Spain. It consisted of a handful of shops, a café, and a passport-control office with a striped pole barring the way. Beyond that, there was a short stretch of no man's land, another striped pole, and another cluster of buildings, under a Spanish flag.

As a rule it was not a busy place; Grace had chosen it for that reason, in preference to the coast road, but she had not reckoned with the long queue of cars, carts and motor coaches lined up at the barrier, or the crowds of anxious refugees besieging the police station.

"It seems we must expect a long wait," she said. She told the driver in precise and formal French that they would not need him any longer; he could go back to Collioure. They would find other transport, once they had crossed the frontier.

Pepé pocketed the handful of francs she gave him, but said he would not leave until he had seen them delivered safely into Spain. He had nothing else to do; he would remain here and wait with them. They would surely be more comfortable, sitting in his taxi, than out on the road under the blazing sun.

The ladies were very touched, and Grace said: "In that case I shall go across to the café and fetch a bottle of wine and some Evian water. Waiting is thirsty work."

"I'll come with you," said Edith. "You'll need another pair of hands to carry the glasses."

It took some time to get served in the crowded café, and by the time they left the bar with their bottles and glasses, the traffic had crawled on a few yards. As they walked back to their taxi, they heard raised voices – an Englishman and an American woman sat in an open Buick, behind a uniformed chauffeur. The passengers were arguing about three restless Cairn terriers who shared the back seat with them, and the American woman was saying: "For Pete's sake, they have to go walkies, darling. Can't the chauffeur take them to find a lamppost or something?"

Her husband protested: "Suppose the convoy moves on while he's out of the car? We don't want to miss our turn."

She dabbed irritably at her knot of raven hair: "We shouldn't *have* to wait our turn! – Don't these people know who we are? . . . Oh, well – then you'll have to do it. But for heaven's sake be *quick!*"

Obediently, the man stepped out of the car, coming face to face with Edith and Grace.

Edith nearly dropped the tray of glasses: "Oh, Your Majesty —" she began: "No – I beg your pardon – I mean, Your Royal Highness – oh, dear. . . ."

Confronted by a flustered but clearly aristocratic English lady, the Duke of Windsor retained his poise.

"Hello – how are you?" He smiled politely: "Forgive me; I'm sure I should remember – have we met?"

"No, sir – but I think you know my family; my brother is Lord Minster – we had the pleasure of entertaining His Maj —" She broke off and corrected herself again: "Your brother – when he was the Duke of York – at Crown House."

"So you're Lady Minster's sister-in-law? What a small world. . . ." Turning, he included the Duchess in the conversation: "Hear that, darling? This is – um – let me see —"

89

"I'm Lady Edith Gaunt, and this is my friend, Miss Duncan," said Edith.

"I see you've been getting drinks," said the Duchess. "Now that's what I call a really bright idea – I'm simply parched."

"Allow me," said Grace crisply. "With or without Evian?"

"Without," said the Duchess. "I need something to give me a lift . . . Would you believe, we left our villa at Antibes four days ago? It's taken us all this time just to drive across France – simply ghastly!"

She took the glass of wine Grace poured for her, raising it in salutation: "Cheers," she said – and a moment later: "Boy – that hit the spot."

The Duke refused a drink, saying to Edith: "Oddly enough, Lady Minster was one of the last people I spoke to before we set out; she telephoned me from London." He explained Alice's anxiety over Miranda, adding: "I did what I could – I sent a message to the American Consul; he'll probably be able to track the girl down. There was no time to do anything else; we left in rather a rush."

"*Jeepers!*" Suddenly the Duchess sat bolt upright. "I just remembered – I left my best swimsuit hanging up to dry in the bathroom . . . God, how could I be so dumb? If this weather keeps up, I'm going to need that costume in Spain – whatever shall we do?"

"Surely you can buy another bathing-costume, darling?" suggested the Duke.

"But it was my very favourite – the nile-green one – practically brand new. Listen, why don't we ring the Consul at Nice and get him to send one of his boys round to the villa, to pick it up? I know exactly where I left it – he can have it sent on to us in Madrid or Lisbon or wherever the hell we're going. . . . Oh, look – the traffic's moving at last. . . . Thank you so much – that was really darling of you."

She handed the empty glass to Grace with a dazzling smile: "Maybe we'll all meet up again when we get through . . . Honey, hop back in the car – the dogs will just have to hang on a while longer, that's all . . . Bye for now!"

90

The Buick moved slowly forward, and Grace and Edith walked back to their taxi.

Grace said: "He seemed pleasant enough – I can't say I cared much for her. All that fuss over a swimming-costume, when Miranda's vanished into thin air!"

As they reached the taxi, Edith said: "We can't go . . . we can't run away and leave Miranda on her own. We must go back and find her."

"But my dear – we've no idea where she is —"

"We know the address of the school; that's a start. We'll go there and make enquiries."

"Yes, but – Annecy is practically on the edge of the Occupied Zone – the place will be crawling with Germans."

"All the more reason to go and look for her," said Edith doggedly. She turned to Pepé, who was eyeing the opened bottle of wine hopefully, and addressed him in schoolroom French: "We will not go to Spain. We wish to go to Annecy instead – it is near Switzerland. Will you please take us there?"

The weeks went by; William and Alice waited at Crown House, hoping against hope for news of Miranda – but they heard nothing. Alice was anxious about Edith and Grace as well, though William felt certain they would have had the sense to get out of France while the going was good. But if they had reached Spain safely, surely they would have been in touch?

Early in July, Alice received a message from the Queen, asking if she could carry out some further duties; they arranged to meet at the Royal Lodge, in Windsor Great Park.

When Alice arrived, the Queen began apologetically: "I always seem to call on you when there's furniture-moving to be done – as if you were a branch of Pickfords! – but could you bear to take on one more packing-up job?"

By now the Royal Family had settled in at the Castle, making themselves as comfortable as possible, but the Queen explained: "As you see, we still have all this furniture to go into store. Perhaps we might make a start in here?"

They were in the Tent Room – an octagonal drawing-room,

decorated to resemble a marquee, with long windows opening on to the garden. They began to make a list of the furniture, but they hadn't got far when they were joined by the Princesses.

Princess Margaret raced in first, skidding to a halt when she saw her mother had a visitor: "Oh, good – it's Lady Minster – hello!"

Her sister followed more sedately, and shook Alice's hand, saying: "How lovely to see you; Mama hoped you might come and help." She looked enquiringly at the Queen: "Have you told her yet – about *our* house?"

The girls had to pack up their own house; the little play house which had been given to Princess Elizabeth by the people of Wales, on her sixth birthday.

"We've got to store all our furniture too – everything except the pots and pans," Margaret broke in. "They're going to be turned into an aeroplane."

"You see, our little saucepans – and the kettle and the teapot and the hot-water jug – they're all made of aluminium," Elizabeth explained. "So we're handing them in as scrap metal, to be made into planes for the RAF."

Alice couldn't help smiling; eight years ago, Lillibet had been enchanted by the pots and pans in her miniature kitchen; now she was fourteen, thinking and talking like a young lady.

"What's the matter?" Elizabeth had seen her smile. "Did I say something funny?"

"No, not at all. I was just thinking how very grown-up you are, all of a sudden."

Margaret nodded: "Everybody grows up sooner or later. I shall be grown-up too, quite soon. . . . Are your children grown-up now?"

"Yes, they are."

"Don't they live at home any more?" she wanted to know.

"No, not now. Nick's in the Navy – he's gone to sea; and Caro is a nurse in a hospital in London. Martin's just taken his final exams at Oxford, and now he's going to join the Air Force – and Miranda. . . ." She stopped, unable to go on.

Her Majesty came to the rescue: "Miranda's grown-up too

– so she's left home as well. . . . Now then, how about some tea?"

Something in her tone caught Margaret's interest, and she asked: "So – where's Miranda gone?"

"Annecy – seven kilometres. . . ." Grace pointed to a signpost. "Not much further now."

They had been travelling for nearly three weeks. At times it seemed that their journey would never end, but now they had almost reached their goal.

At first, Pepé protested that it would be madness for them to drive right across the country, but Edith refused to listen to any argument. If they left France without trying to find Miranda, she would never forgive herself. They had enough money to pay their way; Grace had withdrawn all their savings from the bank three days earlier, and had prudently sewn most of the notes into the lining of her full, old-fashioned skirt.

And they had one great advantage; they would be travelling in the opposite direction from the flood of refugees, who were being continually stopped for interrogation and documentation. Not many people were heading north-east.

Grace smiled to herself; Edith's natural timidity had been swept away by fierce family loyalty, and she had found a new courage. For years, Edith had relied on Grace's strength and followed when Grace led the way; now, in a moment of crisis, Edith had taken command.

Pepé finally agreed to take them as far as he could, without putting himself in danger. He had to think of his wife and family; for their sake, he could not run any risks.

So they set out, driving briskly along the road to Perpignan, past lines of traffic crawling the other way. They stopped for food and drink at Narbonne, and Pepé was uncomfortably aware of the curious glances directed at the two old ladies.

They had intended to continue through Béziers and Montpellier, but Pepé said it would be wiser to avoid police checkpoints in the major towns, and keep to the side roads. So they took the slow route along the coast, through Agde and Sète, between salt lagoons fringed with reed-beds; and when the sun went down, they reached a desolate, wind-raked village in the middle of nowhere, called Aigues-Mortes.

Pepé stopped at a small hotel, and they took two rooms for the night; one double, and one single. The beds were hard and the mattresses lumpy, but the sheets were fairly clean.

Madame la Patronne wanted to know where the travellers had come from, and where they were going. Pepé told her that his ladies were Americans on holiday, who had been overtaken by the sudden rush of events, and that he was driving them to Marseilles, where they would catch a boat for New York.

Madame expressed a desire to see their American passports; it was a legal obligation for all hotel-keepers, and there was no knowing when the police might drop in to check up.

Pepé gave her a long and complicated explanation, regretting that by an unfortunate oversight, the ladies had left their passports in Paris, but that these were even now being sent on to Marseilles, where they would collect them. He then ordered a bottle of *marc*, and poured her a large glassful.

Madame narrowed her eyes, but asked no more questions.

The following morning they settled the bill and left promptly – Pepé did not think Madame would report them to the police, but he did not wish to wait and find out.

All that day they pressed on, taking side roads and trying to keep out of trouble; they bypassed Arles successfully, but at Beaucaire they had to take the bridge across the Rhone, into neighbouring Tarascon – and that was where they hit trouble.

A roadblock awaited them, and a policeman flagged them down. Strolling over to the car, he asked Pepé where he was going, and the purpose of his journey. When Pepé repeated his story about the American tourists, the policeman frowned; why were they heading north-east towards Avignon, instead of south-east to Marseilles? He wished to see their travel documents.

Again, Pepé told him the circumstances of the ladies'

departure from Paris, and assured the officer that the passports were doubtless awaiting their arrival in Marseilles.

The policeman took detailed notes, then allowed them to proceed, adding that when they reached Arles they must go immediately to the central police station. He would telephone ahead to explain, so the Chief of Police would be expecting them.

When they had left Tarascon, Pepé stopped the car, pulling up at the side of the long, dusty road. He was sweating profusely as he apologized; he was desolate, but he could take them no further. For the sake of his wife, his children, and his innocent grandchildren, he must return at once to Collioure, before he found himself in prison for assisting the escape of two "enemy aliens".

Edith began to panic: "But you can't leave us here – what ever shall we do?"

Grace said quietly: "No, dear – he's right. We must not put him in any more danger – and we may do better on our own."

As they discussed the situation, an old farm wagon piled with cabbages overtook them, pulled by a lumbering horse and driven by an elderly woman in rusty black. Pepé sprang from the car and hailed the woman, asking if she would help his passengers on their way.

She shrugged; if they wished to go as far as Avignon market, they were welcome to sit in the back of the cart with the cabbages. Pepé helped Edith and Grace scramble on board, and loaded their luggage beside them; then he wished them good luck and a safe journey, and hoped he would see them again some day.

With that, he jumped into the taxi, did a U-turn in the road, and set off; they saw a cloud of white dust fly up as he took the first side road he came to. He would travel all the way home on byways and cart-tracks, rather than risk any more encounters with the authorities.

The old lady clicked her tongue and flicked the reins to set the horse ambling on, and Grace said: "We must follow Pepé's example – keep away from towns and main roads. Better safe than sorry."

So their weird, dreamlike journey began.

They begged lifts from strangers on deserted country lanes, and were seldom refused. Generally, they covered no more than a few miles at a time; if they made ten miles in a day they thought themselves lucky. Each evening they would find a labourer's cottage where they could rent a room; sometimes they paid for a solid, satisfying meal – a stew of meat and vegetables that had been simmering in the pot all day – at other times they bought themselves bread, cheese and fruit from a village shop.

It was a slow expedition, but not unpleasant; people are only hostile to strangers if they have reason to be afraid of them, and no one felt threatened by these two quaint elderly ladies.

Edith's English accent was a problem, and it was agreed that she should only speak when it was absolutely essential; Grace's clipped, correct French was harder to identify, and they stuck to the story that they were American tourists, and prayed that nobody would ask to see their passports.

But the journey had some unpleasant moments too.

Near Valence, a patriotic veteran of the First World War cornered them in a barn, accusing them of being German spies, sent into the Unoccupied Zone to stir up trouble. He was armed with a rook rifle and a pitchfork, and it was only after Grace's eloquent speech in their defence that he realized they were allied against a common enemy, and offered to shelter them for the night.

Worse was to come when they reached the outskirts of Grenoble.

A couple of youths in a back-street café eyed them for some time, then got into conversation; Grace parried their questions, until one of the boys admitted that they were deserters, on the run from the French army, and had overheard the ladies exchanging some incautious remarks in English. The two louts tried to turn the situation to their advantage, suggesting they should travel on together and pose as a family – "We'll say we're taking you to the Old Folks Home" – but Grace and Edith rejected this kind offer, saying they preferred to travel alone.

Unabashed, the boys insisted on treating them to supper, and would not take no for an answer. After the meal, Edith and Grace found that their generous hosts had disappeared, leaving them to pay the bill – and had also stolen their suitcases.

"Our clothes —!" cried Edith in despair: "They've taken everything!"

"We must make do with what we've got on our backs," said Grace. "It will be less to carry. Thank goodness they didn't bother with the old carpet-bag – I suppose it wasn't worth stealing. Just as well, since it has our passports in it."

As they moved north, the weather broke; without raincoats or umbrellas they were often cold and wet, and always tired. When they could not get a lift in the right direction, they trudged on foot – up the narrow valley of the Isère, and along a winding road that took them high into the mountains. There they hitched a ride on the back of a timber lorry, driving towards Annecy.

"Annecy – seven kilometres . . ." Edith read the signpost which Grace had pointed out. "Miranda must be very near us now."

They saw the roofs and spires of the city reflected in the waters of the lake, against a panorama of mountains. On the peaks, there were still patches of snow.

Tired as she was, Grace smiled: "So beautiful," she said. "Just as I always imagined them."

"Imagined what?"

"The Swiss Alps. I always had a fancy to see Switzerland some day."

The lorry slowed down, turning into the open gateway of a lumber yard, and the old ladies alighted.

Grace thanked the driver, and asked: "Can you direct us to *Les Gentianes*? It's a school – near a village called Pas-de-Loup."

It turned out to be a long way from Annecy, and by the time they reached the school the sun was going down.

They walked up the drive to the front door; a typed notice announced that the school was closed until further notice. They tried ringing the bell, but without any result.

"They can't have left the place empty," said Edith. "Miranda told us there were riding-stables here – someone must look after the horses. What was the name of the riding-master she was so keen on?"

"Alain Lafitte," Grace remembered. "You're quite right – let's find the stables."

They followed an unweeded path which led them to a cobbled yard; through a stone arch they saw a row of loose-boxes. Somewhere, a horse whinnied.

Edith was triumphant: "There *must* be someone here."

Then a side door opened, and a grey-haired woman emerged, wiping her hands on the front of her apron – she had once been pretty, and now looked old before her time.

"What do you want?" she asked.

They explained that they were looking for Miranda Gaunt.

"Miranda Gaunt . . ." The woman repeated the name without any inflection. "She is not here."

"This lady is her aunt," said Grace. "Do you know where we can find Miranda?"

"Do you know a Monsieur Alain Lafitte?" added Edith.

The woman paused, before replying: "Alain Lafitte is my husband. He has gone to the village; I do not know what time he will return. If you wish to talk to him, you must go to the Café L'Aiglon. . . . You must ask him about Miranda Gaunt."

With a curt nod of the head, she went in and closed the door. A moment later, Edith saw the lace curtain twitch at the window.

"She's watching us," she murmured. "Grace, I'm frightened – there's something wrong. . . . Something's happened to Miranda."

Pas-de-Loup wasn't much of a place – a few shops, a handful of chalet-style houses with overhanging upper storeys and pointed roofs – and facing the village square, the Café l'Aiglon.

The moment they stepped inside, they knew it was a mistake.

In contrast with the deserted square, the bar was crowded; men in dungarees or navy blue blousons stood about, muttering to one another – the air was thick with cigarette smoke

98

and the smell of cheap red wine. And there were two uniformed policemen, conferring with two men in dark suits and steel-rimmed spectacles.

As the ladies entered, they all stopped talking and stared at the newcomers. Grace realized that they must present a strange appearance; dishevelled and travel-stained, with uncombed hair, wearing the clothes they had lived in for nearly three weeks. Trying to appear unconcerned, she led Edith to a bench seat against the wall, and they sat down.

The landlord stepped out from behind the bar: "Yes?" he said.

Grace cleared her throat and said as firmly as she could: "Two coffees, two cognacs, if you please."

He grunted and went away; the buzz of voices began again. To her horror, Grace realized that the policemen were going round the room, carrying out a routine inspection; every customer was being asked to produce his identity card.

She thought of getting up and walking out, but that would seem suspicious. Then her heart missed a beat, as she heard the men in spectacles talking to one another in low tones, and recognized that they were speaking German. Even in the Unoccupied Zone, civilian "observers" were allowed to investigate.

Behind the bar, a young woman in a red checked headscarf and a grubby apron was pouring cups of coffee, while the Patron measured out two tots of cognac.

The senior policeman addressed Grace: "Your papers, please."

For once, she was completely at a loss: "Papers —?" she repeated stupidly.

The policeman frowned: "Your documents – your identity cards."

"I – that is to say – we—" She stopped again, frantically trying to think of some excuse.

"Where are your papers?" the second policeman asked. "In here?" – and he made a move to pick up the bag that lay at Grace's feet.

Then a new voice broke in: *"How dare you!"*

In three long strides, the girl in the headscarf had crossed the room and snatched the carpet-bag from the policeman's hands. But she was not addressing him; she was scolding the two old ladies, in a torrent of swift, furious French.

"How dare you come in here again, making a nuisance of yourselves? How many more times do I have to tell you – you are not allowed in here – now get out – be off – leave us in peace!"

She hustled them to the door, explaining over her shoulder: "Take no notice, they're completely mad – always coming in and ordering drinks they can't pay for – but don't you worry, I'll get rid of them – leave them to me. . . ."

She flung the door wide, following them out into the square.

"Don't let me catch you round here again . . . I'm taking you to the backyard – that's where you belong!"

She dragged them down the alley into the yard. As soon as they were alone, unseen and unheard, she spoke to them again – quietly, and in English.

"I couldn't believe my eyes . . ." said Miranda. "Aunt Edie – Grace – what the hell are you doing here?"

Chapter Seven

Thursday, 11 July to Friday, 2 August 1940

Without waiting for an answer, Miranda took the two old ladies into the woodshed, shut the door, and said: "Right – now we can talk. How did you get here? How did you know where to find me?"

They perched on a mound of logs stored for the winter; they were exhausted, hungry and frightened – but none of that mattered now they had found Miranda – and in the dusty half-light, with the last glimmer of sunset coming through the cracks and knotholes of the plank walls, they poured out their story.

When they had finished, Miranda said: "You've done very well – but do you realize what a terrible risk you were taking? You might have been picked up by the police at any time."

"Oh, we would have managed somehow," said Edith. "We decided to say we were Americans and we'd lost our passports. They would have had to send us to an American consul, and then we'd have thrown ourselves on his mercy and asked him to help us get away."

Miranda shook her head: "It's not as simple as that. You haven't heard the latest news – four days ago, they announced that the entry of all foreigners into the Unoccupied Zone was forbidden – and all travel visas issued before then have been cancelled. You'd probably have finished up in an internment camp."

Edith looked at Grace helplessly: "Whatever are we going to do? How will we all get out of France?"

"I don't want to get out of France," said Miranda. "I'm staying here."

Edith's lip trembled: "But your family – your mother and father . . . They're so anxious – you must go home —"

"I've made a new home here; I have a new family."

As simply as possible, she told them about Marianne's death, and how she had grown close to Alain and Germaine in the past eighteen months, concluding: "You see, they really need me. Nobody needs me in England; I'm just another member of the Minster clan. But I'm all the Lafittes have got now; if I went away, it would be almost like losing Marianne all over again."

"Even if that were true—" Grace tried to speak calmly: "You're overlooking the fact that you're British; if those Germans in the café had questioned you —"

"I've been here long enough to pass for French. Alain and Germaine say I'm their niece – and the villagers would never give the game away. Besides – I shall soon make myself useful."

"Useful—?" Grace frowned.

"They're going to need someone who speaks English, when the first agents arrive." They looked at her blankly, and she continued: "Do you really think the French are going to let the Germans walk over them? They haven't lost this war – they'll never give up until they drive the enemy out. Already they're setting up resistance groups, but they need reinforcements – weapons – money. . . . Soon there will be help from overseas; the Free French who got away will come back to carry on the fight. Then the British will follow – and that's where I come in. I shall be a go-between, and —"

Somewhere outside a guard dog barked, and she broke off, listening. They heard a car starting up in the street, then driving off into the distance.

"That's good; the police and the Germans have gone. Now it will be safe for me to take you home. Wait here till I've explained to Alain; the fewer people who know about this, the better."

The ladies sat and waited for what seemed a very long time. Edith began to cry a little, overwhelmed by their impossible situation. Grace put her arms round her, murmuring: "It will be all right, my dear; you'll see – everything's going to be all right."

She tried to sound confident, and Edith closed her eyes, falling asleep with her head on Grace's shoulder.

Grace forced herself to stay awake. Presently she heard low voices, and footsteps; the beam of a lantern penetrated the cracks in the walls, setting up dancing patterns of light and shade.

The door squeaked open, and Miranda said: "We can go now. This is Monsieur Lafitte – he has agreed that you can stay at Les Gentianes for a few nights."

In the village square a horse and cart stood waiting; Alain Lafitte and Miranda helped the ladies to climb aboard, then took their places in front. With a subdued rattle of harness and the clip-clop of hooves, the vehicle set off. There were no lights in the village; it was like a ghost town.

When they reached the school, nobody spoke – they stepped down on to cobblestones, and Miranda led the way into the house while Alain stabled the horses.

After the darkness and silence, the Lafittes' kitchen seemed bright and loud. Miranda explained the situation to Madame Lafitte in rapid, colloquial French that even Grace found hard to follow; and when Alain returned, he joined in. Madame Lafitte looked from one to the other, then subjected the strangers to a long, hard scrutiny. She seemed to be arguing with Alain and Miranda, and they all talked at once, adding to the confusion.

Finally she threw up her hands, exclaiming: "Do as you please! Nobody ever listens to me. . . ."

Then she turned away, clattering the pots and pans on the kitchen range, while Miranda spread a tablecloth and laid the cutlery for supper.

Under cover of the noise, Edith whispered to Grace: "Monsieur Lafitte isn't quite the sort of man you expected, is he?"

103

Grace smiled wryly; certainly, their host was not the young Romeo she had imagined when Miranda spoke of him, at Collioure. A man in his mid-fifties, whose wife was ten years younger – lean and tanned, with deep lines scoring his face, he might once have been handsome in a rugged way, but he had lost some teeth in his nutcracker jaw. As the result of a bad riding accident many years earlier, he moved awkwardly; his right leg had never knitted properly.

Too old and lame for military service, with nothing to do but look after the string of horses in the stables – at least until the Germans decided to commandeer them – he had only one ambition left. He would form a resistance group here in the mountains above Annecy, and he would not rest until the Boches had been driven out of France.

Over supper, he chatted to the ladies, praising Grace's command of French and saying: "I would find your accent hard to place – from Scotland, you say? You could pass yourself off as a Breton – the Celtic races are very similar. As for Lady Edith – if she meets any strangers, it might be wise to say that the good lady cannot speak at all. She can pretend to be deaf and dumb – even a little touched in the head, perhaps?"

He gave a bark of laughter, and described a circle round his temples with thumb and forefinger. Wistfully, Edith accepted her non-speaking role.

When the plates were empty, Miranda pushed back her chair, saying: "I'll go and make up the beds. Since the school closed, there's no shortage of beds, or bed-linen."

"I'll come and help you," Alain volunteered, following her from the room.

Germaine had been silent for some time. Now, as she made a jug of coffee, she asked: "Did Mademoiselle Miranda tell you of our tragedy?"

Grace nodded: "We are very sorry."

"Everyone was sorry. Mademoiselle has been so kind – she has done all she can to help us to forget – but I can never forget. In time, my husband may do so; for me, it is impossible."

104

"Miranda is fond of you both," said Edith. "She told us that."

"We are fond of her – I shall always be grateful for her sympathy – and for her company. These rooms would have been empty without her."

Carefully, Grace added: "Miranda told us she will not leave. She says there will soon be work for her to do here."

"So they say. We would find it hard if she were taken from us – but who knows what may happen, from one day to the next?"

"That's true . . ." As Edith sipped her coffee, there were tears in her eyes. "We don't even know how we shall get back to England."

"Alain is already making plans. He will have a plan for your escape, without doubt."

As there was no shortage of accommodation, the ladies were given a bedroom each on the top floor, but some time later Grace rose from her narrow iron bedstead and crept into Edith's room.

"Thank goodness," whispered Edith. "I'd never have had a wink of sleep if I'd been on my own . . . I keep worrying about Miranda – how could she be so ungrateful to William and Alice? – making it sound as if they didn't want her. . . ."

"There's a grain of truth in it, for all that," remarked Grace. "The twins have never been close to their father."

"But whatever shall I say when we get home? How can we tell them she's chosen to stay in France and live with strangers?"

"Miranda's not a child any more; she's a young woman, and she must make her own decisions. Why don't you stop fretting, and try to get some sleep?"

Edith moved a little closer, saying: "All right – though I'm afraid we shan't be very comfortable in such a narrow bed."

"It's never troubled us in the past," retorted Grace.

Edith began to giggle – then the giggle turned into a yawn and before she knew it, she was fast asleep.

By the following afternoon, Alain had made his plans. Miranda spread out a map on the kitchen table, which showed

Annecy to the south-west, and in the opposite direction, the curving blue scimitar of Lac Leman. Beyond that lay Switzerland.

"Alain has contacts everywhere; he knows a man who knows one of the frontier guards. After some money changed hands, it was all fixed; there will be a path left open for us, leading down to the lakeside, where a fisherman will be waiting with a rowing-boat. But you'll have to wait until the guard is on duty alone. Every Friday night, the officer in charge visits his girlfriend, and leaves our man on his own for a couple of hours – that will be your chance."

Friday was almost a week away, and the enforced wait was even harder to bear than the journey across France. They had to stay away from the village, in case any passing police or German observers should start making enquiries – so for five days and nights, the ladies never left Les Gentianes.

"I feel as if I were in a prison camp already," Edith said to Grace, as they paced the overgrown garden paths.

"Compared with the camps, I imagine this is paradise! You must be patient – we've only one more hurdle to get over."

"I'm so frightened of crossing the lake," Edith admitted. "I can't swim more than half a dozen strokes without sinking."

"I shall hang on to you with one hand, and the boat with the other," said Grace. "But I've no doubt the fisherman knows his business."

"Madame Lafitte said there are police patrols on the lake all the time – suppose we get caught —"

"Stop supposing!" Grace scolded her. "Look on the bright side – I dare say there will be no problems at all."

But for once Grace was wrong.

"Suppose they come down by parachute?" asked Queen Wilhelmina. "What then?"

The question fell into the sitting-room at Buckingham Palace like a stone crashing into a pool, shattering the peaceful afternoon.

Alice stood by a console table, pouring cups of tea. The King

106

and Queen were entertaining two royal visitors, both exiled by the Nazi invasion – the Queen of the Netherlands, and King Haakon of Norway.

The occupation of France was on everyone's mind. Where would the Germans attack next? King George maintained that Hitler would never cross the Channel, but his visitors did not agree. As Queen Wilhelmina said – they could send an advance party in by air.

"German paratroops – here?" asked King George.

"They might arrive at any time." King Haakon looked out at the cloudless summer sky. "Their planes could fly over, and within minutes the enemy would be inside these grounds."

"Let's hope it never comes to that," said Queen Elizabeth. She turned to Alice: "I think we might have our tea now, my dear."

"Yes, Ma'am – it's quite ready." Alice began to hand cups and saucers to the visitors, but Queen Wilhelmina was not to be put off.

"Such things happen!" she insisted. "I have seen the planes and the parachutes – they would try to take you as hostages!"

King Haakon supported her: "We only tell you so you should be on your guard. In this island, you feel secure – but perhaps you are not sufficiently prepared."

"We are deeply grateful for your kindness," Queen Wilhelmina chimed in, "but we think you should take every precaution. . . . Thank you, Lady Minster."

The cup shook a little in Alice's hand, and as a drop of tea slopped into the saucer, she apologized, about to fetch another cup.

The old lady's eyes searched her face, and she said: "Please do not trouble yourself – it is nothing . . . and you are anxious."

Alice tried to pull herself together; the discussion of an enemy invasion reminded her of the German troops who had overrun France. There was still no word from Edith and Grace – or from Miranda. With an effort, she moved on to give King Haakon his tea.

King George rose to his feet: "I promise you, we are prepared for all emergencies," he said. "If such a thing should ever happen – which G-G-God forbid – if we were attacked by paratroops, we would not be in danger."

He pointed to a red bell-push on the writing-desk: "I only have to touch that button, and this room will be surrounded by armed guards. Would you care to see a demonstration? I warn you – this will be rather dramatic."

He pressed the red button. . . . Nothing happened. After a few moments he pressed it again, more urgently. Then he pushed it very hard, several times. . . . Still nothing happened.

King Haakon cleared his throat, and he exchanged meaning glances with Queen Wilhelmina. A muscle twitched in King George's cheek.

"What the devil has g-g-gone wrong?" he exploded. "When I find out who is responsible for this —"

He was interrupted by a strange noise; something between choking and snorting. He glared at Queen Elizabeth, who had a handkerchief to her lips.

"Tea – went down the wrong way—" she gasped.

With commendable restraint, her husband said: "I shall just – um – make a few enquiries. . . ."

As he walked out of the room, Alice heard herself say, in a tone pitched a little too high: "Would Your Majesties care for a cucumber sandwich?"

Queen Elizabeth gave way to giggles; the visitors stared, utterly mystified – and were even more astonished when Alice caught the Queen's eye, and they both dissolved in laughter.

It was nice to know there were still things to laugh about.

When Friday came, it seemed to Edith to go on forever. Soon after breakfast, the old carpet-bag was packed, and then there was nothing for them to do but wait. She counted the hours, longing to be off – yet fearful of the dangers that lay ahead.

They studied the map; their road would take them down the valley and across the River Arve – Alain had warned them to be prepared for a police checkpoint on the bridge at Bonneville

– after that they would make for the southern shore of Lac Leman, and their rendezvous with the fisherman.

The journey would cover some 30 miles; as they were travelling by horse and cart, it would take several hours. They had to be at the meeting-place by ten o'clock, and Alain advised them to set out during the afternoon, to allow for unforeseen delays.

Germaine made up a basket of food for them, while Alain gave Miranda her instructions: "The fisherman's name is Jean-Jacques; he has been told to take you across to Switzerland – when you get there, he will stay with the boat. Once ashore, you must go straight to the authorities and explain the situation. The ladies have their British documents, and you must also show your own passport to the police, to prove that you are telling the truth. The ladies can make their own way to the British Consul in Geneva, and arrange their passage home to England. As soon as your part of the job is done, and you know they are safe, you will return to the boat. I shall expect you back some time tomorrow morning."

He held out his arms, kissing Miranda on both cheeks and clinging to her fiercely. Germaine, who had been watching them in silence, turned away.

"I won't let you down," said Miranda. "This is my first test as a courier. If it goes well, I hope to do the journey often, with many more travellers."

"Good fortune be with you, my darling girl," said Alain, and let her go.

Miranda took the basket from Germaine and kissed her too, saying: "Thank you for your help, Maman."

Germaine embraced her, saying: "Goodbye, my child – God bless you."

The Lafittes shook hands with their English guests, and the little party set out.

When they reached Bonneville, a policeman barred the way, wanting to know where they came from and where they were going.

They had worked out their story already; remembering the deserters who stole their luggage, Edith suggested they should swallow their pride and say they were on their way to an Old Folks' Home. There were plenty of sanatoria for elderly people in the district, and when Miranda offered this explanation, the policeman accepted it without question. He gave the ladies a cursory glance; two weatherbeaten crones in travel-stained garments.

"*Ca va bien?*" he asked.

Grace gave a guttural croak: "*Ca va.*"

Edith stared at him vacantly, her jaw sagging; and the policeman passed them through.

"Well done," said Miranda under her breath, as the cart rolled on.

"I did my best to look stupid," Edith whispered modestly.

After Bonneville, there were wide roads with flat farmland stretching away on either side. Miranda had memorized the route, and once through the village of Louvaine, she pulled on the reins, guiding the horse on to a dirt-track which sloped away into a tangle of scrub and a cluster of pines. The tree-trunks were silhouetted against a streak of silver – the waters of the lake, touched by the setting sun.

"Look out for a stone cross," said Miranda.

The light was fading fast, and they had almost passed it when Grace exclaimed: "Would that be it?"

The crumbling wayside shrine, topped with a broken cross, was smothered in briars and brambles.

"This is where we leave the cart. Now we walk." Miranda led the horse under overhanging trees, and tethered it to a low branch. "This way," she said, picking up the carpet-bag. "And keep as quiet as you can."

The path became more and more overgrown as they followed it, and Edith started to say: "Are you sure this is the way to — oh, look!"

Just ahead, a barricade of barbed wire ran along the water's edge.

"Don't worry – there's a way through," Miranda told them.

They continued in single file, trying to keep their skirts away from the wire; suddenly Miranda stopped.

"We must get down on our hands and knees," she said. "Can you manage?"

At one point the wire had been lifted off the ground by wooden stakes and broken branches; it was the only way through.

"Grace – your bad leg—" said Edith anxiously.

"Blethers!" said Grace. "I'm not incapable!"

One by one they crawled through the gap and emerged on the other side, where lakewater lapped at their toes. There, moored to a tree-stump, was a rowing-boat; and a figure in a navy-blue jacket sat in the bows, waiting for them.

"M'sieur Jean-Jacques—?" began Miranda.

The figure stood up, and they saw that he was only a boy, not more than twelve years old.

"Jean-Jacques is my brother; he has been taken by the police, for questioning . . . I am to say that he is very sorry not to be here."

"But – he was supposed to row us over the lake. . . . Can you do it?"

The boy shook his head, taking off the heavy canvas jacket and dropping it into the boat.

"My parents would not permit it. But you may row the boat yourself, Mademoiselle, if you bring it back safely. I will leave this coat for you to wear, in case anyone sees you."

"But it's a long way – perhaps if you and I take it in turns —?"

"It is not permitted," he said. "I am here to pass the message – now I must go."

With that, he turned and ran back up the path, until the darkness swallowed him.

The ladies looked at one another in dismay – and Miranda lifted her chin.

"Very well," she said: "We'll go on our own" – and she began to help them into the boat.

"But do you know how to row?" asked Edith, tremulously.

"Don't you remember the boat on the lake at home? Martin and I used to go out in it all the time – it's very easy," said Miranda. "And if I get tired on the way —"

"Then I shall take the oars and give you a rest," finished Grace.

"Certainly not! I shall stop rowing and let the boat drift, until I feel energetic again. . . . Hold tight – I'm going to cast off."

She untied the painter, and gave the tree-stump a hefty push; as the boat slid easily into deeper water, she fitted the oars into the rowlocks, saying: "Nothing to it . . . and it's not that far – you can see the lights on the opposite shore."

The lake was about three miles wide at this point, and the lights of Switzerland looked very bright, reflected in the water.

"Doesn't it seem strange to see places lit up again?" said Edith.

"Mmm – the Swiss manage very well," remarked Grace. "They have a great knack of staying out of wars."

The crossing took a long time. Luckily there was hardly any wind, and at first Miranda found it easy enough to send the boat gliding across the smooth surface; but because the air was so still, every sound carried over the water, and they could only speak in whispers.

After a while, they heard the thud-thudding of an engine, and a launch loomed out of the darkness, heading towards them.

"The police—!" gasped Edith.

"Lie flat in the bottom of the boat – both of you!" snapped Miranda.

She slipped the canvas jacket on, turning up the heavy collar. Seconds later, a spotlight cut through the night, and a rasping voice shouted something she could not understand – but the tone sounded friendly enough.

Hunching her shoulders and keeping her head down, she raised a hand in salute; caught in the circle of light, she looked like a solitary fisherman going about his business. The spotlight swung away, and the launch chugged on.

Time passed slowly; after a while Miranda became very

tired, her arms and shoulders aching and protesting – but she couldn't stop now.

"I'll count up to a hundred," she told herself, and with every pull on the oars she counted: "One . . . Two . . . Three . . ." until she had reached a hundred. Then she began another hundred.

"The lights look ever so much nearer," Edith encouraged her.

She glanced over her shoulder; it was true – she could see lighted windows, and the headlamps of a car.

"Are you sure you wouldn't like me to take a turn?" Grace offered.

"Quite sure – I'm enjoying the exercise," lied Miranda, keeping up the steady rhythm.

Then she heard the sound of a marine engine, and her heart sank. The police-launch was on its way back – and this time there could be no possible doubt; clearly, the rowing-boat was crossing the lake. She redoubled her efforts, trying to increase their speed, but it was hopeless. The launch was getting nearer by the minute, and the passengers had to get down, out of sight – not a moment too soon, for the spotlight picked them up once more.

"Attention!" This time the voice was far from friendly. "You must stop immediately!"

Gritting her teeth, Miranda carried on.

"Stop at once – or I fire!"

Again she ignored the command; there was a flash of light, and an explosion. In the bottom of the boat, Edith gave a smothered cry, and Grace gripped her hand.

Then, somewhere behind Miranda, another voice broke in, issuing conflicting orders – and another searchlight was turned on their boat. From the shore, a Swiss frontier patrol was taking a hand in the game.

A fierce argument broke out, raging across the water, as the Swiss protested that the vessel was now inside their territorial waters; the French at first denied this, then gave way sulkily and retreated, while the rowing-boat reached its destination, tying up alongside the wooden pier.

Then there were lights everywhere; a lakeside restaurant switched on its floodlights, and the headlamps of a dozen parked cars were turned on to the boat. As Miranda helped the old ladies ashore, flashbulbs exploded, and cameras recorded the scene for tomorrow's newspapers.

"What's happening—?" Miranda was dazzled and bewildered.

A reporter ran up to them, exclaiming: "You are the Englishwomen – the Ladies Miranda and Edith Gaunt —?"

She flinched: "I don't understand – how did you know —?"

"We were given information that you would be arriving tonight. That is why we are here; you must tell us the whole story."

Several hours later, when the sun was high above the mountains, Alain Lafitte returned to his wife at Les Gentianes.

"Where have you been?" she reproached him. "I was so worried – why did you not tell me you would be out all night?"

"I did not intend to be late," he said; his face was grey with fatigue, and drained of emotion. "I waited at the café; we had arranged that Jean-Jacques should telephone as soon as they returned safely. . . . We waited all night, and at dawn the telephone rang. It was Miranda – calling us from Switzerland. The plan went badly wrong; they could not return the boat."

He explained that Miranda had to row them across the lake herself – and when they reached the other side, the police and the press were waiting for them.

"It will be in the Swiss newspapers by now. . . . Her photograph will be published everywhere. She did not realize – she said she would try to get back to us as soon as she could – that was when I lost my temper."

Germaine put her hand on his arm: "Oh, no —"

He shook her off angrily: "I shouted: 'Don't you see, you can never come back now? You will be recognized everywhere you go! You must never call this number – do you understand? Go home to England where you belong!'

114

—then I slammed down the telephone. . . . We shall never speak to her again."

He slumped across the table, letting his head fall on his arms.

Germaine put her hand on his shoulder, patting him as if he were a child.

"What I cannot understand," he said presently, "is how the story got out. How did the newspapers know where to meet the boat – and when? It's as if someone deliberately tried to keep the girl from coming back to us – but who would do such a thing?"

Germaine said nothing, but went on patting his shoulder.

"I always thought the Swiss were such efficient people," said Edith – not for the first time.

"We must try to be patient, my dear. They must have a great many problems to deal with," said Grace. She stretched her leg – her arthritis had been playing up again, and sitting for so long in one position made it worse. Unfortunately, as she straightened her knee, her foot shot out and nearly tripped a passing airport official; he glared at her, and hurried on.

"But they keep saying we shall get on an aeroplane – why do we have to wait like this?" Edith wanted to know. "We might as well have stayed at our hotel – it would have been far more comfortable."

By now Grace, Edith and Miranda had been in Geneva for three days and nights; their cash soon ran out, since they had not foreseen that they would be paying for Miranda as well, but the British Consul had been very helpful, advancing them enough money to pay their hotel bills and buy a change of clothes.

Every morning the Consulate Secretary tried to put them on a plane to England; every afternoon they waited at the airport, hoping to get away – and every evening the last fully-booked flight took off without them, and they had to return to the hotel and start all over again.

"The trouble is, so many people are travelling from one

country to another across the war zones," Grace tried to explain, "and they all have to pass through Switzerland . . . it's like Clapham Junction."

Twisting her fingers nervously, Edith asked: "If we have to fly across the war zones – do you suppose they'll shoot at us? How will they know we're not an enemy aeroplane?"

Grace would not admit that the same thought had already occurred to her – what was to prevent some keen young officer in an anti-aircraft unit losing his head and sending up a few shells as they flew over? However, she had no intention of sharing this anxiety with Edith.

"Nonsense, dear – it's bound to be perfectly safe, or they'd never take the risk – don't you agree, Miranda?" she added, leaning forward.

Miranda, sitting on the other side of Edith, did not reply; she had not been listening to their conversation. She had said very little, ever since that first night – or early morning – when she finally managed to put through the call to her friends in Pas-de-Loup, and returned some time later – white-faced, and fighting back tears.

"I let them down," she told them. "I let everybody down . . . Now I've got to go home to England – because I failed the first job they gave me."

There was nothing more to say; after that, she had shut herself away in her own private misery.

Sitting in the passenger lounge with her eyes closed, she was scarcely aware of the crowds, the discomfort, the endless boredom and frustration. She had only one thought to console her; soon – very soon – she would see Martin again. He would understand – Martin always understood everything.

For some time, the indefinable link between Miranda and her twin brother had been stretched too far; though she was always aware of him, he seemed faint and far away. Lately, she sensed that he too had been confused and unhappy, but while she was so deeply involved in her own problems, she had pushed him to the back of her mind.

Now she realized how much she missed him, and how badly she needed Martin – the one person in the world she could be sure of – the one who would always be there for her – the one who never changed . . . and she longed to be close to him once more.

"Miranda, dear. . . ." Edith broke in upon her thoughts. "Didn't you hear? – Good news at last!"

She came to with a start, as if awoken from a dream, and found a uniformed airport official standing in front of her, ticking off names on his list. Bowing from the neck, he announced formally:

"Mesdames Gaunt – Madame Duncan – your flight is ready to depart. You will please to follow me to Passport Control."

They looked at one another like gamblers whose winning numbers had come up at last, hardly daring to believe their luck. . . . They were going home.

By a lucky chance, Lady Minster was not on duty at the Palace that week. William was out in the long meadow, helping Ken Stubbs and his diminishing team to get the hay in, and Alice had just brought them a large jug of beer. The men gathered round her, holding out their tin mugs, when she heard Alex calling her.

"Grandma – Grandpa!" he shouted, running across the field at full tilt. "They're here!"

"They –?" Alice repeated; then her hand began to shake, and Ken took the jug from her: "Who's here?"

"Aunt Edith and Miss Duncan – and Miranda!" he said impatiently. "They caught an earlier train and took a taxi from the station – and they're here!"

The travellers had already telephoned Crown House from Geneva, and again as soon as their plane touched down; Alice had promised to meet them off the five-twenty-five at Medford.

"Already —?" Alice found that she was running; William too broke into a jog-trot, and she had to stop and scold him, telling him to remember his heart – and that was how they continued, linking arms, walking and trotting and walking again, talking and laughing – until they met Polly coming towards them from the house, with little Harriet swinging on her hand, and three strangers by her side.

"Look who's here!" Polly exclaimed.

They stared at the newcomers, and realized that they were not strangers at all. It was six years since Edith and Grace left England, and they had changed so much; they were thinner, for one thing – leaner and sun-tanned, stronger and surer than when they went away. As for Miranda . . . Alice and William had last seen their daughter eighteen months ago; then she was still a schoolgirl – now she had grown up.

Alice ran to her, holding out her arms and hugging her as if she would never let her go: "Thank God," she said, again and again. "Thank God you're safe."

William embraced Edith and planted a kiss on Grace Duncan's cheek. Then, as the group broke and reformed, he turned to his youngest daughter: "Miranda – my dear girl. . . . Welcome home," he said.

He held her for a moment; they searched each other's faces – and smiled.

"Hello, Daddy." she said. "Sorry I've been so long."

"Let's find Lilian and see what she's got in the larder." Polly gathered up her children: "It's about time we had a family party!"

Miranda looked around hopefully: "Where's Martin?" she asked. "Isn't he here?"

Her mother replied: "He sent you his love. When we told him you were on your way, he applied for a weekend pass – I do hope he gets it, but he's on a training course now, learning to be a pilot – and he has to work terribly hard."

Miranda tried not to show her disappointment. She'd waited so long – she told herself that a few more days wouldn't make any difference.

"I expect you've noticed a few changes, eh?" asked her father. "The house – the gardens. . . ."

"Yes – of course," she answered, though she had hardly taken anything in; the fields that had once been lawns – the potatoes and cabbages where peonies and roses used to be – the uncurtained windows criss-crossed with gummed-paper strips

– the empty, echoing rooms. . . . "Yes," she said: "It all looks very – very —"

She could not think how to finish the sentence, and Grace came to her rescue: "It looks as if Crown House is in uniform!" she said – and William chuckled, gratified by the description.

Remembering her duty as a hostess, Alice was saying: "I expect you'll want to wash and change after the journey."

"Where are you going to put us?" Edith wanted to know. "You wrote and told us someone had moved into the Lodge Cottage."

"Yes – Mr Stubbs, our estate manager – such a nice man, he's been sharing it with Dennett. You remember Dennett, who used to be our chauffeur in the old days?"

"Of course – has he retired?"

"No, he's gone to work as an engineer in the new arms factory, outside Medford. He's earning twice as much, *and* doing his bit for the war effort!"

"So you're without a chauffeur?" said Grace. "That must be a great inconvenience."

"Not really; petrol's rationed, so we only use the car on special occasions, and then I do the driving – though I still hate driving in the blackout," Alice admitted. "Anyway, when he heard you were coming home, Ken Stubbs said the Lodge was too big for one person, so now he's living in the village – the Wilkinsons had some empty bedrooms over the shop, since their evacuees went back to London – and Ken's moved in with them. Polly and I spent all day yesterday getting the Lodge ready for you both . . . I hope that's all right?"

Edith looked radiant: "I can't imagine anything nicer. . . . What a lovely homecoming."

In some ways, Miranda was glad to be home again – but she still felt very ill-at-ease. She didn't seem to belong at Crown House any more; she had nothing to do here – and she was no use to anyone. . . . Even now, she could not bear to remember her last telephone conversation with Alain.

On Friday, she took a train up to town and had an early lunch

119

at Eaton Square with Caro and Jenny, before they went on duty at the hospital. She enjoyed their company, and they all laughed a lot, but she couldn't help envying them. Caro was now a fully-qualified nurse, hoping to be promoted to Staff Nurse if she got through her next exams – and even though Jenny assured her that working in the canteen was soul-destroying in its monotony, Miranda felt that any job must be better than no job at all.

In the afternoon, she decided to amuse herself with a little shopping spree in the West End, but that only made her cross – partly because the dresses she looked at all seemed to be uninspired and overpriced – and partly because there were expensive clothes for sale at all; she couldn't help thinking of the shops in Annecy, with empty windows and empty shelves. Angrily, she turned away, resenting the unfairness of it all.

Deciding that she wasn't in the right mood to buy anything, she abandoned the whole idea and went to catch the next train back to Medford.

When she reached Charing Cross, she discovered that she had over half an hour to wait, and thought about trying to get some tea in the buffet, but it was very crowded and she didn't feel like queueing. She would have liked to sit down, but the benches on the concourse were all occupied – by uniformed servicemen, or office workers on their way back to the suburbs, with gas masks in cardboard cases slung over their shoulders. For a while she wandered about aimlessly, looking at the indicator board, and then, quite suddenly —

Even before she saw him, she knew he was there. She could feel his presence – so close, it almost overwhelmed her – and she spun round like a magnet swinging towards the north.

"Hello, Mandy," said Martin. "I got my weekend pass."

He looked so handsome in his RAF uniform; all around them, other couples were embracing – soldiers about to embark on a troop-train were kissing their girls goodbye – and Miranda fell into her brother's arms.

"Oh, Marty – I've missed you!" she whispered. "I've been needing you so much. . . ."

"I know – I need you too," he said, cupping her face in his

120

hands and bringing his mouth down to hers – and then she felt the tip of his tongue slide between her lips.

No one had ever kissed her like that before; it was shocking – it was intimate – it was exciting – and it was completely unexpected. She didn't even know if the sensation was pleasant or unpleasant – and she didn't know what to do.

She only knew one thing for certain. During the long, lonely time while they had been separated, something had happened to change their relationship. And Martin – her own Marty, who had always been the same, and who would never change – Martin had changed too, in some inexplicable way.

He had become a stranger.

Chapter Eight

Monday, 29 July to Thursday, 29 August 1940

The hot, sunny weather seemed to be lasting forever. There were no clouds in the sky, except the white vapour trails scrawled by the fighter-pilots.

"Another lovely day, Mama," said Edith brightly.

She and Grace had helped to wheel Old Bea out into the sunshine, to sit in her invalid chair beside the summer-house.

"Why do I have to sit outside?" complained the Dowager Countess. "Why can't I stay indoors and listen to my wireless?"

"The fresh air will do you good, Mama."

"You all treat me as if I were a child – anyone would think I was feeble-minded," croaked the old lady. Watching Grace Duncan's back disappearing down the path, she added: "Your friend has better things to do, I see – she has more sense than to sit in the sun, frying her brains."

"You're not in the sun, you're in the shade – and Grace has to go in to Medford to collect our ration books."

The arrival of Edith, Grace and Miranda posed some problems for officialdom, and they had to make repeated applications for their new documentation.

"Hmph . . . I trust you'll take me in again before the one o'clock news; I must know what's going on." As an afterthought, Lady Beatrice added: "Not that I approve of these newfangled announcers telling us their names – Stewart

122

Somebody and Alvar Something – the men who read the news in the old days knew their place!"

"I think it's so that – in case the enemy invaded us – you'd be able to tell the difference if they took over the wireless," Edith tried to explain.

"Rubbish!" snorted Old Bea. "I should soon know if a man with a German accent read the news, shouldn't I?"

She was interrupted by a distant metallic rattle, and Edith glanced up, asking: "What's that funny noise?"

"Machine-guns," replied her mother laconically. "Up in the sky – our boys and the Germans shooting each other. . . . The bullets will start tumbling down presently."

Edith turned pale: "Isn't that very dangerous? Should we take shelter?"

"Nonsense – it happens all the time; we're well protected under the trees." She screwed up her eyes as two small figures scampered up the path. "Ah – here come the children. . . . What have you got for me today? Any more bullets?"

Alex arrived first; at twelve, he was beginning to grow into a young man – loose-limbed, with his mother's looks and his father's energy.

"They aren't bullets, GreatGran – I told you, they're empty cartridge-cases," he said patiently. "Only we haven't got any today."

"But we've got a huge bit of shrapnel for you!" Breathlessly, little Harry caught up with her brother: "Show her, Alex."

He produced a jagged splinter of metal, saying: "It's still warm – perhaps the plane blew up in mid-air."

Old Bea examined the fragment and sniffed: "I've got plenty of these already – you said you'd try and find me some parachute silk."

"No luck so far," said Alex. "But we'll go on looking. . . . That'll be half-a-crown for the shrapnel."

"Not worth it." His Great-Grandmother shook her head. "I'll give you sixpence, but I warn you, I don't want any more shrapnel."

Edith was shocked: "You *pay* the children to find these awful things?"

"Certainly. I don't want to be left out of this war altogether – I'm building up quite a collection. I do wish I could get a parachute – there must be plenty of them about – you see them coming down all the time."

Harry said in an awestruck whisper: "One of the village girls knows a boy in Maidstone who found a German airman's flying-helmet – and it had still got his head in it — !"

"I won't listen!" Edith closed her eyes: "You shouldn't encourage them, Mama – it's too horrible!"

That afternoon, since Grace had not returned from Medford, Edith had tea with Polly and Miranda in the flat above the garage.

"I've never been what you'd call a dab hand at cooking," said Polly, bringing a plate out of the kitchen. "And I had to go easy on the marge, 'cos it's the end of this week's rations, so they're as heavy as lead . . . I s'pose that's why they're called rock-cakes."

She handed them round, and Miranda said politely that they were delicious.

"May you be forgiven!" Polly grinned: "Don't spare my feelings, Aunt Edie – I can see from the look in your eye that they're disgusting."

"Oh, no – I wasn't thinking about the cakes, they're very nice. . . . But I am worried about Grace – what can have happened?"

"I expect she had to wait. Those places are all the same – they keep you hanging about for hours," Polly assured her.

"But with this dreadful battle going on over our heads all the time – how can you bear it?"

"You went through a lot worse in France," Miranda reminded her.

"That was different; we expected that sort of thing over there – but not here, in our own home . . ." She told them what Harry had said about the German flying-helmet; to her amazement they both laughed.

"That tale's been going all round south-east England," said Polly. "I bet it never really happened."

124

"But there are aeroplanes being shot down – people *do* get killed —"

She broke off as a heavy thud shook the mews cottage. It was not an explosion, but a flock of rooks flew up from the treetops, complaining loudly.

"What ever was that?" gasped Edith.

"Haven't the foggiest. . . . Go on with what you were saying," Polly prompted her.

"Well – I do think it's wrong of Mama to send the children scavenging for those ghastly relics."

"I don't think it does them much harm," said Polly. "And it's given Her Ladyship a new lease of life. She likes to be part of everything that's going on."

"I know the feeling." Restlessly, Miranda stood up and moved to the window. "I ought to be doing something. . . ."

"You and me both," sighed Polly. "When the kids go back to school after the holidays I'll have more time on my hands – but what is there in Medford? I don't see myself stamping ration books in the Food Office, somehow."

"I know – that's the worst of living in the country; I'll never do anything as long as I stay here."

Miranda looked out at the elm trees; still complaining indignantly, the rooks were beginning to settle on the upper branches again, but she hardly noticed them. She was thinking about Martin.

She remembered their unexpected meeting at Charing Cross, and how shocked she felt – betrayed, almost – by the realization that they had grown away from one another. But after that initial sense of loss, they had moved very quickly into the old familiar pattern of acceptance and understanding. All the way home in the train, they had talked, filling in the gaps, telling each other what had been happening; they shared childhood stories and family jokes, and laughed together – by the time they arrived at Crown House she didn't know why she had ever been upset.

He was still the same dear old Marty; there was nothing to worry about – and now she was missing him more than ever.

He had told her that he sometimes slipped up to town for

a few hours when he was off duty; perhaps she might meet him there.

Aloud, she said: "I think perhaps I'll go up and stay at Eaton Square for a while – and see if I can get a job in London."

Half an hour later Grace arrived – tired and thirsty. The tea was stewed and half-cold, so Polly made a fresh pot, defying the "two ounces per person per week" regulation.

"Did they make you wait all this time?" Edith was horrified.

"It was nobody's fault; they're up to their eyes," said Grace, sinking into an easy chair. "Then I missed the bus and had to wait nearly an hour for the next – and just outside Ebony the road was closed, and the driver took us on a diversion through Fallowfield."

"Why was that?"

"An unexploded bomb – someone said it landed near the church. I'm surprised you didn't hear it."

"Oh, dear – poor William!" exclaimed Edith. "He's on ARP duty today – he'll have to deal with it."

Beside the churchyard, Lord Minster and Ken Stubbs made their way cautiously towards the hole. A makeshift roadblock had been set up; wearing their dungarees and tin helmets, they ducked under the ropes to take a closer look. The bomb was embedded in soft earth; only the tail-fins were showing.

"Do be careful!" called the Vicar, sheltering under the lychgate at what he trusted was a safe distance. He too wore a tin hat, which looked rather incongruous with his clerical collar. "Is it ticking?" he asked. "Are you sure it's all right?"

"It depends what you mean by 'all right'," said William. "But it's certainly not ticking – this isn't a time bomb."

"Looks like a big'un," added Ken Stubbs: "Five-hundred pounder, I'd say."

"Dear me. . . ." The Vicar stepped further back. "Shouldn't you *do* something? Perhaps – if you were to throw a bucket of water over it — ?"

"I hardly think so," said William. "I phoned District Head-quarters; the bomb-disposal squad are on their way."

"Yes, but – until they get here. . . ." The Vicar ran a

126

finger round the inside of his collar: "What shall we do if it goes off?"

William and Ken looked at one another.

"If it goes off," said William carefully, "I rather fancy there won't be a great deal any of us can do."

When the bomb-disposal unit arrived, the explosive charge was defused quickly and efficiently, and William and Ken were free to return to Crown House.

Polly met them halfway up the drive.

"Are you all right?" she asked.

"Oh, yes – just a routine incident to enter in the log," William told her. "Nothing dramatic."

"But it might have been. . . ." Polly walked back to the house with them. "Maybe Aunt Edie's right to be anxious. Suppose that bomb had landed on Saturday, when the kids were at the Salvage Drive in the Church Hall – and suppose it *had* gone off. . . ." She took a deep breath: "Miranda's going up to London tomorrow, and I'm going with her. We want to find some war work we can do – and as soon as I get fixed up, I'll come back for the kids. They can stay with us at Eaton Square until these daylight raids are over."

The Queen had disappeared.

She wasn't in her sitting-room at Buckingham Palace, and no one had seen her for the last half-hour. She couldn't have gone far – perhaps she had taken the corgis for a run?

Alice went out into the grounds; when she heard a dog barking, she followed the sound.

A corgi was scratching at the door of the private chapel, protesting at being shut out; Alice did her best to quieten him – but then the door opened, and the Queen stepped out into the sunlight.

"My dear – have you been looking for me?" She stooped to pat the dog: "What a noise you've been making, you rascal – just when I wanted to be quiet."

"Nobody knew where you were, Ma'am," Alice explained. "I was rather worried."

"I'm so sorry – it was silly of me to slip away without a word. But sometimes, when there are difficult problems, it helps to be alone for a while, and have a little pray . . . It's very peaceful in the chapel."

"Problems — ?"

The Queen managed a smile: "Ever since the trouble over the security guard, the King has been concerned about my safety, and now he's arranged for you and me and some of the other ladies to have lessons in marksmanship – rifles and pistols and so on – so we can defend ourselves if necessary. I'm sure it will never come to that, but it never hurts to acquire a new skill, does it?"

She led the way through a sandbagged doorway into the royal air raid shelter, where they could talk privately. "An instructor is coming on Friday afternoon – will you be here, or are you going home to your family this weekend?"

"I shall be here, Ma'am – in fact, most of my family seem to be coming to London," replied Alice. "Miranda and Polly are moving to Eaton Square, hoping to find jobs in town – if all goes well, Polly's children will join us, so we shall be quite a houseful."

"How very nice. You must be so relieved to have them all safe and sound again. I know you went through a terrible time when they were abroad, and you couldn't get news of them. . . ."

A shadow of anxiety crossed her face for a moment, as she confessed: "Sometimes I'm afraid for the King. . . . If the Nazis came here, he would never collaborate with them; I think he would rather die . . . and there are other possibilities. . . . We don't know what David might do under those circumstances; that's the fear that haunts me."

Alice said cautiously: "I believe the Duke is in Spain now — ?"

"No, he's in Portugal. He moved on from Madrid, which was a great relief, because General Franco's sympathies with Hitler are well-known – at least Portugal is a genuinely neutral country. The Prime Minister discussed all kinds of possibilities with His Majesty, and they have offered David the post of

Governor-General of the Bahamas."

She went on: "You see, they have reason to believe that – through their Spanish contacts – the Nazis have been making overtures to him." Seeing Alice's bewilderment, she explained: "It seems that if the worst happened – if the Nazis actually invaded us – they would offer David the throne of England again. . . . A coronation in Westminster Abbey, with his wife beside him as his Queen – in return for his co-operation."

Alice struggled for words: "Surely – he would never agree to that — ?"

"We can't be certain. I suspect *she* would like nothing better. She never made any secret of her links with the German Embassy when she was living here; and we know how much power she has over David. If she could make him accept the offer, it would be her final triumph."

"It would be shameful. I can't believe it would ever happen."

"Let us hope not." The Queen touched Alice's hand lightly: "I shouldn't be telling you this; I must ask you to try to forget what I have said. But I've kept it to myself for so long, it's a relief to be able to talk – to someone I can trust."

"Thank you, Ma'am. . . . May I ask one question? What is the next step?"

"As I say, David has been offered the Bahamas. Walter Monckton is on his way to Lisbon, to persuade him to accept. And he has arranged a passage for David and his wife on an American liner, sailing the day after tomorrow. Until then, all we can do is wait – and pray."

On the first of August, Walter Monckton arrived at a villa near Estoril, which the British Ambassador had put at the disposal of the Windsors during their stay in Portugal.

He expected to find the Duke and Duchess ready to leave, but to his surprise half-filled suitcases were still scattered about – and another visitor had arrived ahead of him.

"Do you two know each other?" asked Wallis. "Walter Monckton – the Marques de Estella —"

The two men inclined their heads, but did not shake hands.

"I understand, sir, that you are one of the leaders of the Falangists in Madrid?" said Monckton. "And that you have been sent here by the Spanish Government?"

"That is correct, Senor."

"Sent here, in fact, to warn His Royal Highness of a plot against his life? A plot supposed to have originated in London?"

The Marques shook out a silk handkerchief and wiped his upper lip: "Perhaps, Senor, we should continue this conversation in private?"

"I see no necessity for that. It's an absurd idea, so let us discuss it openly." Monckton turned to the Duke: "If Your Royal Highness agrees — ?"

"The sooner we thrash it out, the better." The Duke took his wife's hand and drew her down beside him on the settee. "We're supposed to be catching a ship in an hour's time, but —"

"David, don't be ridiculous!" Wallis broke in. "If your life's in danger, we can't possibly sail on that ship."

"*If* your life is in danger . . ." repeated Monckton. "The Government have already heard of this alleged plot, but the Marques has been unable to furnish us with any hard evidence whatsoever."

Estella crossed his legs, adjusting the crease in his trousers, and said: "I assure you, the evidence exists, but it is in Spain. If His Royal Highness wishes to verify it, he has only to accompany me to Madrid —"

"That's not good enough," said Monckton. "Once in Madrid, His Royal Highness might find pressure being brought to bear upon him to remain there – within the hospitality of the German Embassy perhaps? No – if such evidence exists, you must produce it here."

"That will take time – I can bring it to you within ten days —"

"And the ship sails in an hour." Monckton remained

130

implacable. "Time and tide cannot wait – and neither can the Duke."

"Of course we can wait!" The Duchess's voice became shrill: "What do ten days matter, when David's life is at stake?"

Monckton faced the Duke: "Well, sir – it's up to you. What do you say?"

The Duke studied the pattern in the carpet, then asked the Marques: "Are you telling me that the British Government is sending me to the Bahamas in order to have me done away with by hired thugs? With the full knowledge of Mr Churchill – and of my brother?"

"Alas!" The marques shrugged: "According to our information – yes."

"Then you are mistaken," said His Royal Highness – and turned to his wife. "My darling, you may be right about a good many things – you generally are – but this is one thing I can be sure about. If they claim that my brother is planning to have me assassinated, I can only say – I know Bertie better than that."

Facing the Marques de Estella, he concluded: "I'm sure your intentions were excellent, but I'm afraid you have been misinformed. The Duchess and I will be sailing this morning – as arranged."

In the basement at Eaton Square, the Minster women were hard at work. Since it was the housekeeper's day off, they had the kitchen to themselves, and Jenny announced over breakfast that today was "Salvage Day" and everyone was expected to contribute to it – except Lady Minster, who was on duty at the Palace.

Jenny had taken time off from the canteen, as she had an appointment with her doctor in Harley Street at noon; he suspected she had a tendency to anaemia, and proposed to take a blood sample. Caro was on a late shift, so she had a free morning; and Polly and Miranda, who had spent two frustrating weeks looking for war work without success, were willing to make themselves useful at home.

"We've got to make up four parcels," Jenny told them. "Paper, metal, string – and bones."

Miranda wrinkled her nose: "What do they want bones for?"

"I believe they're melted down for glue," said Jenny "Anyway, Miss Kendall has been saving bones for ages – after she's boiled them for stock, she stores them in the old dustbin at the bottom of the area steps."

"I thought I noticed a bit of a niff out there," remarked Polly.

Jenny sighed: "All right, I'll deal with the bones if nobody else wants to – thanks to the Canteen kitchen, I'm getting used to peculiar smells!"

"I know what you mean," agreed Caro. "I gave up eating their fish pie long ago. Can I do the paper collection?"

"Yes, please – there's a huge pile of newspapers and paper bags in the cupboard under the stairs, to be done up into bundles. You'll need some string – oh, that reminds me – Polly, could you sort through the string bag and untangle it? Then it's got to be wound up into useful lengths, for the WVS."

"You know, when I came to town to find some war work," said Polly dreamily, "I never thought I'd finish up unravelling little bits of string . . . Oh, well – I suppose it's all in a good cause."

"That leaves you to do the metal salvage, Mandy," said Jenny. "It's mostly old tins – use a tin-opener, then squash them flat. I know it's a dreary job; just keep telling yourself – every tin you flatten will finish up in a Spitfire one day!"

"Like Martin – he's going to be flying Spitfires, isn't he?" asked Polly. "When he finishes his training?"

"If he's lucky," said Miranda. "They don't all get accepted."

"Oh, he'll manage," said Polly. "Martin always gets what he wants!"

"I wouldn't be so sure – people never stop turning *me* down," muttered Miranda, searching for the tin-opener. "Either I'm too young, or not young enough, or I haven't got the qualifications – sometimes I think they just don't like my face."

"I told you – why not try nursing?" Caro was busy folding newspapers. "The hospitals are crying out for volunteers."

"I don't think I've got the patience for—" Miranda broke off, hearing a knock at the front door. "There's the post – shall I — ?"

"I'll go." Jenny wiped her hands and ran up the basement stairs.

"She's expecting a letter from Nick," said Caro. "He hasn't written for ages. . . . Neither has Scott, come to that. I suppose it's difficult, when they move around all the time."

"Where is Scott now?" asked Polly.

Caro shrugged: "I never know! In his last letter, he said he was going back to the States – something about a new job."

"It must be rotten for you and Jenny, with your husbands away all the time," Polly sympathized. When Jenny came downstairs, she asked hopefully: "Anything from Nick?"

Jenny shook her head: "Not today. He writes as often as he can – I know that." Smiling, she turned to Caro: "But this is for you – from Washington."

She handed over a large parcel, which had been opened and re-sealed by Customs. Grabbing a kitchen knife, Caro ripped it open. Inside was a tin, and the tin contained a cake; a rich fruit cake, decorated with a glistening pattern of candied peel, glacé cherries and sticky pecan nuts, colourful as a stained-glass window.

"Isn't it beautiful?" said Polly. "Almost too good to eat."

"But not quite!" said Caro. "We'll cut it tonight, when Ma gets home – and she can take the rest back to Crown House – the children will think it's Christmas."

"Was there a letter with it?" Jenny asked.

"Just a card – '*All my love – see you soon . . .*' I wonder what 'soon' means?"

Caro replaced the cake in its tin, and they went on working.

"The postman said there was a very bad raid on Croydon last night," Jenny remarked.

So far, air raids over south-east England had been scattered and indiscriminate; but a concentrated attack on Croydon sounded more ominous – and uncomfortably close to London.

Miranda exclaimed: "I just wish I could hit back at them somehow! It's so infuriating, not having a proper job!"

"Come with me to the hospital," Caro urged her. "I'll introduce you to the Probationer Sister —"

"No, thanks . . . As a matter of fact, I've still got one more interview tomorrow, at the Foreign Office – so keep your fingers crossed."

But the following afternoon, she came home, tired and depressed.

"You can uncross your fingers," she said. "They wouldn't take me. They said I ought to try Civil Defence."

Alice wanted to hear all the details, but Miranda didn't feel like talking; after supper, she said she had a headache, and went up to bed early.

A little later Martin arrived unexpectedly, and they improvised a meal for him from the leftovers, followed by a generous slice of the American cake. He was on an overnight pass before a posting to an airfield somewhere in the Midlands, and had to leave very early in the morning. When his mother told him Miranda had already gone to bed, he said: "I'll just tap on her door – she might not be asleep yet . . . I'd hate to leave without seeing her."

Miranda had been lying awake in the dark; when Martin came in, she didn't bother to turn on the bedside light, but sat up eagerly, saying: "Marty! – I thought you were hundreds of miles away."

"So I was – I'm only here overnight. Sorry if I woke you – but I need to talk."

"Why – what's happened?"

"It's all pretty bloody." He sat beside her, on the edge of the bed. "I've finished my training course, and I've got a new posting, on my own. . . . All the others have been sent to Biggin Hill."

"Why not you?"

"Some damn fool who thinks he's a psychologist told me I wasn't the right type for a fighter pilot. He said you need very special qualities to fly solo – when you're on your own, making your own decisions, you need a cool head and bags of self-discipline. And the silly bugger said that's what I haven't got. . . . Oh, I argued – in fact I lost my temper and yelled at him – but he just nodded and said: 'That proves my point. You can't always get your own way. You must learn to be part of a team; that's why I'm sending you to a bomber squadron . . .' Damn him!"

"Is it really so terrible? You'll still be flying —"

"Along with a whole crew of tail-end Charlies, navigators, bomb-aimers – all the odds and sods. . . . God, it's humiliating."

"What are you going to do?"

"There's only one thing I can do. I'm going to prove I'm the best bloody bomber-pilot in the RAF – and then I'll apply for a transfer to fighters, and they won't dare turn me down. . . . Only – till then – life's going to be fairly hellish."

"I'm sorry." She felt for his hand, and gripped it. "I sort of knew you were going through a bad time, but I thought perhaps it was just me. I've been having problems too – I got turned down today myself."

"What for?"

"I'd been trying to pull some strings and get back into France."

"For God's sake – why?"

"They're going to start flying people in to work with the resistance fighters. I speak the language – I'm the obvious person to act as a courier. And today I managed to see this very important chap in Whitehall; he told me they're recruiting men and women to do special jobs out there – they're going to be dropped by parachute, with money and ammunition . . . and then, after all that – he turned me down."

"Did he give you any reason?"

"Oh, yes. It's because of that muddle when I went through Geneva. He said now the Germans know what I look like, they'll be watching for me – I wouldn't last five minutes. And I'd be putting other people's lives at risk – so he advised me to get a nice job with the ARP. . . . Isn't it *stinking*?"

"Poor old you."

"Poor both of us."

Martin put his arm round her shoulders; side by side, they sank back against the pillows.

"I suppose you were trying to get in touch with your Frenchman? Were you in love with him?"

"Alain —? Goodness, no! He's *old* – he was like a father to me!"

"He might not have felt so fatherly about you – we all know what Frenchmen are like. Did he ever try to —"

"No! – he's not like that. . . . Yes, he loved me – so did his wife. I was like another daughter to them; one of the family."

"You don't need another family; you belong here with us . . . You belong to me."

Her head was on his shoulder, and he began stroking her hair; it was extraordinarily comforting, and Miranda felt her bitterness and disappointment beginning to float away.

In the darkness, time ceased to exist, and they were together again, as they had always been. It might have been the old night nursery at Crown House; Miranda could picture the doll's house, the rocking-horse, the two little beds, side by side.

Nestling closer to him, she whispered: "Dearest Marty – I've been so unhappy."

"I know. Me too."

Then they heard their mother calling from the end of the corridor:

"Martin – your room's all ready for you!"

"Blast . . . I'll have to go." Reluctantly, he stood up, calling out: "Thanks, Ma!"

When he had gone, Miranda settled down again, trying to sleep; but sleep was elusive, and when it came at last, she was troubled by strange dreams.

Towards the end of August, life at Eaton Square took a turn for the better. They were having a snack supper – salad and corned-beef sandwiches on their laps in the drawing-room –

136

when Polly came in and announced dramatically: "Guess what – I've got a job!"

They all congratulated her, and Miranda said: "That's given me some hope – perhaps it will be my turn next."

"You mean, if I can get a job, anybody can?" Polly grinned: "Actually, it was a sheer stroke of luck. I ran into an old friend of mine in Charing Cross Road – he was in the Cochran show all those years ago – Dickie Pitts, you wouldn't know him, he did a fantastic tango speciality. . . . Anyway, I asked him what he was up to these days, and he said: 'Well, darling, I've stopped painting my face at last!'" Seeing their expressions, she explained quickly: "What he meant was, he's not on the boards any more; but he's still in the business – he's got a job as an organizer at Drury Lane."

"I thought the theatre was closed?" said Alice.

"Yes, it is – Basil Dean's taken it over as the Headquarters of ENSA – they send shows round the Army camps and RAF stations and all that. Dickie said he was sure they'd take me on, with my experience of running an office – so he dragged me back to the Lane to meet his boss – and to cut a long story short, I start on Monday!"

"What are you going to do about the children?" Alice wanted to know.

"I'll give myself a week to learn the ropes, then I'll bring them up to town. I know it'll mean a bit of an upheaval – but if we could move the beds round a bit, I don't mind sharing a room . . . Jenny, when's your next day off? – p'raps you could give me a hand — ?"

"Well – I'm off duty on Tuesday," said Jenny. "But I've got another appointment at Harley Street at twelve o'clock, so. . . ."

They all looked at her in surprise, and Caro said: "I thought the doctor put you on iron tablets and vitamins and things? There's nothing wrong, is there?"

"Nothing at all – only he wants me to have another check-up . . . And I'm not sure about moving furniture." Jenny found she was blushing, and began to laugh: "I wasn't going to say

137

anything yet – I know it's stupid to be superstitious, but – I'm going to have a baby."

"Jenny dear – how absolutely wonderful!" Alice hugged her daughter-in-law. "You and Nick have been waiting so long – when is the baby due?"

"At the end of March, if all goes well – and the doctor says as far as he's concerned there's no reason why it shouldn't."

"Does Nick know about it?" asked Caro.

"Not yet; I couldn't tell him until I was certain, so I didn't write until last weekend . . . I hope he gets my letter soon."

Polly exclaimed: "Two bits of good news in one day – this calls for a celebration! Let's all have a Saturday night on the town; it's a bit short notice for this weekend, but I'll book seats for a show next Saturday – and supper afterwards on me – how about that?"

Chapter Nine

Saturday, 7 September to Friday, 13 September 1940

"Good evening, ladies and gentlemen!" boomed the Chairman.

"Good evening, Mr Sachs!" shouted the audience.

Dark and debonair, Leonard Sachs welcomed them to the Players Theatre for an evening of *Late Joys*, and opened the programme:

"Number One on your song sheets – the Players Theatre Anthem – 'Covent Garden In The Morning'!"

Polly had found it hard to decide on a show they would all enjoy – in the end she had settled on something a little different.

"The Players Theatre is in King Street, Covent Garden," she told them. "It's a supper club, with old-fashioned music-hall turns – and the audience join in the choruses. I haven't been there myself, but everyone tells me it's marvellous."

The pianist played a rousing introduction, and the audience plunged in with a will:

"Cherries so red, strawberries ripe –
At home of course they'll be storming;
Never mind the abuse – you have the excuse –
You went to Covent Garden in the morning!"

At first, Jenny thought she was going to hate it; the idea of community singing did not appeal to her – but the audience's enthusiasm soon melted her inhibitions.

She sat at a small round table with Polly, Miranda and Caro, half-pints of beer in front of them and song sheets in their hands; as the show continued, they applauded a talented bill of artistes, supporting them in old favourites like "My Old Man Said Follow the Van" and "By The Light Of The Silvery Moon".

Some time later, the Chairman announced: "A short interval for refreshment; during which Ladies and Gentlemen will find the ample means provided to satisfy the needs of the inner Ladies and Gentlemen" – and they made their way to the bar to refill their glasses.

That was when the air raid siren moaned. As the second part of the programme began, they heard anti-aircraft gunfire in the distance. Mr Sachs announced that the performance would continue during the alert, but that the audience were welcome to go down to the basement shelter if they wished to take cover.

Half the audience were in civilian clothes; the rest were all members of the armed services. Hardly anyone left – nobody in London took air raid warnings very seriously – so Mr Sachs went on: "It gives me much pleasure to resume the programme proper. . . . It gives me particular pleasure tonight, Ladies and Gentlemen, since our next guest is a favourite and very distinguished lecturer – none other than His Grace, the Archbishop of Limpopoland!"

In the guise of the aged Archbishop, a talented young comedian called Peter Ustinov shambled on to the stage and began an absent-minded account of his missionary exploits in darkest Africa. Carrying on the pretence that time had turned back half a century, he paid a devoted tribute to "Her great and glorious Majesty, Queen Victoria – God bless her!" Halfway through his lecture, there was a very loud explosion, and the building shuddered. Without stepping out of character, Mr Ustinov paused, raised an admonitory finger, and mumbled: "Mmm . . . the Wright brothers appear to have gone wrong again. . . ."

After a split second, the audience roared with laughter, and sat back to enjoy the rest of the show. However, the Chairman reappeared, saying that it might be advisable for the audience to proceed to the basement. Amid groans of disappointment, he explained that as soon as the all clear sounded, they would continue the entertainment.

The basement shelter was small and crowded; Miranda found seats on a wooden bench along the wall, then noticed that Jenny was looking rather pale.

"Are you all right?" she asked, under cover of the general chatter.

"I feel a bit sick; it's so stuffy down here . . . I think I'll just slip into the ladies."

"I'll come with you."

In the cramped conditions of the ladies' lavatory, a WRNS officer was combing her hair at the mirror; she made room for Jenny to get by, saying: "I'll be out of your way in a jiff; I've got to nip over to Waterloo, bombs or no bombs – I'm due back at Pompey at the crack of dawn, and if I miss my train there'll be hell to pay."

"Do you think you should go out – during a raid?" asked Miranda.

"Oh, lor', yes! I'd rather face a few tons of high explosive than our CO if I'm late back off leave!"

She pulled on her tricorne hat, brushed a loose hair from her lapel, and was gone.

Miranda watched her go, and sighed: "It must be nice to be as confident as that. . . ."

Coming out of the cubicle, Jenny asked: "Sorry – did you say something?"

"Nothing important. . . . How are you feeling now?"

"Much better. I was probably more scared than anything; that bomb shook me rather."

"Of course – sudden shocks aren't good, in your condition."

"That's the worst of it; I know I've got to stay calm, because of the baby."

They heard the whistle of another bomb falling, followed by

the *crump* as it went off; it was further away, but the building still quivered.

"I do hate air raids," Jenny began. "You feel so helpless – there's nothing to do except wait for it to go away" – then another explosion made her catch her breath.

"I think that was one of the anti-aircraft guns," said Miranda. "Let's go back to the shelter; it's so noisy in there, you won't hear a thing!"

As the raid continued, the Chairman announced that they would conclude the evening with songs and recitations; there was no piano in the shelter, so they would perform without musical accompaniment, but he hoped the audience would make up for this by singing louder than ever.

By the time the improvised concert was over, they were all feeling very tired; some people fell asleep, curled up awkwardly on the narrow benches or stretched out on the floor. At half-past four the sirens sounded the all-clear, and they stirred themselves, preparing to leave.

"We'll never get a cab now," said Polly. "Do you think you can walk home, Jenny?"

"Oh, yes – it's not far, the exercise will do me good."

They emerged into cool, fresh air; there were still a few searchlights cutting through the night sky, but in the east they could see a faint glow, promising dawn.

King Street had been cordoned off; a hundred yards away, a small fire had started in a warehouse, but the Fire Service had it under control. Early-morning lorries were starting to unload; the work of the market went on.

There was no serious damage, though a good many windows had been blown out and the pavements were thick with broken glass. As they picked their way down the Strand, they heard it crunching underfoot, and the occasional tinkle and crash as someone swept the road clear.

"What a night," yawned Caro. "Thank goodness I'm not on duty till teatime – I can sleep all morning."

"Ah, well – at least we had our night out," said Polly. "Even if if wasn't quite the way I planned it."

*   *   *

142

When the sun rose, Nick was on the bridge of HMS *Sabina*, watching the amethyst coastline of Scotland emerge from its morning haze.

The destroyer had been working the Atlantic convoys for several months now, and today she was heading back for Scapa Flow, where she would spend a couple of days, provisioning and refuelling, before turning round and setting off on another trip.

Convoy work was monotonous, with sporadic moments of drama; the navy patrols acted as sheepdogs to flocks of merchant ships bringing in food from overseas. Every night, *Sabina* had to steam the entire length of the convoy, making sure there were no stragglers, and looking out for enemy attack at all times.

Now First Lieutenant Gaunt prepared to bring the destroyer in, leading the rest of the flotilla into harbour. He checked their position, double-checked the wind-force and direction, and estimated that they should make land within the next half-hour.

When one of the lookouts reported: "Enemy aircraft on starboard bow!" he was immediately ready for action.

He spotted the plane, flying low over the western sea; a single Heinkel 111 bomber, obviously shadowing the convoy. Swiftly and succinctly, Nick gave the crew their orders, and the four-inch guns swung round. On the command to fire, the gunners put up three salvos – and the third found its mark.

They saw a flash as the shell exploded above the wing, and the plane dropped like a diving bird, plummeting into the sea and sending up a column of white water. A shout broke out from the deck-crew, and Nick felt a surge of triumph. Bombers were fair game; they came at you out of nowhere, sowing death and destruction – he felt no more compunction than if he had swatted a wasp.

As *Sabina* entered the natural harbour of Scapa Flow, most of her crew were eager to get ashore, but there were sacks of mail waiting for them, and when these came aboard, Nick was content to stay in his cabin, reading his letters from home.

Scanning the envelopes, he was disappointed not to see

Jenny's handwriting; as a rule, she was a regular correspondent – it wasn't like her to miss a post.

He picked out a letter from his mother, hoping for the latest family news. One of the items was about Martin:

" . . . *afraid he still feels resentful that he wasn't picked to train as a fighter pilot, though I can't help feeling relieved that he's joined a bomber squadron instead – only don't tell him I said so! I hated the idea of him, all alone in a Spitfire; a bomber seems more solid somehow – if Martin were injured (which heaven forbid) it helps to think that the rest of the crew could still bring the plane home safely. . . ."*

So Martin was flying a bomber . . . In his mind's eye, Nick saw the Heinkel plunge into the sea again; the German pilot could have been the same age as Martin – but there was no question of his being brought home safely; no one in that crew would have escaped death.

Slowly, he put aside the letter; he would finish reading it later.

A knock at the door – and one of his fellow-officers entered the cabin with another envelope, saying: "Sorry, old man – this one's for you – it got in with mine by mistake."

Nick smiled; so she hadn't missed the post after all.

After a few fond words, Jenny came straight to the point:

". . . *the best news of all – we are going to have a baby. The doctor says everything's going according to plan, and the baby is due in March. I wonder if every proud mother expects her firstborn to be a boy? I have a hunch that ours will be – and I can't help feeling you've been secretly hoping for a son, haven't you?"*

A son . . . a child of their own at last. He looked at the two letters; within a few moments, he had been presented with two conflicting ideas – a man's death and, God willing, a child soon to be born – one life ending, another about to begin. And he was responsible for both. The situation was too big, too complex for him to take in all at once – but he was sure of one thing.

He loved his wife very much, and he couldn't wait to tell her so.

*   *   *

Alice put down the telephone and turned to William: "That was Polly, ringing from the station. Their train was delayed, and now there are no taxis on the rank, so they're coming on the bus – which means they won't get here till two o'clock."

"They —? I thought she was coming on her own?"

"Jenny's with her – so that means one more for lunch." Looking round the little sitting-room in the west wing, Alice did some mental arithmetic: "You and me – Mama, Grace and Edie – Alex and Harriet – and Polly and Jenny make nine. We can't possibly get nine chairs round this table."

It was going to be a feast; Ken Stubbs had supplied a capon from the farm, and cream from the dairy herd, while Alice had used the last of the month's sugar ration to sweeten the plums from the orchard. Since Polly had decided to take Alex and Harry back to Eaton Square with her, this might be their last Sunday at Crown House for some time.

Alice went on: "I suppose we can have lunch downstairs in the Servants' Hall – but if they don't get here till two, the chicken will be overdone, and the plum pie will have burnt to a crisp . . . and I wanted everything to be specially nice today."

Of course the Dowager Countess was scandalized – ("A family luncheon party – in the *Servants' Hall*?") – but everyone else welcomed the idea.

"We must congratulate you, Alice," said Edith, at the end of the meal. "I thought the chicken was a great success – not at all overcooked."

"And the plum pie was a triumph," said Grace. "Anyone can push a bird into the oven, but pastry takes talent!"

"Our compliments to the Chef!" said Polly. She turned to her children: "We're going to have some boring grown-up talk now, so you can run along to the farm and find Mr Stubbs. Tell him I'll come over to see him presently, but I want a word with Grandpa and Grandma first."

As soon as they were out of earshot, William said: "Well? What's the problem?"

Polly turned to Jenny: "Who's going to begin?"

"It was Nick who began it, really," said Jenny. "He phoned this morning, when his ship docked; he'd just got my letter about the baby, and he rang to say how pleased he was – but then he asked about the raid on London last night. It's amazing how quickly the news gets round."

"I dare say he heard it on the wireless, like me," Old Bea chimed in. "Not that they tell you much – just 'scattered damage in London's West End' – whatever that means. . . ."

"It means, when we went to the theatre we got caught in Covent Garden and had to spend the rest of the night in a shelter," said Polly.

Jenny continued: "I'm afraid I told Nick, without stopping to think – and he said that if they've started to bomb London, he wants me to come back here till things quieten down . . . I've brought my luggage; it's in the hall."

"It's not just you Nick's worried about – it's the baby as well," said Polly. "I feel the same; I don't want my kids to be in London – Alex will be off to school soon anyhow, and Harry will be happier down here." Throwing Jenny a quick smile, she added: "So we worked out a plan. At first I thought I'd have to come home and look after Harry – but now I'm starting this ENSA job, I can't very well let them down, can I? So we decided – I'm going to stay in town Mondays to Fridays, and pop down to Crown House at weekends – and Jenny can move into our flat over the garage. We haven't told Alex and Harry yet – Alex won't like it when he hears he's not going to London – but Harry will be thrilled that Jenny's going to stay with her. . . . Only we thought we'd better tell you first – is that OK?"

Alice said: "Of course it is. . . . If Nick wants Jenny to stay here, I'm sure we shall be delighted – won't we, William?"

He nodded: "It seems to be the best solution . . . I can't say I like the idea of Polly travelling up and down to London, but since my wife has been doing it for God knows how long, I can hardly object!"

"Thanks – you're a love." Polly planted a kiss on his cheek. "Wish me luck while I break the news to my offspring."

Jenny helped Alice to clear the table, and they began the washing-up, while William helped his mother negotiate the narrow staircase up to her room. After a long struggle, he eventually got her settled in her chair by the window, but it was some time before she could get her breath back.

At last she managed to croak: "Not right – not right at all. . . ."

"What's not right, Mama?"

"Polly – gallivanting off to London every week – she should be here, looking after her family; and she shouldn't put it on to Jenny. That girl's not strong at the best of times – and she lost her first child, didn't she?"

"Oh, come now – the doctor is very satisfied with her state of health."

"You won't be told, will you? Your father was just the same – Minster never listened to a word I said. . . . No good will come of this arrangement, you mark my words . . . ! But there – no doubt you're delighted at the way things have turned out?" she concluded, with a gleam of malice.

"What d'you mean by that?"

"You'll have your precious Jenny at your beck and call, helping you with the garden – walking round the estate, holding your hand. . . . You're soft on that girl, you always were. . . . Still, they say there's no fool like an old fool."

"There I must bow to your superior knowledge, Mama," said William dryly. "Let's see – is it next year we celebrate your ninetieth birthday —?"

"Hold your tongue – and mind your manners!" snapped his mother. "You know very well, I won't be ninety till the year after next!"

Meanwhile, Polly had followed her children down to the farm; she found Alex riding one of the shire horses, digging his heels into its sides and trying to urge it into a canter, with Harry perched in front of him.

Ken stood by the paddock gate, lighting his pipe; he nodded cheerfully at Polly as he puffed away.

"You're looking well," he grunted.

"Am I? I feel like the wrath of God, after a night in a shelter."

She told him about last night's raid and explained the change of plan, while Ken concentrated on his pipe, his head wreathed in smoke. At last he said: "Do you have to work in London? Couldn't you find something nearer home?"

"Nothing I'd enjoy so much – this ENSA job will suit me down to the ground. And I know Harry will be in safe hands."

He misunderstood her: "Thanks – I'll certainly do my best to keep an eye on her while you're away."

"No – I really meant – Jenny. . . . But you too, of course. You've always been very good with the children."

He still seemed to be having difficulty with the pipe, and struck another match as he said: "Mrs Jenny will look after your daughter very well – no doubt of that. But if there's anything I can do, you've only got to say."

"I know – I'm very grateful." She noticed he was wearing an armband with the letters "LDV" – the initials of the Local Defence Volunteers. "I thought you were in the ARP?"

"I'm in both; defending Crown House against the enemy, and learning how to round up German parachutists with a couple of pitchforks and a rook rifle! Next week they might even issue us with uniforms. . . . Only they don't call us LDV any more – we're the Home Guard now."

"I bet you'll look very smart in your uniform – when you get it." Polly began to wave; Alex had just seen her, and was pulling on the reins, persuading the carthorse to lumber across the paddock. "Here they come – you can help me explain to them . . . and – thanks. . . ."

"Thanks? What for?"

"I don't know – for everything. . . . For being in the ARP – and the Home Guard," she said awkwardly. "For being here, really."

"There's trains running to Ashford – or to Maidstone," said

the man at the ticket-office window. "But no through trains at present."

Alice and Polly stared at him: "But we're going to London!" began Alice.

"I'm starting a new job today!" said Polly. "I've got to be there!"

"Sorry, ladies – the Southern Railway is in a right old mess this morning. Two nights running, they've had real heavy raids, and there's track damaged all over the South-East. So until they get it repaired – no London trains."

"You're on duty at the Palace, aren't you?" asked Polly, as they left the station.

"Yes – I'd offer to drive up, but there isn't enough petrol in the tank, and I've used up this month's allowance."

"There's only one thing for it – we'll have to thumb a lift."

As the petrol rationing tightened, it was quite common to see little bands of travellers by the roadside, hoping some public-spirited motorist would come along. Alice and Polly walked to a roundabout on the outskirts of Medford, and began to wait.

Most of the traffic seemed to be going the other way; the vehicles heading for London were already crowded with passengers – apart from a convoy of army lorries which would not pick up civilians.

"I suppose they're moving in troops to help clear up the damage," said Alice, thinking of Miranda and Caro, alone in the town house. "I wonder what it was like last night, in Eaton Square."

"If there was any bad news, you'd have heard – oh, look —" Polly broke off as a milk-tanker slowed to a halt. The driver wound down his window and said: "London?"

"Yes, please – whereabouts are you going?"

"Depot in Lewisham," he replied. "Hop in."

They accepted his offer gladly, and as they climbed aboard, Alice asked: "Do you think we'll get a bus to take us into Central London?"

"You'll be lucky," grunted the driver. "Lots of roads are

closed – gas mains on fire, water mains burst, broken glass everywhere. . . ."

In the end it took two more lifts to get them as far as Waterloo – then Alice picked up a taxi at the station, and Polly ran across the bridge, towards Drury Lane.

The tanker driver had not exaggerated; squads of volunteers had set to work – clearing roads, boarding up broken windows, or shepherding bewildered, homeless people to a temporary refuge. The people of London had been badly shaken, but they were not defeated, and the city was slowly coming back to life.

That night the sirens wailed again, and Alice accompanied their housekeeper down to the cellars, now converted into a shelter. Polly and Caro joined them; presently Miranda ran down the stairs, saying brightly: "I'm back! . . . Isn't anyone going to ask what I've been doing today?"

"All right," said Caro kindly. "Tell us, Miranda – what have you been doing today?"

"Well – if you really want to know – I've been to the Recruiting Office," she replied. "I've signed up to join the WRNS. And I'm off to Portsmouth on Wednesday, to start basic training – won't Nick be surprised when he sees me?"

They all congratulated her; Miss Kendall said she felt sure she would look lovely in that smart uniform, and Miranda sighed: "If I'm lucky! There are so many girls joining now, they're short of uniforms, and I don't know when I'll get mine."

Then it was Polly's turn to report on her working day; she told them that ENSA was simply marvellous, and Mr Basil Dean had actually condescended to smile at her – briefly: "So p'raps he's not such an ogre as people say. . . . Anyway, I probably shan't see him again – unless I make an awful mistake, and get hauled over the coals."

"But what do you actually do?" Caro asked: "Rehearse new shows?"

"Goodness, no – there are some people rehearsing on the stage, and some more in the Circle Bar, but I share a tiny office with three other people, and we get the artistes kitted out to go on tour, to army camps and ack-ack units and dockyards – they all have to be fitted up with khaki, and I have to check their ration books and identity cards and travel passes —"

"Talking of travel – did you hear about our nightmare journey up from Medford?" asked Alice.

"You were lucky to get here at all – it took me nearly an hour, just going to the hospital," retorted Caro, "thanks to the roadblocks and diversion signs."

"God bless the Underground," said Polly. "I can go on the District Line from Victoria to the Temple, and then walk. I came home by tube this evening." She grinned suddenly: "Trouble is, you can't see out of the windows, 'cos they've stuck some sort of netting over them in case of flying glass, so people keep peeling off the net, and London Transport have put up a poster with a po-faced little man called "Billy Brown of London Town" and he's saying —

'I trust you'll pardon my correction —
That stuff is there for your protection . . .

"– only underneath that, some bright spark had written:

'We thank you for your information —
We want to see the bloody station!'"

Everybody laughed – and then they heard a distant rumble that might have been thunder, but was not.

After a moment, Polly asked quietly: "What was it really like – last night?"

Caro and Miranda looked at one another; but it was Miss Kendall who spoke.

"It was dreadful," she said. "I don't think I could have stood it, if I'd been on my own – the bombs whistling down – and those terrible bangs. . . ."

"It was pretty grim," Caro agreed. "I was glad Jenny wasn't here. Still, we kept each other entertained – I told them all the juicy gossip about the senior medical staff at the hospital, and we tried to see how many old jokes we could remember."

More explosions, closer than before, made a shower of plaster dust fall from the ceiling. Out in the Square, above their heads, an ambulance drove past with its bell clanging.

"It seems so extraordinary, having raids every night." Miss Kendall's voice trembled: "I wonder how long they'll keep it up."

"Perhaps Hitler's planning to give us a whole week of it," said Caro.

Miss Kendall stood up abruptly: "I think I'd like a cup of tea – would anyone else care for some?"

She went into the makeshift kitchenette and put the kettle on. None of them could have guessed that these air raids were only the start of a blitz on London which was to continue, almost without a break, for the next eight months.

As it turned out, that night was comparatively peaceful; after a picnic supper, they played cards, and eventually rolled up in blankets and eiderdowns on camp-beds, dozing fitfully until the all-clear roused them at dawn, and another day began.

Caro, on early duty, was the first to leave the house. As she climbed the basement stairs, she heard a resounding knock at the front door.

"There's the post!" she called to the others, who were finishing breakfast. "I'll go."

But it wasn't the post. A red-bearded man, in a loud check shirt which did not match his equally loud check sports coat, stood on the top step, laden with suitcases, shoulder-bags and parcels.

"Hi there, Mrs Hanson," he said.

"*Scott — !*"

He let the luggage fall and took his wife in his arms, holding her tightly and kissing her again and again.

"Why didn't you let me know?" she began, when she could speak. "Oh, it's so lovely to see you – you look absolutely dreadful – what have you been up to?"

"Travelling too much, and not sleeping enough, I guess," he said, following her into the house.

His face was lined with fatigue, and there were white hairs in his red whiskers.

152

"And I hate the beard, it ages you – that's got to go," she added firmly.

"Really? I thought it made me look distinguished."

"No – just old." She took him into the drawing-room. "Sit down and put your feet up. As a medical expert, I diagnose extreme exhaustion – I prescribe a lot of sweet, weak tea —"

"Yuck! Make that coffee – black and strong – and you've got yourself a deal. But not right now – we have things to talk about."

"I can't stay long; I'm on duty at eight, and the Ward Sister is a dragon."

"Ring up and tell her you just cracked a rib." He reached out for her: "Better yet, come here and let me crack one for you."

She laughed: "I'd love to, but I really must go —"

He grabbed her hand: "I'm serious – pick up the phone and tell your dragon with my compliments to go jump in a lake. You are handing in your notice at that hospital, honey-lamb – and the sooner the better."

She sat beside him: "I haven't the faintest idea what you're talking about."

He spelled it out for her: "Listen, I just got in from Berlin, by way of Rome, Madrid, Lisbon and Dublin, so I'm kinda travel-worn – but the news is that the phony war is over, and the Nazis mean to hammer this city into the dirt. So you're coming back to the States where you belong, before all hell breaks loose."

She stared at him: "I can't possibly – I've got a job to do."

"Sure – your job is being my wife – that's why I'm taking you with me."

The drawing-room door opened and Alice walked in, saying: "Scott! – I thought I heard your voice – what a wonderful surprise. . . . Oh, you've got a beard. . . ."

He scrambled to his feet: "That's only part of the surprise. I've also got supplies of American cigarettes, silk stockings, bourbon, and assorted goodies." He embraced her warmly: "You're looking swell, mother-in-law – I'm sorry this is only a flying visit."

153

Her face fell: "Don't say you're not stopping!"

"I have to get back to the States; in the past few months I've collected enough material to fill a year's issue of *Life* and *Time* – and still have enough left over to produce a best seller at the end of it. . . . And my dearly-beloved wife is coming back to Washington with me – right, sweetheart?"

"I'm afraid not." No longer smiling, Caro stood up. "I'm sorry, Scott. I'm not going."

"What happened after that?" Her Majesty wanted to know.

"Oh – they started arguing – but then Caro had to leave, because she was late for the hospital. When she came home, the argument began again, and I'm afraid it's been rumbling on all the week."

On Friday morning, Alice was working in the Queen's office. When they broke off for elevenses, Her Majesty had enquired after the family, so Alice told her about the deadlock between Caro and her American husband.

"How very difficult." The Queen sipped her coffee. "One sees both points of view – naturally, he wants to take his wife out of danger, but she's doing a useful job here, and she doesn't want to run away . . . I sympathize with both of them."

"So do I – and I also feel like banging their heads together!" sighed Alice. "Scott's staying with us at present, and it's rather wearing when they keep squabbling."

"Let's hope they manage to sort it out." Her Majesty shivered: "There's a draught coming from somewhere – though I suppose that's hardly surprising."

The window was temporarily covered with transparent sheeting. Three days earlier, a delayed-action bomb had fallen outside the north wing and exploded before it could be defused; no one was injured, but a great many windows had been shattered.

Since the raids on London were now so frequent, most people ignored the sirens and carried on with their work – at least until the raiders were actually overhead. The Royal Family were no exception, and though there had been another warning an hour ago, their motto was "Business As Usual". After lunch, their Majesties would visit the East End, to see the hardest-hit areas and meet some of the people who had been bombed out.

"One side of the sheeting has come adrift – I'll put in some more drawing-pins," said Alice. As she struggled with the material, she added: "I'm just hoping that Caro and Scott don't blow up into a real quarrel, today of all days."

"Today — ?"

"Well, Ma'am, it *is* Friday the thirteenth!"

The Queen began: "Thank goodness I'm not superstitious —" but then she frowned, and crossed the room to join Alice at the window. "What's that strange noise?"

There was a zooming sound overhead; they both looked up – and gasped, as the shadow of a low-flying aircraft flickered across the courtyard, and they saw a stick of bombs falling on the opposite side of the Palace.

The Queen gripped Alice's arm, and they heard a series of explosions, followed by one last resounding crash.   As the echoes died away, Her Majesty said: "What fools we are – standing by a window in the middle of a raid! We're lucky there was no glass left to break . . . Let's go and find out what's happened."

Outside was a scene of devastation. Two of the bombs had fallen within the main quadrangle, while another landed just beyond the royal apartments, bringing down tons of rubble, and completely destroying the private chapel.

The King was already on the spot, surveying the damage. The Queen slipped her hand in his, saying quietly: "Are you all right?"

"Of course. No one was hurt, thank God."

Alice noticed that, for the moment, he had mastered his stammer.

"That's all right then," said the Queen.

A duty policeman hurried up, reporting that the German pilot had taken an extraordinary risk; under cover of low cloud, he had flown straight up the Mall and dropped a stick of bombs into the heart of the Palace.

Turning to the Queen, he said breathlessly: "It was a magnificent piece of bombing, Ma'am – if you'll pardon me saying so."

Her Majesty said: "Good – I'm very glad."

The King laughed: "Glad we've been bombed?"

"Yes, I am . . . Now I feel I can look the East End in the face."

Chapter Ten

Wednesday, 9 October to Tuesday, 15 October 1940

With Ken Stubbs at his heels, Lord Minster climbed the tower of the village church in silence. There were forty-three steps in the spiral staircase, and he knew from previous experience that he must save his breath.

In addition to his other duties, he had put his name down on the village rota, taking his turn to keep watch on the sky from this Observation Post. Over his shoulder was a folded tartan rug, and in his free hand he carried a shopping bag containing sandwiches and a flask of coffee; his other hand followed the knotted rope which served as a handrail.

When the two men emerged, panting a little, the Vicar struggled up from his deckchair: "Ah, there you are, gentlemen – you come most carefully upon your hour," he said, in the special voice he used whenever he quoted the Bible or Shakespeare. "Well, Mr Wilkinson – we may as well take ourselves home to our beds."

Mr Wilkinson, from the village stores, collected up his picnic basket and his blanket.

"Going to be chilly tonight," he muttered. "A real nip in the air."

"Ah, well, it's been a wonderful summer – we can't expect miracles," said the Vicar. "By the by, there was a telephone call earlier – there are reports of parachutists sighted along the Kent coast, and we're told to keep a sharp lookout for enemy activity. We haven't seen anything yet, but one never knows. . . . Anyway – I hope you have a peaceful night!"

Glad to be off duty, the two old gentlemen scrambled through the door and disappeared, while William and Ken settled in the deckchairs and prepared for the long night ahead.

Tucking his blankets around him, Ken grumbled: "How are we supposed to see paratroops coming down in the pitch dark?"

A little later, they heard a steady drumming overhead, which grew steadily louder, and they looked up, but there was nothing to be seen.

"Bombers," said Ken. "Sounds like London's in for it again. . . ." Too late, he realized that he had been tactless, and bit his lip.

"Yes – I'm afraid my wife will be in Eaton Square tonight," said William.

"She deserves a break, after that narrow squeak at Buckingham Palace. . . . It's a pity the whole family can't move down here until it's all over."

"They're all the same – Caroline won't give up her hospital job – and Polly seems equally determined not to desert Drury Lane."

Ken grunted: "I admire her spirit – I just wish she'd found a job where she could live at home."

They went on talking for a while, trying to keep themselves awake; gradually they lapsed into a companionable silence, and it was after midnight when William roused himself, straining his ears.

"What's that?" he asked.

Ken had heard it too. They moved to the parapet; the noise was directly below them – a scraping sound, accompanied by heavy, asthmatic breathing.

"He's got a cold on his chest, whoever he is," Ken said quietly.

"What would anyone be doing in the churchyard at this time of night?"

"Could be one of those German paratroops . . . We'd better go and see."

They stumbled down the forty-three steps as cautiously as possible. Ken had a torch, but the arrow-slit windows were not blacked out, so he dared not use it. At last they reached ground level and groped their way out through the porch; they could see no sign of movement among the glimmering tombstones, but then —

"There it is again!" whispered Ken.

They froze, listening to the scraping and the heavy breathing – only a few yards away, though they could see nothing.

Ken challenged the intruder: "Who goes there?"

Instantly there was silence. They waited for a moment, then William added: "Who are you, and what are you doing here?"

He took a step forward, but Ken put a hand on his arm: "Steady, sir – he might have a gun – there's only one thing for it!" – and he switched on his torch.

There, transfixed in the beam, was an old badger, disturbed as it grubbed up crab-apple windfalls from the stone-flagged path. It glared at them indignantly, then lumbered off, wheezing, into the undergrowth.

As they began to laugh, they heard an angry cry: *Put that light out!*

Coming through the lychgate, the Vicar was shocked to find them apparently neglecting their watch, and flouting the blackout regulations. They tried to explain that they had come down to investigate a possible enemy intruder, but the Vicar interrupted them: "No, no," he said. "There will be no invasion tonight – I've just had another call from Thanet – the sightings along the coast were not paratroops, but parachute-mines, dropped into the sea. . . . That's what I came to tell you."

As they began to climb the tower once more, William said to Ken: "I don't think I'll tell anyone about this little incident – and I'd be obliged if you'd keep quiet about it as well."

The following afternoon, Caro and Scott were sitting side by side on a bench at Waterloo Station, looking pale and tired. Above them, the glass roof had been replaced by tarpaulin, casting a thundery twilight over the waiting passengers. Scott glanced at his watch, and Caro tried to smother a yawn, but failed.

"Am I boring you?" he asked.

"Don't be silly. I'm a bit sleepy – that's all."

"It was lousy luck, you having to do extra night duty last night – and it was *my* last night, too."

"It couldn't be helped. Nurse Potts had an impacted wisdom tooth – somebody had to take over."

"Yeah – but why you?"

Caro yawned again, and said: "I'm sorry."

"Me too. It wasn't the way I'd imagined our last evening." Then he added: "I wish you were coming with me."

"You know I can't."

"We ought to be together."

Caro sighed: "Yes, but for how long? How long will you be in New York?"

"How do I know? Couple of weeks, maybe."

"And then where will you go?"

"Wherever they send me. They're making noises about Moscow."

"Could I go to Moscow?"

"Well, no, honey, but —"

"Exactly. So I'd be alone in New York, with a million strangers."

"You'd be with my friends. And you'd be safe."

"I'd sooner be here, with my own friends – with my family."

He looked at his watch again, and said no more.

When Caro got back to Eaton Square, Polly met her in the hall saying: "Oh, it's you – I was hoping you were your Ma."

Caro smiled wearily: "I seem to be a disappointment all round today."

"No, there's someone waiting to see her, in the drawing-room. I told him she wasn't back yet, but he said he'd wait." A little embarrassed, she explained: "It's Paul Weyman."

"Paul – ? What does he want?"

"He didn't say. But I know this must be awkward for you – I mean, you and him having been. . . ." She began again: "You could go up to your room, if you want – he doesn't know you're here."

Unexpectedly, Caro felt suddenly confident: "That's all right – I don't mind seeing him."

She ran upstairs to the first floor, and opened the drawing-room door.

For a moment, she thought Polly had made a mistake. The man by the fireplace, with his back to her, couldn't possibly be Paul; he was too old – round-shouldered, stooping a little. . . . Then he turned and stared at her, momentarily disconcerted; she hand't seen him for nearly four years, but he seemed to have aged much more than that.

"Caro – my dear—" he began.

They shook hands with absurd formality. Even his smile was different; with a shock, she realized that he now had false teeth.

"How are you?" she asked. "Do sit down – would you like some tea?"

"Thank you, no – Polly offered me some, but I can't stop – I only called to see your mother on a business matter . . . Polly said she's expecting her home shortly."

"I hadn't realized you and Polly knew each other."

"Good lord, yes – the first time I came to Crown House was Polly's wedding day. . . . It seems like another world, doesn't it? So much has happened to us since then."

"To us — ?"

"To all of us."

They sat on the sofa and made small talk; he told her about his job at Broadcasting House, and she told him about her hospital work – and all the time, she was thinking: "Is this the man I lived with? The man who taught me about love?"

She was relieved when the door opened again and Alice came in, brightly determined to carry off an awkward situation.

"Paul – how nice – I hope Caroline has been entertaining you?"

He stood up and took her hand, saying: "I do apologize, but

161

there are one or two things which – well, I thought if you were at home I might trespass briefly on your time — ?"

"Of course. . . . Caro, darling – why don't you go and see about tea?"

Paul began to explain that he wouldn't dream of imposing upon them, but Caro was glad of an excuse to escape. As soon as the door shut, he said in a different tone: "I wouldn't have come, but I felt I should warn you; I've been at Windsor this afternoon, to discuss next Sunday's broadcast – I expect you've heard about that?"

"No – tell me."

"Princess Elizabeth is to speak to the children of Great Britain; it was Derek McCullough's idea – 'Uncle Mac', you know – and the King has graciously given his approval."

"How splendid – no, I hadn't heard – I've been busy at WVS headquarters today."

"Ah – well, Her Majesty said she would ask you to join them at Windsor on Sunday; she remembered that you and I are old acquaintances, and thought you would like to see me again."

Alice walked over to the windows and straightened the blackout curtains, saying: "That was very kind of her."

"Of course I knew you would prefer *not* to see me, but I could hardly say so. That's why I called in – I thought you might like to be prepared, so you could make your excuses."

Alice turned to face him: "That won't be necessary. It was very considerate of you, Paul, but I shall do whatever Her Majesty asks me to do. After all these years, I think we are old enough and wise enough to put the past behind us, don't you?"

"I can truthfully say to you all that we children at home are full of cheerfulness and courage. . . ."

Princess Elizabeth's voice was being broadcast throughout the British Isles, and to every part of the Empire; she sounded young for her fourteen-and-a-half years.

Her father's study had been used as a studio on several occasions; in an adjoining room, Paul Weyman stood with the engineers at the control panel, while the King watched and listened; only a muscle that twitched in his cheek betrayed his nervousness.

Elizabeth showed no sign of nerves; with her mother's help, she had rehearsed her speech over and over again, learning to pause for breath at the right moments, and remembering not to drop her voice at the ends of sentences.

"We are trying to do all we can to help our gallant sailors, soldiers and airmen" – (pause) – "and we are trying too" – (pause) – "to bear our own share of the dangers and sadness of war."

At the other side of the room, the Queen was willing her daughter not to make any mistakes; sitting next to her, Alice could sense her relief as each tricky hurdle was safely negotiated.

"We know, every one of us, that in the end all will be well."

Her Majesty smiled; the Princess was in the home stretch now, and coming up to the finishing-post. Elizabeth turned to her ten-year-old sister, who sat swinging her legs beside her, and said: "Come on, Margaret."

Princess Margaret, who had been silent throughout the broadcast, took a deep breath; this was her big moment.

"Good night, children," she said – and grinned broadly.

Then they were off the air, and everyone crowded into the study to congratulate the girls; Paul complimented Princess Elizabeth on her professional delivery. Tea and sandwiches were served, and Alice handed the Queen a cup and saucer, saying: "I expect you need this, Ma'am."

"Oh, yes – I had terrible stage-fright for both of them – isn't that ridiculous?"

"It was an historic occasion," said Alice. "And I'm sure the broadcast will have cheered everyone up."

"Let's hope so. I wish the girls could come with us when we tour the bomb-sites; but of course that would never do." Since the Blitz began, the King and Queen had gone to visit the devastated areas every day, but the suffering they witnessed was impossible to share with their daughters. She continued briskly: "We must make an early start tomorrow, my dear – can you be ready by half-past eight? I'm afraid you'll be late tonight, by the time you get back to Eaton Square."

Her eye fell on Paul Weyman, whose team were already packing up their equipment, and she asked: "Mr Weyman – could I beg a favour? If you're driving back to Broadcasting House, would it be possible to drop Lady Minster in Belgravia, on the way?"

Half an hour later, Paul and Alice were travelling through the blackout, towards West London. He was an experienced motorist, and kept up a steady pace, following the white lines in the middle of the road.

They made conversation for a while, and then he said: "I was glad to see Caroline and Polly the other day. How are the rest of the family? How's William?"

"He's very well indeed. After his heart attack, he had to take things easy for a long time – but now he's taken on all kinds of responsibilities. He does his share at home, helping to run the estate, and he works for the County Agricultural Committee and the ARP – and he even takes his turn at the Observation Post. . . . . It's as if the war had given him a new purpose in life."

"I'm glad; I would say: 'Give him my regards' – but perhaps that might not be a good idea."

They drove on for some time, and Alice told Paul various items of family news. As they entered the Chiswick High Road, heading for Hammersmith, Paul said abruptly: "You've told me about the whole family – except the two people I care about most. How are the twins?"

Alice stiffened: "I'm sorry – I can't discuss Martin and Miranda with you."

"Surely you can tell me how they are – where they are – what they're doing? I think I have a right to know."

"You have no right at all," she said quietly.

"But we're talking about my children! Dammit, they're probably the only children I'll ever have – I can't help taking a certain pride in them —"

"*Pride— ?*" Alice threw the word back at him. "You take

pride in the greatest shame of my life – the greatest wrong I ever did to William?"

It had happened during the First World War, not long before the Armistice. Paul, a young subaltern in William's regiment, had been sent home on sick-leave – and that was when Alice received the telegram, saying that William was missing, believed to be killed. In her misery, Paul had comforted her, and she fell into his arms.

A few weeks later the war was over, and – miraculously – William returned, alive and well. By then Alice was pregnant. The following summer, the twins were born; though it was another twelve years before Alice was able to tell her husband the truth – and he was able to forgive her.

But if William lived to be a hundred, he would never forgive Paul.

In despair, Paul exclaimed now: "I don't understand you! You were able to accept my relationship with Caro, in the end – surely, after all this time, William must accept that Martin and Miranda —"

"He will never accept it – why should he? In every way that matters, he is their father; nothing can change that."

"So – they still don't know the truth?"

"Of course not! How can you even think such a thing?"

"Caroline found out; she might have said something."

"Caroline would never tell them – they must never know." Alice struggled to control herself: "I said I hoped we had put the past behind us – obviously I was wrong. And I warn you – if you ever try to take advantage of the situation, I will never see you or speak to you again."

The car was slowing down as they reached Hammersmith Broadway, and she said: "Please stop here. Thank you for the lift; I shall go home by myself. Good night, Paul."

He did not try to argue; he pulled in to the kerb, and watched her walking into the Underground station – and then she was gone.

It wasn't only the air raid which kept Alice awake that night.

165

She lay on her narrow bed in the Eaton Square cellars, thinking of Paul – and the twins – and of William's love and forgiveness. Morning came all too soon; suddenly it was seven o'clock, and she had to report for duty by half-past eight.

When she arrived breathlessly in the Palace courtyard, where the gleaming Daimler awaited them, their Majesties were coming down the steps.

"Good morning, Alice; what a gorgeous dress – is it new?" the Queen wanted to know.

"No, Ma'am, I've had it for some time, but I've never found the right occasion for it."

It was a summer dress, with a pattern of poppies and wheatstalks in bold splashes of scarlet and gold, and would not have been Alice's first choice for a tour of the bombed areas, but all her other dresses were being cleaned – they never survived more than a day or two of floating soots and brickdust.

"You both look very stylish," said His Majesty, following them into the car. "I feel we should be g-g-going to a party."

"That's the whole idea!" said the Queen, who wore a dress and jacket of power blue, matching her eyes. "People want to see us looking our best – they need cheering up."

As the car moved off, she continued: "Bright colours – no blacks or greens. Black would give quite the wrong impression, and green is supposed to be unlucky."

"I thought you weren't superstitious, Ma'am?" Alice ventured.

The Queen smiled: "I'm not – but some people are, and one mustn't hurt their feelings."

The East End had taken another night of punishment, and there were signs of damage on all sides; broken windows, holes in roofs, and hideous gaps in the terraced houses, like missing teeth. Alice saw one building which had been ripped open; no floors remained in the upper rooms, but there were still pictures hanging askew on the walls, and a clock stood on a mantelpiece, above a fireplace that hung in mid-air, two storeys up.

The car slowed to walking-pace, negotiating piles of debris, then stopped at a barrier stretched across the road.

"This is where we walk," said his Majesty, opening the door.

Only a few people had been told to expect the royal party, and there were no crowds – but word soon got round, and men and women appeared at every street corner. An elderly postman on his rounds had just stopped at a pillar-box, isolated in the middle of no-man's-land, surrounded by rubble. As he cleared the box, he saw the King and Queen; pulling himself together, he straightened his peaked cap and made a sketchy salute.

The King returned his salute, and the Queen waved; then she saw a small crowd round what was left of a public house, and changed direction, going over to join them.

They all welcomed the Queen, but one man had other things on his mind; his dog was under the fallen masonry.

"He's all right, 'cos I can hear him whining – but he's scared out if his wits, poor little beggar. I've called him, but he won't budge – suffering from shock, most like . . . and if I try and dig him out, I might bring the whole lot down on top of him. . . ."

"Let me try; I'm quite good with dogs," said the Queen, dropping to her knees – and she began to talk gently and soothingly, until she had coaxed the terrified animal from its hiding-place.

Meanwhile the King was asking the ARP workers about last night's raid, anxious to hear everything that had happened.

All the morning, Alice followed the royal couple wherever they went. One woman saw them passing, darted into her house and came out again with a single bronze chrysanthemum, which she pressed into the Queen's hand. Her Majesty admired it, then as the tour went on, gave it to Alice to keep safe.

By the time they got back to the car, Alice was carrying several flowers, a good-luck horseshoe, a sprig of white heather – and a bag of toffees for the Princesses.

The car was already covered with a thin film of dust, and Alice's dress would need cleaning when she got home – but what did that matter?

The chauffeur started the motor, and a little band of

onlookers raised a cheer. One man called out: "Thank God for a good King!"

The King said softly: "Thank God for a good people."

As they drove away, the Queen took his hand, saying: "The destruction is awful, but the people are so wonderful – they deserve a better world."

"Gaunt! You're wanted!"

Miranda scrambled to her feet. In her fatigue overalls, she had been cleaning the components of a carburettor; she clutched an oily rag, and there was a black smear from her left ear to her chin.

"Better clean yourself up pretty smartish." CPO Molloy was one of the oldest instructors aboard HMS *Pomfret*, and he deplored the slapdash behaviour of the young female trainees under his supervision. "You're to report to First Officer Banner – chop-chop!"

Miranda groaned: "What have I done this time?"

"Just a routine interview, I reckon. Nothing to worry about – provided you wash your face. So jump to it!"

Miranda dropped the oily rag, and ran.

Ten minutes later, her hair combed and her face scrubbed pink, she entered the office. Gazing at a point on the wall just above the officer's head, she stood to attention and saluted, bringing her hand up to her ridiculous pudding-basin hat. There was a rumour going about that the WRNS were soon to be issued with proper sailor hats, but so far these had not materialized.

"No need to salute, Gaunt. Stand easy – you may sit down."

Miranda sat in the chair facing the desk, her shoulders well back and her feet planted side by side. If there were such a thing as "sitting to attention", Miranda was doing it.

Not that FO Banner was particularly ferocious; she had the reputation of being a stickler for neatness, but there was a hint of amusement in her eyes as she asked: "How are you enjoying life on board?"

168

"It's very interesting, ma'am," said Miranda.

That was an understatement. Her first few weeks as a raw recruit in the Women's Royal Naval Service had been more than interesting; they were an introduction to another world.

She had spent a fortnight at the Training and Drafting Depot, trying to cope with incomprehensible rules and regulations and learning a new language. The rooms were cabins, the floor was the deck, and a trip into Portsmouth was known as "going ashore", even though the depot was on dry land. She even had to learn a new way of telling the time, for the day was split up into "watches" marked by "bells".

For a fortnight she was kept continually on the move – being drilled on the parade-ground (which was called the quarterdeck) – being exercised in the gymnasium until every muscle ached – being sent to work in the stores, and the galley, and the sick-bay – and learning to ride a motor bike.

At the end of the fortnight, when she had to decide which branch of the Service she wished to join, she put her name down for "Motor Transport and Maintenance". After that she was sent for specialist training to HMS *Pomfret* – a group of hideous brick buildings in a sea of tarmac, somewhere between Reading and Newbury.

"You're now halfway through the course – I have several interim reports here from your instructors – and I'm glad to say they are all quite favourable."

"Thank you, ma'am."

"You have shown some mechanical aptitude; you are willing to learn, and one of your instructors describes you as 'a good mixer'."

Miranda tried not to smile; CPO Molloy had been pleasantly surprised to discover that she played a tough game of poker in her off-duty moments.

"On the other hand, you have been reported for untidiness; on one occasion you were reprimanded for not laying out your kit in the regulation manner."

"Yes – I'm sorry, ma'am."

"But if you are prepared to smarten yourself up, I see no reason why you should not get a good posting. Have

169

you any particular preference about where you might like to go?"

"I'd like to serve overseas, ma'am – if possible."

"Ah, yes – many girls would like to do that, but the opportunities for travel are very limited. However, there will soon be some vacancies for Dispatch Riders at the Admiralty . . . I notice you gave Eaton Square as your home address. On entry, ratings are either classed as "mobile", which means they can be sent anywhere – or "immobile", when they live at home and carry out their duties at a nearby depot. If you were given a London posting, you could be billeted with your own family."

Miranda said nothing; the prospect of returning to Eaton Square and spending her war service running errands in Whitehall did not appeal to her – but then, in a moment, everything changed.

It was as if lightning had struck, out of a clear sky – and Miranda's future no longer mattered, because the nightmare had begun again. . . . She struggled to concentrate on the officer's words, trying to ignore the dryness in her mouth and the sickening emptiness at the pit of her stomach.

FO Banner frowned, and said: "You're very pale – are you feeling ill?"

"No, ma'am – it's nothing. Indigestion, probably."

She clenched her fists, determined that the officer should not see her hands were shaking.

"Have you told the Medical Officer that you suffer from indigestion?"

"No, ma'am."

"I think you should. Report to the sickbay when you leave here, and say I sent you. Very well, Gaunt – you may go."

When Miranda left the cabin, the First Officer sighed; she had seemed such a bright, sensible girl, with a promising future ahead – and then, for no apparent reason, her whole manner had changed, and she had looked as if she were about to faint.

The officer began to make some notes on the girl's personal file; but how should she describe her? Nervous? Unstable?

The word that sprang to her mind was "Frightened . . ." But of course that was absurd.

On Thursday evening, Alice was late again. Today, their Majesties had refused to turn back until they had seen all the latest damage, as far east as Dagenham. Too tired to eat, she went down to the kitchen to make herself some cocoa. Caro, in her nursing uniform, was filling a kettle at the sink.

"Have you only just got back?" Alice asked. "I thought you finished at seven?"

"I should have, but some of the night staff were late – more bombs on the railway, so they couldn't get a through train. We had to hang on till they turned up."

Alice looked around: "Where's Polly? And Miss Kendall?"

"They've gone down to the shelter with the portable wireless; there's an ENSA concert for the RAF on the Forces Programme. Have you had supper?"

"Not really – I've snatched the odd sandwich – I think I'll have cocoa."

"I'm just making some for myself," said Caro, fetching another cup. "I warn you, we're almost out of milk; there was a bomb at the Express Dairies, so they were short of supplies."

Polly appeared in the doorway, saying: "Did I leave my *Woman's Own* up here?" Then, seeing Alice: "Hello, you're back – what sort of day?"

"Don't ask," said Alice.

"Oh, that sort. . . . Listen – something really weird happened just now. Bruce Belfrage was in the middle of reading the nine o'clock news, and suddenly there was this bang and a sort of rumbling noise in the background. Seemingly a bomb had landed on part of Broadcasting House – but he just carried on with the bulletin as if nothing had happened."

Caro and Alice looked at one another, but said nothing.

When Polly had found her magazine and returned to the cellar, Alice said: "I know what you're thinking."

"Do you?"

171

"We're both wondering if Paul was on duty at the BBC tonight . . . and hoping he's all right."

Caroline passed a cup and saucer across the table, and asked: "Do you still care about him? After all these years?"

"No – of course not – not in that way. . . . Sometimes he makes me very angry . . . But if he were injured, or – or anything. . . . That would be terrible."

Caro sipped her cocoa and said: "I don't feel like that about him . . . I don't really care about anyone, any more."

"Of course you do – you care about Scott —"

"I don't think so. I don't hate anybody – and I don't love anybody either." She pushed her cup aside, letting her head drop onto her arms. "I feel as if this war had been going on for years and years . . . and I'm too tired to bloody well care."

In Dormitory B Block, on board HMS *Pomfret*, Miranda lay awake, staring into the darkness.

Around her, she could hear the gentle, rhythmic breathing of the other girls, fast asleep. But she could not get any rest.

The feeling was stronger than ever tonight; the nauseating fear that gripped her mind and body. She tried to think of other things, but it was no good; every other thought was swept away by the nightmare that overwhelmed her. . . . It was as if she were in two places at once; her physical body trapped in a Berkshire Naval Establishment, while her mind was hundreds of miles away – no longer tied down to earth, but soaring up – onward, and upward. . . .

Then the explosions began. Although she could see nothing, she could *feel* the dazzling flashes – and her body was as heavy as lead. She wanted to scream for help, as terror engulfed her, but she could not utter a sound.

And she knew that Martin was flying with the bomber squadron again tonight.

Chapter Eleven

Friday, 10 January to Friday, 17 January 1941

"Bloody sirens – seem to be earlier every night," grumbled the Chief Petty Officer, blowing on his knuckles. "Let's hope our boys are giving 'em a taste of their own medicine, over there."

Miranda thought of Martin – and steeled herself. Time enough for that later.

It was the worst time of the year; the temperature was well below freezing, the hours of daylight were all too short, and the sirens warbled every evening at nightfall. This evening she had been sent to deliver sealed orders to the Captain of a troopship sailing from Tilbury; she was told to wait in case there was a reply, and was sheltering in a wooden shack which served as a guardhouse. The CPO had given her a cup of tea, so hot she was unable to drink it, but at least it was keeping her hands warm.

"Bad last night up west, I hear?" he enquired. "Out in it, were you?"

"No, Chief, I was on maintenance in the garage – but I believe they caught a packet round St Paul's."

She put down her cup and sprang to attention as a Wren Third Officer opened the door, saying: "Nothing to go back this time. Report to Base and await further orders. . . . All right – carry on."

Miranda saluted, then went out to find her motor bike in the darkness.

"Mind how you go!" the CPO called after her.

She buckled her crash-helmet more tightly under her chin and swung her leg over the saddle before switching on: "I always do!" she retorted, and opened the throttle.

Above her, searchlights swept the night sky. So far there had been no sound of bombing, but it wouldn't be long now. There was a temptation to scorch along the empty roads, but during a raid you never knew what might be round the next corner – a fizzing incendiary, or a smoking crater.

As she headed back towards the West End, the fear began again; she tried to ignore it, but it would not go away.

Ever since Martin had begun flying night raids over Germany, she had shared his terror. She wondered if she should write to him, telling him she understood and sympathized – but she wasn't sure if letters to an air-base might be opened and read by the censor, and she couldn't risk that.

Over Christmas, their leaves had not coincided, and she had not seen him for months. Occasionally he phoned home to reassure his mother that he was well, and everything was fine; Miranda had spoken to him once, but he said there were other chaps waiting to use the phone – and anyway, what could she possibly have said?

All she could do, when the fear began, was to concentrate on thoughts of love and comfort, and hope that he might receive them.

They were going back to the Ruhr tonight. The briefing had been concise and simple; the target was the oil refineries at Gelsenkirchen, on the Dortmund-Ems Canal. The squadron were due to take off at nineteen hundred hours.

In the Officers Mess, men clumped about in heavy flying boots, wearing thick rollneck sweaters under sheepskin jackets; they were smoking rather too fast, and making loud jokes.

Flight Lieutenant Gaunt made the silliest jokes, and laughed louder and longer than anyone. Suddenly he realized he had to go to the bog again; it was the third time in half an hour – he hoped nobody had noticed.

When he returned, the crew were being issued with ration packs, including cartons of orange juice.

Flying Officer Caldicott – their navigator – gave Martin a quizzical look, saying: "Go easy on the juice, Skip – you'll be busting for another pee before take-off!"

Martin retorted easily: "I need the vitamins, Caldy – got to keep my energy up."

"Save it for tomorrow night, old son! – Haven't you got a date with that little popsie from the Feathers?"

"Mind your own damn business," said Martin, with a cheery grin.

The daughter of the local butcher, Sue helped out as a part-time barmaid in the local. She was a bit scatty, but definitely easy on the eye.

As the crew were bussed out on to the tarmac, Martin concentrated on tomorrow night. Another twenty-four hours, and he'd have that gorgeous body in his arms. . . .

The ground crew had finished loading the bomb-bays; Martin and his team climbed aboard, and began the take-off procedure.

In the navigator's seat, Caldicott sorted out his maps; Saxby, the Flight Engineer, settled himself in the cockpit; beside him, Martin switched on his mike, making contact with each member of the crew:

"Test oxygen masks . . . Test helmet intercoms."

Their voices came back to him, one after another – Davidson from the rear-turret, ckecking his guns – Longhurst from the bomb-aimer's bay, stowing his parachute – Matthews the radio operator, at the W/T set.

Below them on the tarmac, the ground crew moved away to a safe distance. Their leader gave the thumbs-up sign, and Martin switched on the port outer engine, which roared into life, then each of the other engines. The chocks were pulled away, another thumbs-up when they were clear, and the huge plane rolled slowly forward on to the runway.

Martin felt his heart pounding, and concentrated on the image of Sue – first undressing, then naked, and kissing him, and curling her legs around him – he felt desperately excited;

175

tomorrow night seemed suddenly very near. . . . As long as he was still alive tomorrow night.

The plane gathered speed – the runway lights flashed past like the glittering whirl of a merry-go-round, and Martin felt the tail-assembly leave the ground.

He pulled back the stick: "Climbing power . . . Wheels up . . . Flaps up. . . ."

They were airborne. Fear and excitement combined in a climax that was almost sexual; Martin held his breath, afraid Saxby might hear him panting.

Caldicott's voice came over the intercom: "Five minutes to rendezvous point. Steer 051 magnetic."

He tried to think ahead to the next manoeuvre, when they would join the squadron in formation, but his head was full of Sue . . . of tomorrow night . . . of staying alive.

Inside the Stage Door at Drury Lane, another little group was preparing to leave the country.

The two men and six girls who comprised the "Starlight" concert party were checking their bags, suitcases and prop-baskets and tying on luggage-labels.

The oldest of the girls, who was the show's pianist, asked: "Where do you think we're going? I hope it's not West Africa – I've heard some very nasty things about West Africa."

"P'raps they'll send us to Gibraltar," said the youngest dancer hopefully. "My friend Valerie went to Gib with 'Swingtime Follies' – she said they had a lovely time."

Polly hurried along the corridor to round them up: "Have you all got your medical certificates? Best to make sure – no use getting there and being turned back because you can't show your pink form."

"Getting where?" asked the pianist. "Do you know where they're sending us?"

"Secret and confidential, that is," said Polly firmly. "All got your identity cards? Right, then – the motor coach is all ready."

Out in the street, they watched their baggage being stowed in the back of the charabanc.

176

"We can't be going to West Africa," said the tenor thoughtfully, as he climbed aboard: "I was told to bring two sets of winter underwear."

Polly had been wondering when this thought would occur to someone; she knew their destination was the Reykjavik Garrison Theatre, Iceland – but she was keeping that to herself.

"So long, boys and girls – and *bon voyage*! Thanks, driver – off you go."

The driver switched on the dim blue sidelights and started the engine. Polly gave a last wave and watched them until they turned the corner; she always felt sorry for them when they left England – under these conditions of secrecy, they were not allowed friends or families to see them off.

As she turned to go back into the theatre, a man in a black overcoat hurried out, nearly colliding with her.

"Starlight Company?" he barked.

"Just gone, Mr Birtwhistle," said Polly sweetly. "I'm afraid you've missed the bus."

The Security Officer was a pain in the neck, and she was delighted to be able to put him in his place.

He glared: "Is that meant to be funny?"

"No, honestly – the bus left about a minute ago. . . . What a shame."

"But I have to check their identity cards before they're allowed to leave!"

"Oh, that's OK – they all had their cards – I checked them for you."

She walked into the theatre, pursued by the furious Security Officer.

"It's my job to make the final check!" he shouted. "I am going straight to Mr Dean's office, and I shall leave a strongly-worded complaint on his desk – and don't walk away while I'm talking to you!"

"Sorry, can't stop!" Polly called back: "Haven't you heard? We're starting shows for the people sheltering in the tube stations tonight – I've got a date in the Underground, with George Formby!"

*   *   *

177

Miranda was doing nothing.

Her bike was parked in the street outside the Admiralty. When she reported back, she had been told to sit and wait for further instructions, and she had been sitting and waiting ever since.

On her way back from Tilbury, she had made three separate detours, by-passing roads closed by ARP wardens, or signs saying: *"Danger – Unexploded Bomb."* She longed to slip away to the canteen for a coffee and a currant bun, but she had been told to wait, and she dared not disobey an order.

When a Wren Chief Officer suddenly appeared, Miranda jumped up, saluting smartly.

"Stand easy," said the Officer. "Is my car outside?"

"I beg your pardon, ma'am?"

"Car – my car!" snapped the officer. "It was supposed to pick me up ten minutes ago – have you seen my driver?"

"No, ma'am. I've been waiting much longer than ten minutes; no drivers have gone through this way."

"Really." The officer raised an eyebrow. "I shall go and see what's happened."

She vanished into outer darkness, and an icy blast whistled round Miranda's ankles. Somewhere outside, she could hear heavy gunfire, and a series of little tinkling crashes.

Quite unruffled, the officer returned, saying: "Shrapnel coming down – and not a car in sight. Detained by the raid, I presume. I shall wait here."

Miranda offered her the bench: "Would you care to sit down, ma'am?"

"We shall both sit down," declared the officer. "Special circumstances. . . . Sit."

Awed, Miranda obeyed. The Officer subjected her to a close scrutiny, then said: "Your hair's too long. Almost down to your collar. Either have it cut, or knot it up in a bun."

"Yes, ma'am." Eyeing the crash-helmet on Miranda's lap, the officer asked: "How long have you been a dispatch rider?"

"Since I finished basic training, ma'am – last October."

"Did they teach you to drive a car as well?"

"Yes, ma'am. But I prefer bikes – you feel more independent."

"Really. What is your name?"

"Gaunt, ma'am. Miranda Gaunt."

"Any family connection with the Service?"

"Yes, ma'am – my brother Nicholas is First Lieutenant on board HMS *Sabina*."

"In that case, Gaunt, you should know by now – you are part of a team. Independence may be a good quality in civil life; it is not how naval battles are won."

"Except . . ." Miranda began, then stopped herself.

"Except — ?"

"I – I was thinking of Nelson, ma'am. . . ."

There was a pause, while Miranda wished the earth would open and swallow her up.

Then the officer remarked: "Quite right. I shall now go and look for my driver."

At that point the street door opened to admit a Leading Wren. Seeing the Officer, she threw up a salute and reported: "I've just come from St Thomas's Hospital, ma'am. Your driver was on her way here when a bomb fell behind Waterloo Station. The car was hit by flying debris and crashed into the side of a building. They took the driver into hospital immediately, but she was dead on arrival . . . I'm very sorry."

For some time the Chief Officer neither spoke nor moved; she seemed to have turned to ice. At last she said: "Thank you. I shall go and make some phone calls. You'd better order another car – and I shall need a replacement driver."

She brushed past Miranda without a glance, and went back to her office.

"Pyjamas lying side by side —
Ladies' nighties I have spied —
I've often seen what goes inside
. . . When I'm cleaning windows!"

A last shower of notes from the ukulele, as George Formby

179

brought his turn to a triumphant close, and the shelterers on the platform of Aldwych tube station broke into wild applause.

A temporary stage had been put up, just big enough to hold George, his accompanist, and a mini-piano. As he took his final bow and stepped down, the audience surrounded him, wanting to shake his hand. For a little while, he had brought a touch of magic to their dreary subterranean routine, and they hoped some of his magic might rub off on them.

Polly was afraid their enthusiasm would sweep him off the platform, but George's wife Beryl – never far from his side – had already taken charge. Kindly but firmly, she helped him slip through the crowd and make his escape.

They were all talking and laughing and humming snatches of his songs as they returned to their places; some would be sleeping along the platform, on mattresses and eiderdowns laid out in orderly rows – others along a side passage in two-tier wooden bunks.

They would all spend the night there, until the all-clear sounded at dawn, then pack up their shopping bags and attaché cases, and take themselves off home, to wash and shave, and snatch some breakfast, and face another day.

Polly caught up with Mr and Mrs Formby, thanking them again for giving ENSA's latest venture such a wonderful send-off.

"Are you coming back to Drury Lane? Because I know Mr Dean would like to see you before you go – so he can thank you personally."

When they reached the Lane, they found it was cordoned off. A Special Constable tried to stop them, but Polly explained that she worked in the theatre, and they had to get through. They were still arguing when Basil Dean appeared at the stage door, and hailed them.

"You must have given 'em plenty of encores tonight, George," he said, as they shook hands. "Thank God you did – if you'd finished half an hour earlier, we'd all be in hospital."

"Why? What's up?"

"I'd just gone down to the theatre wardrobe, and while I

was out of the office, a bomb fell over the road and blew my window in, frame and all – it sailed clean through the room, and smashed to bits across my desk . . . If we'd been there at the time – well, it doesn't bear thinking about."

"Oh, dear – has it done much damage?" asked Beryl.

"Plenty. The place is covered in broken glass and plaster dust – everything's in smithereens – the files and papers on my desk look like confetti."

Polly remembered Mr Birtwhistle and his "strongly-worded complaint" – and for a moment she felt almost grateful to the German Luftwaffe.

"I'll murder those bloody boffins at the Met Office one of these days," said Martin. "Why can't they do their homework?"

There had been no warning of fog, but as the bomber squadron flew east, the cloud had been closing in, and now visibility was practically nil.

Through the intercom, he received a crackly message from the Wing Commander in the leading plane: "Conditions hopeless. . . . Abort the mission and return to base. . . . Jettison your bomb-load over the sea, not – repeat not – over occupied territory."

"Of all the lousy luck . . ." grumbled Martin; but secretly he was overjoyed. They were not to enter enemy territory; they would live to fight another day.

"Heading for open sea, Skip – we're over the Friesian Islands now," reported Caldicott, through Martin's intercom.

Suddenly there was a brilliant flash directly ahead, almost blinding Martin; it was followed by another, off the port wing, and the whole plane shuddered.

His hands tightened on the controls: "Damn. . . . Ground defence sending up flak."

Then a third shell burst on the starboard side with a deafening bang, and the aircrat was hurled sideways – away from the rest of the formation. If they had been flung into the slipstream of the nearest plane, the collision could have been fatal.

"What the hell was that?" Saxby rubbed his head, which had hit the instrument panel.

"Bloody silly question," snapped Martin. "We copped one, fair and square."

He called up the crew one by one; each man replied – except Longhurst.

"I'll go and see what's wrong," said Caldicott, and left his position to scramble down to the bomb-bay.

A few moments later his voice came through again; this time he was using the bomb-aimer's mike.

"The shell's torn a hole in the fuselage a yard wide. He's spark out, and bleeding pretty badly – I think they're mostly superficial cuts from splintered perspex, but I can't be sure. I'll drop the bomb-load presently – but first I'm going to rip out the intercom – I can use the cord as a tourniquet for the poor sod. . . ."

Another loud crackle, and the intercom went dead.

A sub-zero wind was tearing through the aircraft from the broken observation windows. Trying to sound nonchalant, Martin said: "So that's where the perishing draught's coming from. . . . This is going to be fun."

"Better peel off and leave the formation." Saxby was being infuriatingly calm: "At least we'll have visibility once we get out of this lot."

Martin reported the situation to the Wingco; permission was granted, and moments later they were above the cloudbank, flying in bright moonlight across what looked like an arctic sea.

Although he could now see ahead, Martin was aware that any night fighters in the area could see him too – a solitary black dot against unbroken white . . . a sitting target.

On Saturday morning, Miranda reported for duty at the Admiralty garages in Albany Street, and was told that she was to be relieved of her duties as a dispatch-rider. She was being transferred to drive a staff car; someone high up in the Cipher Unit had put in a request for her, and she was to report to Chief Officer Pinnegar's office at 0800 hours on Monday week.

"Chauffeuring one of the Top Brass!" sniffed one of the other dispatch-riders. "Some people have all the luck."

"Not if she's the one I think she is," said Miranda – and gave a brief account of her meeting with the Wren officer, and the way she had reacted to the news of her driver's death.

"What a cow – must've got a swinging brick for a heart. . . ." The other girl changed her tune: "Sooner you than me."

On Saturday evening, Martin was waiting for Sue to finish work.

He had brought the plane back without much difficulty; there had been no further incidents. Thanks to Caldicott's improvised tourniquet, Flight Sergeant Longhurst had survived the journey, and a waiting ambulance had rushed him straight to hospital. After debriefing and a token breakfast, Martin fell into bed and slept through the day; by the evening, he was ready for a little recreation.

He sat in the saloon bar at the Feathers, with Caldicott and a couple of other chaps from the Mess, playing bar billiards and buying rounds of drinks. Throughout the evening, he kept his eye on Sue. The waiting was the worst part; he watched her reach up for clean glasses from the shelf above the bar, and the sight of her breasts lifting under her silk blouse was a delicious torment. . . .

When "last orders" were called, the customers began to disperse; then it was "Time, gents, if you please", and the lights went out one by one. Finally he escorted Sue off the premises.

She had everything organized. Her best friend Linda had gone away for the weekend, leaving Sue the key of her cottage; when she led the way into Linda's neat little parlour, the embers of a fire still glowed in the grate.

"Shall I put some more logs on? I'll make some tea, if you want," she offered.

He took her in his arms: "There's only one thing I want."

So they went up to the spare room, where a double bed awaited them, the sheets and blankets invitingly turned down.

"Come here," said Martin, and began to undress her.

She began to protest – she'd expected some kissing and cuddling first – why did he have to be so impatient? Removing her underclothes and lifting her on to the bed, he didn't bother to reply.

She watched him strip off his uniform, and asked: "You do love me, don't you, Martin?"

He wasn't listening – naked, he threw himself upon her.

Night after night he'd been imagining this moment, and yet – now it was here – something was different. . . .

In the cellar shelter at Eaton Square, Miranda was asleep and dreaming. She had been swimming in a lake – gliding through soft, warm water – but now, inexplicably, something was wrong. . . . She tried to move her arms and legs, but could not – she was paralyzed – she was dying – perhaps she was already dead —

In her camp bed, Alice woke to hear her crying out in her sleep: "I can't – *I can't* — !"

She went over to Miranda, putting her arms round her and whispering: "It's all right, darling – you're having a bad dream."

But when she awoke, Miranda could not remember it.

In Mavis's spare bedroom, Sue switched on the bedside light, and sighed.

"I'm sorry," said Martin. "I don't know what's wrong with me."

"It doesn't matter." She smiled unconvincingly: "I expect you're a bit tired, that's all."

Lying back, he said: "You must think I'm a bloody idiot."

"Of course I don't . . . but – you really do love me – don't you?" she added anxiously.

The following week, while the Minsters were having breakfast

184

in the kitchen, they heard the telephone ringing in the hall, and Miranda got up from the table, saying: "I'll get it."

"If it's the Palace, say I'll be there by nine," Alice called after her. She took a slice of toast, and said: "Oh, dear – is that all the butter that's left? I'd better just have marmalade."

"Go easy on it – that's going to be rationed next," Caro told her. "At the hospital, we're dishing out carrot jam instead; the patients are furious."

"It sounds disgusting," said Alice. "I must bring back some apple jelly from home next weekend."

When Miranda returned, she was smiling: "The post's come as well – you've got one from New York, Caro."

"From my wandering boy?" Her face lit up, and she tore open the airmail envelope. "Let's hope he's on his way back to London."

"Who was on the phone?" Alice wanted to know.

"It was Martin."

"Oh – what did he want? Is he all right?"

"Yes, fine – he sent you his love . . . But it's such ages since I saw him – he asked me to go up there for the weekend."

"Will you be able to get time off? Aren't you on duty?"

"No, I finish dispatch-riding on Friday, and I don't start chauffeuring till Monday, so it fits in very well. I'll go up by train; Marty's going to book me in to an hotel."

"Damn and blast . . . !"

Caro's sudden exclamation startled them all, and Polly asked: "What's wrong? Isn't Scott coming to London?"

"No, he is not. . . . You know he wanted me to go to the States and I said I couldn't? Well, now my dear husband has got himself some top secret job in Washington, and he's staying there indefinitely. . . . Right – if that's the way he feels, the hell with him. . . . What do I care?"

And Caro tore the airmail letter into tiny little pieces.

On Friday, when Miranda scrambled out of the train, Martin was on the platform, chilled to the bone.

"I've been waiting ages."

"Sorry – the train was terribly slow – *and* I had to stand in the corridor most of the way . . . but it's lovely to see you."

"I've missed you like hell," he said, and kissed her on the lips.

She pretended to scold him: "You've been drinking!"

"For medicinal purposes – I'm freezing. Come on, let's go; I warn you – the hotel's a bit ramshackle."

The Ring o' Bells was very old-fashioned, but Miranda rather liked it, though dinner was a disappointment; she had expected the traditional roast-and-two-veg, and was disconcerted to find that everything was "off" except spam fritters, tinned peas and chips. The second course was a choice of bread-and-butter pudding (with marge instead of butter, naturally) or mousetrap cheese and water-biscuits. When the meal was over, they returned to the lounge, which was occupied by a crowd of local farmers and a sprinkling of airmen from the nearby RAF station.

"So – what's been happening?" Miranda asked, making herself comfortable on a wooden settle by the fireplace.

Martin squeezed in beside her, with two glasses of something dark red and sticky, saying: "Cherry brandy – to take away the taste of the cheese . . . they've run out of scotch."

She sipped it: "Ugh – it's a bit sickly."

"Never mind. If we get sloshed, it might cheer us up."

"Is it really that bad, Marty?" She searched his face: "Tell me about it."

"We can't talk here. Let's go upstairs."

There was only one basket-chair in the bedroom, so Martin took that, while she sat on the bed.

He lit a cigarette, and said: "It's hard to know where to begin. . . . You don't know what it's like."

"I think I do – some of it. I've been getting – you know – feelings. . . . In the evenings, and during the night. It's been going on for months, hasn't it?"

He nodded.

"And you're frightened," she said gently.

"I – well, yes. . . . But the worst thing is, having to keep it to yourself – you daren't let anyone know."

Her heart went out to him. She got up and knelt beside him, saying: "I know it's awful – but it must be the same for all the others."

He held her tightly, like a drowning man clutching a lifebelt.

"Yes – they probably feel the same way – nobody wants to die, do they? But once the raid's over, they manage to throw it off, somehow. They get drunk – they pick up girls, and have a bit of fun, and get their nerve back, ready for the next time. . . . Only —"

He stopped, and she knew he was close to tears.

"Only what? Don't you ever want a bit of fun?" She rubbed her cheek against his. "Don't you want to go with girls sometimes?"

"Oh, yes, I want to!" His voice broke. "God, I want to so much, I feel as if I'm going to explode, but . . . when we – when we're in bed – I can't. . . . Why can't I do it, Mandy?"

Then she remembered the bad dream – the feeling of helplessness – and a voice that called out: "I can't – *I can't*. . . ."

She cradled him like a baby, rocking him in her arms, soothing him, and saying: "Perhaps . . . perhaps it's because you don't really love them."

He made a contemptuous sound, between a sob and a laugh: "Love? Who said anything about love? I ought to be able to do it. . . ." She felt his body go taut, and his voice changed: "Of course you're right – I don't love them . . . I love you, Mandy – nobody else. . . . It's you I want."

He began to kiss her hungrily, and his hands fumbled for her breasts.

"No, Martin – don't —"

Driven by some inner fury, he was pulling at her dress, muttering incoherently: "Now – I could do it now. . . . Help me, Mandy – I want you —"

She knew she must break free, before his obsessive passion dragged her down with him. Summoning all her strength, she hit him across the face, and his head jerked back; shocked, he loosened his hold, and she struggled to her feet.

187

"Don't – ever – do that again. . . ." she said.

He looked up at her, and she saw the madness and the lone-liness in his eyes. His face puckered, and he started to cry.

For a moment she did not move; then she stretched out her hand and began to stroke his hair – soft, blonde hair, so like her own.

"Don't cry, Marty," she whispered. "It's over now. . . . Please, darling – you mustn't cry. . . . It's all over."

Chapter Twelve

Monday, 20 January to Tuesday, 15 April 1941

The junior Wren officer put down the internal telephone and said: "All right, Gaunt – you can go in. She'll see you now."

Nerving herself up, Miranda tapped at the inner door.

"Come," said a voice from within.

Chief Officer Pinnegar was at her desk; as Miranda entered, stood to attention and saluted, she glanced up.

"Stand easy, Gaunt. I'm glad to see you have put up your hair, as I suggested."

"Yes, ma'am."

"I have some urgent papers here which must be dealt with. When that is done, you are to drive me to an address in Bucks. Here is a sketch-map which will show you the most efficient route; you'd better memorize it. . . . You may sit down."

She did as she was told. The office had no unnecessary decoration, and a minimum of furniture – a bookcase, two filing cabinets, a desk and two bentwood chairs. There were no pictures on the walls; CO Pinnegar had not added any personal touches.

Miranda studied the sketch-map, trying to familiarize herself with the various landmarks and changes of direction; the route was reasonably clear, and she wondered whether the map had been drawn by her predecessor in the job. It was an uncomfortable thought.

After a while she felt a spasm of cramp, and changed her position, pressing her foot hard on the floor.

"Please don't fidget," said the Chief Officer, without looking up.

Miranda gritted her teeth and tried to turn her mind to other things. She remembered her return journey to London, yesterday morning. Martin had not come to the station to see her off, since he had to report for early duty at the airfield. They had said their goodbyes on Saturday evening, after another cheerless dinner at the 'Ring o' Bells'. He did not suggest going up to her room, and when he was about to leave she lifted her face, expecting a kiss – but he only gripped her hand and turned away. Remembering the look in his eyes, she sighed.

"Try not to communicate your impatience," said the Chief Officer. "I have almost finished." A few moments later she closed the file she had been working on. "No doubt we shall become accustomed to each other's habits in time . . . I understand you left your previous post on Friday? Perhaps you were able to spend the weekend with your family?"

"Actually, ma'am – I went up to Lincolnshire, to see my brother."

"Really?" A lifted eyebrow. "I thought you told me he was on board HMS *Sabina?*"

"I'm sorry – I've got two brothers – Nicholas is in the Navy; my brother Martin is a pilot in the RAF."

"Ah." Chief Officer Pinnegar lost interest immediately and rose to her feet. "Very well, please fetch my car and wait for me at the front entrance." As Miranda jumped up to open the door for her, she added: "Have you heard from Nicholas recently?"

"No, ma'am – he's been at sea for months . . . but he should be due for some leave soon."

The Navy were engaged in convoying supplies from Alexandria to Crete and to Greece, and the Italian High Command had decided to ambush them on the way. A heavy task force, headed by their flagship, *Vittorio Veneto*, left Naples, intending to surprise the British battle fleet; but Admiral Cunningham had advance intelligence of this move, and an aircraft-carrier, three battleships, four cruisers and four destroyers were already steaming towards Cape Matapan to meet the enemy.

In the early evening of March 28th, planes from the aircraft-carrier *Formidable* attacked the *Veneto* and scored a direct hit; the flagship listed heavily, settling by the stern, and her engines had to be stopped.

Cunningham's fleet, still more than fifty miles away, raced ahead at full speed, eager to locate the stricken battleship, but by eight o'clock darkness had fallen and they had difficulty in sighting the enemy fleet.

At ten p.m. the battleship *Valiant* picked up the stationary vessel on her radar equipment, and twenty minutes later the accompanying destroyers picked out the line of ships on the starboard bow. Cunningham gave the signal and swung his fleet into line ahead, closing in on the Italians.

On *Sabina's* bridge, Nicholas passed along the Captain's orders to switch on searchlights. Not far away, on board *Valiant*, nineteen-year-old midshipman was in command of another searchlight battery; if Nick could have seen him, they might have recognized each other, for they had met briefly almost two years earlier, when Prince Philip came to meet the Royal Family at Dartmouth.

One after another, the support vessels turned the searchlight glare on to the enemy; one after another, the Italian cruisers, *Zara, Pola* and *Fiume* stood out – silvery-blue against the surrounding darkness. The British guns roared, and Nicholas could see shells whizzing through the air; five of them exploded below the *Fiume's* upper deck, and the ship burst into a sheet of flame. After this broadside, *Valiant* turned her guns on *Zara*, which was equally unprepared; Nick saw her blazing from stem to stern, until her boilers exploded.

Through the overwhelming thunder of the guns, he could hear the screams of injured men, and cries for help from those who had jumped overboard and were floundering in the water. By the light of the blazing vessels, he saw boats, rafts and swimmers bobbing about in the waves, and the British destroyers were ordered to stand by and pick up survivors.

191

On the nearest Italian ship – the cruiser *Maddelena* – there was no sign of life; drifting, completely out of control, she seemed to be a ghost ship.

Sabina's Captain gave Nick his orders: "I'm going alongside – prepare wires and fenders."

Nick needed no further bidding. Within minutes he had ordered a boarding-party, armed with cutlasses, to stand to and prepare to take *Maddelena* by force.

The approach was made; a heaving line spanned the narrowing gap between them, and the British crew jumped over the ship's rail and swept across the enemy decks, yelling threats and bloodcurdling oaths.

Nick had an absurd desire to laugh – he felt as if they were schoolboys, playing at pirates.

Exploring *Maddelena*, he found the ship deserted; locker doors hung open, sea-chests had been rifled, and empty Chianti bottles rolled around the deck.

Ten minutes earlier, there had been a thousand men aboard; now the ship was silent, apparently lifeless. Nick investigated further, making his way cautiously below decks. A half-eaten sandwich on a plate – a pair of boots thrown into a corner – reminded him of the *Marie Celeste*. Then he heard an uncertain tenor launch into a Neapolitan ditty; other voices tried to hush the singer. Nick squared his shoulders and pushed open a door into the fo'c'sle – and found a gang of frightened men staring at him in mute appeal. All the rest had jumped overboard, preferring to take their chances in the sea, rather than risk going down with the ship; of those who remained, many were hopelessly drunk, and they were all taken prisoner, putting up no resistance.

Within a few hours, the most sweeping naval victory since Trafalgar was over.

"Hello, Jenny? Can you hear me? This is a terrible line."

"It's a bit faint, but I can hear if you speak up."

Nick took a deep breath, and shouted: *"Has the baby arrived yet?"*

He was ringing from the Officers' Club at Gibraltar, and his question produced a sudden hush – then a roar of laughter and applause from the men crowded round the bar.

Nicholas turned crimson, as Jenny replied: "Not yet – I'm afraid he's overdue."

"Like my blasted leave," he muttered.

"What – ? I didn't quite catch —"

"I said *'Like my leave!'* . . . Anyway, this is a lucky break – perhaps I'll be home in time for the great day."

The baby should have arrived before the end of March, but by the first week in April, the youngest Gaunt still seemed reluctant to face the world.

When Nick arrived at Crown House, Jenny met him in the entrance hall, torn between tears and laughter: "Don't look at me – I feel like a baby elephant."

"You look more beautiful than ever," he told her.

It was true; her eyes were bright and sparkling, and her skin had a kind of bloom he had never seen before.

"But are you really all right – and the baby? What does the doctor say?"

"Everything's fine – there's nothing to worry about."

"You're absolutely sure? You know what an old fool Dr Parry is – shouldn't we get a second opinion?"

"I'm not going to Dr Parry now; Polly sent me to Dr Hilliard instead, and she's absolutely marvellous. She's certain there won't be any complications."

"Let's hope she's right . . . I've been going frantic, stuck out in the Med, wondering what was going on. Why didn't you tell me you'd changed doctors?"

"I did – I wrote about it ages ago."

"I never got that letter. The mail does go adrift sometimes, when things are a bit fraught."

"Have things been fraught – lately? You never said. . . ."

He shrugged: "Oh – it wasn't worth writing about."

Over the next day or two, the story came out gradually; he told her all he could remember about the battle of Matapan – or as much as he wanted her to know. It wasn't until Alice

193

came down from London with Polly on Friday evening that Jenny heard the sequel.

The family were sitting round the supper-table, when Alice asked Jenny: "Aren't you proud of your husband? Going on board an enemy ship and capturing the crew single-handed?"

"For goodness sake, Ma!" Nick protested: "I had twenty other chaps with me – and the Italians didn't even put up a struggle. . . . Anyway, who told you?"

"His Majesty called me in as soon as the news came through. . . . Do you mean to say you haven't told Jenny?" She turned to the rest of the family, and announced: "After the battle, Lieutenant Gaunt was mentioned in dispatches!"

They all exclaimed with surprise and delight; Lord Minster shook his son's hand, and Lady Beatrice screeched: "William – this calls for champagne! – You must have a few cases left?"

After that, it turned into a very jolly evening. When William had filled their glasses, Polly proposed a toast – "To our hero!" – but William amended it: "To Nicholas. . . ."

"To Nicholas . . ." repeated Alice. "Oh – I nearly forgot the most important part. When I said you were home on leave, their Majesties asked if you and Jenny would like to visit them at Windsor; nothing formal – just a private tea party."

Nicholas frowned: "That's very kind, but – when?"

"Next Tuesday. You'll still be here, won't you?"

"Well, yes, but I'm not sure if – I mean, in Jenny's condition. . . ."

"I don't see why we shouldn't," said Jenny. "As long as I take things easily."

"But all that travelling —"

"William broke in: "I think we might be able to solve that problem. Ken Stubbs has to go up to a regional conference at the Ministry of Agriculture on Wednesday; he's got to take a load of reports and confidential documents, so he's going to use some of our precious petrol coupons and drive up. . . . Which means he could give you both a lift."

"But if his meeting's on Wednesday —"

"He can go up on Tuesday – you can all stay at Eaton Square overnight, and come back on Wednesday evening.

Then Jenny won't have to do the journey twice in one day."

Nicholas was still not very happy about it – London had been raided every night for the past six months – would it be wise for Jenny to enter the danger zone?

"The blitz has cooled off a bit lately," Alice assured him: "And our cellars make a very good air raid shelter."

On Saturday morning, Jenny and Nick were taking a walk through the grounds when a sudden shower sent them hurrying for shelter in the farm office.

They found Ken Stubbs at his desk, talking to Polly. He stood up to shake hands with Nicholas, and congratulated him on his recent exploits – then added, slightly embarrassed: "I hope I'm not breaking any confidences?"

Nick looked very hard at Polly: "Some people just can't keep their traps shut . . . I suppose it'll be all round Drury Lane on Monday morning?"

"That's where you're wrong!" Polly tossed her head: "As it happens, I'm not going up till Tuesday – so there! . . . Well, with Alex home for Easter, I want to spend as much time down here as I can – and Ken's kindly offered me a lift in the car, so you'll have the pleasure of my company as well."

Nick turned to Jenny: "D'you think we'll survive it?"

"Oh, shut up – it's going to be fun!" Polly said firmly. "Listen, I've just had an idea – when you get back from your tea party at Windsor, why don't we all go out to supper – the four of us? There's a really swish restaurant I know – the Eden-Roc in Bond Street – so we can celebrate Nick's dispatches in style – whatever they are. . . . This will be on me – my treat!"

That night, as they were getting ready for bed, Nick said to Jenny: "Are you sure we're doing the right thing – going up to town? You don't think we ought to make our apologies and cry off?"

Their bedroom in the old stable block was rather cramped for space; he had to move aside so Jenny could squeeze past and get into bed.

"I wouldn't dream of it," she said. "Crown House is lovely, but I still miss the excitement of London sometimes."

"Well . . . just as long as it isn't *too* exciting. . . ."

"Anyway, Polly's planned her dinner party; we can't possibly disappoint her now."

Nick switched out the light and climbed in beside her: "That's another thing. Don't you think it was a bit strange – Polly inviting Ken to join the party? I thought he looked rather embarrassed."

"Nonsense – I expect it's a sort of thank-you to him, for helping to look after the children while she's away."

"I thought that was your job?"

"Oh, I do my bit, but they need a man around the place as well. Ken's very good with them; I watched them the other day, when he took them fishing on the lake, and I thought what a marvellous father he would have made."

"How about me? Will I make a marvellous father?"

"The very best." She found his hand and placed it on the curve of her abdomen. "Can you feel your son there – moving about?"

"I'm not sure – there's a little flutter. . . ."

"That's his heart beating."

"You're very sure it's going to be a boy."

"Oh, yes. And he's going to be strong and well. . . . It won't be long now."

Nick put his arms round his wife, holding her gently against him. For the first time, he was aware of the third person who lay between them, soon to be their firstborn child; and he felt a surge of joy and pride that meant far more than any battle honours.

Jenny had never been to Windsor Castle, and she was overawed by the size and splendour of the building; but once they were inside the royal apartments, she felt that she was visiting some old and dear friends. For Nicholas, it was like a second homecoming.

The King came to meet them, congratulating Nicholas on his exploits.

"I want to hear all about it," he said enthusiastically. "After tea, you must tell me all the things that never g-g-get written up in the official records."

The Queen steered Jenny firmly towards the sofa: "Between ourselves, my dear, the daily bulletins are quite enough for me; I'd rather hear about your baby. Lady Minster tells me he's being a little bashful?"

"Yes, Ma'am – I'm afraid so. But my doctor thinks he might decide to make a move quite soon —"

Seeing her expression change, the Queen asked: "Are you sure he isn't moving already?"

"I don't think so – I get these niggles occasionally, but they never come to anything. It's probably indigestion."

"Sometimes it's hard to tell the difference. Perhaps you're hungry – shall we have tea early?" She turned to her husband, already deep in conversation with Nicholas, and said: "I don't know about anyone else, but I'm dying for a cup of tea. The girls are in the playroom – why don't we go and join the party?"

The King led the way along a shadowy corridor. There were several blank patches on the walls, showing where paintings had been removed and put into store; in their place, Jenny noticed some more homely pictures – coloured prints of Mother Goose and Simple Simon.

"Portraits of my ancestors," said the King, as they strolled past.

"We let the girls put them up – well, we had to brighten the place up somehow," the Queen explained.

She opened a door, and they found themselves in a light, airy room, with cozy chintzes on the armchairs, and the walls covered in pictures and shelves of books – old favourites, brought down from London.

At a round table, the Princesses were playing "Racing Demon" with a tall, fair young man in midshipman's uniform. He stood up as the visitors entered, and Margaret burst out: "You can't stop now – it's my turn next!"

Her mother hushed her: "Put the cards away, darling – we're going to have tea. . . . Philip – I don't think you know our friends, Jenny and Nicholas Gaunt?"

197

They shook hands, and Prince Philip said to Nick: "I've met you before, sir, a couple of years ago – at the Naval College."

"Of course," said Nick. "I remember you very well."

"You may not realize it, but you two have something in common," the King informed them. "You were both at Matapan – and you were both mentioned in dispatches."

"It's an awful lot of nonsense, really," said the young officer apologetically.

"Absolutely," agreed Nick, and they both laughed.

"I don't think it's nonsense at all," said Princess Elizabeth. She looked up at Prince Philip: "It's nothing to laugh about – you might have been killed."

Then the door opened again, and the tea trolley was wheeled in; the girls cleared the table, and conversation became general.

Some time later, the guests returned to the drawing-room for a glass of sherry before their journey back to London. Once again, the King monopolized Nick, and they stood by the huge fireplace, reminiscing about some of the things that happened during Nick's time as a royal equerry, while the Queen entertained Philip and Jenny.

During a lull in the conversation, Philip said awkwardly: "Excuse me, Ma'am – could I ask you a question?"

A little surprised, Her Majesty said: "Of course – what is it?"

"Well – after tea, Elizabeth and I were talking. . . . She's a fine girl, isn't she? Very intelligent – and so interested in everything."

The Queen smiled: "Her father and I think so – I'm glad you agree."

"Yes. . . . Well, the thing is – when we said goodbye just now, she asked: 'Would it be all right if I wrote to you sometimes, while you're away at sea? She thought I might like to have news from home, every now and then – so of course I said yes . . . But afterwards I thought – well, perhaps I should have asked you first — ?"

"I take it you will reply to her letters – every now

and then?" asked Her Majesty, showing the hint of a dimple.

"Well, yes, actually – she seems rather keen on the idea; a sort of – cousinly correspondence, so to speak. . . . Providing you and His Majesty don't have any objection?"

"I think it's a very good idea. Thank you for telling me."

The nineteen-year-old midshipman leaped to his feet, saying: "I'll just go and have a word – will you excuse me, Ma'am?"

The Queen and Jenny exchanged glances as he raced off.

"A charming boy," said Her Majesty. "I'm so glad he and Lillibet have become friends."

Polly had suggested that Ken might come to Drury Lane and collect her at the end of the afternoon – ("It will save time if I don't have to struggle home on the tube") – and at five o'clock he made his way to ENSA's headquarters.

When Ken had produced his credentials, the stage doorkeeper gave him a series of complicated directions to Miss Harvey's office.

He got lost in the maze of dressing-rooms and rehearsal-rooms, and had to knock on a half-open door for assistance. A young lady in tights, some wisps of net, and a few strategic spangles kindly redirected him, and he continued on his quest, feeling even more nervous.

He climbed to the third floor, and was wondering which way to go next, when he heard Polly's voice – she was speaking with a brisk authority which took him by surprise, and he hovered in the doorway until she had finished her phonecall.

"Is that Greenock? This is Polly Harvey, at the Lane – what's your problem? . . . Yes, the 'Piccadilly Revels' are already on their way; they should reach you tomorrow with any luck, but it's a very old van. . . . Dartboards? No, I didn't forget the dartboards – we packed them in at the back, under the spare wheel. . . . Not at all – glad to be able to help . . . Ta-ta for now!"

When she rang off, Ken tapped on the door and looked in.

"Ken—! Oh, I'm so glad to see you – I've been on the phone

all day, and I think my ear's going to drop off. . . . Have you come to take me away from all this?"

"Well – yes – if you're ready. Sorry if I'm late; it took me a while to find you."

"I'm not surprised – this office is a complete madhouse." She snatched her coat from a hatstand and threw it round her shoulders: "Let's get out of here before that phone rings again, and somebody asks me for a replacement tap-dancer at Catterick!"

They went downstairs and crossed the back of the stage; from the other side of a painted cloth they could hear animated voices, and suddenly a girl emitted a piercing scream, which was followed by the thud of a falling body.

Ken stopped dead in his tracks and looked at Polly, who explained: "They're trying to find a girl to go on tour in an Agatha Christie. . . . She's being auditioned."

"I don't know what that means . . ." Ken scratched his head: "But it sounds painful."

Polly laughed, and opened the pass-door, saying: "Here, this is the quickest way out."

They crept up a side-aisle, through the auditorium, which was shrouded in tarpaulins and scaffolding.

When they emerged into the street, Ken asked: "What's going on there? Rebuilding the place, are they?"

"No, just shoring it up. We had a five-hundred-pounder through the roof – it went straight through the gallery, both circles, and finished up in the back of the stalls."

Ken was horrified: "You never told me the theatre had been bombed?"

"Well, we've only had one direct hit; the rest were just incendiaries. Apart from that – and having the windows blown in every now and again – we've been pretty lucky." She looked around: "Where did you park the car? This is what I call luxury – getting a lift home."

It was the first time Ken had visited Eaton Square, and he felt a little apprehensive – but he needn't have worried; the chaotic family atmosphere in the kitchen was reassuringly familiar.

Polly burst in, saying to Jenny: "I've got to have a bath and make myself look gorgeous – bags first go at the hot water . . . I've been toiling through a lot of dusty old card indexes, and you look gorgeous enough already."

"I don't feel very gorgeous," Jenny told her. "I've been getting little niggles from the son-and-heir all day – I think he's looking forward to a night on the town. He must have caught it from you, Polly – including your talent for tap-dancing!" She turned to greet her husband as he came downstairs: "Do you fancy a cup of tea, Nick? Caro's making a fresh pot. . . ." Then she saw the look on his face, and the telegram in his hand: "What's happened?"

"There's been a change of plan – new sailing orders. I have to rejoin the ship."

"But this is your leave – they can't do that —"

"It's an emergency. I've got to report to Alexandria tomorrow."

"*Tomorrow?* —"

"There's a special flight leaving tonight, from Northolt. . . . Jenny – I don't know what to say – I wouldn't have had this happen for worlds."

"Bang goes your night out," said Caro.

"The hell with that – I wanted to stay here till the baby arrives."

Jenny hugged him: "I know . . . but the Navy has first call on you." She tried to make light of it: "We know our place – women and children last!"

"Well . . . I'd better go up and pack."

Ken spoke for the first time: "What about all your other luggage – at Crown House?"

"Oh, hello, Ken – I didn't see you there – sorry about all this. Could you have the rest of my gear sent on after me?" He turned to Jenny: "There's a staff car on its way to pick me up and take me out to Northolt. . . . Of all the bloody rotten luck. . . ."

He left the kitchen abruptly.

After a moment, Polly said: "I suppose we can still go and have dinner? I mean, it's no good us sitting here, brooding about it. Caro, why don't you come as well, to make up the foursome?"

"No, thanks – I've been on duty all day, and I'm dead beat," said Caro.

Jenny said: "I think I'll give it a miss as well – do you mind if I cry off, Polly? I've been feeling a bit uncomfortable anyway; I'd rather stay in and have an early night. . . . Couldn't we postpone it until Nick gets his next leave?"

"Good idea," said Ken. "We can have supper here instead, can't we? – We don't want to go gallivanting —"

"You speak for yourself!" said Polly indignantly. "Honestly, what a mouldy lot – I've booked the table, and I'm not going to waste it – Jenny and Caro can do what they like, but you're coming with me, Ken Stubbs, and that's that!"

Nick rejoined them ten minutes later, carrying his suitcase, with his coat slung over his shoulder. When Jenny explained that she was going to stay at home after all, he looked very relieved.

"You'll be safe enough in the shelter," he said, "and you'll have Caro and Miss Kendall to keep you company."

"And me and Ken, when we get back," Polly pointed out.

"Of course – so you'll be very well cared for." He kissed Jenny, who was about to go up to see him off. "No, don't do that; I hate doorstep goodbyes – they're as bad as railway stations. You stay here and have a good night's rest . . . and – good luck. . . . Let me know as soon as the baby arrives – send me a cable."

"You know I will."

The others made themselves useful in the scullery, while Jenny and Nicholas clung to one another in a last embrace – and then Miss Kendall came down to say that a car had arrived for Lieutenant Gaunt.

"That's that, then," he said. "Goodbye, my love – God bless."

He went upstairs very quickly; after a few seconds, Jenny heard the front door slam.

"I think perhaps I'll have a lie down before supper," she said carefully. "Miss Kendall – could you take me to the cellar and show me which is my bed?"

*   *   *

When Polly met Ken in the hall, he was quite taken aback. She was wearing a flamboyant evening-dress of black lamé, shot with purple, which glittered with every move she made. He was wearing his best three-piece suit, in sober clerical grey, and she said at once: "I've gone too far, haven't I? I know it's a bit much, but I don't often get the chance to glam up these days . . . Alex loves this dress – he says I look like a giant blackcurrant pastille."

"No, you look magnificent – but I should have hired a dinner-jacket."

"Rubbish! – Nobody bothers about that nowadays. I'm the one who's overdressed, but who cares? This is our night out, and I'm going to enjoy it even if it kills me!" When the sirens wailed, she added: "Oops – only joking."

Ken looked even more unhappy: "Are you sure you want to go out while there's a raid on?"

"Of course I do – we can't let Hitler ruin all our fun, can we? People just carry on regardless. . . . Though I'm glad you've got the car; taxis are a bit few and far between during an alert."

Ken was surprised to find that she was right; in the streets, life seemed to go on as usual, and they reached Bond Street without any trouble. Heavily disguised behind sandbags and camouflage netting, the entrance to the Eden-Roc was almost invisible, but once they went through the blackout doors, they stepped into a kind of dream.

Under some imitation palm trees, a three-piece band – piano, bass and drums – played the latest hits; a dapper headwaiter ushered them to their table. Around the miniature dance floor, white napery gleamed on pink tablecloths; above, a circle of chandeliers threw a rainbow glitter over the scene.

"I didn't know there were still places like this," said Ken, as they sat down. "What does the name mean – Eden-Roc?"

"I think it's somewhere in the South of France, but I wouldn't know – Brighton rock's more my line. . . . Now then – what are we going to eat?"

When they opened the menus, Ken had another shock: "It's

not right, you paying for all this – look, let me do it —"
he began.

"Will you shut up? I'm a working girl now – I can spend
my own money, can't I? Right, then – put a sock in it and tell
the waiter what you fancy."

"Well – I see they've got steaks – I wouldn't mind steak
and chips."

"Actually, they're Vienna steaks – what you and me would
call rissoles, only tarted up a bit." Polly beckoned the wine
waiter: "We'll have a bottle of the Burgundy, please."

He bowed and withdrew, and she continued: "Cheer up, Ken
– you've had a face like a wet week ever since we left the office
– what's the matter with you?"

"Nothing. It's just – I wish I'd known about the bombs on
Drury Lane – it gave me quite a shock. . . . You should've
told me."

"What good would that have done? You'd only have lectured
me about packing it in and coming back to Crown House. Up in
town, I feel I'm doing a useful job."

"Sending out concert parties and dartboards — ?"

"What's wrong with that? The boys need cheering up –
they're the ones who are fighting this war."

"Some of us try to do our bit at home," he growled, then
broke off as the waiter poured some red wine into his glass.

"He wants you to taste it," Polly prompted him.

"Oh – I don't know much about wine, but. . . ." He sipped
it: "Yes – very nice – thank you."

The waiter filled their glasses and vanished again, as
Ken continued: "All I know is, I'd like you to be somewhere safe."

"I *am* safe. I've been in town ever since the Blitz started,
and look at me – not a scratch! What I say is, if a bomb's got
your name on, it'll get you wherever you are."

After that, the conversation languished, until the band began
another selection of familiar tunes, and Ken suggested: "D'you
feel like a turn on the floor before supper? I warn you, I'm not
much good at this – Marion always said I'd got two left feet
– but I'm willing to have a go."

"Will you stop running yourself down? . . . And who's Marion, when she's at home?"

"My wife."

"Oh, yes – I'm sorry – sometimes I forget you're still married."

"So did she – that was the trouble. . . . Well, what do you say? Do you want to dance?"

She hesitated, then answered: "It's a nice idea, but – I'm a bit tired, actually. I think I'll give it a miss at the moment, if you don't mind."

"I see. . . . Oh, well – it was just a thought."

To lighten the mood, she commented: "Pretty tune, though—" and began to sing softly, along with the band:

"There were angels dining at the Ritz,
And a nightingale sang in Berkeley Square . . ."

Then there was a deafening explosion, and she clutched at him for support – the dance floor seemed to rise and fall like an ocean wave – the lustres on the chandeliers tinkled like wind-chimes, and a nervous woman gave a stifled scream.

"Bloody hell!" exclaimed Ken, adding lamely: "Beg your pardon . . ."

Polly managed a shaky laugh: "That's the first time I ever heard you swear. . . . Anyway, we seem to be all right – just another near miss."

But most of the diners were on their feet, and the dance band had stopped playing; the head waiter suggested that the ladies and gentlemen might care to go into the basement shelter until things quietened down.

Ken grabbed Polly's arm: "I'm taking you downstairs."

There was no panic, and they all filed out in an orderly manner; just in front of them, the nervous woman was saying to her escort:

"I'm sorry, Reggie – I lost my head for a moment . . . I couldn't help remembering the Café de Paris, last month."

Ken asked Jenny: "What did she mean? What's the Café de Paris?"

"Oh – another restaurant – well, more of a nightclub, really. . . . They got a direct hit – thirty-four people were killed."

He turned and stared at her.

"You *knew* about that? And you invited Jenny here tonight? . . . I'll never understand you, as long as I live."

Jenny and Caro were making up their beds in the cellar. Alice, not on Palace duty this week, was at Crown House, and Miranda was away for a few days too; Chief Officer Pinnegar had to make a tour of inspection in the West Country, visiting several WRNS training establishments, and Miranda was driving her.

"So it's just you and me this evening," said Jenny.

"You and me *and* Miss Kendall," said Caro, with a long-suffering look.

Jenny smiled: "Oh, she's not that bad!"

"Wait till you've spent a night with her – she snores. . . ."

A series of explosions made them both jump, and Jenny asked nervously: "Is that just anti-aircraft guns? They sound awfully close."

"I'm not sure." Caro was evasive: "Anyhow, we'll be perfectly safe down here. We had steel girders put in to reinforce the ceiling."

They heard footsteps on the stairs, and Miss Kendall appeared in the doorway, looking very flustered and saying: "It's getting awfully loud, isn't it? I'll just fetch my knitting, then I'll come down and join you – if that's all right?"

"Of course," said Caro, adding as soon as she was out of earshot: "That wretched knitting . . . she calls it her war work – khaki socks for Our Brave Boys, made of horrible scratchy wool. Our boys will have to be very brave to wear them."

She looked up as Jenny gasped and sat down suddenly on her bed: "What's the matter – are you feeling faint?"

"No – I've been getting these pains rather a lot today." Jenny tried to ease herself into a comfortable position: "They seem to be coming quite often now."

"How often?" Caro asked sharply. "When was the last one?"

"I'm not sure – about twenty minutes ago, I think." Jenny turned to Caro, frightened and excited at the same time: "You don't suppose — ?"

"If they're coming at twenty-minute intervals I'd say we ought to get you into hospital, my girl. Let's time the next one, to make sure."

"And then what? Ring for an ambulance?"

Caro shook her head: "Not much hope of that; they'll all be out on casualty work, I expect – but we might pick up a taxi if we're lucky. I wonder what time Ken and Polly will get home; perhaps he could take you in the car."

Miss Kendall hurried downstairs again, carrying her knitting-bag, a bundle of shapeless khaki socks, some brown paper, and a ball of twine.

"I thought I might as well start making up a parcel to take round to the Women's Institute tomorrow. . . . Oh, dear – is something wrong?"

"Mrs Gaunt's getting some pains; I think perhaps I ought to get her into hospital."

"Oh, dear – in the middle of an air raid too. . . . How ever will you get there? It won't be safe to walk – there's a lot of shrapnel coming down outside. At least, I suppose it's shrapnel – it's a sort of pop-pop-pop noise, like peas being dropped on a tin plate."

Caro frowned: "That's not shrapnel, that's incendiaries; they drop them in clusters – dozens at a time. Let's hope the fire-watchers get them cleared up before we have to go out . . . *if* we have to – it could be just a false alarm, Jenny."

"Perhaps. . . . But I hope the baby comes soon – I've been waiting such a long time." She lay back on her camp-bed, smiling dreamily. "If he arrives tonight, I can send a cable to Alexandria, and it will be waiting for Nick when he gets there."

They tried to talk about other things, and Miss Kendall began to make up a brown-paper parcel, asking for help when it came to tying the string.

"Could you put your finger on the knot while I pull it tight?" she asked Caro.

Then there was a very loud bang, quite unlike the earlier explosions. This time the house rocked, and the ceiling-light swung on its flex.

"I wish they wouldn't do that," said Jenny.

"That wasn't a bomb," said Caro. "It sounded as if something had fallen down, upstairs. I've never known the house to shake like that before."

"Should I go up and see?" asked Miss Kendall, doubtfully.

"Perhaps you'd better —" Caro began, when Jenny interrupted her, making a sound that mingled pain and satisfaction.

"Was that another one?" asked Miss Kendall, and Jenny nodded speechlessly.

Caro checked her watch: "Nineteen minutes – that settles it – hospital, here we come," she said. "I'll try to ring for a taxi – you get your coat on."

She went up the cellar stairs and opened the door at the top. They heard her call out – a short, wordless cry – and when Miss Kendall looked up the darkened staircase, she saw her silhouetted against a blaze of light . . . Caro took a step forward, and then there was nothing but the fierce orange glow, and a loud roaring and crackling.

"What's that noise?" Jenny struggled to sit up: "What's happened?"

"I – I don't know." Miss Kendall was trembling: "Don't move – stay where you are."

"But where's Caro? Is she all right?"

Before the housekeeper could reply, Caro came down the stairs. When she rejoined them, her face was quite expressionless.

"The house . . . It's on fire, isn't it?" whispered Miss Kendall.

Caro nodded: "That noise we heard was a wall caving in. Some of those fire-bombs must have landed on the roof – the whole place is alight. I went in to see if I could put the flames out, but it's hopeless."

"How are we going to get out?" Jenny asked.

"Through the kitchen – the area steps —" Miss Kendall grabbed her coat: "Quickly — !"

Caro stopped her: "The kitchen's blazing; we can't get out that way. We shall have to stay down here."

Miss Kendall began to whimper: "We shall be burned alive. . . ."

"Of course we shan't. Heat rises, doesn't it? – the fire will go upwards. We shall be safe here; it's just a question of sitting it out until – until the Fire Service come and deal with it." She wasn't sure she believed her own confident assertion, but the others seemed to be a little reassured. "After all," she continued: "we've got an electric kettle down here, and emergency rations, and a first-aid box —"

As she spoke, she wondered what use a first-aid box would be if Jenny went into labour – and Jenny must have read her thoughts.

"What about the baby?" she asked.

"The baby – oh, this is dreadful. . . ." Miss Kendall's hands were shaking: "Whatever shall we do?"

"Well, I fancy a cup of tea myself," said Caro. "Would you like to make some?"

As the housekeeper scurried off to fill the kettle, Jenny asked: "I'll be all right, won't I?" Then she answered her own question: "Of course I will – you're a qualified nurse – you know what to do."

"That's right," said Caro.

Her thoughts raced. She had never taken a midwifery course; the nearest she had come to an actual childbirth was when she started as a probationer, helping out on the maternity wards, and listening to the old hands swapping stories in the staff room. She racked her brains for useful scraps of information. . . . Whatever happened, Jenny mustn't know that she was totally unqualified.

"There's nothing to it," she said. "It's just a question of passing the time and waiting for nature to take its course."

She tried to remember what was in the first-aid box. There was a pair of scissors – she could sterilize them in the boiling water from the kettle – you had to cut the umbilical cord, didn't you? The important thing was to tie off the end afterwards – she had a hazy idea that the mother might bleed to death if the cord wasn't fastened tightly. And she could use pieces of lint to clean up the baby's nostrils and mouth, to make sure it could breathe properly. . . .

"Nothing to it," she repeated.

As soon as the kettle boiled, they drank cups of tea. Jenny seemed quite serene; as if she were detached from the goings-on around her – intent upon the only thing that mattered. When the contractions became more frequent, she actually smiled, confidently awaiting the next stage of labour.

Then the lights went out.

The darkness was absolute, seeming to bear down upon them like a physical weight, and Miss Kendall squeaked with alarm.

"Damn – the mains cable must have gone," said Caro.

"What can we do?" asked Jenny.

"We're prepared for all emergencies," Caro told her. "There's a torch here somewhere."

She groped along the wall until she reached the food cupboard. There was a two-gallon jar of drinking-water – that would be useful later – a tin of biscuits, and – thank goodness – her fingers closed around the torch, and she switched it on.

"I don't know how long the battery will last. Didn't we put some candles in here somewhere? And matches?" When she found them, she lit one of the candles, and the little flame cast a soft glow over the whitewashed walls.

"Lucky there are no draughts down here," she said. "It'll take longer to burn."

"That's because there's no ventilation," said Miss Kendall. "You don't think we'll suffocate, do you? It's getting ever so warm."

Caro had already noticed this, but she replied casually: "It will be perfect for the baby – a nice warm atmosphere. . . . How are you feeling, Jenny?"

"Fine. . . . What time is it?"

"Half-past two. A few more hours, and it will all be over."

By seven o'clock Jenny's contractions were almost continuous, with brief periods of respite in between. In those moments she felt quite drowsy, for the muscular spasms were hard work. Caro remembered seeing one of the nurses in the maternity ward rubbing a mother's back, and tried to do the same for Jenny, but she picked the wrong place, and Jenny had to direct her to the right spot.

Soon after that, the waters broke, taking them all by surprise and soaking Jenny's bed.

Caro pretended she had been expecting it, saying: "That's no problem – we've got spare beds made up already."

With Caro and Miss Kendall helping her, Jenny shuffled across the cellar to lie on Caro's bed.

"I think I'd like another cup of tea," she said. "My mouth's so dry."

"Oh, dear – I can't boil the kettle, with no electricity," the housekeeper reminded her.

"Is there any tea left in the pot? I don't mind if it's cold."

By now she had reached the second stage of labour, and Caro urged her to push as each contraction reached its peak. When she saw the baby was about to emerge, she told Miss Kendall to bring the candle a little closer.

By the light of the yellow flame they watched, almost hypnotized, as the little head began to appear. The raid, the fire-bombs and their situation were temporarily forgotten – carried away by the wonder and excitement of the moment, Jenny did not feel any pain, only a kind of exultation she had never known before.

Caro prayed that the baby might be in a normal position, with no complications – and the next moment, as if in answer to her prayer, the head emerged. Jenny's cervix tore slightly, although she was not aware of it; at the next push, the shoulders came free, and Caro put out her hands to receive the baby.

As she took the tiny body in her hands, a dim memory returned to her, and she gave the baby a slap; he took his first breath, and uttered his first cry. Miraculously, his skin colour changed from purplish and chalky-white to a deep rose-red.

"It's a boy," said Miss Kendall, awestruck.

"Of course he is," said Caro.

"My son," said Jenny.

It was almost eight o'clock when Ken and Polly came home;
the roads into Eaton Square were barricaded, and they had to
leave the car in Elizabeth Street, walking the rest of the way.

As they approached the house, they saw the fire-engine
outside, its hoses snaking across the road, and puddles of
water everywhere – but the building was a blackened shell,
with charred timbers still smoking in the chilly morning air.

Polly began to run, and Ken had to grab her, holding her
back as she tried to climb over the rubble.

"I must find them!" she shouted. "They'll be in the cellar
– Caro and Miss Kendall – and Jenny. . . . Oh, God –
Jenny — !"

One of the firemen wiped his face and said: "The cellar
wasn't touched, miss. It's just a question of clearing the debris
away. . . . If there's anyone down there, we'll find them – three
people, did you say?"

There were not three people, but four.

Caro finished swabbing the baby's eyes, nose and mouth;
he needed washing, but they had no warm water, so that would
have to wait. Carefully, she placed him in his mother's arms.

Jenny lay back against the pillows, gazing ecstatically at her
son. Miss Kendall had unpacked her parcel of knitting, and she
handed some pieces of twine to Caro, who tied the cord in four
places. She was very scared, but she knew this had to be done
as soon as possible; holding her breath, she used the first-aid
scissors to make the cut.

"There . . ." she said – and waited, fearfully.

There was no bleeding. It was all right.

"You've done it," said Miss Kendall.

"Jenny's done it," said Caro.

Jenny said nothing; smiling down at her son, she could not
see or hear anything else.

212

Chapter Thirteen

Friday, 18 April to Sunday, 22 June 1941

Carrying two heavy cases, and a briefcase tucked under her arm, Miranda was very glad when she walked into the office at the Admiralty, and was able to put them down.

The tour of the West Country had taken nearly a week – longer than Chief Officer Pinnegar had anticipated. Wherever they went, the Chief had been provided with first-class accommodation, while Miranda had slept in barracks; they had scarcely spoken to each other, for even in the car the Chief was usually "doing her homework," as she called it. They exchanged very little conversation, and Miranda had not learned much more about her superior officer during these six days.

She stacked the luggage neatly, and asked: "Will there be anything further, ma'am?"

"No, thank you, Gaunt – you may go." The Chief sat down and began to go through her in-tray. "It is Friday today, so I shall see you here at eight o'clock on Monday. I hope you have a pleasant weekend."

"Thank you, ma'am."

As Miranda turned to go, the Chief called her back: "Wait – there is a message here for you."

"For me, ma'am?" Miranda was bewildered.

"Normally it is not permitted for your family to reach you through this office – I can only suppose these must be exceptional circumstances." Chief Officer Pinnegar read aloud: *"Message received Wednesday, April 16th., at fourteen hundred hours: to Wren Gaunt, M. from her sister Mrs Caroline Hanson. Please ensure that the above-named Wren is informed as soon as possible. Upon her return, Wren Gaunt is to proceed to her sister's flat at 17A Markwick Terrace, Chelsea. She is not – repeat not – to go home to the family house in Eaton Square under any circumstances."*

Miranda frowned: "It doesn't make sense – surely I can go by way of Eaton Square and drop my suitcase in, before I —"

"It seems that is precisely what you must *not* do. I suggest you carry out these instructions; there must be some good reason for them."

Her expression changed slightly: "I hope this will not mean bad news. I shall be here for another two hours; if you are in difficulties, do not hesitate to call me."

"Yes, ma'am. . . . Thank you, ma'am."

Twenty minutes later, Caro opened the front door of the second-floor flat, in a quiet street off the Kings Road, saying: "Thank goodness you got my message. I didn't know how else to get hold of you."

"What's happened? Why have you moved back to your own flat?"

"I didn't have any choice." Caro offered her a chair: "You'd better sit down. . . . First of all, some good news – Jenny's baby has arrived."

"While I was away? – Oh, no! – she might have hung on a bit longer – now I've missed all the excitement."

"That's putting it mildly. He was born at a quarter to eight on Tuesday morning – six pounds, four ounces."

"Marvellous – I must see them. Which hospital are they in?"

"They're not in hospital. They're at Crown House."

"Why did they let her go home so soon?"

"Look, will you stop interrupting, and let me tell the story?" Caro was at the sideboard, busy with a bottle and glasses. "And have a drink – you'll probably need it."

"Brandy – ? But —"

"There were some bottles in the cellars at Eaton Square – I

214

rescued as much as I could, after the fire, and Ken helped me bring things round here. . . ."

So Miranda heard the news – the incendiaries that had almost gutted the house – the bombs in the West End, which had kept Polly and Ken in a deep underground shelter off Piccadilly until dawn – and, most important, the birth of Jenny's baby.

Caro concluded: "And the best news is that nobody was hurt. We're all alive and well – if a bit shaky."

"Thank God for that. . . . But – the house — ?"

"It will be a long time before anyone lives there again. I managed to salvage a few bits and pieces, but what the bombs didn't wipe out was pretty well finished off by the firemen's hoses. Part of the roof has gone; a couple of walls collapsed, and the top two floors fell in . . . That's why I couldn't let you go there – it would have been a terrible shock."

"Yes – I see. . . . Thank you."

"Did you leave anything valuable in your room? We weren't sure – but I couldn't get up to the second floor to check – there's hardly any staircase left."

"I didn't have anything much. . . ." Miranda took a sip of brandy, and her teeth chattered on the rim of the glass. "You're quite sure everyone's all right? How's Ma?"

"Still dazed, but bearing up; it was a stroke of luck she was off duty. For two pins, she and Pa would have come rushing up to town to inspect the damage, but I talked them out of it; it would have upset Ma dreadfully to see the house like that. . . . They've both been splendid – bloody but unbowed . . . Grandmama, I need hardly say, was unbowed and twice as bloody!"

Miranda smiled faintly: "Bloodier than usual?"

"Breathing fire and demanding vengeance. Her first reaction was to tell Pa he must whack the Government with a huge demand for compensation! She says it's not only the material damage, but the personal loss to her – family treasures, souvenirs of the past – all irreplaceable. . . . Which is a bit steep, considering she's hardly set foot in the place for donkey's years." Her eye fell on Miranda's suitcase: "Is that all the luggage you've got?"

215

"I was only away for five nights – I've got a few bits and pieces in my locker at the Admiralty – spare uniform, and so on. . . . Why?"

"I thought you might make this your address, for the time being; the spare room's quite reasonable – and frankly, it'll be nice to have someone here to talk to. . . . If you'd like to?"

Miranda hesitated: "Don't you think you ought to ask Scott? I mean, this is his flat too, and he might —"

"Turn up? No – he's still sulking in Washington. I wrote and told him I'd moved back, in case he felt like dropping me the odd postcard – but I didn't explain why I'd left Eaton Square."

"Oh, but he ought to be told —"

"No, thanks! That's all he needs – he'd be over on the next boat, to drag me off to the States by brute force . . . I'm not giving him the satisfaction of saying 'I told you so!'."

Miranda changed the subject: "Where's everyone else going?"

"Polly's moved in to the shelters at Drury Lane; several girls on the ENSA staff have been bombed out, so they're making do there until they find somewhere else. And Miss Kendall finally gave in her notice; she's gone to live with her married sister in Hereford, on a dairy farm. . . . She should feel quite at home there."

Miranda couldn't help laughing: "Oh – that's unkind!"

"Yes, it is, isn't it? Actually I nearly changed my mind about her when the baby was born; she didn't go to pieces, like I thought she would – of course she didn't know anything about obstetrics, any more than I do, but it helped somehow, just having her there."

"But you said you delivered the baby?"

"More by luck than judgment. Jenny still doesn't realize I'd never even seen a child being born – I did it all by guess and by God."

Later, during a supper of baked beans on toast, Miranda asked: "Now Ma's living at Crown House – I suppose she's given up her job at the Palace?"

"Not her! She didn't want to; and their Majesties said she

can stay at Windsor whenever she's on duty. I think Pa would like to keep her at home, but she says it's her war effort, so that's that."

They went on talking all the evening, and had some more brandy before they went to bed; in spite of the news about Eaton Square, Miranda was unexpectedly cheerful.

For weeks now, she had been very lonely; tonight she was able to gossip and share jokes with someone close to her – for the first time since her weekend with Martin, she did not feel isolated.

Before that, she had never really known what loneliness meant. Martin was always there – if not in person, he had been continually in her mind and in her heart – but since that night, everything had changed. She still loved him, but the special bond that linked them seemed to have broken – and for the first time in her life, she knew what it meant to be alone.

Caro's offer of friendship and hospitality had come as a lifeline, and she clung to it gratefully.

Next morning she rang one of the other Admiralty drivers – Wren Patricia Blair – to ask a favour.

"Patsy – if you're not too busy this afternoon, could you help me shift some of my gear back to Chelsea? We've been bombed out at home, and I'm going to stay with my sister for a while. Would you like to come to tea?"

Caro used her last precious egg to make a sponge sandwich, and it turned into quite a jolly tea party.

Patsy was a chubby blonde with curly hair and childishly wide blue eyes. Her fiancé was a Gunnery Officer on board HMS *Hood*, and she showed them a recent snapshot he had sent her – a grinning young man, holding up a huge teddy bear.

"Derek won it at a fairground, on the rifle-range – he's ever such a good shot. Of course he couldn't tell me where he was, but he says he'll bring it home for me, as a souvenir. It's ages since his last leave – I wish I could wangle an overseas posting; I might stand more chance of seeing him if I could go abroad."

"That's what I'd like," Miranda agreed. "But as long as I'm

classified as 'immobile', I haven't got a hope." She explained to Caro: "'Immobile' means living at home. 'Mobile' means they can send you anywhere they like."

"Well, you're not living at home now," Caro pointed out. "If you tell them the house is a wreck, they might reclassify you."

"That's an idea . . ." Miranda considered this: "I suppose it's worth trying."

Patsy giggled: "It's better than being stuck with the Chief Iceberg for the duration!"

"Oh, Pinnegar's not that bad," said Miranda. "It's just that she doesn't show her feelings."

"That's because she hasn't got any. She hasn't got any friends either – they say she lives on her own. I mean – can you imagine her having a family? She's really weird, that one. . . . The sooner you get another posting, the better."

When Miranda reported for duty on Monday morning, she told Chief Officer Pinnegar that she intended to ask the central administration department to reclassify her as "mobile" – and explained about the Eaton Square house.

Chief Pinnegar, correcting a memorandum, paused with her pen in mid-air: "I hope no one was hurt?"

"No, ma'am."

"Good. Houses are only bricks and mortar; it's the families who live in them that matter."

Something in her tone made Miranda ask: "I hope – your own family are well, ma'am?"

The officer put down her pen and looked at Miranda: "What makes you say that?"

"I beg your pardon, ma'am – it's only. . . . You often ask about *my* family, but – well, I was talking to one of the other girls from the Motor Pool, and we were wondering if you —"

Chief Officer Pinnegar cut in sharply: "I'd be grateful if you would refrain from discussing me with other people!" She paused for a moment, then continued more calmly: "To satisfy your curiosity – I was an only child. My father was a Naval Officer; he was killed in 1916, at the battle of Jutland. My

218

mother died six months later; I imagine she no longer wished to go on living . . . so I have no family."

Miranda managed to blurt out: "I'm very sorry, ma'am."

"You didn't mean any harm, I realize that. But you're an intelligent girl – you shouldn't waste your time chattering to the little nitwits in the Motor Pool. You had a very good education; why didn't you apply for a post where you could put your brain to some purpose?"

"I – I didn't know what else to do, ma'am."

"Perhaps you should think it over. In my opinion, the greatest sin of all is to waste your natural abilities. . . . Very well, Gaunt – you may dismiss."

"He's still very small, isn't he?" asked Harriet.

It was a splendid May morning, and Jenny had brought her baby son out onto the terrace to enjoy the sunshine. Polly, on Whitsun leave from ENSA, had just come back from the village shop with her children, and they were admiring their new cousin.

"When is he going to get bigger?" Harriet wanted to know. "I'd like him to start walking and running about, so he can play with us."

"Give him a chance!" said Polly. "He's only a few weeks old."

"Next Thursday, he'll be exactly one month," Jenny reminded her.

"Already? And when's the christening going to be?"

"Soon, I hope. I'm waiting to hear when Nick will get his next leave," Jenny replied.

"Have you decided on a name yet?"

"Well – I'll have to talk it over with Nick first – but I thought perhaps – Edward."

"*Edward — ?*" A harsh voice broke in: "What ever for?"

The interruption took them by surprise; Lord Minster had pushed his mother's wheelchair along the terrace, and Lady Beatrice was not going to be left out of the conversation.

219

"Edward. . . . A very strange choice," she sniffed. "We've never had an Edward in the family."

"A very good choice, in my opinion," said William. "It's an old and honourable name – eight Kings of England, no less!"

"As a matter of fact, it was my father's name," said Jenny. Mr Webster had left home to seek his fortune in Canada, soon after she was born, and had never been heard of again. "Of course I don't remember him – but I believe he was known as Ted."

Lady Beatrice was affronted: "By all accounts, the man was a ne'er-do-well – no, that wouldn't do at all . . . *Ted Gaunt* – it sounds like a jobbing gardener."

"What's wrong with that?" asked her son, who would have been very happy to be a jobbing gardener. "Ted – or Edward – I should be perfectly satisfied with either."

The old lady tossed her head: "In any case, I didn't come out to here to bandy names about – I have some news; a message just came through on my wireless. One of those Nazis has had the impertinence to fly across from Germany; he landed in Scotland, by parachute – a fellow called Hess."

"Rudolf Hess?" Jenny looked at William for corroboration. "Isn't he one of Hitler's top men?"

Lord Minster nodded: "Apparently it's true. He arrived a couple of nights ago, but they've only just released the news. He was captured by the Home Guard, and is now in custody."

"A great mistake," snorted Old Bea. "They should have shot him on sight; he's an enemy, isn't he?"

"It seems he was trying to propose some kind of peace plan to our Government, in an attempt to bring the war to an end," William explained.

"Nonsense! They say the Home Guard who arrested him was armed with a pitchfork – it's a pity he didn't polish him off there and then."

Polly glanced quickly at the children; Harriet had lost interest by now, and was trying to amuse the baby by making a daisy-chain, but Alex chimed in: "Wouldn't that be a good thing – to stop the war?"

Lady Beatrice looked scandalized: "This war will stop when we have won it and not before," she announced. "Britain will go on fighting to her last drop of blood."

"That's just silly," said Alex. "What's the good of people killing each other till there's nobody left?" Knitting her bony fingers together, his great-grandmother glared: "I blame you for this, William. . . . You've been filling the child's head with pacifist nonsense!"

"I don't believe Alex and I have ever discussed pacifism, Mama," he said mildly. "Though he certainly has a valid point – I should welcome an end to the war, before any more lives are lost." Deaf to his mother's scolding, he turned to greet Ken Stubbs as he walked up the gravel path: "Good morning, Ken – were you looking for me?"

Ken took off his tweed cap as he joined the ladies, saying: "No, sir, I was looking for Lady Ebony. She's kindly invited me to lunch with the children."

"Help!" exclaimed Polly. "Thank goodness you reminded me – there's a roast chicken in the oven, and it'll be done to a crisp. . . . Come on – let's go!"

Lady Beatrice scowled as Polly and the children set off with Ken along the path: "I don't know why Polly encourages that man – it will only put ideas in his head."

"Try not to be such a snob, Mama," said Lord Minster. "Ken's an excellent chap, and I'm sure he'd never get any 'ideas', as you call them."

As they approached the old stables, Alex and Harry raced on ahead; Polly gave Ken a sidelong glance and asked: "What's wrong?"

Staring straight ahead, he replied: "I heard at the Wardens' Post this morning – the raids on London last weekend were the heaviest yet."

"So what? I was down here, out of the way, wasn't I?"

"But you'll be going back there. Twice now, you've had a narrow escape – I just wish I could make you see —"

She laid her hand on his arm: "Ken . . . Please."

"I know. . . . Wasting my breath. But how do you expect me to feel? You up there, facing danger – and me down

221

here, safe and sound . . . I don't care what you say – it's not right."

A fortnight later, news came through from the North Atlantic that was both good and bad. In a naval action somewhere off Iceland, the new German battleship *Bismarck* had been sunk; but not before the British battle-cruiser *Hood* was blown to pieces.

Miranda was waiting in the staff car outside the Admiralty; as Chief Officer Pinnegar left the building, she sprang out to open the door for her.

As they drove away, the Chief passed on the latest news bulletin; Miranda said nothing – but all day, as they travelled to Buckinghamshire and back, she kept thinking of Patsy Blair, and remembering the blurred snapshot of a young Gunnery Officer, laughing, and holding up a teddy bear.

That evening, after work, she went to the canteen and found Patsy with a cup of cold coffee in front of her. She looked up at Miranda with her usual bright smile: "I suppose you've heard — ? His Mum rang me at midday; she'd just had the telegram."

Miranda, expecting to find her in tears, was confused: "You mean – he's all right?"

"Oh, we don't know any details yet . . . 'Missing, believed killed' – that's all it said. But I expect he's been picked up by another ship. Derek's always been lucky – he'll turn up soon."

"Yes – I see. . . ." Miranda could not think what else to say.

"The ship went down very quickly – I don't suppose I'll ever get that teddy bear now! . . . Still, as long as Derek's all right. . . ."

Her fixed smile never wavered. She had been smiling steadily ever since midday.

"Don't you think – perhaps – you should go home?" Miranda asked.

"Oh, no – I'm fine . . . I'm sure I'll hear from him – any time now."

She went on smiling when Miranda went off to find the Welfare Officer; and when they sent Patsy home in a taxi, Miranda saw her little, childlike face looking back through the rear window – still smiling.

Jenny read the newspaper reports next day and thought of Nick. There was plenty of activity in the Mediterranean too; at the end of May, the British were driven out of Crete by combined air and naval forces. The press described their withdrawal as "a glorious evacuation"; some people were wondering privately whether it might have been a dress rehearsal for the invasion of England.

At the beginning of June, Jenny received a cable saying that Nick would be coming home in ten days time, and the family began preparations for the christening. It was to be held on a Saturday, so as many people as possible could be present.

When Nick arrived on the Friday afternoon he found Jenny beside the lake, on a bench under the trees, gently rocking the perambulator. She looked up – and her face was radiant.

"Nick — !" She jumped to her feet, then glanced at the occupant of the pram, afraid she had disturbed him.

"Is he asleep?"

"Not quite. But he won't be long."

Nick put his arms round his wife and held her for a moment without speaking.

"Don't you want to introduce yourself to your son?" she asked.

"Of course I want to, but. . . ." Almost fearfully, he looked down – then smiled slowly. "How do you do – Edward?"

The baby gave a prodigious yawn, and turned its head away.

Nick grimaced: "He doesn't think much of his father."

"He's very sleepy. He loves being under the trees; he looks up at the leaves, and gradually his eyelids begin to droop – there, you see?" Now his eyes were shut, his tiny hands quite relaxed. "Your mother says he looks like you at that age, and Polly thinks he takes after me, but I think he just looks like himself and nobody else."

"I think he looks amazing," said Nick. "He's a real person . . . I've tried to picture what he'd be like, but seeing him like this – he's even better than I imagined."

"And you're happy about calling him Edward?"

"Of course – what else could you call him? It's his name, isn't it?"

The following afternoon, in the village church, the Vicar intoned: "I baptize thee Edward George Richard. . . ."

As the water trickled over his forehead, Edward George Richard Gaunt puckered up his face in disapproval.

Afterwards, Nick confided to Jenny: "For an awful moment, I decided he didn't take after either of us – when he's feeling tetchy, he looks exactly like Old Bea!"

Jenny smiled contentedly at the bundle in her arms, swaddled in a white lace shawl that had been handed down through many generations of Minsters, and said: "Your grandmother's pleased that we called him George, after her husband – and Polly was very touched that we remembered Richard as well."

Polly was Edward's godmother; Martin, who had been given weekend leave to attend the christening, was to have been his godfather, but as he had not arrived when the ceremony began, William stood in for him, as a proxy godparent.

"What a pity Martin didn't get here in time," said Alice, as they strolled back across the village green. "I do hope nothing's happened to him."

"I expect the trains were held up," suggested William. "I'm sure he's on his way."

Caro whispered to Miranda: "What d'you bet Martin's picked up some gorgeous girl on the train?"

Miranda said nothing. She had been nerving herself up all day to see Martin again, and his non-arrival was worrying.

Several friends and neighbours had been invited to the christening party; it was the first social occasion at Crown House since the war began, and the Minsters had taken advantage of the fine weather to entertain their guests outdoors, in the walled garden.

Grace Duncan congratulated William: "I don't think I've ever seen your roses looking so beautiful."

"Yes, they make a good show, don't they?" William filled her glass with champagne. "When we turned over the rest of the garden to vegetables, I couldn't bring myself to grub up the roses – and there wouldn't have been much space in here for turnips or potatoes anyway. So the roses were reprieved at the last minute, and I must admit I'm delighted. We need a spot of colour in our lives, these days."

Standing beside the sundial, Ken Stubbs was looking rather lost, and Polly came over to join him, saying: "Your glass is empty – so's mine. Why don't we both get a refill?"

"I'd better not, thanks all the same." Ken looked at his watch: "I'm due at the village hall in half an hour, and I've got to go home and change first."

"Your life is one long social whirl," she teased him. "What is it this time? The Mothers Union throwing a cocktail party?"

He smiled: "You're almost right. Only it's not the Mothers Union – it's the Home Guard – and the cocktails are the Molotov variety. It's a training session."

"What's a Molotov cocktail?"

"A home-made bomb – in case there's an invasion. You fill a bottle with some inflammable liquid, like paraffin, and stick in a piece of flannel for a wick, then you put a match to it and chuck it at the enemy tanks."

"Sounds a bit risky to me."

"Yes, I admit it's fairly unreliable – but we've got to show the Jerries that we mean business."

"Oh, dear. . . . You will be careful, won't you? Promise me you will."

She looked really concerned, and suddenly Ken was a happy man.

"I'll be all right, don't you worry. In fact, I'll be calling in to see you later, when the practice is over; I've got a little present for you."

225

"Oh, Ken, you shouldn't – what is it?"

"Something I picked up last night at the whist drive; I drew the winning ticket in the raffle – a string of onions! I'm afraid they couldn't run to a Rolls-Royce."

Polly laughed: "I'm very glad – where would we get the petrol? Onions are a real luxury – you can't get them for love or money." As William passed them, carrying another bottle of champagne, she held out her glass and asked: "Why have all the onions disappeared? You're the agricultural expert – why don't we grow our own onions?"

"A good question. In the old days it was cheaper to import them from Spain, or Brittany," said William, replenishing her glass. "But we've learned our lesson – we'll have plenty of onions next year, won't we, Ken?"

At the far end of the garden, Jenny sat with Nicholas, who had Edward on his lap. Dipping his little finger into his champagne, he put it to the baby's lips. A small tongue appeared, investigating the new, unknown taste.

"He likes it," said Nick.

"Shame on you!" Caro and Miranda joined them, and Caro continued: "You're teaching him bad habits already – the acid might give him colic."

"Nonsense!" said Nick. "Look at him – he's smiling."

"People always think babies are smiling, but it's usually wind," said Caro knowledgeably.

"Oh, I beg your pardon – I was forgetting, you're an expert! . . . Darling, can you take him for a minute?" Nicholas passed his son to Jenny, then stood up and kissed Caroline formally on both cheeks. "Seriously, though – I never thanked you properly for your sterling work when our son was born. If it hadn't been for your medical skill —"

"Medical skill?" Miranda smiled: "Come on, Caro, own up – tell them the truth."

When Caro explained, Jenny stared at her blankly: "You mean – you'd never done it before?"

"Never! I was absolutely petrified, though of course I didn't dare tell you that. Afterwards I felt simply marvellous; as a matter of fact, I'm thinking of applying to go on

226

a midwifery course, so I can learn how to do the job properly."

The girls laughed; but Nicholas cut in coldly: "You can think yourself damn lucky nothing went wrong. If anything had happened to Jenny – or the baby – I should probably have killed you."

Caro's face changed: "Well – I'm sorry – I did my best —"

"Oh, yes, it was a wonderful chance for you, wasn't it? Qualified or not, you couldn't wait to experiment on my wife and child!"

Jenny interrupted: "Don't be silly, Nick – it wasn't like that – Caro had no alternative. We were trapped in that cellar; she had to do what she could."

"You weren't trapped when the labour pains first started. She could have got you into hospital then, but – oh, no – she had to show how bloody clever she was." Miranda broke in fiercely: "That's a rotten thing to say! You should go down on your knees and apologize —"

Disturbed by this angry exchange, the baby began to cry, and Caroline turned and walked away without another word. Hearing raised voices, some of the guests were looking round, and Jenny tried to hush her husband, her sister-in-law, and her baby, smiling brightly at the same time.

William and Alice were out of earshot, under the pergola with Edith and Grace; Old Bea turned her wheelchair towards her son, asking querulously: "What do you mean – there isn't any more champagne?"

"Exactly what I say." William shrugged his shoulders: "You've just had the last of it. I doubt if we shall see any more until the war is over."

"In that case, you should have laid down some more when you had the chance!" snapped the old lady. "I call that gross mismanagement on your part."

Edith tried to mollify her: "Never mind, it's been a lovely party, hasn't it? I'm sure everyone's enjoyed it."

Her mother scowled: "Oh, yes – just look at them all, enjoying themselves at our expense . . . And that's another thing, William – Alice tells me you're planning a garden fete in aid of charity. Ridiculous! – We don't want a lot of strangers barging in here, eating and drinking us out of house and home."

"A garden fete . . . ?" William turned to his wife: "It's the first I've heard of it – whatever gave you that idea?"

"I'm sorry —" Alice apologized: "I knew you'd been talking to little Mr Whats-his-name from the Red Cross; somehow I got the impression that —"

William smiled: "Yes, I offered to help the Red Cross, but not with a garden fete. They need some sizeable properties for conversion into hospitals – convalescent homes – that sort of thing – and I'm considering the possibility of offering them Crown House."

"Worse and worse!" His mother was not appeased. "We shouldn't be able to call our souls our own – a horde of vandals moving in, turning the place upside down. . . ."

"But William – you never said a word to me about—" Alice began.

"It may not happen; there's nothing definite. They only sent their representative to draw up a report on the house – that's all. But there's no point in keeping the place empty when it might be turned to some useful purpose."

"I hope you made it clear that it must be a convalescent home for officers only?" asked Lady Beatrice. "We can't have the riff-raff tramping all over the place, breaking the windows and scribbling on the walls. . . ."

William took a deep breath and stood up.

"I'm sorry to have to say this, Mama, but you are talking balderdash – and very unpleasant balderdash, at that."

The old lady spluttered: "How dare you speak to me in that tone —"

But William had not finished yet: "The other day I said you were a snob – at the time, I still regarded it as faintly comic – but after your latest remarks, I have to say I am deeply ashamed of you. If Crown House is turned into a hospital, it will certainly be open to all ranks – and if that offends you, I'm afraid I don't give a tinker's cuss!"

Alice grasped the back of the wheelchair, saying firmly: "I expect you're feeling tired, Mama – I think it's time for your rest."

"Take your hands off my chair!" The old lady's face was suffused with rage: "I'm not going in until he apologizes — !"

"Perhaps you'd like to come with us instead, Lady Beatrice?" suggested Grace. "Edith and I were saying only last night, it's high time you visited us at the Lodge Cottage, and we'd be delighted to offer you a cup of tea – wouldn't we, Edith?"

Swiftly and efficiently, she trundled the wheelchair away, with Edith hurrying after them, and the old lady's indignant squawks died away in the distance.

"William, dear – *really*. . . ." sighed Alice.

"I'm not sorry," said Lord Minster stubbornly. "She's been getting steadily worse, and it's about time someone told her so."

The party was breaking up; the guests were drifting away, nodding and smiling, telling each other it had been a charming afternoon – quite like old times. The last stragglers paid their respects to the baby, and then Jenny and Nick were left alone, looking at one another.

"We'd better go in too," said Jenny – and added quietly: "How could you be so unkind to Caro – after all she did for us?"

He passed his hand over his forehead: "I don't know. . . . I suppose I still feel guilty about not being there – leaving you to cope on your own. And I thought – suppose something had gone wrong? If anything had happened to you – or to Edward. . . . It was a sort of brainstorm – suddenly I couldn't think straight . . . I'm sorry."

She touched his hand. "You don't have to tell me that. But perhaps we should go and tell Caro."

As she cradled the baby in her arms, a familiar voice broke in: "A classic picture – the Holy Family!"

In his RAF uniform, Martin stood under the rose-arch; his face was red, and his speech a little slurred.

"Bit late, I'm afraid. Missed my train, and had to wait nearly an hour – then I got talking to some chaps in the buffet, and somehow I managed to miss the next one as well . . . So this is young Edward, eh?"

He lurched towards them, peering down at the baby, who was fast asleep. "What a world to be born into – poor little bugger . . . Ah, well." He slapped Nick on the back: "Congratulations – I bet you're feeling very proud of yourself – and congratters to the pretty lady – don't I get a kiss?"

He hugged Jenny, and she smelled the whisky on his breath.

"You'd better come indoors," said Nick. "Bath – change – have some black coffee – if you run into Pa like that, there'll be hell to pay."

"What are you burbling about? I'm all right – perfectly all right . . ." Suddenly Martin turned his head, looking back over his shoulder; a moment later, Miranda appeared under the archway.

She managed an uncertain smile: "Hello, Marty . . . Where have you been?"

"Hello yourself . . . Got here late, and missed all the fun. Always doing the wrong thing, aren't I? – famous for it . . ."

Miranda saw at once that he was drunk, and she knew why. He had been as nervous as she was, at the prospect of this meeting. They looked at one another in silence, and then his eyes slid away from her. They had so much to say to one another – and they could not say it.

Miranda reported for duty on Monday morning with a feeling of relief. Chief Officer Pinnegar asked if she had spent a pleasant weekend at home, and she replied: "Not exactly, ma'am. Everyone seemed to be on edge, somehow – family squabbles kept flaring up – you know what it's like sometimes —" Then she bit her lip, and said: "No – I beg your pardon, ma'am."

The Chief said with the ghost of a smile: "I've heard that family life occasionally has its disadvantages. . . . But you all finished up on good terms, I hope?"

"Oh, yes, ma'am," she lied.

Nick had made his peace with Caroline, and even Old Bea

230

reached some sort of grudging truce with William, but the twins had avoided one another throughout Saturday evening and most of Sunday, until it was time for Miranda to return to London with Caro. Martin suggested they should share a taxi to the station, but when the train arrived, he muttered something about grabbing a snack at the Medford Arms and catching a later train. At the barrier, he embraced Caro, then turned to Miranda, holding her awkwardly by the shoulders and kissing her cheekbone.

"Good luck, old thing," he said. "I'll give you a ring – we must have a proper talk."

All that week, Caro was on nights again. Miranda went to the cinema a couple of times, but she spent most evenings on her own at the flat. She still hoped Martin would get in touch, but there was no word from him.

The following weekend, Caro had some time off, and they pooled their meat ration to make a stew; there weren't enough coupons for a joint, but with plenty of vegetables they managed to stretch some stewing steak into a good, nourishing hotpot – there might even be enough left over for another meal, disguised with curry-powder and rice.

Miranda was scraping carrots when Caroline rushed into the kitchen, saying excitedly: "I've just heard the most glorious news on the wireless!"

"Let me guess. . . ." Miranda put down the vegetable peeler and wiped her hands. "Hitler's been assassinated?"

"No – but it's nearly as good. You remember how fed up Scott and I were when the Russians signed that pact with Germany?"

"Well, I know it was a blow for all the left-wingers – so what?"

"Well, it's obvious now that was only a diplomatic move; it didn't really *mean* anything. Because they've just announced that Hitler's invaded the Soviet Union, so now the Russians are our allies – the Red Army are on our side – how about that?"

"Very nice." Miranda was not particularly impressed.

"No, but don't you see? – The Nazis can't possibly fight

231

against us *and* the Allies *and* Russia. . . . They haven't got a hope in hell now!"

At that moment the telephone rang in the living-room, and Miranda said: "I'll get it – it might be for me."

When she picked up the phone her hands were shaking: "Hello – who's that?"

Silence. She announced the number carefully, and asked: "Marty – is that you?"

After a moment, she heard the phone being replaced, and then there was nothing but the dialling tone.

When she went back to the kitchen, Caro, who had taken over the vegetable peeler, looked at her in surprise.

"That was short and sweet – who was it?"

"Nobody," said Miranda. "It must have been a wrong number."

But she knew that wasn't true. At the last moment, Martin had lost his nerve.

Caro went on scraping carrots: "Oh, well, never mind – what was I saying when we were so rudely interrupted? Oh, yes – Hitler hasn't got a chance now – isn't that absolutely wonderful?"

"Yes," said Miranda, flatly. "Wonderful."

Chapter Fourteen

Monday, 23 June to Sunday, 21 September 1941

Lord and Lady Minster were having breakfast in the house-keeper's flat as usual; William had a soft-boiled egg from their own chickens – even in his mid-sixties, he still cut up his bread and butter into "soldiers", to dip into the yolk – while Alice was content with cups of tea, two slices of toast, and sharp, homemade plum jam.

She had also boiled an egg for her mother-in-law, and handed this over to Lilian Brooks, who was making up a tray for Lady Beatrice. Every morning, Lilian – who slept in the room on the other side of her Ladyship's – went in to wake Lady Beatrice, helped her to wash and dress, and gave her her breakfast in bed.

William was grateful to be spared his mother's company at this hour of the morning. She had been particularly difficult lately; since their altercation at the christening party, she had hardly spoken to him at all, maintaining a furious, resentful silence most of the time.

Lilian carried the breakfast tray in to Lady Beatrice, and through the half-open door they could hear Old Bea wheezing and grumbling unintelligibly as she prepared to face another day. A few moments later Lilian returned, looking rather startled.

"Excuse me, sir – my lady —" she began. "Her ladyship has asked me to tell you . . . she won't be requiring her bedroom any more. She says I'm to pack all her clothes

233

and toilet things and suchlike. . . . She's moving out this morning."

William and Alice looked at one another blankly.

"What's she up to this time?" asked William.

With one accord, they rose and entered the old lady's room. Sitting up in bed, with her tray on her lap and a dribble of egg on her chin, Lady Beatrice smirked with quiet satisfaction.

"You've heard my news, then? No doubt you'll be glad to be rid of me; but I've never been one to stay where I'm not wanted. If my son no longer appreciates my company, I shall go to my daughter instead; I can't think why it never occurred to me before. When I visited Edith the other day, I was quite impressed by that little cottage – she and her friend have made it very comfortable – very welcoming. . . . And they have invited me to go and stay there whenever I like, for as long as I like."

This wasn't strictly true. After tea and three buttered scones that Saturday afternoon, Old Bea had looked appraisingly round the cosy sitting-room, and remarked abruptly: "You do yourselves very well here, I must say. You're not cramped for space, like William and Alice, cooped up in those little boxrooms in the servants' wing – I've never been happy there. . . . Let me see, how many bedrooms do you have?"

"Well, Mama, there's the big bedroom, which we share . . ." Edith glanced nervously at Grace: "And there's the second bedroom, only we don't use that at present."

"Excellent – that will suit me very well. I've had quite enough of my son's bad temper; between ourselves, I've never felt really comfortable in that poky little apartment, with William and his men banging about at all hours . . . It's not what I'm used to; I prefer the peace and quiet of female companionship myself."

She twisted her features into a wicked, conspiratorial smile, confident that she had won the ladies over, and concluded: "Perhaps you'll be kind enough to make it ready for me; I'd like to move in as soon as possible. Shall we say Monday?"

Edith demurred anxiously: "Oh, dear – well, of course that would be very nice, Mama, but perhaps Grace and I should discuss it first. . . ."

234

Old Bea turned to Grace: "Do you have any objections, my dear?"

Grace looked at Edith, and knew that there was no point in fighting a battle which they would inevitably lose.

"We shall do our best to make you welcome here, Lady Beatrice," she said politely. "For a short stay. . . ."

Afterwards, when they were on their own, she told Edith: "We couldn't very well say no. And I dare say it won't be long before she gets fed up with us, and goes back to your brother. Until then, we'll just have to make the best of it."

"Yes . . . I suppose – in one way – it's rather flattering she should want to come and stay with us. She's never seemed to be very interested in me until now," Edith mused. "Perhaps this means she's getting more motherly as she grows older."

"I hope you're right," said Grace. "Though I rather doubt it."

Having got her own way, the Countess now continued to give the housekeeper her instructions, telling her to begin packing at once.

"But where shall I be sleeping, my lady?" Lilian was still confused by this unexpected turn of events. "Surely there won't be room for me at the cottage?"

"No, no – you can stay here," Old Bea told her. "You will come down to the lodge each morning to get me up, and look after me during the day – and return here every evening, after you have put me to bed."

"But suppose you should need anything during the night, my lady? As long as you were sleeping here, you only had to bang on the wall, and I came in at once, but —"

"I shall not need you during the night, thank you; I shall have my daughter to look after me," said Old Bea smugly. "In fact – I shall probably not need you a great deal in future. Perhaps you should offer your services as a nurse at Lord Minster's new Red Cross hospital. . . ." She threw William a baleful glance: "I'm happy to say I shall be well out of the way during all that commotion and upheaval!"

William and Alice left the bedroom without a word, to finish their interrupted breakfast.

"Tch!" Lord Minster grimaced: "This damn egg's practically stone-cold."

"I do think Mama might have given us a little more warning," said Alice, pouring another cup of tea. "Oh, I'm not complaining about that," said William. "The sooner the better, I say – it will make a very pleasant change."

"Ssh! She'll hear you—" Alice began, glancing at the bedroom door; then broke off as Ken Stubbs came in with the morning mail, and some papers that required Lord Minster's signature.

"Ah – morning, Ken – thank you. . . . Hello – what's this?" William tore open an official-looking envelope with "Red Cross" printed in one corner. "I must say, they haven't wasted much time."

The letter was brief and to the point; their representative had decided, after careful consideration, that Crown House would not really be suitable for conversion to a hospital or convalescent home without extensive alteration – additional plumbing, staircases, service lifts, and other amenities – and that in view of this, they must therefore regretfully decline Lord Minster's generous offer, which had nevertheless been much appreciated – *et cetera, et cetera.*

William showed the letter to Alice and Ken, saying: "So that's that."

"I can't pretend I'm altogether sorry," said Alice. "It would have been a terrible upheaval – your mother was right about that. She's going to be delighted when she hears the news."

"Good lord – don't tell her about this, whatever you do!" exclaimed William in alarm. "She might change her mind – and stay put!"

When Miranda came home from the Admiralty on Monday evening, she found Caro getting ready to go off on night duty as usual. She was already in her uniform, brushing her hair back into a knot, and pinning it up under her starched cap; their eyes met in the mirror above the fireplace.

"No, he didn't," said Caro, before Miranda could speak.

236

"What are you talking about? Who didn't what?"

"You were going to ask me if Martin had phoned – I was trying to save you the trouble. He didn't."

"What makes you think I was going to —"

"Because you've asked me the same thing nearly every evening for the past week." She turned to face Miranda: "Now sit down and tell me – what's going on?"

Miranda perched uncomfortably on the edge of a chair, and studied her fingernails: "Nothing's going on. The last time I saw him, he said he was going to ring me – but so far he hasn't. That's all."

"Oh, come on – I'm not a complete idiot. There's obviously more to it than that. You and Martin have always been as thick as thieves – now all of a sudden you're not talking to one another. . . . Have you had a row?"

"No, we haven't – don't be silly."

"Miranda, I was there when he left us at Medford Station, remember? You were both so tense, I felt as if I was walking through a minefield. Come on, own up – it was because he turned up late for the christening, wasn't it? – *And* he was plastered. I suppose you gave him a ticking-off, and he's been sulking ever since – is that it?"

Miranda shook her head: "No – it's got nothing to do with the christening. Of course it was stupid of him to miss the train and get drunk, but that wasn't why we —"

She stopped short, afraid she had already said too much, and Caro picked her up quickly: "That wasn't why you've fallen out with him? So what is the reason? You might as well tell me."

"I can't. . . . It's sort of private – I really don't want to talk about it. . . . Sorry."

"I don't understand – you and Martin hardly said a word to each other last weekend – so what happened to start a row? It doesn't make sense – you two always see eye to eye about everything – you never quarrel!"

"I keep telling you, we haven't quarrelled. It's more of a – a difference of opinion. If you really want to know, it began weeks earlier – that time I went up to see him in Lincolnshire; there was something we disagreed about – something personal.

237

Ever since then, I've been hoping we could sort it out – talk things over quietly . . . I know Martin wants to – well, you heard him, he said we had to talk. . . . But I'm still waiting for him to ring up."

Caro put her arm round Miranda's shoulders: "It's important to you, isn't it?"

"Of course it is. And it's important to Marty as well."

"I wonder. . . ."

Startled, Miranda looked up: "What do you mean?"

"However close you and Martin are, there's still one big difference between you. He's a man, and you're a woman. Women take things like this to heart; we brood about them and worry about them – we feel we've got to try and put things right – but men just aren't like that. Oh, they may be upset for a while, but they soon get involved with other things, and then they gradually push the whole thing aside and forget about it." She stood up, shrugging into her cape: "Let's face it – men can be selfish bastards sometimes."

"No — !" Miranda was shocked. "Martin's not like that – he's just as unhappy about it as I am, I know he is – it's just that he's terribly busy at the moment —"

"Darling, they're always terribly busy," said Caro. "And I speak as one who knows – Scott's been terribly busy for so long, I can't even remember the last time I heard from him. . . . Anyway, I can't stop now, because *I'm* terribly busy."

As she opened the front door, Miranda called after her: "You're wrong about Marty – he *will* ring up!"

"If you say so. . . ." Caro smiled sadly: "Anyway – good luck!" – and she went out.

With a sinking feeling, Miranda began to make herself some supper, then sat all the evening by the telephone, which never rang.

In the lodge cottage, Old Bea was having her first supper with Edith and Grace.

"Cold ham and salad?" She studied her plate without enthusiasm: "Lilian always makes me something hot in the evening."

238

"The salad's fresh from the garden, Mama," Edith said encouragingly. "Very good for you – full of vitamins."

"Raw vegetables at night? Most indigestible," said her mother, in a tone that brooked no argument.

"There's hot jam tart to follow," Grace told her.

"Really. . . ." said Lady Beatrice, bleakly. "Any cheese?"

"Not until we get this week's ration, Mama," said Edith.

"And cheese at night is far more indigestible than salad," added Grace firmly.

Thwarted, the old lady cast about for another topic of conversation.

"I can't say I care for the cardigan you're wearing, Edith," she said at last. "That grey-green doesn't flatter you – very drab. You should buy yourself something more cheerful; perhaps we could all drive into Medford and look round the shops? I dare say my wheelchair would fit into the back of William's car."

"I think Lord Minster only uses his car for essential journeys these days," said Grace. "In any case, since they started clothes-rationing at Whitsun, you have to think twice before you waste any precious 'points' coupons."

"Anyhow, I'm very fond of this cardigan!" Edith defended it hotly. "It's lovat green – a well-known Scottish colour – and Grace knitted it for me, last winter."

"Very clever, I'm sure – but such an unfortunate shade; it makes your skin look sallow. . . . Would you kindly pass me the pickled onions?"

Some time later, when the old lady had finally been settled for the night, Grace took Edith back to the sitting-room and shut the door, saying in a low voice: "Get out two glasses." She had a small bottle of malt whisky put by for special occasions and medical emergencies. "I think we deserve a wee dram."

"I think you're right, dear." Edith sighed: "Of course, it's very nice to be able to help Mama, but I have been wondering. . . . Do you suppose perhaps we've made a terrible mistake?"

The summer ripened into autumn, and early in September

Chief Officer Pinnegar called Miranda in to her office for a talk.

"How are you enjoying your work?"

"Quite well, ma'am, thank you."

"I only ask, because you have seemed a little – how shall I put it? – withdrawn lately. You used to have a certain sparkle; I miss it when it's not there."

Miranda blinked: "I – I don't quite know what you mean, ma'am."

"No? Perhaps it's my imagination, but I can't help feeling you are dissatisfied."

"Not exactly, ma'am. But when I was reclassified as 'mobile', I thought I might get moved around occasionally; I applied ages ago, but I haven't heard anything since then."

"That's probably because the authorities have decided that you are doing a good job where you are. . . . Still, I appreciate your feeling of frustration; I suspect that your particular duties as a driver don't stretch you sufficiently. Do you agree?"

Uncertain what to say, Miranda said nothing.

"That is why – with your permission – I am proposing to put your name forward as a candidate for an Officer Training Course. I hope you have no objection?"

"I don't know, ma'am – I never thought about it . . ." Suddenly Miranda brightened up: "If I did get a commission – would that improve my chances of being sent overseas?"

"I can't guarantee anything. But it is perfectly possible."

"In that case – yes, please, ma'am. I'd be happy to try."

"Excellent." Chief Officer Pinnegar flashed one of her rare smiles. "I'm sure you will do very well; I shall put in the pro forma today, and we might hear something next week. . . . Let me see – you're on duty this weekend, I believe?"

The drivers took the weekend shift in turn; Miranda had to be on call at the Motor Pool from Friday night until Monday morning.

It was fairly boring, and as a rule she did not look forward to it; but she had actually welcomed this particular weekend duty, since she had learned from her mother that Martin would be going home on a 48-hour pass. By now a couple of months had

240

passed without a word from Martin; she had come to think that Caro was right – obviously, he was not going to get in touch with her – and she was glad to avoid another agonising, tongue-tied weekend with him at Crown House.

When she reported at the Motor Transport garage on Friday evening, she was surprised to find Wren Blair was also on the weekend roster.

"Hello, Patsy – it's lovely to see you – how are you?"

"I'm fine, thanks. The Medical Officer signed me off the other day; I've been looking forward to getting back to work."

Miranda was relieved; Patsy looked very well – cheerfully confident, she seemed to have thrown off the horror of her fiancé's death at last.

"I'm very glad. We all missed you, while you were away."

"Yes, I'm fine now," Patsy repeated. "Really I am."

"We must have a good old gossip later on; you've got a lot to catch up on."

At weekends, they spent most of the time carrying out general maintenance duties – cleaning and polishing the cars, checking engines, doing an oil-change or adjusting the timing – and it was not until the supper-break that Miranda found herself sitting next to Patsy in the canteen.

"Now!" Miranda began. "Tell me what you've been up to."

Patsy shrugged and laughed: "There's nothing to tell. I've been leading a very quiet life at home. That's why I'm so glad to be back at work."

She asked after Caroline, and Miranda politely enquired after Patsy's mother; then the conversation flagged, and there was a long pause.

At last Miranda said awkwardly: "Everyone was terribly sorry about . . . you know – Derek. . . ."

"Yes," said Patsy simply.

Miranda looked at her, and found that Pasty had not stopped smiling. But the smile only reached her mouth; it was not in her eyes – and she realized with a sudden chill that there was nothing in Patsy's eyes. They were empty of all warmth, all emotion.

For a frightening moment, she felt that Patsy wasn't there at

241

all; this was not the bubbly, impulsive girl she used to know, it was a smiling automaton. . . .

Desperately, she cast about for another topic of conversation; then she began to relate some of the more entertaining incidents that had taken place in the Motor Pool during Patsy's absence.

Patsy nodded and smiled, and said: "Yes – go on – what happened next?" She even laughed in the proper places – but all the time Miranda had the horrifying sensation that the real Patsy Blair was somewhere else altogether, somewhere very far away.

Home from London for the weekend, Polly got out of the train at Medford; as she walked along the platform a man's voice said in her ear: "Hello, gorgeous – want to have a ride in a taxi with a desperate man?"

Polly whirled round indignantly, about to give him a piece of her mind – then burst out laughing: "Martin – ! I thought I was being picked up!"

"So you are," he told her, taking her attaché case and carrying it as they went through the barrier together. "I was perfectly serious – do you want to share a cab?"

"Of course. I didn't know you were coming down this weekend?"

"Only a short one; I've got to go back on Sunday evening; still, it makes a break." He looked over his shoulder: "Sorry I didn't spot you on the train. . . . Or Mandy, come to that – wonder where she's got to?"

"She's on duty this weekend. And your mother's staying at Windsor – some special do at the Castle, I believe."

"Oh – pity," he said carelessly.

When they got to Crown House, they found Lord Minster hard at work in the housekeeper's flat, puzzling over a pile of forms from the Ministry of Agriculture which all had to be completed in triplicate.

"These things are enough to drive you stark, staring mad," he complained. "I usually leave Ken to puzzle them out, but he's busy Home-Guarding this weekend, and they've got to be returned by Monday, so. . . ."

"Is Ken still spending every spare minute square-bashing?" Polly asked.

"Oh, he's keener than ever now, because they've just issued Number Three platoon, 'A' company, with a machine-gun."

"Goodness!" Polly looked dismayed. "I thought they did all their drilling with pitchforks and broomsticks?"

"No, no – it's the real thing at last. At least, I gather it's a fairly antiquated specimen – a BAR, to be precise."

"What the hell's a BAR?" asked Martin. "I never heard of it."

"I'm not surprised; it's full name is a Browning Automatic Rifle – the last time I saw one was on the Western Front in 1918. . . . ." William gazed out of the window at the clouds, seeing ghosts from the past. When he turned back to Martin, he said: "I hope you know you're in for a very quiet weekend. Quieter than usual, in fact – since your Grandmama moved into the lodge cottage, thank heaven."

"It won't stay quiet for long, once Harriet discovers Uncle Martin has arrived," said Polly. "Do you happen to know where I can find her?"

"I believe Ken took her to the village hall," William replied. "He promised he'd show her how the Browning works."

"Oh, he did, did he?" exclaimed Polly. "In that case I think I'd better find them right away – excuse me, won't you?" – and she set off purposefully.

"Polly tells me Ma isn't coming home this weekend?" said Martin. "And neither is Mandy?"

"That's right. To make matters worse, this is my night on duty at the Wardens' Post, so I shan't be home till breakfast-time tomorrow. Still, I expect you can make yourself comfortable here, can't you? I thought you might like to move into your Grandmother's old room – Lilian's made up the bed, so it's all ready for you."

"Thanks," said Martin.

He walked into the adjoining room, chucking his suitcase onto the bed, while his father continued: "I've got to report at seven, so I thought we could have supper about six-thirty – if you don't mind eating early?"

"Six-thirty's fine by me," said Martin.

"Well – if you're quite sure. . . ." William lingered for a moment, adding apologetically: "As I say, I'm afraid you're in for rather a dull weekend – there's not much going on in this part of the world."

"That's fine by me," Martin assured him. "I get all the excitement I want when I'm on duty; when I'm on leave, a nice bit of dull is just what the doctor ordered."

He didn't elaborate on this; he certainly wasn't going to tell his father that he had been so desperate, he'd actually reported sick, hoping he might get some medical advice.

But then he changed his mind; if he confessed his nightly fears, the MO would probably have grounded him – and possibly put a black mark on his official records: *This officer has been removed from active service, owing to lack of moral fibre*" – wasn't that the official explanation for cowardice?

So at the last moment, he merely complained of a spot of insomnia – disturbed nights – and the Quack had prescribed a very mild sleeping-draught, which did absolutely no good at all.

Smiling, he told his father: "Don't you worry about me – I'll probably go out later on, and have a couple of noggins at the Crown . . . See if there are any of the old familiar faces around."

But he knew he wouldn't be able to let rip and enjoy himself; if he knocked back too many pints, the gossip would go round the village like wildfire, and Pa would soon get to hear of it.

After his one abortive attempt to telephone Miranda at Caro's flat, he had decided that there was only one way he could straighten things out – he had to talk to Mandy, face to face. That was why he had finally nerved himself up to come home – but it had been bloody silly of him not to make sure beforehand that she would be at Crown House this weekend. . . . Obviously, the 48-hour pass was going to be a dead loss; the sooner it was over, the better.

When Polly walked into the village hall, Harriet greeted her joyfully, racing towards her mother at top speed and calling out: "Mummy, mummy – have you brought me any chocolate?"

"Now that's what I call a real old-fashioned welcome. . . . Just you wait and see, young lady!"

Polly hugged her daughter – and registered that Harry seemed to be taller than ever. Even though she saw her every weekend, Polly could never get used to the fact that she was growing so quickly.

"Did you have a good journey?" Harry chattered on. "What's for supper? . . . Tell me honestly – did you really bring me some chocolate?"

When she grinned, Polly recognized the warm, wicked smile that crinkled her eyes; Richard could always get round her when he smiled like that.

The sudden stab of memory was like a physical pain; she didn't often think of her husband nowadays – it was almost exactly eight years since his death – not all that long, measured in terms of a lifetime, but so much had happened in those eight years, it seemed to be a million years away.

She pretended to scold her daughter: "Talk about cupboard love – is it me or my sweet ration you care about? . . . I told you – you'll have to wait and see!"

With Harriet swinging on her arm, she walked in to the middle of the hall, where Ken Stubbs sat on the floor, surrounded by a great many pieces of mysterious mechanism, spread out on a khaki groundsheet. In her mind's eye she could still see Richard – her splendid young husband, handsome and golden – and when Ken scrambled clumsily to his feet, she couldn't help making an absurd comparison.

Poor Ken – how could he possibly have hoped he might take Richard's place?

They shook hands, and a split second later, he apologized: "Sorry! I shouldn't have done that – I'm a bit greasy, I'm afraid."

"Never mind, my hands are filthy already; I don't know why railway carriages are always so grimy." She took the lump of cotton waste he handed her, and wiped her fingers. "So this is the famous machine-gun I've been hearing about? I'm not sure I approve of you demonstrating firearms to my daughter."

"I promised to show her how it works; we've been stripping

245

it down and oiling the moving parts." He assured her: "It's perfectly safe – you know I'd never let her run any risk."

"Yes – of course I know that." She turned to Harriet: "Anyway, it's time for you to get yourself clean before supper. Run home and tidy up; I'll be there in five minutes. And you can take my attaché case with you – you'll find a bar of Cadbury's inside, only don't eat it all and spoil your appetite."

Harry rushed off at top speed, and Polly resumed her conversation with Ken.

"Just between you and me and the gatepost – don't you think you're letting this Home Guard lark go to your head?" she teased him gently. "I mean to say – a grown man – playing soldiers at your age!"

"My age . . . I suppose that's the whole trouble, really," he said, unsmiling.

"What do you mean by that?"

"Seems like I've always been too young – or too old. I just managed to get called up in 1918, but the war was over before I saw any fighting . . . and this time around I'm too old for it – and exempt from military service on account of being engaged in work of national importance . . . growing vegetables and feeding livestock – that's my war work."

"So that's why you're doing all this." She indicated his denim fatigues, and the dismantled machine-gun. "Strikes me you're pushing yourself too hard, Ken. Go on like this, you'll wear yourself out."

"I enjoy it," he said defensively.

"Yes, but you ought to take it easy sometimes. Why not give yourself a treat now and then? Don't you ever go to the flicks nowadays? – or go dancing at the Palais?"

"Don't fancy it. Anyhow, I've got no one to go with."

"You used to take Lilian with you once. You're still on good terms with her, aren't you?"

"Well, yes – but it's a bit awkward, isn't it?" Ken frowned: "I don't think she'd fancy taking up with me again – not after what happened."

He and Lilian had been going steady at one time, until he realized that he didn't love her, and broke off the engagement.

It had been an embarrassing and unhappy experience for both of them.

"All the same, she might be glad of your company," Polly suggested. "I don't think she's got many close friends – men friends, I mean."

"I wouldn't want her to start getting the wrong idea. . . ." He shook his head: "No, it wouldn't do – that's all over and done with now."

"Perhaps you're right. Well, then – you'll just have to find somebody else – there's plenty of nice girls about, you must start looking – why not?"

He looked at her mutely, then turned away. Of course they both knew why not – but that was something they never mentioned.

"I'd better pack this lot up," he said at last, indicating the scattered parts of the machine-gun.

"Sooner you than me. I wouldn't know where to start."

"I thought I did," he said ruefully. "It all seemed pretty straightforward when I took it to bits, but now. . . ."

She stared at him, trying not to laugh: "You mean you can't remember how to put it together again?"

"I'm not absolutely sure. . . ." Sheepishly, he admitted: "I think I might have mislaid one of the parts." Then his face cracked into a grin: "Goodness only knows what the Sergeant will have to say about it! Have me court-martialled, he will."

"Here, let me help – they do say two heads are better than one." Relieved that the atmosphere had lightened, Polly dropped to her knees and began to pick up various metal objects. "You know, when I go back to work on Monday, and they ask if I had a nice weekend in the country, I'll be able to say: 'Oh, yes – very nice, thanks – very peaceful . . . I spent most of my time helping to put a machine-gun together!'."

The Blitz on London was not nearly as intense as it had been; once the Luftwaffe stopped coming over every single night, people began to relax a little. That was why a sudden, unexpected attack seemed even more shocking.

Late on Friday evening, an emergency call came through to the Motor Pool; there had been an incendiary raid on a WRNS hostel at Mill Hill, and the number of casualties was not yet known. The building was severely damaged, and all available drivers were being called out to North London, to ferry the survivors to temporary accommodation in Hampstead.

"That means us," said Miranda, grabbing her tin hat.

"Good," said Patsy, pulling on her duffle-coat.

"What's good about it?" Miranda asked.

"I'd sooner be working than sitting here all night, doing nothing. . . . Have you got the address?"

They set out in convoy; while the alert continued, the streets were fairly empty, and they made good time – but when they reached Mill Hill, they were flagged down by Civil Defence workers and policemen, and had to show their passes before they were allowed through.

The Wrens were housed in a late-Victorian mansion surrounded by woodland, and this had created its own problem, since most of the trees had been set alight by floating sparks, and the Fire Service had to clear a way through the ring of fire in order to reach the house.

Patsy and Miranda parked their cars at the end of the drive, alongside NFS floats and waiting ambulances. As they watched, a massive pine, ablaze from top to bottom like an infernal parody of a Christmas tree, fell to the firemen's axes, with pennants of flame streaming from every branch.

Suddenly Miranda caught her breath, remembering an incident from the distant past; once, after a long, hot summer, a blaze had broken out in the shrubbery at Crown House, and spread very quickly – now she felt that time had rolled back – as if she were a small child again, watching with a mixture of fear and fascination as the fire raged. . . .

"It's terrifying, isn't it?" she said, almost to herself.

Beside her, Patsy replied: "I don't think so. It's sort of thrilling, somehow."

Miranda glanced at her; Patsy was staring, wide-eyed, at the silhouetted figures of the firefighters – her eyes shone, reflecting the flames – her lips, slightly parted, curved into a smile.

"OK, lads – now we're getting somewhere!" shouted the Fire Officer in charge, as his men moved in through the channel they had opened up.

A little group of Wrens were huddled together in front of the house, in various stages of undress; some of them had already gone to bed when the incendiaries fell, and there had been no time to do more than pull on outdoor clothes over nighties or pyjamas.

They stood about helplessly, mesmerized by the intense heat and the glaring light that spilled from the open front door and the shattered windows.

"Let's have those women moved, right away!" the Fire Officer barked, above the roar of the flames. "Where are the relief drivers?"

Miranda and Patsy stepped forward: "Here, sir."

"Right – how many can you take in your cars? The sooner we get 'em away from here, the better."

Already, the survivors were being shepherded down the drive by a couple of NFS men; some of them in tears, others looking completely dazed, as if they could not comprehend what was happening to them.

One of the senior Wren officers looked back and exclaimed suddenly: "My bag! – I left my shoulder-bag behind —"

"Never mind that now, miss; just get into the car, please," said the Fire Officer, and gestured impatiently at Miranda to help her.

"Let me take your arm, ma'am—" began Miranda, but the Wren officer pulled free, protesting: "No, no – you don't understand – I must get my bag, it's got my keys in it – all my valuables – I must go back —"

"Where did you leave it, exactly?" Patsy asked.

"Under the stairs; we were sheltering under the stairs, when – when —"

"All right, ma'am," said Patsy. "I'll find it."

And without a moment's hesitation she set off, walking very quickly towards the house.

The Fire Officer yelled after her: "Come back – are you crazy? *Come back here – that's an order!*"

But Patsy ignored him, and continued up the drive.

"Stop that girl, somebody – do you hear? Stop her, can't you — ?"

Miranda began to run after Patsy; although she was very frightened, she knew that she had to catch her before she reached the house. Running as fast as she could, she grabbed Patsy by the arm, just as she was going up the front steps.

"Don't be silly, you can't go in there!" she began, shouting against the tumult.

The heat was overpowering now; she felt it scorching her face, and with every breath she took, burning smoke scalded her throat. Then Patsy looked at her – and she was still smiling.

"Let me go," she said calmly.

She struck Miranda's wrist, throwing off her restraining hand, and moved towards the open door. The last Miranda saw of her, Patsy was walking into the house, into the heart of the fire, her face transfigured with joy – on her way to meet her lover.

Martin did not know where he was.

Some time earlier, he had been in the pub – he had tried to play a game of darts with some of the villagers, but after he'd had a few beers, his aim was uncertain, and he had made a poor showing.

But win or lose, he had insisted on buying drinks all round – and from then on things got a little hazy. He seemed to remember making his way back to the housekeeper's flat – throwing off his clothes – flopping into bed, and trying to sleep – but it seemed to be unusually warm tonight, and he couldn't get comfortable.

After that, everything got very muddled; one moment he was lying awake in the darkness, aware of the room revolving around him like a giant wheel – and then it was no longer a wheel, but a bomber on a night mission – and he was sitting in the cockpit next to Caldicott, flying over the Kiel Canal.

They were rolling and lurching badly, and he fought with the joystick, trying to bring the old crate back under control – why wouldn't she respond?

Starbursts of light exploded all around them – there was a deafening roar, and the plane began to drop like a stone.

"*Christ!*" shouted Caldicott: "We're going into a nose-dive – pull her back, Skip. . . . *Come back here – that's an order!*"

His words didn't make sense; Martin turned to his navigator and realized with horror that it wasn't Caldicott at all – how could it be Caldy, who had been shot down over Bremerhaven, months ago – Caldy, who was already dead?

Then he saw that it was Miranda who sat in the seat beside him; Miranda, her face illuminated by leaping yellow flames.

"Mandy — !" He called to her, but she couldn't hear him – she was staring ahead, with a look of absolute terror in her eyes.

Following her gaze, he saw the cockpit windows ablaze with a dazzling incandescent glare – and he felt the searing heat as the plane hurtled on – down and down – into the heart of a blazing furnace. . . .

"Help me — !" he screamed. "Somebody – *help me* — !"

Then there were cool arms about him, and a voice broke through the darkness of the little bedroom – a woman's voice, saying:

"You're all right – you'll be all right now – you were having a bad dream, sir, that's all. . . ."

At first he did not know where he was; then, bit by bit, it all began to fall into place – he was at home, sleeping in the housekeeper's flat – and someone had woken him from a nightmare.

"Who are you?" he managed to ask, hoarsely.

"It's Lilian, sir – Lilian Brooks. I was sleeping in my room next door, and I heard you calling out. Shall I put the light on?"

"No – no, don't do that. . . . Stay here for a minute," he whispered.

"Yes, sir." Holding him tightly, she could feel the sweat on his body. "Why, you're wringing wet. . . . Feverish, you are – aren't you well, sir?"

"I'm all right . . . been drinking a bit too much – sweating it out. . . ."

He began to shiver, and she said: "You'll be catching your death, lying here wet through. Let me fetch a towel."

"Don't go —" he said urgently, as she moved away, but she returned almost immediately, pulling back the bedclothes and dabbing his body with the soft bath towel she had put out for him, earlier in the day.

"You'll feel better soon," she said soothingly; and as she rubbed the towel over his wet skin, she discovered that he was completely naked.

"Yes. . . ." he said, and began to breathe faster. "Better soon. . . ."

He stretched out his hands to find her in the darkness, and held her; she wore nothing but a thin cotton nightdress, and presently he slipped it off her shoulders.

She said nothing, but allowed herself to be drawn into the bed, still stroking him, and they continued to embrace one another, giving and receiving comfort. They exchanged no more words until Martin reached his climax – then he burst into tears and sobbed:

"Thank you . . . Oh, thank you! . . ."

Still she said nothing, but went on holding him in her arms, rocking him very gently until he fell asleep.

Early next morning, when Miranda started work in the garage, there was a message waiting for her. Chief Officer Pinnegar wished to see Wren Gaunt in her office as soon as possible.

"What does she want now?" she asked the CPO mechanic who had passed on the message. "I thought she'd got the weekend off."

But she smartened herself up and reported to the Cypher Unit as instructed. Before she could salute, Chief Officer Pinnegar looked up from her desk and said: "I think we may dispense with formalities this morning. Please sit down."

Bewildered, Miranda obeyed, and the officer went on: "I received a telephone call soon after midnight, telling me what

252

happened at Mill Hill. Some of the officers in that hostel had been members of my staff; it was a terrible shock."

"Yes, ma'am."

"But far worse for you, I'm sure. They tell me that your friend Wren Blair died in the fire – and that you were with her at the last moment."

Miranda stared at the floor; she had been lying awake most of the night, trying to forget that last moment – and the radiant look on Patsy's face. . . .

"This was one of my reasons for coming in to the office today. I do have some work to finish – but I also wanted to tell you personally how very sorry I am, and to ask if there is anything I can do to help. I know you are on call until Monday morning, but perhaps you would like me to have a word with the duty officer? I'm sure that under these circumstances, we could arrange for you to be temporarily replaced —"

"No, ma'am – it's very kind of you, but that won't be necessary."

"Are you quite sure? I'm asking you – not as your superior officer, but as a friend. Perhaps if you were to go home and talk to your family, it might help you to come to terms with this dreadful experience."

Miranda looked up, and was startled by the expression of deep concern and sympathy in the older woman's face.

"Really, ma'am – I shall be all right. To be honest, I'd rather have something to do – I want to keep busy."

"I see. Well, if you're quite sure. . . ." The Chief Officer sighed: "I realize it's small consolation, but at least you know your friend died very bravely. They tell me she was trying to go back into the building to fetch something one of the officers had left behind."

"Yes, ma'am – a shoulder-bag, with keys and valuables in it."

"So I understand . . . I wonder just how valuable they were, compared to that girl's life. She met her death accidentally, trying to do her duty. . . ."

The officer continued to talk, in an attempt to soften the blow for Miranda; but Miranda was no longer listening.

She knew that Patsy had not met her death accidentally; she had gone to meet death quite deliberately – because for her, life had ceased to have any meaning, four months ago.

When Martin awoke the next morning, he felt happier and more relaxed than he had been for a long, long time; but then he started to think about Lilian Brooks – and that was when he began to worry.

By the time he woke up, she had gone back to her own room, so he had never had a chance to speak to her again, after . . . after what had happened.

Now, lying in bed, he had a sinking feeling at the pit of his stomach; how could he have been so stupid? Of course it was his own fault – he had still been half-drunk at the time – and in the dark it had all been so easy and inevitable. . . . Thinking back, he struggled to picture Lilian in his mind's eye, and was ashamed to realize that he could not even remember very clearly what she looked like.

He had never really given her a moment's thought until now; she had been at Crown House for so many years, he had taken her for granted, as if she were part of the fixtures and fittings.

He wondered how old she was. He had vaguely thought of her – in so far as he had ever thought of her at all – as middle-aged; a slow-moving, slow-speaking countrywoman, heavily built, with a plain, homely face. He tried to remember how long she had been in service with the family, and decided she would probably be in her late thirties.

Martin was twenty-two, so there must be at least fifteen or sixteen years between them; last night that had been completely irrelevant and unthinkable, but this morning he could think of nothing else. With growing alarm, he imagined her hanging about during the day, waiting to speak to him on his own – perhaps she imagined that last night's encounter was the beginning of a love affair. . . . He wondered if she would try to turn the situation to her advantage; he dreaded the demands she might make upon him. He would have to leave the house at once; he could pretend there had been a phone call early this morning, summoning him to return to duty immediately.

From the next room, he heard the sounds of someone moving about, and the chink of crockery. He remembered his father saying he would be home in time for breakfast. . . . Well – he'd better get this over as soon as possible.

He stumbled out of bed, slightly hungover, groping into the sleeves of his dressing-gown, then went out into the sitting-room.

To his dismay, he found Lilian there, wearing her starched housekeeping apron over a plain black dress, putting out bowls for cereal. There was no sign of his father.

Lilian glanced at him briefly, then looked away again, saying: "Good morning, sir. His Lordship isn't back yet, but I expect he'll be here directly."

"Oh – yes – I see."

"Will you be wanting cornflakes or porridge, sir?"

"Er – cornflakes, I think . . . I'd better get washed and dressed." About to retreat into the bedroom, he hesitated, feeling called upon to say something, but wondering what on earth he should say. "Um . . . Lilian – about last night. . . ."

"Yes, sir; you'd had a drop too much, I expect," she said cheerfully. "Well, we all make mistakes sometimes, and I don't suppose it'll happen again. Least said, soonest mended, eh?"

"Oh . . . yes."

He hovered in the doorway a moment longer, half-expecting something further, but she kept her eyes fixed on the table as she concluded: "I'll make the tea as soon as His Lordship arrives. Will there be anything more, sir?"

"No, nothing more. . . . Thank you, Lilian."

"Very good, sir." She nodded, and walked out of the room without looking back.

Chapter Fifteen

Saturday, 17 October to Thursday, 25 December 1941

"Isn't it wonderful to have the afternoon off?" said Miranda.

"And such a perfect one," said Caro.

It was a Saturday; a golden October day, with the sun shining and the sky bright blue. In St James's Park, the autumn trees were a firework display of gold, orange and crimson; everyone was taking advantage of the fine weather, and the girls were still wearing their summer dresses.

"I'm glad I changed into civvies," said Miranda, as they passed two senior Naval Officers. "I'd have been saluting every other minute – I've had quite enough of that lately."

"Has the Vinegar Queen been keeping you busy this week?" asked Caro.

Miranda laughed: "Oh, yes – Pinnegar's been dashing about all over the place. I had to drive her to Bletchley Park and back every day."

"What goes on at Bletchley Park?"

"Haven't the remotest idea – but it's something to do with the Cypher Unit – all terribly hush-hush. . . . But today was different – you know I told you she was putting me in for an officer-training course? Well, this morning they suddenly sprang it on me – I had to go before the viva-voce board."

"What on earth's that?"

"A sort of interview, to see if you're good enough. Only it's much worse than an ordinary interview – there were six Wren

Officers sitting at a long table – and me on my own, facing them – like the Spanish Inquisition."

She had been told to report to a tall, gloomy house in Kensington, somewhere near the Victoria and Albert museum; when she got there, she found a dozen other girls awaiting the ordeal. One by one, they were summoned to go before the board, and the group in the waiting-room slowly dwindled. When there were only three candidates left, a clerk called out: "Gaunt!" – and Miranda jumped to her feet.

She hoped her collar was still clean, and that her shoes hadn't lost their polish; surreptitiously, she rubbed one toe behind the other calf, before marching in to the boardroom.

The six officers regarded her coldly; one of them said: "Good morning. You may sit down."

Then they began to fire questions at her, asking what she had been doing since she joined the WRNS, and whether she enjoyed her work; why had she transferred from being "immobile" to "mobile" (when she told them she had been bombed out of her house, none of them said they were sorry to hear it, but they all made notes on the sheets of paper in front of them) – where did she go to school – could she speak any foreign languages – was she good at games – and, most important of all, why did she wish to become an officer?

Miranda remembered a phrase Chief Pinnegar had used: "Because I don't think my duties as a driver are stretching me enough, ma'am. I'd like to do a job where I can really use my brains."

They wrote that down too, without comment.

As she told Caro: "They asked so many questions, I can't remember them all; and then they told me to go and wait in the canteen. Half an hour later, they sent for me again – and told me I'd passed – so now I'm being sent to Greenwich."

"Oh – is that good? . . . What happens at Greenwich?"

"It's the Royal Naval College. That's where they try to turn me into an officer."

Miranda's first sight of the Royal Naval College took her breath away. She had not known what to expect; nobody had told her about this magnificent display of buildings, designed by Sir Christopher Wren – the white stonework, touched with pink in the setting sun, the colonnades, the domes and cupolas. . . . She gasped at the sheer splendour of it all – and exhaled a cloud of frosty vapour that hung in the wintry air. The training course at Greenwich lasted for two weeks, and they were the coldest two weeks of her life.

The College had suffered some damage during the Blitz – although the outside looked as glorious as ever, inside, the building was uninhabitable, and the officer cadets, who should have slept in well-proportioned "cabins" overlooking the Thames, now spent their nights in an underground shelter, sleeping on mattresses spread out upon an icy stone floor.

Of course there were compensations. They took their meals in the Painted Hall, seated at Queen Anne tables carved from ships' timbers, illuminated by silver candlesticks that gleamed on the polished wood and glimmered on the panelled walls.

But there was no time to enjoy it; never a moment when Miranda could stop and stare, and appreciate the glory surrounding her. She never stopped running, yet she was perpetually late.

The daily timetable was divided into so many different periods, and everyone had to be at the right place at the right time – but the timetable did not make any allowance for the distance between point A and point B, so Miranda always turned up, panting and red-faced, a few minutes past time – which was a cardinal sin.

From the moment she awoke, while it was still pitch dark, stumbling in a daze to the bathroom and praying that the hot water hadn't all been used up, then racing through the frozen dawn to breakfast in the Painted Hall – from morning to night, Miranda kept on running.

After breakfast there were lectures, on such topics as Navigation or Admiralty Procedure, or more practical matters like Organizational Management, or Health and Hygiene. There were physical training sessions which were sometimes in the gymnasium and sometimes out on a windswept football pitch –

and every day they spent an hour or more on the parade-ground, drilling under the command of a hefty Sergeant from the Royal Marines, who yelled at them to lift their arms higher, and keep their shoulders back, and put "bags of swank" into it.

By temperament an individualist, Miranda found it very hard to become part of a single-minded, well-oiled machine; she did her best, but as the two weeks dragged on, one question was uppermost in her mind – "Will I be good enough to get through?"

At last the great day arrived; the Duty PO stamped into the air raid shelter at six a.m, telling them all to rise and shine. This was it – the moment they had all been waiting for – the moment of truth.

It was like the viva-voce board all over again; the girls waited in a long corridor outside the Superintendent's office, to be called in one at a time.

"I hope I get posted overseas," said the Wren on Miranda's right. "I'd like to go to North Africa."

"I'd rather go to Gibraltar," said the one on her left. "They say it's lovely – just like England."

"I don't care where they send me, as long as it's somewhere warm," said Miranda.

When at last she entered the office, she faced the Superintendent and the Director of the WRNS, Mrs Laughton Matthews, who smiled and said: "You'll be pleased to hear that everyone has given you a favourable report – though there were one or two minor reservations about punctuality and tidiness. But I'm sure you understand that as an officer, you would be expected to set a good example to others."

"Yes, ma'am." Miranda hardly dared to breathe.

"Very well – in that case, I have no hesitation in approving your promotion." Mrs Laughton Matthews turned to the Superintendent: "Have we selected a posting for Third Officer Gaunt?"

The Superintendent ran her finger down a typed list.

"We have indeed. Since there is a shortage of suitable candidates for the Cypher Unit, she is to be returned to Whitehall to join Chief Officer Pinnegar's staff."

Miranda said in a small voice: "But – forgive me, ma'am – now I'm reclassified as 'mobile', I thought – I mean, I hoped – I might get an overseas posting. . . ."

The Superintendent shook her head: "The Cypher Unit is crying out for extra help, and I know you'll do an excellent job there. Thank you – you may dismiss."

So Miranda had to return to the Admiralty, where Chief Officer Pinnegar welcomed her affably, and she began to study the mysteries of cyphering and decoding, and to accustom herself to her new life as a Junior Wren Officer. Haughty young ladies behind desks, who had scarcely given her the time of day when she was a mere driver, were now her colleagues and her equals – but it was still a big disappointment.

The only silver lining was that she could continue to be Caroline's lodger at Markwick Terrace, pooling their rations and exchanging confidences.

One Sunday evening at the beginning of December, they sat at the kitchen table, making their Christmas lists.

"It's going to be ghastlier than ever this year, finding presents for everyone," said Caro. "I tell you what – let's cross each other off our lists for a start – don't give me anything, and I won't give you anything – all right?"

"Very sensible," Miranda agreed. "Perhaps we could make the same arrangement with Polly and Jenny."

"That's a good idea." Caro began to cross names off her list – then paused. "Except – if we take that to its logical conclusion, we'll finish up with no presents at all, and that's going to be awfully dreary, isn't it?"

"True. . . . Oh, well – we'd better carry on, then," sighed Miranda. "I've started crocheting a scarf for Ma, but it's going to be more like a dishrag by the time it's finished."

Later that evening, when they turned on the BBC news, they heard that Pearl Harbor had been attacked by the Japanese; after a long period of careful neutrality, the United States would now be joining the Allies in the war against Fascism.

"And about time too!" said Caro.

"What do you think will happen?" asked Miranda.

"I don't know – but whatever it is, it's got to be good. In

the last war, it was the Americans joining in that swung the whole thing around; the Germans soon asked for an armistice after that."

"I really meant – what will happen to Scott?"

"Oh, Scott's been saying for ages that the States couldn't stay on the sidelines – I bet you, at this very moment he's sitting at his typewriter, banging out a leading article under the headline: *'What Did I Tell You? . . .'*"

As it happened, she had misjudged her husband.

At breakfast time, the telephone rang, and when Caro answered it, her face lit up.

"Scott! – How are you? Where are you? What's happening?"

His voice sounded thin and metallic, but his words were crystal-clear: "I'm fine – I'm a happy man – I guess you heard our news?"

"We certainly did. I hope you realize what this means – I'm not just your wife now – I'm your co-belligerent!"

When he laughed, her heart danced; she had not heard Scott laughing for a long time.

"Hey, listen —" he went on, "I can't talk long, 'cos I'm using a phone in the office of a good friend of mine at the Pentagon – for the past few months I've been trying every which way to get myself a commission in the Army. I was sure as hell we'd be pitching into the fight, and I wanted to be there when it happened. Now I reckon I'll be in uniform within a matter of days, so put a light in the window for your wandering boy, 'cos I'm on my way!"

When Caro hung up, she relayed this message to Miranda, saying happily: "He still doesn't understand about the blackout, but he'll learn. . . . Isn't it wonderful? – he might even be home for Christmas."

The night before Christmas Eve, Alice was doing her best to make the housekeeper's flat look a little more festive.

"Needs more holly," said William, surveying his wife's handiwork critically. "Over the mantelpiece – and what about the bookcase?"

"I didn't dare touch the bookcase; the top shelf is full of Ministry of Agriculture pamphlets – you never even let me dust up there."

"I'm not likely to need any pamphlets for the next few days. Let's have plenty of holly."

"In that case you'll have to fetch in some more. . . . It's a pity there isn't any mistletoe," Alice said wistfully. "It won't seem like Christmas without that."

"It's not the decorations that make Christmas – it's the people," William told her. "Wait till the family arrive – you'll soon cheer up then."

Alice looked at her watch: "It's getting awfully late."

Soon after that, they heard the sound of the station taxi pulling up on the cobblestones in the yard, and a murmur of voices; Caroline ran up the stairs, dropped her suitcase, and kissed her mother and father.

"Home at last!" she said.

"Darling, your poor face is freezing – and where are the others?"

"Miranda's just paying the driver. . . . We didn't see Martin."

Alice looked stricken: "But that's the last train – you don't suppose they cancelled his leave — ?"

"Oh, no – I expect he'll be here tomorrow." Caro looked round the room. "You've made it all very jolly – what a lot of cards."

"Yes, I think there are more than ever this year – it's amazing, we've had cards from all over the world."

"Anything from Washington?" asked Caro.

"From Scott? No, not yet – but there's still time."

"I wasn't really expecting him to send cards. He said he'll try to get here for Christmas – his ship's probably docking at Southampton this very moment."

Caroline spent a restless night, alone in a double bed – thinking of Scott, and wondering when he would arrive. Having taken so long to get to sleep, the next morning she overslept, and apologized to her mother:

"Sorry I'm so late – you should have woken me."

"Why – what does it matter? You don't have to report for duty at the Hospital today – why not make the most of it?"

Over her tea and toast, Caro asked: "Were there any messages — ?"

"Not exactly, though I rather think – Scott —"

Before she could finish, Caro cut in: "Scott? You've heard from him? Where is he?"

"Oh, no – nothing like that . . . but I think he's sent you a parcel. . . . It's from America, and it looks like his writing on the label."

It was a large cardboard carton, covered in American stamps, Christmas seals, and customs declarations. Scott had sent the family a food hamper; it contained a tinned ham, a Christmas cake, a plum pudding, some corned beef, some salami, some peaches bottled in brandy, various slabs of chocolate, tins of candies and cookies, and a pound of coffee.

"God bless America!" exclaimed Alice. "And God bless your dear husband – it's an absolute banquet. . . ." Then she saw the look on Caro's face. "Why – what's the matter?"

Caro was reading the letter Scott had enclosed: "He says getting into the Army is still complicated – Washington's got too many goddam bureaucrats. . . . There's no hope of seeing him at Christmas, but perhaps – in the New Year. . . ."

"Darling – I'm so sorry."

But Scott wasn't the only absentee.

During the morning, Martin telephoned from Lincolnshire, and when Alice put down the phone, she explained to William: "He says they drew lots to decide who had to stay on duty over the holiday – and he was one of the unlucky ones. . . . Well, I suppose that's the only fair way to do it, really. He sends his love to everybody, and wishes us all a merry Christmas; he hopes he'll be able to get down here some time soon – but he couldn't say exactly when. . . ."

She had tried very hard to sound calm and sensible about it, but as she spoke the last few words, her voice cracked a little.

William put his arms round her. Neither of them said anything; there was nothing to say.

*　　*　　*

263

On Christmas Day, the Minsters gathered for lunch in the old Servants' Hall – the only room in the west wing large enough to accommodate everyone. Lilian Brooks and Ken Stubbs had been invited to join the family, and the Dowager Countess presided at one end of the long table, propped up with cushions in her wheelchair, while at the opposite end Lord Minster carved the turkey.

For weeks now, Alice, Jenny, and Lilian had been saving items from the family rations, to produce something as near the traditional Christmas menu as possible. They had even provided crackers; and although Old Bea grumbled that the mottoes were feeble, the paper hats uninspired, and the "gifts" inside – wire puzzles, penny whistles or imitation jewellery – were very tawdry, the children enjoyed them enormously.

After the pudding and the mince pies, they sat on, gathered round the wireless set which Ken had moved downstairs for the occasion, and listened to the King sending his annual message to the nation and the Commonwealth.

His theme this year was "Absent Friends"; when the speech was over, the family remembered all those who could not be with them.

"It's a shame about Martin," said Caro. "And I know Scott wanted to be here."

"So did Nicholas." Jenny had to take what comfort she could from the long letter Nick had written her, and the silk shawl in peacock colours which he had sent from North Africa; but her best consolation came from eight-month-old Edward, who slumbered peacefully beside her in a pram throughout the meal. "He was so sorry to miss Eddie's first Christmas," she said. "But I'm sure all our men will be home soon."

Across the table, Polly sat between her son and her daughter, smiling fondly and taking great pleasure in their company; too late, Jenny recognized the aching loneliness behind Polly's smile, and knew that she was remembering one man who would never come home again.

"The King sounded rather tired, I thought," said Miranda. "I felt quite sorry for him."

"It's a terrible ordeal for him, every year," Alice reminded her. "He dreads having to speak in public."

"Does Paul Weyman still help to organize the royal broadcasts?" asked Polly.

After a short pause, Alice replied evenly: "Yes, I believe so."

"It's funny, we used to see Paul so often in the old days," Polly continued. "I remember he came to my wedding – but now we seem to have lost touch with him altogether. . . ." Silence fell once more, and then she said quietly: "Sorry, Caro – I am a fool."

"Forget it." Caro pushed back her chair and stood up, saying briskly: "I'm going out for a walk. I need some exercise after that enormous meal."

"Good idea!" Miranda joined her. "Let's go down to the village and try to work up an appetite for tea."

After that the party soon broke up; by half-past four it was almost dark, and as Alice drew the heavy blackout curtains across the sitting-room windows, she said to William: "I was expecting the children to be back by now; we've got a splendid Christmas cake – but it seems silly to cut it, just for you and me."

"They'll probably drift in presently, in ones and twos." William caught his wife's hand, and held it. "And the cake will keep. Sit down and talk to me."

She sat beside him on the sofa near the fire. After a while he continued: "You were quite right – it doesn't feel like Christmas . . . Caro – Jenny – Polly – all lonely, all trying to pretend nothing's wrong."

Alice gave him a sidelong glance: "I wish Polly hadn't started talking about Paul. Of course she wasn't to know, but – it still upsets you, doesn't it? – even to hear his name?"

William frowned: "Every time I think I've put him out of my mind once and for all, he manages to crop up again somehow – and it always catches me off my guard. . . ." He drew Alice closer, and they gazed into the heart of the fire, where a log of applewood spat and settled. "But it wasn't only that . . . I can't

265

help feeling there's something badly wrong – and I don't know what it is."

That evening, they heard on the nine o'clock bulletin – Hong Kong had fallen to the Japanese.

At the lodge cottage, Caro was having supper with Edith and Grace; Lady Beatrice, who had been listening to her own wireless, wheeled herself into the parlour to tell them the latest news.

"This dreadful war. . . ." Edith put her hand to her mouth. "It seems to be nothing but one disaster after another – do you think it will ever come to an end?"

"We must hope and pray," Grace said simply. "The tide will turn, in God's good time – I've no doubt of that."

"Of course it will!" Old Bea cracked her knuckles impatiently. "I'm surprised at you, Edith – a daughter of mine, giving way to despair? Remember what Queen Victoria said: *'There is no depression in this house. . . . We are not interested in the possibilities of defeat; they do not exist'.*"

Caro did her best to cheer her aunt, saying: "Now the Americans have got into the war, it will soon be over."

Then they heard someone knocking at the front door, and a moment later Alex's voice called through the letter-box:

"Auntie Caro – are you there? It's me!"

When Caro brought him into the little parlour, the boy was pink with excitement, proud to be the bearer of an important message.

"Mum says I'm to tell you – there was a telephone call for you – from America! Person-to-person, she said; Grandpa told them to ring again in twenty minutes – so you've got to come back right away!"

Holding Alex's hand, Caro ran all the way; she went straight to her parents' sitting-room and waited breathlessly by the phone as the minutes ticked by.

When it rang, William and Alice disappeared into the kitchen, leaving her to talk to Scott on her own.

"Hi there!" he began. "Merry Christmas, honey."

"Happy Christmas, my darling – and thank you so much for that fantastic hamper. . . . How are you? What's your news? How soon will I see you?"

266

"I wish I knew. I thought by now I'd be on my way, but – it didn't work out like that. . . ."

"Why – what's happened?"

"They rejected me. Unsuitable for military service. I thought maybe I could appeal against the decision, but it seems not."

"Unsuitable? Did they tell you why?"

"They don't have to give a reason. Could be on account of my age. Maybe they think I'm too old to start life all over as a Serviceman, at the grand old age of forty!"

"That's not old! I bet the Army's full of forty-year-old men – lots of Generals and Colonels are older than forty!"

"Maybe they didn't consider drafting me in as a three-star General. . . . But most likely it's on account of my political record. The Pentagon aren't any too keen on Commie sympathizers."

"But that's ridiculous – the Russians are our Allies now!"

"You try telling that to the Pentagon. . . . Like I say, there's no way of knowing, but the sad fact remains, sweetheart – they gave me the bum's rush."

"Oh, Scott – I'm so sorry. What will you do now?"

"God knows. Looks like I'll be stuck here for the duration. . . . Maybe I'll get me a job in a factory – making munitions." She heard the surge of longing in his voice, as he added: "All I know right now is – I'm missing you like hell. . . ."

"And I miss you – terribly." Suddenly, violently, she exclaimed: "Oh, I hate this bloody war – and most of all – *I hate Christmas!*"

Chapter Sixteen

Friday, 16 January to Monday, 27 April 1942

In the New Year, newcomers began to arrive in London. Day after day, more and more American servicemen appeared on the streets; lean and suntanned as film stars in their smooth, well-tailored uniforms, they strolled through the city like tourists on a sightseeing trip, gazing at the famous landmarks and taking snapshots with the cameras that hung around their necks. Day after day, Caro became more silent and more unhappy; until one Friday night, when she arrived home from the hospital in a towering rage, and reported to Miranda: "Would you believe it? A GI outside Victoria Station actually tried to pick me up!"

Miranda laughed: "You should be flattered. None of them ever dare speak to me; I think it's because I'm an officer – they're afraid I'll whistle up an MP and have them arrested. . . . It's rather funny – they call their Military Policemen 'Snowdrops', because of their white helmets."

"I don't see anything funny about it." Caro threw herself into a chair. "My GI had the nerve to offer me a stick of chewing-gum – and then he said: 'I guess you never met anyone from the US of A. before!'"

"Well, he wasn't to know." Miranda's tone softened. "But I do see it must be beastly for you, seeing all those Americans over here, while poor old Scott —"

"While he's sweating over some dreary desk-job in Washington. . . . It's so unfair! How dare they persecute him, just because of his political viewpoint?"

268

"It might be nothing to do with politics." Miranda tried to console her: "The ways of the Administration are a complete mystery – look at me, for instance – I've applied for an overseas posting three times now, but nothing ever happens, and nobody can tell me why. . . . It's probably just the same in America."

Caro sighed: "I suppose so . . . Heaven knows how the Powers-That-Be are ever going to win this war – when they can't even sort out little problems like yours and mine."

January was a cold, unfriendly month, and February was colder still. The plumbing at Crown House, which was becoming fairly antiquated, could not cope with the drop in temperature; the water tanks froze in the attics above the west wing – and as the ice expanded, the pipes burst.

The Minsters awoke one morning to the sound of water dripping in their little sitting-room, and discovered that it was coming steadily through the ceiling.

Alice and Lilian spent some time clearing all the books and papers out of harm's way, mopping the carpet with old towels, and putting down bowls and basins in an attempt to deal with the worst of the deluge; while overhead William – with Ken's assistance – mounted a rickety stepladder and explored the loft.

Having managed to turn off the water-supply at the mains stopcock, they eventually sealed up the cracked pipes; but there was very little hope of getting the overworked local plumber to do any major repairs in the immediate future.

In the Servants' Hall, Alice gazed in despair at the empty sink in the big old-fashioned kitchen, and asked: "What on earth are we going to do? We can't live here without any running water!"

"If I might make a suggestion," said Ken Stubbs, tentatively, "there's Glebe Cottages, down at the farm, standing empty. They need a bit of doing up, but they're warm and dry, and they had new plumbing put in not so long ago. You could do worse than camp out there for a while."

William smiled for the first time that day, and said: "Thank you, Ken. Oddly enough, I had been considering whether we should use those cottages – though for quite a different reason. So this may prove to be a blessing in disguise – the burst pipes have helped me to make up my mind."

In the old days, Glebe Cottages had been "tied" accommodation for the farm workers, but now that the younger men had gone into the Services, and a good many of the older men and women had moved to better-paid jobs in munition factories, they were no longer tenanted.

A row of three identical cottages, they stood under one long thatched roof, each one having a small parlour and kitchen downstairs, and two little bedrooms above. The original earth-closets at the bottom of the gardens were removed in the 'thirties, and an extension had been built at the back, providing bathrooms and flush lavatories.

At the time, William remembered, his mother had been scandalized by such reckless extravagance, though he tried hard to explain that they would never recruit farmhands if they could not offer these ordinary amenities. Now his foresight was being rewarded.

"This will solve a problem that has been on my mind for some time," he continued. "I still feel that Crown House should be serving some useful purpose – and when the American troops started to arrive, I realized they would need accommodation. So I offered them Crown House, and I've been informed that the United States Army Air Force would be glad to move in – but with one proviso. . . ." He hesitated briefly, before continuing: "For security reasons, they could not share the premises with us; so we shall have to find ourselves other quarters. Now it seems that we are forced to move in any case, and I'm sure there can be no objection to our settling in at Glebe Cottages. The farm is sufficiently far away from the house, and we shall have separate access by the back road."

After a long moment, Alice said: "William dear – I do wish you would discuss things with me sometimes, before you come to these decisions."

He looked at her in bewilderment: "But I'm discussing

it with you now! We must all put our heads together and work out the best way of tackling the situation. Obviously, the Americans are eager to move in as soon as possible."

"Yes, I'm sure they are, but – it's not only *us*, is it? What about Polly – and Jenny – and the children? Will your Americans want to take over the garage block as well?"

"Oh, yes – undoubtedly. But that's why Glebe Cottages will be so convenient; there are six bedrooms altogether – plenty of room for all of us."

"And what about Lilian?" Alice wanted to know. "She'll need somewhere nearer the lodge, to be on call for your mother —"

"But Mama won't be at the lodge!" William corrected her. "The Americans will want to use the lodge as a guardhouse, by the main gates. I'm sure Edith and Grace will soon find somewhere else nearby – and they can take Mama and Lilian with them."

Alice exclaimed: "Really, William! – you can't shuffle people about as if they were pieces on a chessboard – aren't they to have any say in the matter?"

Foreseeing a domestic disagreement, Ken said tactfully: "I think I'll just nip down to the village and see what I can arrange with the plumber – if you'll excuse me. . . ."

As soon as the door shut behind him, William tried to pacify his wife: "My dear – why don't we sit down and have a cup of tea, and talk things over quietly?"

"Certainly – if you're prepared to take the kettle all the way to Jenny's flat and fetch some water," said Alice. "And you might as well break the news to her at the same time that she's got to start packing!"

William struggled to be calm and reasonable: "I realize we shall all have to make some changes in our living arrangements, but that's the way things are now – many people have to put up with far worse hardships."

"Of course they do – but this all seems so unnecessary!" complained Alice. "Just think – all of us, squashed together in those tiny cottages – with two children and a baby. . . ."

"Polly won't be there during the week – and you're

away a good deal yourself, aren't you?" William reminded her.

"So that's it. . . ." Alice folded her arms: "Well, I can tell you one thing – I shan't be there to provide moral support when you try to explain your plans at the lodge cottage. When you tell your mother she's got to move again – you'll be on your own!"

That evening, William set out to tackle the three old ladies – and armed himself with a bottle of sherry.

"Not the first quality, I'm afraid," he said, as he filled their glasses. "But it might help to warm the cockles of our hearts – whatever they may be."

Edith and Grace expressed their appreciation; Old Bea sniffed, gulped, snorted, and pronounced: "I suppose it's better than nothing!" – then held out her glass to be refilled, while William began to expound his plan.

They listened in growing dismay. Edith and Grace exchanged glances, and when her brother had finished speaking, Edith clasped Grace's hand, asking faintly: "But William – where ever shall we go?"

"I've no doubt there are plenty of empty houses in the area," he told her. "A good many people moved down to the West Country when the Battle of Britain began; they'll be only too glad to find some decent tenants."

"All the same – it may be some time before we find somewhere suitable," Grace pointed out. "How soon would you expect us to move out?"

"Oh, there's no immediate urgency," William told her. "It will take the USAAF a while to convert Crown House to their purposes; you won't have to pack up and leave all in five minutes. Take your time – explore every possibility . . . I believe there are some attractive properties near Medford Park – you'd enjoy that, Mama – closer to the town, convenient for the shops —"

But when he turned to his mother, Lady Beatrice was not even looking in his direction.

"Tell my son I refuse to speak to him," she told Edith haughtily. "And you may add that if he thinks he can bribe me to leave my own home with a bottle of third-rate cooking sherry, he is very much mistaken!"

"Now, Mama – let's try to be sensible about this—" began William.

The old lady interrupted him, turning her wheelchair so she had her back to him, and saying: "I am going to my room, Edith – you may come and put me to bed as soon as you please. . . . And you had better begin preparations for my funeral as soon as possible – after this shock to my system, I doubt if I shall live to see another day!"

All the same, Lady Beatrice had no intention of going to meet her Maker quite so soon; by the time Edith came in to help her undress, she had decided upon a plan of action.

"It's very simple," she said. "We are not going to be driven out of this cottage; you can tell your brother that we intend to stay where we are. And since you and Grace are defenceless spinsters, and I am a frail elderly widow, public sympathy will be on our side. If he's looking for a fight, he shall have one – just tell him that!"

Edith cleared her throat, then began: "But Mama – Grace and I were wondering —" She faltered, and stopped.

"Well? What were you wondering? Do you have a better suggestion?"

Edith moistened her lips, and then replied in a whisper: "No, Mama. . . . Not really."

When she went back into the parlour, Grace looked up from her crochet work and asked: "Well? What did she say?"

"I didn't tell her. . . . I couldn't."

"But my dear – we agreed —"

"I know, but – when it came to the point. . . . She says if we all stick together, William can't turn us out."

Grace put aside her crochet: "Come and sit by me. . . . You have to explain to her – tell her we don't wish to stay."

"Yes, but – she never listens to anything I say. . . . Couldn't you talk to her? You know what a coward I am."

"I know nothing of the kind." Grace slipped her arm round Edith's waist, drawing her closer. "When we were about to leave Collioure, it would have been so easy for us to skip across the frontier into Spain – but you were the one who decided to go back and look for Miranda. All the time we were on the road, we were risking our lives – we could have been shot, or sent to a concentration camp, but you would never give up. And I was so proud of you."

"Grace – please – you're embarrassing me. . . ."

"Hear me out, my love. . . . Now you have to face that old lady in the next room, and explain to her. If you give in to her this time, we'll never be able to call our souls our own."

"Very well." Edith held Grace tightly for a moment, then said: "Wish me luck."

When the bedroom door reopened, Lady Beatrice had her bedside light on; she was sitting up in bed, her reading-glasses at the end of her nose, catching up on last Sunday's *News of the World*.

"Well, well!" she exclaimed. "What did you forget this time?"

"Nothing, Mama. There's something I must tell you . . . Grace and I have had a talk, and we decided that we agree with William. It would be wrong to let Crown House stand empty, when it might be helping the war effort. We are very glad he has offered it to the Americans."

The old lady took off her spectacles, and glared: "What are you saying?"

"Grace has some relatives in Scotland – some cousins, on a farm near Perth. They have written to her several times, inviting her to go and stay with them – inviting both of us . . . I've never been to Scotland – and everyone says it's very beautiful. I haven't touched my water-colours since we left France; I might take up painting again."

"Scotland? – Water-colours? – I never heard such nonsense!" Old Bea's bony hands clawed at the eiderdown. "What about *me* —?"

"Grace and I will help you find somewhere to live; a nice little house, just big enough for you and Lilian Brooks. William says there are some to let at Medford Park —"

"Don't mention that man's name to me! I don't want to be cooped up in some nasty little suburban villa – you must stay

274

and look after me. I am your mother, and I have first claim on you —"

"No, Mama." Edith drew herself up, looking straight ahead. "Grace has first claim on me. We have made our lives together; I must go where she goes."

At the beginning of March, Miranda received a picture postcard from Lincolnshire – a photograph of the Lincoln Imp, one detail from the great treasure house of carvings in the Cathedral – and even before she turned it over to see the message on the back, a sudden burst of happiness surged through her. After all these months of silence, without any communication between them, Martin had got in touch with her at last.

He must have known that she had been feeling particularly low. Only yesterday, she had been told that her application for an overseas posting had been turned down yet again – and she was beginning to think she'd been wasting her time. For some unknown reason, someone in authority, high in the Olympian upper regions of the Admiralty, had taken a marked dislike to Junior Officer Gaunt, and was deliberately dashing her hopes in order to spite her.

She would have felt a little better about it if she'd had someone to turn to – someone who could advise her – or just a cosy shoulder to cry on. Of course she could pour out her troubles to Caro, but she suspected that Caro, though invariably kind and sympathetic, was getting a little tired of hearing the same old story every time. After all, Caro was equally stuck in her hospital job, with no chance of being posted anywhere more exciting – and no hope of seeing her husband again until the end of the war. . . . No, it wasn't fair to keep moaning to Caro.

But suddenly – here was Martin, holding out a helping hand – Martin would listen to her tale of woe – Martin would understand. . . .

Turning the card over, she read the scrawled message:

"Hello, you! How's tricks? I'm feeling on top of the world

275

now, so I suppose that means you're OK too – ain't life wonderful? I still go to the Ring o' Bells on Saturday nights, and always think of you. I expect we'll meet again one of these days – dunno where, dunno when, as the song says – but until then – lots of love from – Your Lincoln Imp."

Miranda sat down, slightly deflated, and read it through once more, trying to find a deeper message between the lines. Was he suggesting they should get together again – or was he telling her that he was quite happy to go his own way without her? If only she could talk to him. . . .

Suddenly one phrase sprang out: *"I still go to the Ring O'Bells on Saturday nights"* . . . And today was Saturday.

She looked at the clock – twenty past seven – he might be there now. Of course! – that was why he'd mentioned it – he was hinting that if she wanted to speak to him, she could ring him this evening.

Quickly, she found the number of the hotel, and put through the call.

One of the barmaids answered the phone; there was a lot of chatter and raucous laughter in the background, and Miranda had to speak slowly and clearly to make herself heard.

The barmaid asked: "What was the name – ? Oh, Martin Gaunt – yes, of course I know him, he always comes in of a Saturday. . . . No, he's not here yet, dear – but I expect he'll pop in any time now – can I give him a message?"

Very carefully, Miranda spelled out her name and the phone number at Caroline's flat, and the girl promised to tell Martin as soon as he arrived.

Then Miranda made herself some supper, and sat down and waited for the phone to ring.

At the end of the evening, she gave up and went to bed.

So that was that . . . Martin felt he had already done his brotherly duty by scribbling a postcard. It had not been a helping hand after all – more like a slap in the face.

On Monday morning, she reported for work at the Admiralty

as usual, and was given a long and involved report which had to be encoded and transmitted.

Chief Officer Pinnegar went through it with her, explaining carefully what had to be done; Miranda tried to follow her instructions, but she was finding it hard to concentrate.

At last the Chief put down her pen and asked, not unkindly: "Are you feeling unwell?"

"No, ma'am."

"Are you quite sure? You have no colour in your cheeks, and there are dark shadows under your eyes – and you seem to have difficulty in following what I say to you."

"I beg your pardon, ma'am. I – I haven't been sleeping very well lately."

"I'm sorry to hear that. Is there any particular reason?"

Suddenly Miranda had a terrible feeling that she might burst into tears; she struggled to suppress her emotion, and said huskily: "I had some – personal problems – ma'am."

Chief Officer Pinnegar put the report into her pending-tray, and said: "May I offer you some advice? We all have to deal with problems in our private lives – times of anxiety, times of unhappiness – but although it may seem like a cliché to say so, these bad times will pass, you know; and you can make them pass more quickly, if you try not to brood on them. Because there are always other things in our lives – and dare I say? – very often they are more important. In your case, you have your work, which is the best remedy of all. If you can throw yourself into your work, heart and soul, you'll soon be able to forget everything else . . . I can say that with absolute conviction, because I speak from personal experience."

The Chief glanced at her wristwatch, took the report from the pending-tray, and said with the ghost of a smile: "Perhaps we might make a start now?"

"Yes, ma'am. . . . Thank you, ma'am."

Slowly – grudgingly – winter gave way to spring, though April brought more showers than sunshine. The news from the battlefronts was no better; after the fall of Hong Kong,

Singapore followed, and 85,000 British troops were forced to surrender to the Japanese.

At home, life became increasingly grim; rationing was tighter than ever, and there were severe shortages of everything, from cigarettes to crockery, and beer to bananas. Petrol rations for private motoring were withdrawn altogether – and Lady Minster was able to give up driving with a clear conscience.

But this was small consolation while the domestic situation at Crown House continued to be unsettled. Alice did her best to support her husband in his decision to hand over the property to the USAAF, but moving into Glebe Cottages was beset with problems; trying to find space for four adults, two children and a twelve-month baby, she felt great sympathy for the Old Woman Who Lived in a Shoe.

Things were not made any easier by Lady Beatrice's stubborn refusal to leave the lodge cottage. When Edith and Grace packed up and departed for Scotland at the beginning of April, the old lady instructed Lilian Brooks to move into their empty bedroom; she refused pointblank to consider alternative accommodation.

Using Alice as an intermediary, she sent her son a message, saying that if he wished to turn her out, he would have to use brute force – whereupon she would immediately write to all the national newspapers, explaining how Lord Minster had evicted his eighty-nine-year old mother from her family home.

"Goodness knows what I'm going to do," sighed William, after another fruitless attempt to negotiate with his mother. "Can't you talk some sense into her?"

"I do have one little trick up my sleeve," Alice admitted. "Though I don't guarantee results."

The next time she visited the Dowager Countess, she took an armful of tulips and narcissi with her – and a bar of milk chocolate.

Old Bea accepted the peace-offering ungraciously: "I suppose your husband told you to soften me up? You can tell him he's wasting his time. . . . The only way he'll get me out of here is in my box!"

278

"As a matter of fact – I came to bring you an invitation," said Alice.

"Did you indeed!" The old lady sniffed: "So you've persuaded one of your friends to ask me to tea? . . . When we come back, no doubt I shall find all my bits and pieces stacked outside in the drive, eh?"

"You have a suspicious mind," Alice smiled. "Surely you don't suppose their Majesties would conspire in such a plot?"

"Their Majesties —?"

"Princess Elizabeth is about to celebrate her sixteenth birthday; and before that she's going to be confirmed in the chapel at Windsor. Queen Mary will be coming up from Badminton – I understand she's anxious to see you again."

The Dowager Countess preened herself: "Queen Mary and I have always been very good friends. . . . If she wishes to see me, I can hardly refuse."

"Quite . . . I don't think we should travel to Windsor and back in one day; we might stay overnight with my brother – if you have no objection?"

Old Bea considered this: "I've never thought much of Charlie Bowyer, but I suppose – for one evening – I could put up with the man. Lives in a flat in Mayfair, doesn't he? How would I manage the stairs?"

"There's a lift, Mama; I think it will take the wheelchair."

"Ah, well – I suppose it might make a change – and I would enjoy visiting Windsor again. . . . Will they give us lunch?"

When Alice rang her brother and put the plan to him, he reacted in alarm: "Good heavens! – I don't know about that – this flat is an absolute pigsty. I haven't had any living-in staff since the Blitz; only an old crone who drops in once a week to rearrange the dust . . . and I'm hopeless in the kitchen – I live on sandwiches and tins of soup. . . . Your blessed mother-in-law wouldn't care for that."

"Don't worry, Charlie; we'll bring some food with us, and I'll make the supper. It's only for one night; we shall leave early next morning, to get to Windsor in good time."

The trip seemed to rejuvenate Lady Beatrice. She insisted on the hire-car taking a circuitous route, so that she could inspect

279

the shell of the old house in Eaton Square. Alice was afraid this might be a shock for her, but all she said was: "*That's* going to cost somebody a pretty penny. . . . Drive on."

Her meeting with Sir Charles went off quite smoothly. Wisely, he offered Lady Beatrice a pink gin the moment she arrived; she enquired after his health, and then told him in great detail about her own. At one point she ran a finger across the top of an occasional table, to demonstrate the shortcomings of his domestic staff, but he poured her another stiff drink, and took her mind off it.

By the time they sat down to supper, the combination of alcohol and exhaustion was taking its toll, and she nodded off during the meal. When Alice put her mother-in-law to bed, she stayed on to talk to her – and since Old Bea was in a good mood, she ventured to raise the topic of the lodge cottage.

"Ha! I thought we'd come round to that, sooner or later." The old lady shut her eyes. "I'm too old to be whisked from pillar to post; I'm staying put, and that's that."

"I know, Mama, but it's the same for all of us. William has made up his mind that it's our patriotic duty to give up the house – couldn't you think of it as your contribution towards winning the war?"

The old lady yawned: "I've already given up taking sugar in my tea. . . . Now you're asking me to shut myself up in a stucco rabbit hutch at Medford Park with nobody but Lilian Brooks for company – and all for the sake of a lot of Yankees!"

Alice persevered gently: "More and more American troops are arriving now – we should feel proud that they want to stay at Crown House . . . and they really need the lodge cottage as well – do you understand? . . . Mama —?"

But there was no reply. The Dowager Countess of Minster was fast asleep.

Next morning, she woke bright and early. Alice produced a cooked breakfast, and the old lady tucked in heartily, without any trace of a hangover.

She enjoyed the drive to Windsor, and kept up a running commentary on various places of interest along the way, but she never mentioned the lodge cottage. Alice could not decide whether she had forgotten their bedtime conversation, or whether she was deliberately ignoring it.

They arrived at the Castle in good time, and drove through to the inner courtyard; a footman assisted Lady Beatrice into her chair, then wheeled her into the chapel.

The Confirmation Service was a private occasion, restricted to the immediate family and close friends, and Alice felt that, at any parish church, anywhere in the country, she might have witnessed a similar ceremony. Afterwards, they all gathered in their Majesties' drawing-room; Alice wheeled her mother-in-law up to be presented to the King and Queen – and then to the end of the room, where Queen Mary held out a welcoming hand, and smiled: "Dear Beatrice – I am so glad you were able to manage the journey; it's always a pleasure to meet an old friend."

"It's a great privilege, Ma'am." The Dowager Countess touched the outstretched hand. "Especially on such a memorable occasion."

"Yes, I was extremely proud of Lillibet," said Her Majesty. "But then she has always taken her responsibilities very seriously."

"As I was watching her, during the service, I was reminded of someone else, a long time ago," said Old Bea. "The same air of solemnity – the same natural dignity —"

"I think I know what you are going to say; you and I are probably the only ones here old enough to make that comparison. . . . She put you in mind of her great-great-grandmother?"

"Yes, Ma'am – of Queen Victoria."

When Alice moved away, leaving the two old friends together, Princess Elizabeth greeted her warmly.

"Lady Minster – Mummy told me you would be here. How are all your family, at Crown House?"

Alice explained that there were very few of the family at home now; Nick and Martin were both on active service –

Caroline was nursing in London, and Miranda was a Wren Third Officer at the Admiralty.

"Goodness, how exciting for them. . . ." The Princess lowered her voice: "Did you know? – It will be my birthday next week – and then I'm going to register at the Labour Exchange."

"Yes, your mother told me. You'll be setting an example to all the other sixteen-year-olds."

The Princess smiled ruefully: "It would be more of an example if I could volunteer for war work, like your family. I ought to be doing something useful – but Daddy still thinks of me as his little girl. . . . He doesn't realize I've grown up."

By this time, Lady Beatrice too was airing her grievances.

"But my dear – if you are to leave Crown House – where will you go?" Her Majesty wanted to know.

"I have no idea, Ma'am – I could finish up anywhere!" Old Bea protested. "They say it's my duty to move out and let some Americans take over my little cottage, but I'm sure you see my point of view – we're too old to be uprooted at our time of life – don't you agree?"

Queen Mary, who was a mere seventy-five years old, pursed her lips: "Perhaps I shall do so – when I reach your age, Beatrice. . . . At present I can only say that I envy you."

Taken aback, Old Bea repeated: "*Envy* me, Ma'am? I don't understand."

"You are fortunate to have the freedom of choice. You spent last night in London; I am never allowed to do that. I am treated as if I were a priceless national treasure, buried in the country for safekeeping! . . . Whereas you can travel to London – you can be at the heart of things. . . . You don't know how lucky you are."

"Lucky?" Old Bea looked pensive. "I hadn't thought of it like that."

By the end of April, Miranda was feeling desperate.

There had been no word from Martin – no response to her telephone call – and although she tried hard to accept the fact that he was deliberately rejecting her, she was bitterly unhappy.

If only she could get away – a long way away – she might be able to put him out of her mind, once and for all. But the overseas posting she had set her heart on seemed to have become an impossible dream.

Finally she made up her mind. During her morning coffee-break, she slipped away from the Cypher Unit and went down to the Administration Office on the second floor.

Luckily, there was a young officer on duty whom she knew slightly; they had been through the Naval College at the same time. Miranda explained that she had applied repeatedly for an overseas posting, without getting any encouragement.

"If they keep rejecting me, I'd like to know why," she demanded. "Don't they like my face? Has somebody put a black mark against my name? Be a sport – put me out of my misery. Anything's better than this everlasting silence."

The officer smiled and said: "I'll see what I can do. Hang on a tick, while I go and look up your personal file."

Three minutes later she was back again, saying: "You don't have to worry about black marks – just the opposite, actually. You've got such a good report, you ought to be wearing a halo! According to the confidential recommendation, you're so jolly efficient, you've become irreplaceable – that's why she won't let you go."

"Who won't let me go?"

"Your boss – Chief Officer Pinnegar. Every time you put in for a transfer, she turns it down."

Chapter Seventeen

Monday, 27 April to Tuesday, 25 August 1942

Ten minutes later, Miranda tapped on Chief Officer Pinnegar's door.

"Yes, Gaunt? What is it?" asked the officer, as she walked in.

"I should like to speak to you, ma'am. I've just heard that you have been blocking my application for overseas posting."

The officer's face changed: "Where did you hear that?"

"I understand it is in my personal file."

"Who said so?"

"I can't tell you that, ma'am."

"I'm afraid I must insist. Staff records are highly confidential, and if there has been some leakage of information, I must know who —"

Too angry to be diplomatic, Miranda interrupted: "I'm not going to tell you. I just want to know – why did you do it? You knew how much I wanted to get away from London – why wouldn't you let me go?"

"You must not address me in that tone. I realize you are upset, but —"

"You can have me court-martialled if you like – I don't care. Why couldn't you tell me the truth?"

The Chief Officer looked down at the pages of figures spread out before her, then asked, in a different tone: "I don't think you ever met Angela Bennett, did you? She was the driver who worked for me before you arrived – she was killed one evening, during a raid."

"Yes – I'm sorry – I heard about that. But I never knew her."

"She was an intelligent girl; like you, she was too good to remain a driver. I had already recommended her for officer training, before the tragedy occurred. It was a great shock to me, because I had been planning her future. I intended to train her personally; perhaps, in time, to make her my second in command. But of course those plans came to nothing."

Miranda did not know what to say; she could not understand what this unhappy story had to do with her own situation.

After a moment, the Chief continued, without looking up: "And then you took her place as my driver – and as I came to know you, I realized that you could replace her completely. I discovered that you were even more intelligent – even more outstanding. I flatter myself that I saw something of myself in you – as I had been at your age, when I first joined the Service.

"So I gave you your chance to become a junior officer – and you have not disappointed me. In due course you will become my second in command – as and when I am promoted to a higher echelon, you will take my place as Head of Section. Now you understand why I could not let you go; it would have been a terrible waste of your abilities. Your place is here – at my desk, to carry on my work."

It was very quiet in the office; the only sound was the hum of passing traffic in Whitehall.

At last Miranda said: "It's very good of you to tell me this, ma'am, and I'm very grateful, but – you see, I don't want to spend the rest of the war sitting at a desk. I have two brothers on active service – I want to be where the action is."

Then Chief Officer Pinnegar looked up, studying her carefully, and asked: "Are you quite certain about that?"

Miranda answered: "Yes, ma'am – absolutely certain."

"Yes – I can see that you are." The Chief sighed, and lowered her gaze. "Very well . . . tomorrow morning, I shall inform Administration that I am prepared to release you for overseas posting. I wish you every success – wherever you go."

The new posting did not happen automatically; for several weeks, Miranda continued to work in the Cypher Unit. Chief Officer Pinnegar remained courteous and pleasant, but they never had another personal conversation.

When at last her orders for embarkation came through, everything happened very quickly; at the end of May, Caroline went down to spend a weekend at Crown House, and told the family: "Miranda's been sent overseas. To an unknown destination – but she was issued with tropical kit, and had shots for malaria and yellow-fever – so we think she could be on her way to North Africa."

"I wonder if she'll run into Nick while she's out there." Jenny stroked the head of her small son, who was taking a siesta on her lap. "By the time he comes home, he won't recognize Eddie – will he, my poppet?"

Though most of the family had settled in at Glebe Cottages by now, they were enjoying a sunny Sunday afternoon on the terrace, where early bees buzzed contentedly among tubs of wallflowers.

"At least you know that when Nick gets some leave, he'll be coming home," said Caroline. "I haven't the faintest idea when I'll see Scott – he doesn't even write very often."

"How naughty of him!" Alice was shocked. "I hope Miranda sends us regular letters – I shall worry about her, now she's so far away. I expect she'll he homesick for England —"

Her words were drowned by a fusillade of hammering from within the house. Lady Beatrice, dozing in her wheelchair, woke with a start, grumbling: "Are those Americans at it again? Have they no respect for the Sabbath?"

"They're working right round the clock, Mama," Alice told her. "There are so many alterations to be made – and they haven't been able to start on the lodge cottage yet," she added pointedly.

"I shall move when I'm ready, and not before," snapped the old lady. "I need time to find somewhere I like – I won't be rushed!"

"You've been saying that for weeks," Alice protested. "Colonel Schmidt has been very patient, but they really must start work on the guardhouse soon."

"Schmidt! – What sort of a name is that? The man's probably a German spy." The Dowager Countess still took a jaundiced view of Britain's allies. She turned to her granddaughter: "Tell me, Caroline – if Miranda's gone abroad – who's sharing with you, in Chelsea?"

"Nobody, Grandmama. I've got the flat to myself."

"Ah. . . ." Old Bea's eyes narrowed. "How many bedrooms?"

"Only two, but—" Just in time, Caro saw the way her mind was working. "Surely you're not thinking of living in London?"

"You wouldn't like it, dear – London's very noisy," said Alice.

Indoors, a deafening high-pitched whine meant that the workmen were drilling holes through the walls.

"It would be a haven of peace, after this place!" said Lady Beatrice. "It's a pity you only have two bedrooms, Caroline – but I dare say we could fit a camp-bed for Lilian into my room."

"I'm afraid not." Caro was standing firm. "That won't be possible."

The old lady bristled: "And why not?"

"Because—" As Caro searched for a reason, it suddenly fell into her mind. "Because I've decided to go and live in America – with Scott."

As soon as she said it, she realized that it was what she had wanted for a long time; if her husband couldn't come to her, she would go to him.

Alice exclaimed: "But darling – you've always been so determined not to give up your hospital job —"

"Yes, and now I've decided I've done it long enough – I might be able to help in a hospital over there."

"I never heard of such a thing!" Old Bea disliked being

287

thwarted: "If you leave England, people will think you're running away!"

"Rubbish," said Caro calmly. "I'm not running *from* anything – I'm running *to* something. . . . I'm going to my husband."

It was one of life's little ironies, Miranda thought. Not much more than six months ago, she had been aching with cold at the Royal Naval College. Now – in Alexandria at the end of June – she felt she might melt into a little pool of grease.

Lying on her bed in the Wrens' Quarters, with nothing but a sheet over her, she was already wet with perspiration, and the sun had only just cleared the horizon. She got up and went to the ablutions – a cold shower might help her to face the day ahead.

Third Officer Mavis Harmer – a hearty girl from Sunningdale – was already in the showers, wrestling with the control lever.

"I can't make this beastly thing work!" she exclaimed. "There's only a trickle of water coming through."

"Perhaps it's something to do with the air raid," suggested Miranda. "They turned off the electricity yesterday – when the all-clear goes, they'll probably turn the water on again."

Then they both ducked instinctively, as they heard the whistle of a falling bomb, which was followed by a deafening explosion. The building rocked, and the wooden shutters on the windows rattled like teeth chattering.

"That was a near one," said Miranda, shakily. "I wonder where the next one will land. . . ."

They waited tensely, listening to the rhythmic drumming of the German bombers overhead, but the next explosion was further away, and both girls breathed again.

Miranda abandoned the showers, and went to the washbasins instead, where she managed to squeeze a few drops from the tap – enough for what Nanny used to call "a lick and a promise".

"Goodness knows when we'll get a proper bath," she said to Mavis. "This looks like being another difficult day."

*   *   *

288

Ever since she had been attached to the Cypher Unit in Alexandria, there had been problems. The news from the battlefront grew steadily worse; a week ago, Tobruk had fallen to the enemy, and since then the German Army had been moving inexorably onward. Rumours ran round the Naval Headquarters like wildfire; the Germans would continue to advance across Libya, and into Egypt.

Over breakfast, the Wren Commandant issued the orders for the day: "All members of the Unit will suspend normal duties, and prepare to evacuate this hostel, and the Unit Office. You will each be allocated your contribution towards this exercise. Stand by to move off at a moment's notice."

Miranda spent the morning in the Galley, packing up tins of biscuits and corned beef, and making quantities of sandwiches. Whatever else might happen, the Wrens would not starve.

By noon, the heat was so intense, she felt as if she were moving in slow motion, and the Quarters Officer barked at her: "Get a move on – you look half asleep! We haven't got time to hang about – good gracious! – What's that?"

The door to the courtyard had been kept open to let in some air, and now a stringy rooster which had lost most of its feathers strutted into the kitchen, foraging for food.

"Where on earth did that come from?" the officer demanded. "What's happened to it? Do chickens get mange?"

"They keep chickens in the yard next door," Miranda suggested. "Perhaps it got blown over the wall, in the bomb-blast."

The rooster pecked at the Quarters Officer's ankles, and she backed away, exclaiming: "Get it out of here! No – put it out of its misery, then pop it in the oven – it's plucked already. We can take some cold roast chicken on the journey, in case our supplies run out."

Miranda protested: "I never killed a chicken in my life – I wouldn't know how."

"Don't be squeamish – just wring its neck. I'm going to my cabin to start packing; I'll help you clean out the giblets when I come back."

When she had gone, Miranda eyed the rooster, and said:

289

"This is no place for you, my friend – I suggest you leave while the going is good. Go on – shoo!"

She flapped a teacloth at the bird, and it took her advice; when the officer returned, she would tell her it had made a sudden dash for freedom.

Luckily, events moved so fast after that, the ready-plucked chicken was never mentioned again.

A convoy of battered-looking army lorries drew up outside, and the Wrens were told to pile their luggage into the transport as quickly as possible. Vital documents and office equipment were transferred to the lorries, while less important material was destroyed in a bonfire. Within forty minutes, they were on their way.

The journey was hot, dusty, and extremely uncomfortable. They thudded and bumped over potholed roads, heading out of the city, until they reached the single highway which cut across the desert – churning up the sand that drifted over the road – driving into the middle of nowhere. Inside the lorries, it was suffocatingly hot; Miranda's throat was parched, and her mouth felt gritty and dry.

"Where are we going?" someone asked.

"The driver told me we're heading for Ismailia," said another voice.

"What for? Why don't they send us to Cairo? What happens at Ismailia?"

"It's on the Canal – there'll be a boat waiting to take us on to Suez."

Gradually the daylight faded and night fell. In Miranda's lorry, the girls tried to lie down and go to sleep, but there wasn't room to stretch out. Aching with tiredness, Miranda gazed at the black velvet night, bright with stars, while the perspiration trickled down her spine, and asked herself: "Is this what I came to Egypt for? . . . Is this how we're supposed to fight for our country and defend freedom? . . . What's the point of it all?"

Still pondering these questions, she fell asleep.

"One small van should take this lot – I'll tell Ken to get on to the removal firm." William was walking round the lodge cottage with a pencil and notebook, listing the various items of furniture. "You can't put it off any longer, Mama – you've got to move out. How would Wednesday suit you?"

Old Bea looked up at him under her eyelashes, like a naughty child: "It wouldn't suit me at all; I'm not ready to go."

"But there's no reason for you to put it off now," Alice protested. "We've found you that pretty little bungalow at Medford Park – and the work at Crown House is finished; there's nothing left to be done except this cottage."

Apparently changing the subject, Old Bea turned to Alice and asked: "When are you going to town again? Didn't you say something about a christening?"

"Yes, I'm going up on Monday – the Kents' baby is to be baptized on Tuesday."

On the fourth of July, Princess Marina had presented Prince George with another son – a brother for seven-year-old Edward and six-year-old Alexandra; on the fourth of August, the baby was to be christened by the Archbishop of Canterbury.

"Will Queen Mary be there?"

"I believe so – but I really don't see —"

"I'll make a bargain with you. Take me to Windsor again, and I promise to leave here by the end of next week – how's that?"

"Mama, you know I can't do that. It's a private ceremony – only members of the immediate family are invited."

"I went to the Princess's confirmation – I'm sure Queen Mary will be delighted to see me again."

"No, Mama. Last time, she asked to meet you; this is very different."

Lady Beatrice saw the look in Alice's eye, and knew that argument was useless. "Very well. . . . You'll be sleeping at Curzon Street again, I presume?"

"Yes, Charlie says I can stay there any time – providing I cook his supper!"

"In that case, I shall come with you – I'd like to have one more glimpse of London. Surely you won't begrudge me one last fling?"

William and Alice exchanged glances, and William said: "Let me get this quite clear. . . . If Alice takes you to Curzon Street, you promise to vacate this cottage by the end of next week? I have your word for it?"

"I just said so, didn't I? You may tell Colonel Schickelgruber he can move in on Monday week."

So everything was arranged; Alice and Lady Beatrice drove up to London as before, and spent the night at Charlie Bowyer's flat. On Tuesday morning, Alice left her mother-in-law in his care while she went to Windsor. On Tuesday evening, she returned to Curzon Street, and began to tell them about the christening.

"It was lovely – the baby's names are Michael George Charles Franklin – Franklin after Franklin Roosevelt. I suppose they felt it was only right to ask the President to be one of his sponsors, since he was born on the Fourth of July. Of course he couldn't come over in person – though I believe Mrs Roosevelt is planning a trip to London soon. . . ."

By this point, Alice realized that she had not quite captured their attention; Old Bea was nodding and smiling, but she did not seem to be listening – and Charlie had the expression of a man in a state of shock.

Alice asked: "Is there something wrong?"

"No, no – far from it." Lady Beatrice replied. "In fact – your brother and I have had an inspiration – haven't we, Charles?"

"Oh – yes – an inspiration," he repeated gloomily.

"We'd been discussing the war, and our future plans and so on – and it suddenly came to me in a blinding flash . . . I've been buried in the country far too long; it's time I saw a bit of life again. And here's poor Charles with nobody to look after him – so we decided the best solution would be for me to settle here permanently . . . I shall bring Brooks with me – she can move into the servant's room and take care of both of us. She'll cook and clean and do the shopping and suchlike – it's going to be a godsend for you, isn't it, Charles?"

"Oh, yes . . . a godsend," he repeated flatly.

"So that's settled. And he's offered to take us out to dinner,

292

to celebrate the new arrangement. You'd better go and get dressed, Charles – we don't want to be late, do we?"

"No – I suppose not. . . ."

Still in a daze, he wandered off to his bedroom.

When the door closed, Alice said: "I believe you had this in mind all along. You planned it, didn't you?"

"Certainly not! Though I admit, I had been praying for guidance . . . God moves in a mysterious way," concluded the old lady with quiet satisfaction: "And this time I really think He's come up trumps."

Caro counted the days as August ran out; a passage had been reserved for her on a ship leaving Liverpool at the end of the month. She supervized the storage of her furniture, books and pictures, and closed up the flat at Markwick Terrace, then went down to Crown House, to say goodbye to the family.

Polly and Jenny told her to have a wonderful time in the States; the children kissed her, and asked her to send them postcards. Little Harry was convinced that Auntie Caro would soon be rubbing shoulders with Laurel and Hardy – and possibly Mickey Mouse and the Big Bad Wolf as well.

Lord Minster embraced his daughter, and said that she was doing the right thing; a wife's place was at her husband's side. He sent his regards to Scott, hoping it would not be long before they visited Crown House together.

Then Caro said goodbye to her mother – in London, where Alice had just seen their Majesties off to Scotland.

"They really needed a break – they've been driving themselves so hard. The Duke of Kent is going to look in on them – you know he's serving in the RAF? He's off to inspect our airbases in Iceland, so Balmoral will be a good stopping-off point."

"I'm glad you're getting a break as well," Caro told her. "Go home and tell Pa he's got to make a fuss of you."

Alice smiled: "First of all, I want to spend a day with you, my darling – just the two of us."

They made it a special occasion, and visited the National

Gallery, to hear one of the regular lunchtime concerts. Dame Myra Hess played two Mozart sonatas, and a packed audience of servicemen and women, and visitors from overseas, sat in rapt silence. During one of the slow movements, Alice held her daughter's hand – and Caro saw that there were tears in her eyes.

In the afternoon, they took a trip on a river boat to Greenwich and thought of Miranda – when they got back, Caro saw her mother off on the Medford train at Charing Cross.

"This seems all wrong," Alice said. "I should be seeing you off – not the other way round."

"There's no point in your staying up in town, just to put me on the night train to Liverpool," Caro told her. "And today's been lovely – I can't remember when we've spent so much time together."

"Nor can I. . . ." Alice heard a whistle blow. "I expect we'll move off any minute now . . . You will take good care of yourself, won't you? Don't do anything silly."

"I'll try not to." Steam hissed, and more whistles echoed under the arched roof. "And you look after yourself as well."

Alice tried to laugh: "I'm getting to be quite an old hand at this – waving goodbye to the family, while you rush off to the four corners of the earth. . . ."

At the far end of the platform, the guard waved a flag. Slowly, the train began to move; Caro walked alongside, keeping up with it for a few yards, then the train gathered speed and she had to drop back, letting it draw away.

Alice waved, calling out: "Goodbye, my darling – God bless!" – and Caro waved back, and went on waving until the train was out of sight.

She was glad she had nobody to see her off from Euston. Though the Medford train had been quite crowded, it seemed half-empty, compared with the train for Liverpool.

Hoping to get a seat, Caro arrived in good time, lugging two heavy suitcases and a shoulder-bag. The corridors were crammed with passengers, and many of them were in uniform, fully equipped with kitbags, haversacks, and even rifles – squeezing past them was like an obstacle-race.

After she had inched her way along three coaches without finding a seat, she made a place for herself in the corridor, where there was just room to put down her suitcases and sit on them. It wasn't comfortable, but it was better than standing all the way to Liverpool.

Once they had pulled out of the station, she could see nothing, for the blinds were pulled down, and the lighting was very dim; it was too dark to read, so she entertained herself by eavesdropping on her fellow-passengers – two girls in WAAF uniform, who discussed the men at their airfield in amazing detail. Hour after hour, the train rumbled on, occasionally stopping at a station for five or ten minutes; when a soldier in the Scots Guards tried to climb on board, they told him there was no room, but he retorted: "Ah've overstayed ma leave – if ah dinna get back by tomorra, they'll hae me for a deserter!"

So they squeezed into a still smaller space to accommodate him, and the journey continued. Every time the train stopped, someone asked: "Where are we now?" – but nobody knew.

At one of these halts, they heard an air raid siren; after that the train proceeded at a crawl. All the lights were extinguished, and the journey continued in total darkness.

Above the rattle and thump of the wheels, they could make out the regular drone of German planes overhead, the sound of ack-ack guns, and the crump of shells.

"Guid lads – gie 'em a pasting!" muttered the soldier.

Soon after that, they heard the sound of a plane coming down – the long wail of air rushing through the fuselage – the screech of an engine out of control. . . . The same thought was in every mind: "What if it lands on us . . . ?"

To their relief, they heard a shattering explosion some way off, and the Scot grunted: "Puir bastard. . . . Sooner him than me . . ."

The train trundled on, the noise of the guns died away – when suddenly there was another terrifying sound – a high-pitched scream of brakes grinding against the rails; the train lurched violently, and the passengers were flung against one another.

Caro did not know what was happening; she heard another explosion, so loud it seemed to be inside her head – was it just noise, or was it a physical blow, striking her full in the face? She felt herself being pushed against the door – pushed so hard, she couldn't breathe – and then the door gave way, and she fell back, holding the soldier who had fallen across her – he was screaming now, and she could feel his hot breath on her face.

Nothing made sense. She felt as if she were hanging upside-down in space – except she no longer knew which was up and which was down; a vast tearing sound came rushing towards her – and then the sound became light, and the light was the night sky, and the moon and the stars were beneath her feet – and she felt something hot and wet that trickled over her face, and tasted blood in her mouth – and the soldier had stopped screaming at last, because he was dead.

Next morning, Alice and William were having breakfast in their kitchen at Glebe Cottages. They were not listening to the wireless; William preferred a peaceful breakfast, with a copy of *The Times* propped up against the teapot.

As Alice spread home-made blackberry jam on her slice of toast, she became aware of a change in the atmosphere. Looking up, she saw William's expression.

"What is it?" she asked. "Bad news?"

He said gently: "I'm afraid so . . ." He passed the newspaper to her, and she read:

"DUKE OF KENT KILLED IN AIR CRASH
    "Accident to Flying Boat in the North of Scotland
    "The Air Ministry deeply regret to announce that Air Commodore His Royal Highness the Duke of Kent was killed on active service this afternoon when a Sunderland flying-boat crashed in the north of Scotland. His Royal Highness, who was attached to the staff of the Inspector General of the Royal Air Force, was proceeding to Iceland on duty.
    "The Duchess of Kent, the King and the Queen, and

other members of the Royal Family were immediately informed. . . ."

Alice put down the paper: "Oh, dear God – the Duchess will be on her own at Coppins, with the children . . . That poor girl – with a new baby, only seven weeks old. . . ."

She stood up, and William asked: "What are you going to do?"

"I don't know – but I must do something. Someone should be with her – she mustn't be alone. Their Majesties are both in Scotland —"

The sound of the door-knocker made her jump; William went to the front door, and greeted Ken Stubbs:

"Ken – I didn't expect you so early —"

"I thought I'd better come right away, sir. I just had a phone call, a few minutes ago."

When the family moved out of Crown House, the telephone had been installed at the Home Farm, which was now the centre of operations. He looked uncomfortably at Alice: "I'm sorry to tell you – it's bad news."

"We know." Alice showed him the newspaper: "We just read about the Duke. . . ."

Ken began again: "No – it's not that, my lady. . . . This is news of a personal nature. The police telephoned – I said I'd pass on the message. It's about your daughter."

The colour drained from Alice's face: "Something's happened to Miranda — ?"

"Not Miranda, my lady . . . Caroline."

Chapter Eighteen

Tuesday, 25 August to Saturday, 14 November 1942

It took them most of the day to get there.

They had to find a hire car which would drive them all the way from Crown House to a small hospital in Warwickshire, near Kenilworth, and by the time they arrived, it was almost dark.

William asked the driver to wait, saying he had no idea how long they would be; then they made their way up a sloping concrete ramp, through swinging glass doors, and found the Casualty Ward.

The Sister led them into her office, saying: "I'm sure you would like a cup of tea. . . ."

"Thank you, no – we should like to see our daughter as soon as possible," said William firmly.

"We've come rather a long way," Alice explained. "Where is she?"

"She's still in the theatre – I'm afraid I must ask you to wait," said the Sister. "You may as well have some tea anyway."

"Could you tell us what happened, exactly?" Alice continued. "All we know is that there was a train crash —"

"I can't tell you much more than that." The Sister poured the tea as she spoke: "I believe an enemy plane was shot down on the outskirts of Coventry – it crashed on to the railway line, and a few minutes later, the train from Euston ran into the wreckage."

"Yes, but – is she — ?"

"It took some time for rescuers to free the passengers from the overturned coaches; they had to send for a crane and lifting gear, and then they worked all night, cutting through the wreckage. The problem was to find enough beds for the survivors; the emergency services had to call on hospitals and nursing homes all over the West Midlands to cope with them. This is a comparatively small unit – we could only take four patients. One of them was your daughter —" She shot a glance at the notes on her desk: "Caroline – she was unconscious when they found her, and she hadn't regained consciousness when she went into the theatre. . . . At least she wasn't in any pain."

"But do you know the extent of her injuries?" William persisted.

"You will have to ask the surgeon about that, when you see him. Meanwhile you're very welcome to wait here."

"How long do you think it will be, before —" Alice's voice shook: "Before we can speak to him?"

"I'm afraid I couldn't say."

William stood up: "I'd better tell our driver to find himself a room for the night, and some supper – he must be starving."

"When did you and Lady Minster last have anything to eat?"

They looked at one another; it seemed a very long time ago.

"This morning – we were finishing breakfast when – when we got the message."

"Let me send some sandwiches in. You must have something."

"I'm not hungry." Alice shook her head. "This tea is all I need."

William went out to speak to the chauffeur; when he returned, Alice was sitting alone, with her eyes shut. He thought she had fallen asleep, but she opened her eyes and said: "It's all right – I'm only resting. . . . Did you ask the driver to find a room for us as well, while he's about it?"

"No – don't you think we should stay here? We can't leave until we know for certain that Caro's going to be all right."

He took the chair beside Alice; they sat in silence, until he remarked: "This reminds me of that night – it must be nearly twelve years ago – when I came to find you in hospital, after your car had gone into a ditch. You'd been driving Jenny's mother up to town —"

"Poor Mrs Webster . . . I was luckier than I deserved."

William took her hand. "You were in a coma for days. I just had to wait – and pray as hard as I could. On the fourth day, my prayers were answered."

"Four days. . . ." Alice's hand tightened in his. "Do you think – Caro — ?"

"Let's hope the surgeon can tell us."

When Mr Greville came into the little office, it seemed smaller still; he was a large man, with a loud voice.

"This is a bad business," he said, perching on the edge of the desk. "Sorry not to have anything very cheerful to tell you, but we must face the facts. . . . Your daughter has a fractured skull – that should mend, in due course. She also has lacerations on both arms, but she can thank her lucky stars someone fell on top of her and shielded her from most of the flying glass. He was a hefty chap, whoever he was – she's got several cracked ribs, but they'll mend. The real problem is her right leg; she's got a nasty compound fracture – the shaft of the femur is broken in several places, and it's going to be the devil of a job to knit it together tidily. To make things worse, I'm afraid of osteomyelitis setting in – that's a bone infection, and it could be rather grim. However, we're trying her with penicillin —"

"What's that?" asked Alice.

"Our new wonder drug – it only came into mass production about a year ago. That's one good thing coming out of this damn war; they've put time and money into the treatment of wounds and fractures – for obvious reasons. Penicillin's having excellent results, so we must hope for the best – but. . . ."

"But — ?"

He chose his words carefully: "At the moment, your girl's still in a coma – I'm afraid her name is on the danger list. . . ."

*　　*　　*

300

The following morning, Jenny called in to see Ken at the Home Farm.

"Any news yet?" she asked.

"Not since His Lordship's phone call yesterday evening. I suppose she hasn't come round yet."

"But if he tried to phone here during the night—" Jenny began.

"His Lordship's got my number, in the village," Ken assured her. "I told him to phone if there was any change, whatever time it was. I'll let you know as soon as I hear from him."

"Thank you. I'm just taking Eddie to the shops, to collect our rations." From his pushchair, her son looked up with interest. "We're going to buy something nice for dinner – aren't we, my poppet?"

Master Edward made an appreciative noise, which Jenny interpreted for Ken: "That means 'sausages' – they're his favourite."

Eddie crowed with delight, and Ken grinned: "That's right, lad – you eat plenty of sausages, and you'll grow up big and strong, like your Dad."

Jenny's face clouded: "It seems so awful that Nick doesn't know about Caro – neither do the twins. I suppose there's no point in trying to get in touch with them until – until we know for sure."

"What about her husband?" asked Ken. "He ought to be told."

"Scott's somewhere in Washington, but I haven't got a number for him. . . . Oh, well—" Jenny turned the pushchair round, saying: "Off we go, my love! I'll look in presently, Ken – just in case."

It was nearly an hour later when she returned, with a heavy shopping basket on her arm, and saw Ken beckoning at the office window. He met her in the doorway, saying: "I told him to hold on – it's better for you to speak to him."

"Lord Minster –? What's happened?"

As she pushed past him and picked up the telephone, he explained: "No – it's her husband – Mr Hanson. . . ."

At the same moment, a voice in her ear said: "Hi, Jenny! – how's everything? How's the family?"

"Scott! – where are you?"

"In London – got in this morning, at crack of dawn. Hey, listen – where's Caro? I went to Markwick Terrace, but the apartment's shut up; someone said she's gone away."

Jenny took a deep breath: "I'm terribly sorry, Scott, but I'm afraid – there's been an accident. . . ."

At the Hospital, William and Alice sat beside Caroline's bed. Last night, the Matron had given them her own room, in the main building, but this morning they had come back to the Emergency Ward, where Caro lay – pale and horribly still, her face looking very small under a turban of bandages. Only her shallow breathing showed that she was still clinging to life.

The prefabricated wards were newly-built, in the grounds of the original hospital, with open walkways connecting them; outside the windows, nurses passed by, their red capes flapping in the wind. An ambulance drew up, and a muffled figure was carried out on a stretcher. At noon, two orderlies wheeled in food trolleys; the day wore on – and still Caroline did not move.

Some time during the afternoon, a red-haired man in khaki fatigues wandered along the concrete walkway, looking lost. Suddenly Alice said: "William – look! There's Scott!"

"It can't be – that chap's in uniform – Caro said the Army rejected Scott when he —"

"But it is him!" Alice hurried to the door and called: "*Scott*! – she's here – Caroline's in here!"

When he came into the side ward, he put his arms round Alice, but his eyes never left the motionless figure upon the bed.

"Tell me," he said.

They told him all they knew; he found another chair and sat at the end of the bed.

As the daylight waned, he suggested they should go and have something to eat; he would stay with Caro.

When they left the room, he began quietly: "Hi there – it's me . . . I don't know if you can hear me, sweetheart, but I'm here at last. . . . Sorry it took so long." He held her hand, adding: "I wouldn't say anything till I knew for sure – I didn't want to raise any hopes. Your Ma and Pa tell me you were on your way over to join me – while I've been doing my darndest to get back to you. Seems like we both wanted the same thing."

He broke off – was he dreaming, or did the hand within his own return a faint pressure? He waited, but when nothing happened, he continued: "Trouble was – after the Army turned me down, I couldn't settle to anything. For a time I lost interest in journalism – it seemed kinda stupid to be writing about the war instead of fighting it. . . . It took me a while to realize I still had something to contribute. There was a whole mess of red tape to cut through – but I'm in uniform at last. I got sent over with the latest batch of enlisted men – they've given me a permit to travel with them, and send back bulletins as an Official War Correspondent – how about that?"

There was no response from Caro, but he went on: "OK, so I'm talking too much – I guess I always did, huh? But there's another thing that hasn't changed – I still love you, babe."

That was when her eyelids fluttered.

By the time the Minsters returned, the room was full of people – Mr Greville, a Nursing Sister, and two Auxiliaries were hovering round her bed; Scott broke away from the group, and came to meet them, shining with happiness.

"She's OK," he said, over and over. "She's OK – she's going to be OK."

It was a long time before Caroline recovered completely from the effects of the crash, but she and Scott were together again, and nothing else mattered.

By the end of October, winter had begun to tighten its grip; the people of Britain were asked to practise economy measures to save fuel, using as little heat and light as possible.

The Royal Family had to set an example, and when they moved back temporarily into Buckingham Palace, to welcome an important visitor, the huge rooms were partly stripped of furniture – and not many degrees above freezing.

Alice met Cecil Beaton, who had been called in to take pictures of this special occasion.

"Nobody's told me yet who the visitor is," he grumbled, fussing over his camera and re-setting the lights.

"It had to be kept secret," Alice explained, "but now their Majesties have gone to meet her, we needn't hush it up any longer. . . . It's Mrs Roosevelt."

He grimaced: "I see I shall have my work cut out – not exactly photogenic, is she?"

No," Alice reminded him: "Just the First Lady of the United States."

"Well, I'll do my best, but we mustn't expect miracles, must we?" Glancing round the room, he shivered: "This place used to be so gorgeous, and now look at it – no pictures – no flowers – an empty fireplace. . . ."

Then he put a finger to his lips as the Royal Family entered – not only the King and Queen, but the Princesses as well.

"Mrs Roosevelt has gone up to change after the journey," the Queen explained, as they shook hands. The girls greeted Mr Beaton cheerfully – a trip to London was an unexpected treat.

While they waited, he murmured to Alice: "Elizabeth is growing up; I never noticed before – she has her mother's smile."

Soon the President's wife burst in, keeping up a flow of chatter: "Oh, are there going to be pictures? My! – I've hardly put a comb through my hair since I left New York, and I haven't powdered my nose since Washington!"

She continued to talk; Mr Beaton tried to persuade her to remain silent for a moment – or at least to keep still – but in vain.

That evening, there was a dinner party for a few special guests, to meet the First Lady. Alice went up to her room, to escort her, and found Mrs Roosevelt gazing in despair at her reflection, saying: "Well, I've done my best – though heaven knows that's not saying much. . . ." She pulled a woollen stole round her shoulders: "Tell me – is there any kind of heating downstairs?" She indicated the single-bar electric fire in the hearth: "That doesn't do a lot for a room this size – I feel as if I'm sleeping in Grand Central Station."

"I'm sorry – His Majesty is very strict about fuel economy," Alice apologized.

"Ah – would that be the reason for the line painted round the side of the tub?" asked Mrs Roosevelt: "To limit the hot water?"

"I'm afraid so – five inches per person!"

"Maybe it's easier if you're slender," she sighed. "I guess we'd better go down – will you lead the way?"

As they descended, Alice warned her that the dinner was also limited by austerity regulations; the main course would be fried spam fritters – though served on gold and silver plates.

Among the guests assembled to meet Mrs Roosevelt were General and Lady Smuts from South Africa, Lord and Lady Mountbatten, and Mr and Mrs Churchill. Over dinner, Lord Mountbatten told Mrs Roosevelt that he had arranged a film-show in the library afterwards.

"Heavens – do I have to watch myself on the screen?" she asked in dismay. "You're not showing that movie they shot, the minute I arrived?"

The Queen intervened: "Oh, no – Mr Beaton only takes still pictures."

"My! – no wonder he looked at me as if I were half-witted," said Mrs Roosevelt. "That's why I kept talking and bobbing about . . . Franklin says I have to look animated for the movies!"

Her Majesty smiled: "Don't worry, tonight we have the pleasure of watching other people perform." She turned to the King's cousin: "Remind me, Dickie – what's the name of your film?"

"'*In Which We Serve*' – but it's Noel Coward's film," Lord Mountbatten explained. "I only gave some technical advice."

When the closing titles faded from the screen and the lights went up, the Prime Minister asked their Majesties:

"I'm expecting a telephone call, with news from North Africa – may I have your permission to ring Downing Street?"

Ten minutes later they heard him singing loudly and tunelessly along the corridor: *"Roll out the barrel – we'll have a barrel of fun. . . ."*

He broke off as he walked in, and gave them a cherubic smile.

"Great news!" he announced. "Montgomery is advancing from El Alamein – he's got Rommel's army on the run. This is what we've been waiting for – the turning of the tide."

Miranda was on her hands and knees, scrubbing floorboards, when Mavis Harmer found her.

"Goodness, you shouldn't be doing that!" she exclaimed. "Where are the Quarters' staff? Why don't you get one of the Egyptian sweepers to do it?"

"Quarters can't spare anybody," said Miranda, without looking up. "And the sweepers have all gone on strike."

"What on earth do you mean? They can't do that – it's against regulations!"

"Apparently I offended them by burning all the old mattresses – which were crawling with lice and bedbugs. I made a nice bonfire outside, and now I'm scrubbing the floor with disinfectant."

When the Wrens detachment reached Suez, it had been Miranda's job to find suitable accommodation, and she was still wrestling with this task; not only requisitioning vacant premises, but begging, borrowing or scrounging pieces of furniture.

"I'll try and get a working party from HQ to help you," said Mavis. "Oh, by the way – you've got a visitor. . . . Somebody who's driven down from Cairo – I'll send him in, shall I?"

Miranda called after her: "But I don't know anyone in Cairo – did he say who —"

She broke off, as an officer in tropical whites walked in, saying: "Hello, Mandy!"

"Nick — ! Oh, it's so wonderful to see you, but. . . ." She

306

laughed, indicating the bare room, the floorboards smelling of disinfectant – her filthy hands and broken nails. "I wish I'd known – I must look terrible . . ."

"You'd better get cleaned up pretty damn quick, because I'm taking you out for a meal, and I'm only here for a couple of hours."

"But I'm on duty —"

"That's all taken care of – don't argue, or you'll be reported for insubordination towards a senior officer!"

In the restaurant bar, they caught up on the family news, and suddenly Nick asked: "When do you get your next leave?"

"Goodness knows; I'm due for some now, but we've all been told to stand by and await further orders – things are moving so fast now, we might move on at any time."

"In that case, I think you'd better put in a request on compassionate grounds – for family reasons. You and I have both got to get home next month, by hook or by crook – even if we have to develop a mysterious disease, unknown to medical science."

"I don't understand – what family reasons — ?"

"Have you forgotten Grandmama's ninetieth birthday? If we miss that, she'll never forgive us!"

In Curzon Street, the fourteenth of November began quietly; Lady Beatrice spent some time over breakfast, opening her birthday cards. One especially pleased her; affectionate good wishes from Badminton – Queen Mary had not forgotten her old friend.

Sir Charles Bowyer presented her with a bottle of perfume and a bunch of mophead chrysanthemums, golden and glowing. She accepted these tributes graciously, then asked where all the other presents were?

"I have a son and a daughter – grandchildren and great-grandchildren – I hope they haven't forgotten me!"

"Of course they haven't," Charlie assured her. "Alice and William are driving up to town; they're going to take you out to supper – I dare say they'll bring some presents with them."

Old Bea sniffed: "What about the others? Grace is in Scotland – Nicholas and Miranda on the high seas – Martin's up in the sky somewhere – they all sent cards, but where are my presents?"

When Alice and William appeared at six o'clock, bearing more flowers and a very small package, she was not best pleased.

"Red roses – yes, very nice – but where's the rest of the family? I'm ninety years old – and I won't be overlooked!"

"No one could overlook you, Mama," said William. "Why not open your present?"

Inside was a jeweller's box, containing a diamond pendant. She held it up to catch the light, then allowed Alice to fasten it round her neck.

"Bring me a mirror – I want to see how I look," she commanded, then preened with quiet satisfaction: "Yes, you have to have style to carry off diamonds. . . . Well, I'm ready for supper – where are we going?"

"Not very far," he told her. "A little place called the Ritz. As it's rather a special occasion, I reserved a private room."

When the door opened, the family were there to greet her, offering their congratulations, their good wishes – and their presents.

Her sharp features softened into a smile: "Dear me – I wasn't expecting this. . . . Has everyone come to see me?"

"Miranda hoped to get leave," said Nick, "but it seems she couldn't make it."

"And we left Eddie at home," said Jenny. "It's past his bedtime."

Lady Beatrice opened their present; a splendid silk dressing-gown in peacock blues and greens, which Nick had found in a bazaar at Marrakesh.

Corks popped and champagne bubbled; even the children were allowed a taste, for Polly had brought Alex and Harriet to join the celebration. At enormous sacrifice, they had saved their sweet ration for weeks to buy their Great-Grandmama a jar of old-fashioned humbugs.

She thanked them, adding: "I'd offer them round – but we

don't want to spoil our appetites before supper, do we?" – and wedged the jar firmly into her wheelchair for safety.

"My present's a sort of joint one – with Ken," Polly explained.

For some time, Ken had been taking photographs of Crown House, to record the changing scene, showing the grounds as they were now, and as they used to be before the war. Polly had the prints enlarged, and stuck them into a leather-bound album: "In case you ever feel homesick."

"As it was – and as it will be again, God willing," said Ken.

Waitresses were handing round trays of canapés – the old lady stuffed a couple in her mouth and went on opening presents.

Caro and Scott offered a very original tribute; a frozen carton of chocolate ice-cream, provided by the PX store at a USAAF base.

Lady Beatrice licked her lips, then turned on her son accusingly: "Why don't we ever have ice-cream nowadays?"

"Because the Government have put a ban on the manufacture of ice-cream," he told her.

"Thank God the Americans have more sense," grunted the old lady.

Alice smiled: "That's the first good word I've heard you say about our new neighbours."

William teased her: "You're just as bad – you still don't like having strangers at Crown House, do you?"

"At first I hated the idea," she admitted. "But they're so friendly and cheerful – and it won't be for ever. The Prime Minister said the tide has turned, and I'm sure he's right. . . . We're going to win this war."

Old Bea drew herself up indignantly: "Of course we are! The Minsters have always won wars – it runs in the family."

She began to rip open another present – labelled "From Edith and Grace, with all our love." Unable to make the long journey from Scotland, they had sent her a lap rug of softest lambswool, woven in the Duncan tartan.

309

Perching on the arm of her wheelchair, Martin said dismissively: "I don't think much of that – you're not old enough for winter woollies, Gran. And you'll feel warm as toast, when you wear these. . . ."

"These" turned out to be a set of fancy lingerie – a petticoat, a camisole, and two pairs of directoire knickers in slinky black silk and pink lace.

"Oh, Martin – really!" Alice apologized to her mother-in-law: "I'm afraid our son has a rather basic sense of humour, Mama."

She clutched the undies defiantly: "Just because I'm elderly, it doesn't mean I can't enjoy a little luxury now and then. You're a good boy, Martin!" – and she gave him a smacking kiss.

On the other side of the room, the children were getting bored, but Ken Stubbs took charge of the situation, producing a notebook and coloured pencils from his pocket, and encouraging them to play "Heads and Bodies". Polly watched them fondly; their heads close together, all three of them busily drawing and folding the little sheets of paper.

At her elbow, Jenny said: "What would we do without Ken? He's become almost a second father to them."

Polly's smile faded: "Oh, don't — !"

"I'm sorry," Jenny apologized. "Was that the wrong thing to say?"

"Not really." Polly sighed: "You're right – he's a tower of strength, and I'm really grateful, but – sometimes I think he tries to take Richie's place, and of course he can't do that. Ken's wonderful, but he'll never be Richard."

"I'm glad you noticed," said Jenny.

"Noticed what?"

"That Ken's wonderful. Because he is – a good, kind, wonderful man – and he loves you very much."

Dismayed, Polly turned to her sister-in-law: "Did he tell you that?"

"He didn't have to. Years ago, before you ever came on the scene, I thought I was in love with Richard; and Nick used to watch me trailing after him, with a certain look on his face . . . I've seen Ken watching you like that."

Polly looked at Ken – unaware of her scrutiny, he was absorbed in his task, keeping her children happy – and suddenly she saw him in a new light.

Jenny nudged her: "That's it," she said.

"That's what?"

"You're doing it now – you've got that look too."

Polly gasped: "Have I? Are you sure?"

"You're made for one another. I can't think what took you so long."

The waitresses returned, carrying trays of covered dishes, and William suggested that the family should take their places at the table. As Lady Beatrice was being wheeled up to the head of the table, Miranda entered the room, and ran to her Grandmother.

"Gran darling – had you given me up?" Kissing the old lady, she added: "These are for you – I picked them up on my travels. I'm not allowed to say where, but it wasn't a million miles from the Pyramids."

She had come across them in a back-street *souk* in Cairo; a pair of drop earrings made of lapis lazuli, set in gold filigree.

"You must help me put them on – I'm going to be a real bobbydazzler in my new finery!" Old Bea crowed. "It's a pity I'm not wearing Martin's presents as well – he's given me some very stylish unmentionables."

Miranda looked round: "Martin — ? Is he here?"

He appeared at her elbow: "Of course! – It wouldn't be same without me!" – and while the guests gathered around the table, he drew her aside. Under cover of the general chatter, he continued: "Listen, I've been trying to find a way of saying this – but . . . Well, the thing is . . . I'm really sorry."

"For ignoring my phone message?"

"What phone message?" When she explained, he said the barmaid must have forgotten to pass it on – Saturday nights at the Ring o' Bells were always hectic. "I thought you must have torn up my stupid postcard, and I didn't blame you . . . Because of – what happened before."

"You were under a lot of pressure – I realized that."

"Yes . . . I'd been having – you know – problems. I think I was going a bit barmy, but that's all over now, thank God."

311

She squeezed his hand: "I'm very glad."

"That's the real reason I didn't come home at Christmas – don't tell Ma, but I volunteered to stay on duty – well, there's this girl in the WAAF – we've been seeing a lot of one another . . ."

Old Bea interrupted him, calling loudly: "Martin – come and sit next to me!"

"Right away, Gran –!" Urgently he asked: "How about you? Are you OK?"

"I'm fine, Marty . . . Just fine."

As she took her place at the table, she thought: "Yes, I'm fine – and I'm free."

She realized that, during the past few years, she had been trying to find herself. In their different ways, other people had tried to turn her into their own Miranda – a surrogate daughter for Alain Lafitte – a mirror image for Chief Officer Pinnegar – a sexual fantasy for Martin . . . And now she was free of them – free to stand on her own feet, and live her own life.

At the end of the meal, William rose to propose a toast.

"But what should it be? A toast to victory? To a peaceful future? A toast to Crown House, perhaps? Yes, we drink to all these things, but tonight, first and foremost, we drink to the founder of the feast – the head of the family."

They all stood, turning to her as they raised their glasses; and for once the old lady's eyes were bright with tears.

Much later, when the party began to break up, Ken found Polly and said: "I'm fetching the car round – will you bring the children and meet me at the front entrance?"

"Yes – all right." Then she called him back: "Ken – will you do me a favour?"

"Of course – what is it?"

"A very big favour?"

"You know I will. What do you want?"

"Next Saturday night – will you take me to the Medford Palais?" She smiled at him: "I haven't been dancing for a long while . . . I think it's time I started again."